"If you ordered the guards who watch my every move to accompany me home, I would be safe in my Hills, and you would be rid of my inconvenient presence."

Nicholas Rostov's back stiffened. "No."

"Just...no?"

"I cannot spare the men." Still, he did not turn to look at her.

"You already spare the men to watch me. Dear Heaven, why won't you let me go?"

It always caught her off guard, his ability to wheel so quickly, so gracefully, like a large, sleek panther. He loomed over his desk, hands planted on each side of the papers, his eyes burning into her with an intensity that seared her to the very core.

"Tell me who you are. Tell me who your people are. What were you up to when the Nantal found you? Tell me why you know eight languages, and why your horse is of the finest blood stock I have ever encountered, and why you treat a king as an equal, or perhaps a not quite equal. Tell me all that, and I shall think about letting you go."

"It is nothing to you," she said, flinging a look over her shoulder toward the door. Her long braid fell across her breast, and the small thread of hair that held it broke.

Nicholas Rostov's face underwent a subtle change as his gaze fixed on her hair. He walked from behind the desk like a great cat stalking his victim. He loomed over her, large and inscrutable, radiating a force of will both dangerous and seductive. She couldn't seem to move, to breathe. He reached out a hand, lifting her hair, seeming to weigh it in his hands.

"Nothing, you say. I wish it were that simple. There is something about you, Sera with no last name, no history, no family madly searching for you." He leaned close, holding her just by his light touch on her hair. Sera felt the warmth of his cheek, his breath a slow exhalation against the side of her neck. His lips moved, touching, and not quite touching, the hollow there, like the wings of a butterfly.

"Sweet," he whispered. "Soft mystery. Lady in peasant's garb."

For Colin

Heart of Fire

***

Mary Lennox

HEART OF FIRE
Published by ImaJinn Books, a division of ImaJinn

ISBN: 1-893896-91-9

10 9 8 7 6 5 4 3 2 1

PUBLISHER'S NOTE:
This book is a work of fiction. Names, characters, places and incidents are products of the author's imagination or are used fictitiously. Any resemblance to actual events or locales or persons, living or dead, is entirely coincidental.

Books are available at quantity discounts when used to promote products or services. For information please write to: Marketing Division, ImaJinn Books, P.O. Box 162, Hickory Corners, MI 49060-0162, or call toll free 1-877-625-3592.

Cover design by Patricia Lazarus

ImaJinn Books, a division of ImaJinn
P.O. Box 162, Hickory Corners, MI 49060-0162
Toll Free: 1-877-625-3592
http://www.imajinnbooks.com

One

The Hill People are a shy, backward tribe located in the foothills of the impenetrable Arkadian range between the country of Laurentia and Beaureve. They rarely make an appearance in the towns near the foothills, preferring their simple lives of poverty and ignorance to the ordeal of entering even the smallest village on a market day. In all the time I have spent traveling in this area, I have only seen a few of them. Their hair hangs plaited down the backs of both male and female. Without exception, all wear gray cloaks that blend with the mountain from which they come. They have a disconcerting habit of seeming to appear from out of nowhere.

Excerpt from *A Road Well Travelled*
by Countess Irena Volkonsky

October, 1812

"There he is," whispered the mistress of the harem in Iman Hadar's palace.

Sera stared through the intricate latticework of the balcony to the courtyard below. Crossing the brightly patterned mosaic floor was a tall man with dark hair, broad shoulders, and an impatient stride. He walked beside another, a blond whose tousled curls and easy grin contrasted with the dark one's own cool expression and the neat precision of his person. But she could feel the anger seething just below the dark one's surface.

Why should she care whether that man felt anger or joy? All she wished was a chance to escape this prison she had occupied for two weeks, after the cursed Nantal raiders had caught her and brought her to this place. Ever since, she had been guarded like a precious jewel, taught absurd lessons that she would never use—which perfumes to use upon which parts of her body, how to ply cosmetics and how to appear both submissive and seductive to please some Outlander lord.

The blond grabbed his companion, causing him to halt directly opposite her hiding place. As the courtyard fountain muffled their voices, the blond spoke earnestly to the dark one. He appeared to listen intently, but then, just as she thought he'd walk off again with that fierce, long stride of his, he raised his head and stared directly at the latticework hiding her from view.

Sera froze. His gray eyes seemed to pierce the protective screen, as though they could look right into her face. With a shiver, Sera felt the full force of the man's will, daring her to reveal herself.

With the Nantal slavers, with the Outlanders in the bazaars, with the eunuchs and the mistress of the harem, she had felt only disdain, but this man was different. There was something about him—a sense of the power Grandfather and Jacob had.

Taking a soundless breath, Sera stared down into the cold, gray depths of the Outlander's eyes. Two thoughts pounded in her brain in time with the fearful tattoo of her heart. The first was that she would use this man, and through him, escape to find the Heart of Fire—the precious, stolen ruby that protected her kingdom from his brutal world. And the second was that this Outlander, whom, if life had been different, she would have met in dignity and honor, was as beautiful as Apollo himself.

With a quick, impatient turn, the Outlander strode off, his companion quickly following.

"There," said the mistress of the harem with a wave of her jewel-laden hand. "You recognize him now, and you are a bright girl. You understand what you are to do."

Sera gave the mistress a sardonic smile. "I am to seduce this Outlander king, until he is mindless with pleasure."

The mistress frowned. "Don't think you are above this, my girl. Your future, indeed, your very life depends upon your work tonight." She clapped her hands and the eunuch who stood at the archway to the harem came forward immediately.

"She's ready. Take her to him," she said and, in this manner, sent Sera to face the next trial in the Outlander world she could not wait to leave.

***

Nicholas Rostov, the king of Laurentia, masked his rage as he strode through the corridor of Iman Hadar's palace toward his suite of rooms. He had come hoping the ruler of neighboring Jehanna would join him in an alliance against Napoleon. But Hadar had refused, claiming neutrality. And now, it seemed, Hadar's hidden spies watched his every move.

His father's ghostly voice mocked Nicholas with every step down the long corridor. "A real king succeeds in making alliances. But with a sickly fellow like you, Nicholas, Laurentia is doomed. A man who can't control his own body can't rule a nation."

Nicholas clenched his fists, pushing the taunts from his mind and into the past where they belonged. He had controlled his weakness for years. And for better or worse, he was all Laurentia had.

"Tomorrow will be the first day I draw an easy breath," Count Andre Lironsky said as he walked beside Nicholas, his usually cheerful countenance somber. "The sooner we're gone from this place, the better."

Nicholas's gaze raked the corridor as they passed large Corinthian pillars of pink marble. Assassins could easily hide behind each one.

The two friends said nothing more as they walked toward their suite of rooms. As they reached it, the heavy wooden door suddenly swung open. Nicholas tensed and his hand went to the sword slung round his hips. To his surprise, a bald giant of a man, with the soft, undefined musculature and long limbs of a palace eunuch, bowed low in the doorway and backed into the chamber. Eyes still watchful, Nicholas followed him into the room. It was empty aside from the eunuch and a small creature hidden behind his back.

"Most gracious majesty. My master, the great Hadar, begs that you accept this small gift for the evening."

With a great flourish, the man reached behind him and pushed forward a woman. She wore a half veil, but her clothing left little to the imagination.

"Jesu," breathed Andre beside him. "What interesting compensation for frustration—of any kind."

"Quiet, Andre." Nicholas sent him a telling glance. Andre should know better than to speak his mind before anyone in this palace.

Andre gave a theatrical sigh. "Oh, the privileges of royalty."

Nicholas caught himself staring gape-jawed as any country lout at the slave woman. Even with half her face covered, he could see she was incredibly beautiful. Her eyes, a deep blue, were slightly almond shaped and large beneath winged brows. As for the rest of her...He couldn't seem to tear his eyes away from the lush picture of smooth, golden skin and soft curves. His groin tightened just from looking at her. What the hell was wrong with him? With an act of will, he looked back at the eunuch.

"She is a virgin, great king," the eunuch went on in his fruity voice. "The Nantal traders recently found her near the Hill country. As you can see from her bright hair and her soft skin, she is a prize for any man. She knows little of our language, but I was given to understand that you are a fluent linguist and know the Hill tongue. My master, the great Hadar, wished you to be the first to possess this treasure. His greatest wish is that she will please you."

After this astonishing speech, the eunuch bowed low. He shuffled toward the door while still making his obeisance and left the room.

Nicholas' control slipped a notch further on the rack of his outrage. "Hadar knows of my stance on slavery," he muttered to Andre. "Yet, the idiot expects me bed this poor woman. I should have known our cause was doomed from the start."

It had been a miserable week, and Nicholas could wish nothing more than to bury himself in a woman and forget the failures for a night. But control was the creed of his life, and he was not about to take advantage of a woman who had no choice in the matter. He glanced again at her eyes, the dark blue of the sky at sunset, with a look half-fierce, half-terrified in them. And that tumble of bright gold hair falling to somewhere near her hips—was it as warm as it looked?

"What are you going to do, Nikki?" Andre's voice cut into his thoughts. "About her," he added a little louder.

What, indeed. It was hard not to look at her breasts, lifted like an offering in that white halter. Her slim waist tapered to rounded hips encased in a swirling, filmy skirt that swayed as she took a step back from him. His blood seemed to beat to a pounding rhythm.

"I take it you and your...ah...gift will be safe alone?" Andre's voice was pitched even louder, and there was a hint of laughter beneath it.

Nicholas grabbed his cloak, still hanging over the back of a divan, and threw it to the woman. "Cover yourself," he told her in the Hill tongue and turned away from her again. For some reason, he didn't want Andre looking at her. And he didn't like this sense that he was losing control.

Nicholas heard the rustle of his cloak, heard it settle. He turned to the slave and stared only at her face for a long moment, giving her the full benefit of what Andre called the "Rostov frown". Her eyes widened above the veil, and she seemed to shrink into herself for a fraction of a second. Nicholas knew from experience that her next move would be to look for somewhere to run. She surprised him. Slowly, the woman drew herself up to her full height and held her stance, staring back at him.

Intrigued in spite of himself, Nicholas relaxed against an intricately inlaid column, folding his arms across his chest. "You may be calm," he said, again in the language of the Hills, that strange, musical language with something of Greek in it. "I will not hurt you."

She nodded to indicate that she understood.

"I have no plan to bed you, woman," he added firmly. "You may retire to the harem now."

She surprised him again by crossing her own arms across her chest. "If I return, the king of this place will know that I have not pleased you. I will be punished most grievously. It would be in keeping with your reputation for kindness to allow me a corner in your quarters until morning."

He liked the sound of her voice. It was sweet and tart at the same time. He had never heard the Hill tongue spoken by a native of the place, but only learned it from his tutor as an exercise in mastering an almost dead language. When she spoke it, the words took on a lyrical quality he had never heard in any language.

"Why did I never bother to study as hard as you did? If I had, I wouldn't need to ask what in the world you're saying to each other." said Andre, curious.

Nicholas told him quickly while the woman stared at the floor in seeming incomprehension.

"Well, you can't just send her back to that," said Andre.

Nicholas gave him a caustic grin. "Of course not. My reputation for kindness would suffer."

He turned to the woman again. "You may sleep there," he said, pointing to the divan at the foot of the bed. He grabbed a satin quilt and two of the pillows off the bed, shoving them at her. He was relieved that he and Andre were leaving this perfumed den at first light tomorrow morning.

She nodded, holding the bedding to her chest and waiting, her eyes downcast.

"A gentleman would give the lady the bed and take the divan," said Andre as he turned for the door to his adjoining quarters.

"But this is no lady," said Nicholas. He locked the door to the corridor and unbuckled the sword and the knife sheath he carried everywhere, laying both upon the large, canopied bed.

"Take your rest, woman," he said without looking at her. He climbed into bed and placed both sword and knife within easy reach. Blowing out the candle on the small table beside the bed, he heard the rustle of silk as she settled onto the divan.

Nicholas lay awake, staring at the shadowed ceiling for a long time. His body would not let him sleep. The ache in his groin made him restless, made him wonder why he didn't soothe the restlessness. He saw himself as an honorable man, albeit cold. At age twenty-seven, he had experienced the act of love many times without expecting trust or even affection from his mistresses. He never promised what he couldn't give. Professions of emotion were for fools and liars. What would be so wrong if he lifted her from the divan, touched that golden skin and—

"You were wise to reject me." Her whisper came to him out of the darkness. "I could easily be no virgin, but a woman of the bazaars. Everyone knows that the Nantal lie to push the price higher." The soft voice sounded cool and remote. If it weren't for the slight tremor beneath her words, Nicholas would have sworn that she had no fear of him or the situation.

"I could be...diseased. With the...pox. Do you understand what I am saying?"

"What pox? The French?" he asked.

"Yes," she said.

"Perhaps the Italian," he went on.

"Maybe that too," she said, her voice breaking.

Nicholas dealt with enough diplomats to know a liar when he heard one, particularly one who was so unskilled in the art.

"I understand perfectly. I would be a fool to attempt you, wouldn't I?" The darkness masked his grin. Not for a moment did he believe this woman was a diseased harlot. From the little hitch in her voice and the bravado that seemed so much bluff, he had an impression of innocence caught in a trap.

She lay very still, hiding in the darkness. He breathed deeply, scenting her in the warm room. She smelled of lemon and jasmine, and beneath that lay a hint of her own feminine scent. He wished she weren't a slave and could choose a lover of her own volition. He wished he could rub his face against that warm, perfumed skin.

He squeezed his eyes shut and rolled over on his side. "Don't be afraid," he said, more as a reminder to himself than a reassurance for her. "I meant what I said. You're safe with me."

***

Sera lay awake in the dark, listening to the Outlander king's breathing. The depth and the evenness of each breath had told her that he had fallen asleep half an hour ago, but she had to be certain before she took advantage of her sudden good luck.

It was all her fault—from the very beginning. If she had not begged her grandfather to save the ferendi devil who lay dying outside the cliff walls, he would never have ordered the Outlander brought into Arkadia.

After he'd recovered, the Outlander stole away in the night, bearing with him the Heart of Fire.

Without the Heart of Fire, the kingdom was vulnerable to any tyrant seeking Arkadia's destruction. Grandfather would have no recourse but to seal the kingdom shut forever on midwinter's day. And Sera had no recourse now but to chase after the thief and return the ruby before Grandfather did so.

Sera bit her lip. Only two months left! If she didn't find the ruby by then, she'd be banished from the Hills forever. If only Hadar's eunuchs hadn't thought her Hill cloak a dirty rag and burned it, she could fly on the wind from this prison, and she would be searching even now for the ruby.

The Outlander king still slept. His breathing had deepened and slowed into that state of dreamless relaxation when even the most aware cannot hear hushed footsteps in the darkness. She couldn't spare time to think about this king, whose beautiful face outshone that of the Apollo standing in the Temple Square. It had been difficult not to respond to his beauty when she stood hidden by the wooden balcony screen. But up close, the man's dark fringed, gray eyes had shimmered with something both frightening and compelling when he looked at her. It had to be fear that made her respond to his gaze with languid warmth in her belly and a strange weakness in her knees.

Sera rolled into a crouch and rose to her feet. No more nonsensical thoughts, she scolded herself. It was past time to go.

Glancing through the lacquered windows, she saw the moon dip behind a cloud and made her way, step by step, across the marble floor of the bedchamber. There would be a few sleepy guards outside, but she would simply say the king had dismissed her. The walk to the stables wouldn't be a problem. Grandfather had taught her to blend as though she were a part of things.

Muffled sounds came from the corridor—terrible sounds she had heard once before. Heart slamming erratically against her chest, Sera retreated into the room and shrank against the wall to the left of the door. She stood between the sleeping Outlander and the door, listening in horror to the low, choking sobs of the guards as they were killed. And then came a rustle of a key in the lock and the slow creak of the doorknob as it turned.

The dim light in the corridor outlined the doorway well enough for Sera to see four figures dressed in black. A silent scream gathered in her throat, but she could not utter a sound as her worst nightmare crept into the room. She shrank against the wall, thinking only stillness, as Grandfather had taught.

At that moment, the moon sailed out from behind the cloud, limning everything in silver. The men in black were slinking closer to the bed, intent, not even aware of her presence in the room.

Run, run, she thought. The stable was less than three minutes away.

The leader of the assassins was almost past her. She could hear his muffled breathing, smell the sweat of anticipation on him. He slowly made his way toward the bed, his knife raised and ready. She could leave in a moment more and be free. She could—

"No!" The scream ripped its way from her throat.

While the Outlander struggled up from sleep, Sera took a deep breath and hurled herself at the black clad leader who was closest to the Outlander's bed. The vermin was solid and hard. A black hood shrouded his head. She struggled, biting the wrist that held the knife, but the man gripped her hair and pulled back hard, exposing her neck to the knife's blade. Her eyes watered in agony at the cruel pressure on her scalp.

Through the ringing in her ears came shouts and cries of pain. The Outlander king was a blur of motion and unleashed power. The door from his companion's chamber crashed open. In the light pouring in, she saw the king slice through the men coming at them as though they weren't even armed. She caught a gleam of concentration in his gray eyes, a glint of bright sword against her captor's dark-clad side. The knife dropped from her throat, but as the man holding her went down, she felt the icy glide of steel through the flesh of her arm.

The companion, sword raised, joined the fighting. Sera stood swaying in the darkness, while the king whirled, quicksilver swift, and cut down another assailant. Suddenly, there was no sound in the shadowed room but the scratch of tinder as the companion lit a lamp.

"Hell, you're not even breathing hard," said the companion, rushing over to the king.

"They didn't touch me," said the king, shrugging. "The girl sounded the warning and threw herself at the leader."

They both turned to Sera and stared at her. She stared back, her heart galloping unsteadily as the candle flame made swaying shadows on the wall behind them. The Outlander king really was strong, she realized muzzily, and his look could intimidate anyone. His gray eyes had gone the color of dark slate, and his mouth turned down in a fierce frown.

Why was the man angry with her, she asked herself in a hazy sort of defensiveness. It was not fair. All she got from her good deed was the scorching heat of this giant's glare.

The king's eyes were focused on her arm, she realized, not her. Looking down to see what had prompted his fury,

Sera saw the blood coursing down from the slice across her arm right above her elbow. The thin silk of her skirt was already drenched with it.

"It is nothing. A mere scratch," she murmured. "Help me get to the stables, and you've paid your debt."

"It's rather more than a scratch." The king moved to her side, pulled off his linen shirt and ripped it into strips. The blond one held her arm steady while the king wrapped the strips around the wound. Both men paid strict attention to their task, but ignored her weak protests completely.

"The black uniforms, the masks—who else could they be but the bastards plaguing the border towns of Russia, as well?" asked the one called Andre.

"That they would dare! And to do this to a woman..." The king's hands were gentle, but the bandage was uncomfortably tight.

The Brotherhood. That was what they called themselves, the crazed religious zealots who preyed on the kingdoms of Beaureve and this king's Laurentia—as though a word could make jackals seem like men of honor. They spewed hatred upon any of the people who worshipped in traditional prayer houses with those litanies the Brotherhood found offensive. Outlanders! Never in a million years would she understand their antipathies, their brutality.

"Hadar betrayed us," the blond one was saying. "He must have given them access to your room."

"Hadar's a fool and a coward. He could have had an ally, but instead all he's gained is an enemy." The king went to the door, dragging her along with him, holding her close to his side as though he did not wish to let her go. His naked chest was dense with muscle, damp and heated from the battle, and very, very solid. She had a sudden absurd desire to rest her head against the springy scattering of black hair growing there. The blood loss had obviously affected her brain. She looked into the hallway as he pulled her forward within the circle of his muscled arm. Several guards in Iman Hadar's gold and red tunics lay dead outside the door.

The king returned to the room, still holding her steady with one large hand on her shoulder.

"Nikki." The companion threw the king a shirt. He

shrugged into it and then pulled her back against him. Sera swayed, grateful for the support.

"He's in league with them all right, but we'll never prove it," the king said. "These guards died fighting to protect us, so he's got his claim of innocence. But it's the courtesan we must thank. She alone saved us."

Courtesan! Of all the stupid, illogical, Outlander assumptions! Sera felt the room spin out of control. She sank sideways against the Outlander, and the whirlpool sucked her into the dizzying darkness.

***

Nicholas felt the woman slump against him and swept her up into his arms. At the same time, he heard the heavy footsteps of several soldiers in a dead run toward his door.

"Damn, this just gets better and better." Andre lunged forward to shut the door.

"Wait. It's Hadar, come to view the bodies. I want to see his face when he sees which ones lie in this room."

Iman Hadar rushed forward at the center of a troop of his guards. He wrung his plump hands as he passed the guards lying dead in the corridor, his silken shoes making slippery shuffles on the marble floor. As Hadar got closer, Nicholas held the woman tighter against his chest.

He looked down at the slave. She was very small in his arms. The veil fluttered loose, revealing her face. She was, quite simply, the most beautiful woman he had ever seen. Long lashes, blond at the root and darker, like bronze at the tips, curled against her cheeks. Her nose was small and straight and her lips were full, soft, and naturally inclined to curve just a little into a half smile. For some strange reason, she looked oddly familiar, but his first concern was her pallor. He knew how much blood she had lost, and she might even now be dying from it.

He bit his lip, awash in guilt. While he had been dreaming of her, she had faced death alone.

"We leave now," said Nicholas, purposefully fixing Hadar with a look that made stronger men than Hadar quail before him.

Hadar's fat face took on an expression of distress and fear, Nicholas noted. He bloody well should look fearful, for Nicholas was seriously thinking of starting a border war with the turncoat.

"Truly, I don't know how this terrible thing could have

happened, my friend," said Hadar in a soothing voice. "Surely you will allow me to make some reparation for this outrage, both to you and to my honor as master of this palace. Name what you wish, and it will be yours."

Nicholas's lips curled in distaste. "Your slave," he said. "Were it not for her, I'd be dead, and my council would vote for war against Jehanna. I wish her papers, immediately."

Hadar clapped his hands twice, and a servant scurried out of the room, bowing as he left. A short time later, the servant returned, bearing the bill of sale for the woman. Andre accepted it and gathered their belongings, for Nicholas would not let go of the woman.

"Surely there must be something else you wish from me," wheedled a still frightened Iman Hadar. "Jewels? Spices? The brightest, most delicate silk and fine porcelain from the China trade? Name it, and help me to erase this shame upon my reputation."

Nicholas felt a weak tug on his shirt. The woman's eyes were open, blue and limpid as a spring sky. He bent his head to her bloodless lips.

"In the stables, there is a blood red chestnut with flaxen mane and tail. Take him, for there is no finer horse in your kingdom, or any other in your world."

Nicholas froze in place for one moment, intently studying the woman in his arms. He nodded sharply and gave his demand to Hadar, who reddened, but nevertheless gave a command to fetch the stallion. Nicholas stalked down the corridor, now surrounded by his men, who had gathered at the door of his chamber while he spoke with Hadar.

The little concubine lay trustingly against his chest. At the base of his neck, his skin rippled with a small shiver. Here was a mystery within a mystery, a Hill slave who spoke with the cool, pleasing accent of a noblewoman—in Nicholas's language.

When Nicholas reached the stable yard he stopped dead in his tracks. The Hill woman had spoken truthfully. Torches rimmed the area, and in the flickering light stood a magnificent stallion. The chestnut reared, striking out at the grooms who were straining at the ropes they held. He let out a scream of rage, pawed the air again, dropped with lightning swiftness and lunged to the left, snaking his head as he attempted to bite a shouting groom.

"It's obviously my lucky day," Nicholas said to Andre. "My plans for unity are destroyed, but I'm now the fortunate owner of a rogue horse and a slave who orders me about like the kitchen boy."

The woman stirred in his arms. In a voice filled with urgency and insistence, she said, "He is no rogue to a man who deals with him properly."

Nicholas's lips quirked upward. "My apologies, Mademoiselle." He grinned at Andre. "One out of two, anyway."

"Kindly quit dithering and take me to him." The slave's voice was sharp. "Quickly, for I have little strength."

Nicholas startled himself by obeying the woman's arrogant order. Slowly, carefully, he carried her toward the horse. As Nicholas approached with the woman in his arms, the tall stallion sniffed the air, tossed his golden mane and turned to stare straight at them. By the time he'd reached the horse, it had settled quietly enough for the woman to hold her hand right beneath its nose. The stallion sniffed, bowed its head and turned as docile as an elderly maiden aunt.

"Tzirah," whispered the slave, smoothing her palm over its muzzle and up its cheek. "Beautiful boy."

"Tzirah?" said Nicholas.

"His name. It means Wind Rider. You must help me mount, and then swing up behind me. I take it you are not quite a novice rider?"

"Didn't they teach you to soothe a man's pride in Hadar's concubine academy?" muttered Nicholas, lifting the woman onto the horse's back, where she swayed and sucked in her breath.

"They may have taught, but I chose to ignore that lesson."

The stallion wore no saddle and only a halter. Taking a deep breath, Nicholas swung himself up behind her and gathered her close to his body as the horse began to prance. She slumped against him and sighed, then patted the chestnut, whispering soothing words in the Hill tongue. The horse stood at rest, its ears pricked forward.

Andre mounted and moved his stallion up beside Nicholas. His men urged their horses forward until they flanked their king and waited, eager, Nicholas knew, to be gone from this place and across the border before dawn. Nicholas took another deep breath and gathered the ropes of the halter in his left hand. His right arm encircled the woman, pulling her closer against him. He nodded once and squeezed the stallion into a slow canter. With a clatter of hooves, they passed through the high gate of the palace, leaving Iman Hadar and his treachery behind them.

***

When they crossed the border into Laurentia, Nicholas breathed easier. Home. Even the air smelled cleaner, sweeter. He raised his arm high in the dawn's light, signaling his men to halt. He then shifted the limp burden in his arms and ran a hand across his face. His eyelids felt gritty from lack of sleep and the dust from the road, but his body was curiously relaxed, as though he had ridden for an hour rather than most of the night. Aside from the warm sweetness of the woman between his thighs, it was the stallion, of course, that made the difference. Nicholas had never felt such an easy, ground-covering stride.

In his arms, the slave woman moaned and stirred. Nicholas looked down. Her eyes were open but glassy with pain. She moaned again, pushing away from him. The horse stiffened and lunged to the side. Nicholas gave the halter a tug and prayed it would be enough to control the skittish power carrying them.

"We need to find her a doctor," Andre said in a worried voice. "She'll do herself some damage."

"We're miles from a doctor," said Nicholas, fighting his worry and the stallion. "But the lake lodge is close, and it's our best bet if I can get the horse to take the mountain trail without dashing us both to our deaths. We'll take her there and send a few men ahead to Verso for the doctor."

Andre nodded and called to the captain of the guard. Three men set off down the road toward Verso. Nicholas led the rest on the long climb up a narrow trail to the north. The stallion moved under him in an uneasy truce.

The sun rose higher, hot already, with unusual intensity for autumn. The woman was beginning to struggle in his arms. The chestnut snorted and jigged. His muscles turned to iron. Nicholas cursed beneath his breath and used his leg to push the horse forward on the narrow trail.

The stallion's head suddenly pulled against the halter, causing the slave's bandaged arm to bang against her side. She twisted in his arms, shaking her head again and moaning low, and the horse sidestepped the trail, perilously close to the edge.

Tension crept up Nicholas's spine. The hell with the Hill tongue, he thought, wrestling with the horse to keep them from plummeting into thin air. The woman was perfectly capable of understanding anything he said in his own language. "Be still, no matter how much it hurts," he said, allowing the intensity he felt to make his voice hard and cold. "I cannot ride your horse if he thinks I'm hurting you. A minute more of this and I'll leave him behind."

She clamped her mouth together at that threat, shut her eyes and turned her head away from him, effectively dismissing him.

"Good," said Nicholas, as though she were still listening, as though she didn't make him feel like the lowest snake on the face of the earth for threatening to abandon her impossible horse.

They crested the mountain a short time later. The horses behind Nicholas were breathing hard, but the chestnut, now relaxed, never faltered, and his coat gleamed with a thin sheen compared to the runnels of sweat darkening the coats of the other horses.

Andre must have been thinking the same, for he whistled and said to Nicholas, "Jest all you please, my friend. The lady has brought you two gifts already. Your life and this horse. 'Tis not too bad a night's work, eh?"

"She is full of surprises," said Nicholas.

"An interesting lady, I'll agree."

Nicholas nodded glancing down at the woman, who must be conscious, for she kept her face resolutely turned away from him. He remembered her body's nestling acceptance as she slept against him through the long night ride and missed it.

Who was she really? In the bright morning light, he could see the delicate blue veins of her closed lids. Even wounded and exhausted, she seemed to glow like an incandescent flame.

Nicholas caught sight of the lake, its waves sighing as

they lapped at the shore. He sighed in relief. It was cooler already in the shade of the mountain, where the grasses before the large wooden dacha swayed in the lake breeze.

"Dismount, then remove Tzirah's halter."

He shook his head struggling between amusement and exasperation. "How can a woman's voice be as sweet as the scent of jasmine and, at the same time, as cutting as a sharply honed scythe?" he asked her. "Nevertheless, I live to obey."

When he dismounted, she slumped forward against the horses' neck, breathing heavily. The animal stood still as stone while she slipped from its back. Nicholas caught her. Panting heavily, she leaned her forehead against the horse's barrel while he unhooked the halter ropes.

Nicholas turned to the slave again and circled her slender waist with his arm. He was irrationally pleased when she leaned back against him. She might make a show of defiance, but whenever they touched, her body clung to his. The horse nuzzled her hair and sniffed delicately at her bandaged arm. Raising her good hand, she rubbed his mane and breathed into his nostrils. Then she spoke a few words in the Hill tongue too softly for Nicholas to hear, and the stallion made for the lake in a floating trot. Nicholas turned, hesitated, and looked back at the stallion.

"He'll stay close to the lodge until I am ready to mount him again," said the woman softly. "Tell your men to refrain from restraining him, and he'll be as peaceful as your oldest nag."

Nicholas lifted her in his arms and felt that curious satisfaction again as she laid her head against his chest. He fought it down. The woman was stubborn, prideful, and too damned beautiful for a king who needed all his wits about him.

"By all means, My Lady of Humble Mien," said Nicholas, but as he looked down, he realized that his cutting remark had been wasted on her. She had fainted again.

***

Nicholas washed the dust from his face and rubbed it vigorously with a towel the servant handed him. A rap at the door announced Baron Summers, the doctor Nicholas had summoned. He was a small, round man of middle age with a shock of white hair, a small white pointed beard, and twinkling blue eyes.

He shook the doctor's hand. "How is she?"

"Our patient will mend quite well with proper rest and time, never fear. Such a lovely young woman, Nicholas." The doctor produced a long tube and came closer. "Sit down for a moment. I want to see how you do."

Nicholas let out a whoosh of air in exasperation but obeyed as Summers pushed aside his open shirt and held the tube to his chest. "Hold still. You are as much of a fuss-fidget as you were at ten. Hmm. Sounds clear."

Nicholas didn't know why he put up with Baron Summers' ministrations. With the exception of Andre, the doctor was the only person in his kingdom who had no fear of him.

"I'm perfectly fine, Baron. I haven't had a problem in years."

"Still being careful at the first sign of a cold?" the doctor asked, tapping his chest.

"Of course."

"Good, good. All is well. I must say, the exercise regimen you imposed upon yourself has worked beautifully. Astounding. It's almost as though you willed the weakness from your lungs. If you weren't so intent upon secrecy, you'd make a fine case study."

"Absolutely not." Nicholas felt his whole body turn to stone. "No one besides you and Minister Lironsky knows of this, and no one will."

In truth, Nicholas frightened himself sometimes. When he was a boy stricken the second time with pneumonia, his father coldly derided him for his physical imperfection. Nicholas carefully learned the subtle signs of the disease's approach. Through rest and sheer force of will he kept it at bay, and his flaw was a secret from his court and his country. To this day, he had not had another humiliating episode.

"Tush, boy." The doctor patted his arm as though he were ten again. "No need for alarm. It'll be as you say. Now, back to our patient. Get one of the women to stay with her tonight. I gave her laudanum, and she became quite agitated when she learned of it. She fears visions and nightmares. I'm a little concerned, myself, as she mustn't become so upset that she rips her stitches."

"Hmm." Nicholas rubbed his chin. "She'll need someone rather strong. Very well, Baron. I'll see to it. Will you dine here tonight? Perhaps you'll finally reveal the secret of Vladimir's whereabouts. Andre and I are still eager to see him."

"My magnificent grandfather trout? I would no sooner give away his favorite hiding place than slide naked down a snow bank. However, if you'll come fishing with me while you're here, I'll show you a wonderful bend in the stream where the fish are so plentiful they leap at the hook before it hits the water."

"Done." Nicholas walked the doctor to the door and shook his hand warmly. Not two minutes later, Andre Lironsky strolled into his chamber looking fresh and neat, for once, after a cool dip in the lake. Andre took in Nicholas's dusty boots and breeches and his travel-stained shirt.

He raised his brows. "Been waiting for the doctor all this time?"

Nicholas shrugged out of his shirt and cleaned his neck and chest. "She'll need me tonight. There's nobody else who can look after her."

"There are many who can do so, Nikki. Come have a real bath and a decent supper. We've been on the road a night and a day."

"Perhaps tomorrow, when she's completely out of danger. Have them bring a tray to the woman's room," said Nicholas, toweling off and reaching for the clean shirt his aide held out for him.

Andre wore the puzzled look of a man who had suddenly come up against a wall where none had existed for years. "Nikki, I just spoke to the doctor in the hall. The woman will heal. It's beyond your responsibility, nay, it's...improper for you as king to act as a common nurse."

Nicholas concentrated mightily on the buttons of his shirt. "She put herself between me and death. I owe her this."

"And that's all there is to this...labor of yours?"

"What else could there possibly be?" Nicholas felt himself redden. He had not meant to speak so sharply. Ever since the damned disaster in Jehanna, he had been some other person, disgustingly emotional. Like some Eastern fakir, he searched for "signs."

All because he felt that little shiver down his neck.

Andre shrugged and headed for the door. "I'm sure that if you cannot imagine another motivation for your good works, I cannot."

***

The woman's cries roused Nicholas from sleep. He came awake with a start. By the light of the candelabrum, he saw the slave writhing in her bed, her eyes open and unseeing. He rose from the sleeping couch and dipped a cloth into a bowl of clean water. She was muttering now, odd syllables indistinguishable to Nicholas in his state of weariness, her eyes full of fear and anguish.

"Shh..." he whispered, kneeling by the bed and wiping her forehead with the cool, damp cloth. She turned toward him and grabbed his hand.

He rolled his eyes heavenward and knelt there awkwardly. Patting, he thought with a flash of insight. Women like that. He patted her back a few times. "It's just a dream—just visions from the laudanum. It's not real."

But whatever the woman saw was certainly real to her. She cried out sharply in what Nicholas now recognized as a third language—Beaurevian.

"No, no, Mama!" she cried. "Not the closet. Small. Dark. Terrible things—the bad men. There's blood. No, Papa! Don't let her! Oh, gods! I must run, run!"

She was struggling very hard against him. He breathed a sigh of resignation and lifted her up, holding her tightly to keep her from straining against the wound and opening it. He felt her heart pound out its tattoo of terror against his chest. She rubbed her face against his shoulder, then struggled for a moment, batting away his hands, muttering in indecipherable phrases, deep in the nightmare.

How the hell did one soothe a woman? They were all irrational, and this one, of course, was literally so. Perhaps, if he could get that golden mane off her face...

"Shh," he said holding her against him, awkward at the unaccustomed feel of a woman seeking not pleasure, but comfort, in his arms. "No one will hurt you, as long as you're with me. I promise." He smoothed back her hair, surprised at the texture. It felt like rumpled silk. Softer, smoother even than he'd thought it would be. "Have no fear. You're safe."

She sighed and turned her face into the hollow of his neck. And then, quietly at first, the tears began to fall, warm and wet against his skin. She cried, harder and harder, and an odd, tight lump rose in his own throat.

Nicholas was not the kind of man to think in terms of emotion. But here was this woman, fragile in his arms like a bird that had been beating against the bars of her cage for who knew how long. The room was silent and dark in the moonlight, a place somehow out of time. He didn't think or weigh the consequences as he usually did. He just held her.

She let out a little hiccup and a sigh as he dried her tears. Still deep in sleep, she snuggled closer to his body. She took comfort.

From him.

From someplace barren and dry inside him flowed a little spring. He felt his rigid muscles soften like parched earth beneath drops of cool water. His body lifted with his breathing, strange and light.

He laid her back against the pillows, hoping they were soft enough, and stroked her cheek. "Who are you? Why am I compelled to keep you?" he whispered. "And why are you here?"

Two

The Outlander has the desires of a greedy child. He learns only because of his need to possess. Thus, his historic interest in the false science of Alchemy, which he utilizes to acquire gold, or in witchcraft, to seize power. Ever restless, he cannot force himself into the stillness required to understand the essence of a thing—to see how it exists and why. That is why he cannot blend and become a forest, a stone, or even the familiar walls of his own city.
From the Writings of Jacob Augustus of Arkadia

Sunlight crept across Sera's face, warming it. Very cautiously, she opened her eyes and looked around her. She was lying in a soft bed of clean linen, not silk, and there were no bars of wood inlaid with tiny jeweled flowers on the window. She was not in the harem. The room she lay in smelled of pine trees and fresh, clean air. With its oak-paneled walls the color of honey in sunlight, its slightly sloping floor, and its heavy, dark ceiling beams, this room must be centuries old.

Sera jerked upright into a sitting position. The movement set her arm aflame, and she slowly lowered herself back to the bed and took stock of her situation. She was gowned in a long, white linen shift. Beneath the wide embroidered sleeve, her bandaged arm throbbed. Vaguely, she remembered the long journey through the night, how patient and good Tzirah had been carrying the Outlander king mounted behind her.

The brass knob turned, and the door to the chamber swung open.

"Good morning, Mademoiselle." The Outlander king positively filled the doorway. Well, all right, she thought. Perhaps he wasn't quite the giant dear Jacob Augustus was, but he was indeed very tall and broad of shoulder and chest. The king was dressed simply in a pristine linen shirt draped over his wide shoulders, lawn breeches that hugged his slim hips, and tall boots. He wore no stock tie, and his shirt collar was open, showing the strong cords of his neck. Even in this state of informality, his hair was brushed to a glossy sheen and perfectly parted.

"Good morning, Your Majesty. Is my horse settled

well?" The words had risen to her lips before she could call them back. What an idiot she was to question this man as though he were a servant.

Evidently, the king caught the insolence in her remark. His beautiful lips were tight and his eyes were stern. "If you're wondering whether I did as you ordered me yesterday, the answer is yes."

"I did not mean to insult you, and I apologize for my words. Only worry about Tzirah caused them." The king did not seem mollified by her apology. No, he had a heat about him, a shimmering of puzzlement, exasperation, and something else she could almost see in the air surrounding him, which he held perfectly under control. The combination did something strange to her. It made her wish to act badly in his presence.

"And you must also realize that if you had not heeded my advice, Tzirah would have caused you trouble."

He did not deign to answer her. Sera pushed herself back against the carved headboard of the bed and pulled the covers up to her chin, tense and wary. The Outlander's gray gaze lit upon her and took her in—all of her, not just her physical being. He took his time standing silently in the door, as a predator would watch his prey, waiting for the right moment to spring. Sera suppressed a shiver. Part of her felt reckless and excited by his presence. Part of her felt only fear. The man was not what she expected, and in this terrible world, nothing unexpected was good.

"The doctor who treated your wound is waiting to see you. I expect that he will find you somewhat recovered from your ordeal." The king stepped away from the door and leaned back against the wall, crossing his arms over his chest and looming in spite of the distance between them.

"Perhaps you will tell him to come in on your way out."

"I think not."

"Your behavior, sir, is highly irregular, even for a king."

The man merely raised a brow. "But that is the nicest thing about being king in my country. One's behavior is never questioned." Sera felt the Outlander's gaze fix on the heat of her blush as it surged upward from her chest to her neck to her forehead. How dare he remain in her chamber during a medical examination, as though he had a right to be there, as though he owned her! Too weak to fight him, she turned her face away and pretended interest in the vase of flowers on her bedside table.

A small, round man with a cheerful countenance and hair the most wonderful shade of white entered the room and smiled at her. He carried a black bag, and by this, Sera knew he must be the healer the king had mentioned.

The little man bustled over to the bed, took her hand, and bent over it in a kind of bow that looked terribly formal and confused her even more.

"Mademoiselle?" The healer gave her a soothing smile. "I am Dr. Summers, and I am very pleased to see that you are awake and in less pain this morning."

While she tried again to ignore the proprietary concentration emanating from the king, this Dr. Summers held her wrist between his thumb and forefinger and consulted his pocket watch. "Hmm...very nice, but still weaker than we would wish." He carefully unwrapped the bandage and checked the wound. Sera glanced down at her arm and noticed that the slash had been neatly stitched.

"You did that?" she asked.

"I did, last night when I arrived," said the doctor.

In spite of the fact that this man, like every Outlander, had little power to heal a wound, she was impressed with the work he had done. The slash had been long and deep, she knew, and there was no real swelling or heat at the wound's site.

"Thank you," she said. "You are a fine healer."

"Very kind of you, my dear. However, you must help me get you well. That means rest and quiet. By tonight, you must eat meat. As much as you can be persuaded to eat. For the blood, you see. To make more of it."

"I understand, Dr. Summers."

"Good. Until then, rest is the ticket. I am quite satisfied with your progress, but I'll remain just to make certain that you are recovering according to schedule. That, and to take advantage of the fine fishing His Majesty has offered me." The little man grinned over his shoulder at the king, whose fleeting smile in response lightened the darkness in his expression. Then it was gone, and this king was the same overwhelming force against which she must pit her wits.

"If you need me for any reason, please tell the maidservant. Do try to rest, Mademoiselle." The plump little doctor gave her an encouraging smile and left the room.

But the king remained. Although he stood immobile, he again gave the impression of a large, dark cat, and she was the cornered mouse.

She cleared her throat. "I am sure you have much to do this morning. You must not let me take up so much of your valuable time."

He gave her a smile tinged with irony, and he did not move from his place by the wall. "Not at all. Because of you, Mademoiselle, I am on holiday. I have as much time to waste as I wish."

A manservant carrying a tea tray entered the room behind him. The king gave a low order and the servant set down the tray on a table beside her bed and bowed, departing.

The king poured out some steaming tea. After he handed her the cup, he pulled up a large wing back chair and sat down.

He lounged back in the chair, crossing his booted legs at the ankles and resting his chin on his steepled hands as he studied her. His intense scrutiny made her feel like a troublesome puzzle. His long, dark eyelashes fringed his eyes, hiding his thoughts effectively. The flowered porcelain teacup shook slightly in her hand. She put it down on the table, never taking her eyes from the Outlander.

"All night I have been asking myself, who are you? A woman who speaks three languages elegantly. A woman who owns a horse more valuable than a king's treasure. A Hill woman with golden hair and skin so soft and fine you can see the veins through it."

He rose abruptly to his feet and walked to the window. The sunlight played upon his neat black hair, turning it almost auburn at the tips. "Maybe you're a spy, but then, who sent you? Certainly not Iman Hadar, for to pay you would have been a waste of his money. I suspect he was in league with the Brotherhood, and my death, not knowledge of my plans for the future, was his purpose." He began to pace, restless, it seemed to Sera, as though needing to think aloud with his body as well as his mind.

"And if you were a spy—French, or British—why sacrifice yourself for me? My country would be weaker without me."

She realized with a shock of recognition that he was now speaking in French. "Je ne suis pas une agente de Napoleon."

He made no outward movement of surprise and slipped into English. "Nor of the Prince Regent?"

"That libertine?" she scoffed, answering him in kind.

"Of course, were you indeed a spy, what better way to catch me off guard than to save my life and admit to speaking—just how many languages are at your disposal?"

"Eight. I have a small talent for mimicry."

"Mimicry." He raised his brows and slanted her a hint of a smile. "Laurentia is a rich prize, as well as a southern entryway to Russia. Perhaps it wouldn't matter ultimately whether I or some other ruled Laurentia. Napoleon's forces, flush with victory in Russia, would be formidable for anyone."

The king swung around to face her so quickly, she almost gasped. "Why did you throw yourself at the assassin? Why did you take the knife meant for me?"

She shook her head. "How can you ask such a question? All life is precious. I could do no other thing, even though I wished to."

He was looking at her now with the most comical expression—disbelief at war with shock. He gave a bark of laughter. "You're either too good to be true, or the cleverest liar I have yet met. You give me an example of behavior only a saint would follow and then you tell me you didn't wish to follow it, yourself. Why not?"

She could only answer him honestly—there was no other way she knew. "I wanted to escape that prison, and I could have while they...But I couldn't leave you unprotected. Even when I told myself to go, I couldn't." Sera looked down at her hands, unable to explain her actions even to her own satisfaction.

He studied her with that unflagging concentration that made her want to run and hide in a corner.

"No, you couldn't. Spy or unfortunate, I would like to thank you properly, but I don't even know your name."

"Sera," she said, giving him that much. "I don't know your name, either."

"My name is Nicholas Rostov," he said. "I don't know whether they informed you at the summer palace. I am king of Laurentia."

She folded her hands in her lap and looked up at him. "They told me," she said bitterly. "When they—they..." The king stared at her. His nostrils flared slightly, his eyes focused on her with an intensity that seemed to burn. Then he gave her a brief, curt nod.

"You need rest. I'll return later. Perhaps by then you'll be ready to tell me just who you are, and what you were doing in Jehanna that got you captured in the first place."

As soon as Nicholas Rostov quit the room, Sera slumped against the pillows, weak with relief. She was in a terrible state. She had almost lied to this king in Iman Hadar's palace when she felt his body's need for her. She could not lie, but she could not tell the truth, either. To do so would be to endanger all of the Hills. How could she hold strong against that man with his piercing gray stare and his imperial frown? His rare smiles were worse, tugging at her defenses. She must give him a little, but not too much. She must reveal only what she had to. Sera shut her eyes, but her thoughts were whirling too quickly to find rest. What was she to do? How was she to find the thief? How was she to get back home without a Hill cloak to mask her? Why did she ever leave the safety of the Hills in the first place?

***

Nicholas leaned against the pasture fence and watched the chestnut horse gallop in the near field. As Sera had promised several days ago, the stallion was calm. He exhibited a rather distant arrogance with the other mounts grazing near him, and none of the Laurentian horses approached him. They seemed to know he was far too fine for them.

With a bribe of apples in his jacket pocket, Nicholas leaped the fence and approached the stallion. Wind Rider wheeled and galloped away before he could get within twenty yards of the horse.

"Wary fellow, aren't you?" Nicholas left the treats on the ground within the fence. Only when he left the field did Wind Rider approach the little offering and eat.

Andre walked to his side, watching the stallion nibble at the apples.

"Like horse, like rider," said Nicholas.

"What do you mean?"

"Both are fearful and intensely private. Is she a spy or a casualty of war, Andre? Where does she come from? Why was she captured and sold? Who were her parents? I've been trying to figure it out." Indeed, these questions kept him awake the first night at the dacha, watching her as she finally fell into a peaceful sleep. Had it not been for the laudanum and its vivid, drug-induced dreams, he would never have learned about the demons haunting her.

He was a fool to take her home, to keep her in the palace where she might endanger Laurentia.

He shook his head in bewilderment. "Why am I risking the country's welfare, eh?"

"Because if she's a spy, you want to know her contacts and sources," Andre said. "And if she's not, you want to protect her."

"Yes, I've thought of all that," he said. "Whatever she is, I owe her my life. I keep asking myself, why didn't she run when she had the chance? Certainly it wasn't because of my amiable temperament."

"Come, now, Nikki. Surely you are not going to puzzle over this little courtesan any longer. Although she is incredibly beautiful." Andre looked at him closely. "With all your other ruminations, you have noticed that, have you not?"

"Naturally. I'm not totally oblivious to feminine charm."

"Particularly when it's displayed so generously." Andre's lips curved in what could only be considered a smirk.

"Leave off," muttered Nicholas.

"Rather protective, aren't you? And short-tempered, to boot," Andre said as Nicholas turned away from him and began to walk back to the dacha. "There's only one solution for what rides you, my friend, and I suggest you take it as soon as the lady is recovered from her wound."

"I don't know that I can solve this puzzle in so short a time," Nicholas said. "The men I'm sending to gather information won't report back to me for a while."

"I was speaking of a solution to the more obvious problem, Nikki." Andre's face wore an uncustomary look of complete seriousness. "Take your foundling to your bed as soon as possible. Ease your need for her. Then let her go home, wherever that is."

"She deserves better," said Nicholas. "And she's more than you think."

"You really do have a bad case of it, my friend," said Andre.

"No. Do you remember when we were eight, and we decided to climb the old oak in the park?"

"Yes, of course. And you said we couldn't, that there was something wrong. When I asked you why, you said you just felt it. And then that great limb fell from the oak that very afternoon. It was rotted clear through." Andre rubbed his fingers through his hair. "I thought then that to know such a thing before it happened, you must have the Sight."

"Indeed. I didn't see it, Andre. I simply felt a strange prickle at the back of my neck when I looked at that tree. The same one I felt just before the messengers arrived at Oxford to tell me my father was dead." Nicholas kicked at the ground with the toe of his boot. "I felt it the other night, when I held her on the long trip from Jehanna. This time, it's telling me to keep her. And I must pay attention to it, until I know who she is, and why she's somehow mixed up with Laurentia's welfare. Until I do, she stays with me."

Andre let out a low whistle. "This is very strange, Nikki. And you're certain this 'prickle' is in your neck and not another part of your anatomy?"

"Go to hell," Nicholas said, but he couldn't keep his lips from quirking upward.

Later that day in his rustic study, Nicholas nodded to a young lieutenant who folded a sheet of paper and placed it carefully inside his dark blue jacket. "I'll start out at once, Your Majesty."

"Very good, Carlsohnn. As soon as you receive any information about Miss Sera, send word to Montanyard by courier. Interview the families near the Hills, either in Jehanna or in Beaureve. Young Oblomov has already left for the foothills of Arkadia. And don't neglect the nobility."

Sera's nature was too ladylike to indicate low station. There might be a family frantically searching for her. But to own a horse like that chestnut, to speak eight languages fluently, and to instruct a king with cool confidence were the trademarks of something more than just a chit from a noble family. Who the hell was she?

The lieutenant saluted smartly and quit the room. Nicholas walked to the oak wall lined with bookshelves. He picked up a small figurine, a little Minoan earth goddess his father had brought back to Laurentia after a state visit to Crete. He had loved it as a boy, had felt the secret thrill of seeing a woman's uncovered breasts, her small, supple waist, her rounded hips, even if they were made of marble, not flesh. The stone felt warm to his hand.

His thumb played softly over the statue. Round, high breasts, hips flaring from that slender waist. The little goddess bore a striking resemblance to—he almost dropped the precious antique in his hurry to put it down.

It was a damned good thing that Sera was well on the way to recovery. He grew more demented by the day. With a bit of snooping by his agents, he might be closer to what he needed to know about her. He turned and walked into the dacha and down the long corridor to her room. His steps were swift as he traveled the hall, and his knock on her door sounded impatient to his own ears. In a low, musical voice she bade him enter.

Sera tilted her head to look at him as she sat at the bay window, wearing a soft gown of yellow linen. Her long hair rippled in curls down her back. The sun limned her body, outlining her breasts and her hips, turning all of her to gold. Her face had a soft, pink glow like the blush of a rose. Nicholas felt the now familiar tug at his chest as he crossed the room and stood close to her, his back resting against a heavy carved pillar of the bed.

"The doctor was just here with good news," she said to him. "I may travel in a day. I wish to thank you for your kindness, both in saving me from the slave harem in Jehanna and in bringing me here to regain my strength. I owe you a great debt. When I return to my homeland, I shall try very hard to repay you."

"You may repay me by being happy and safe in Montanyard," said Nicholas. He waited, watching the small crease of puzzlement appear between her arched brows

"But Montanyard is in Laurentia," she said.

"Exactly," said Nicholas. He would give orders. While he had her watched for any surreptitious activity, Sera would learn court etiquette, proper court dress, all the necessary foolishness that a lady-in-waiting to a princess was expected to know. She was intelligent. That much he knew from his conversations with her. Until he found out just what Sera was, his sister Katherine would benefit from this arrangement.

"But I am not going to Laurentia. I must return to the Hills." She was holding her hands tightly in her lap, looking up at him with wide eyes. He could see just the beginning of a stubborn set to her rounded jaw.

"Sera," he said, trying to keep his voice reasonable. "A woman, especially one who looks like you, cannot travel these lands alone. Look what happened to you recently. That, or worse, will happen again if you ride off alone."

She rose to her feet and folded her arms in front of her chest. "I made a bad mistake last time, that is all. I promise not to do so again."

Nicholas sighed in exasperation. "I made a promise to you, as well, just a se'nnight ago, as I watched you fight the spell of the laudanum. I promised to keep you safe, and I'll not break that vow any time soon. So you will not ride off alone on that costly stallion."

Her face flushed, and she tapped her foot. "I do not recall you making any promise like that."

"Of course not! You were half out of your mind and raving at the time. Still, I made it."

She stared up at him with wide eyes. Her face grew pale in an instant. "What did I say?" she asked so low that he had to bend over her to hear.

"Something about a terrible punishment—your parents locked you in a closet, apparently. I must say, they sounded like the sort of people I'd put in prison for life."

"Was that all I said?"

Nicholas saw that she was actually shaking. "Yes. But I told you I'd keep you safe, and I shall. Why in God's name do you wish to traipse about the countryside, prey to any villain who sees you?"

"There is something I must do."

He waited for more, but Sera just stood before him, her head down, her hands clasped in front of her.

Nicholas threw his hands up. "You must *do* something? And that is explanation enough for me to send you off, not knowing where you'll wind up, or if you're alive or dead by the side of the road?" God! Which was she—spy or innocent?

Sera shrank back against the wall at this last, and Nicholas came to the realization that he must have been shouting rather loudly. When she raised her head to look at him, her eyes were clouded, but she shook her head and that luscious, stubborn lower lip jutted out.

"First of all, I am not your responsibility, nor your subject. I need not explain anything to you. There are others involved, and my duty lies with them, King, not with you. I can tell you I wish you and your people no harm. My greatest desire is to return to my home and never leave it again. And that is all I can say."

"You will not ride this country alone." Nicholas felt the anger rising in him, hot and potent. He watched her as she blanched and stood straighter.

"You have no right to keep me, Outlander."

"I have every right," he said, working against the heat to keep his voice low and steady. "I own you. Would you like to see the papers?"

She gasped in outrage. "I saved your life!"

"And I plan to return the compliment. Be ready to ride by dawn tomorrow. And don't try to escape tonight. There will be guards at your door and beneath your window, should you be foolish enough to attempt a climb down to the ground."

She had gone from shock to fury to calculation in only seconds. No, Sera couldn't be a spy, Nicholas thought. She was too transparent to last a day.

"Don't even try to think how you might outwit the guards," he told her firmly. "Even if you could get past them, I'd simply ride after you and bring you back. I'm the finest tracker in the three lands, Sera. That's not an idle boast."

She had that helpless look of resentment he had seen before on the faces of his adversaries—the understanding that she had just lost everything and hated the man who was taking it from her.

He turned his back on her and heard his own inarticulate growl. Heaven protect him from emotional women! She'd see the rightness of his decision in time. When he was convinced of her innocence, he would tear up the hateful papers of ownership and free her.

He could almost feel her eyes burning a hole in his

back.

"Soon you'll understand, Sera, and you'll be glad," he said to the window.

Then he turned and walked to the door. Perhaps time alone would make her see sense.

He had his hand on the knob and was halfway out the room when she spoke.

"Barbarian," Sera said, and all the scorn in the world was in that word.

***

Anatole Galerien, king of Beaureve, sat in his opulent study, staring into the fire. He stifled the terrible urge to chew his nails, smoothing the pure white gloves he wore over his ravaged fingers. A servant carrying a coal bucket scuttled across the room to the fireplace and knelt before it. The hod slipped a bit and hit the floor with a loud thump as the man began to set it down.

"Fool!" barked Galerien. "Have a care or you'll be down in the mines bringing the damned stuff up rather than warm and well fed in my palace."

The man rose swiftly, keeping his eyes on the Persian carpet at his feet, mumbling his apology and bowing his way out of the room.

Galerien pulled off his gloves and stared at his hands for a moment. They were cracked and reddened with the rash that had tormented him for the last eighteen years. He scratched at the flaking skin, reached into the hidden cabinet in his parquetry desk and pulled out a brown glass bottle. His hands trembled as he unstopped the cork and poured the lotion from the latest quack on the backs and palms of his hands. The itching subsided a bit, and he sat back in the gold inlaid chair, gnawing at his fingernails.

Someone rapped hesitantly at the door. "Wait," Galerien called. When his gloves were safely on his hands again, he said, "Enter."

A soldier, smartly turned out in parade dress, opened the door. "Count Laslow requests an audience," he said, standing tall but pale with uncertainty and just a hint of fear in his face.

Good, thought Galerien. He wanted their fear, their immediate obedience.

In a swirl of black, Laslow entered and gave him a bow somehow ironic, although correct.

"Well? What news? Of the thief—of the girl?"

Laslow pulled off his black gloves and cloak. He crossed the room to the fire and stood, his back to Galerien, holding his hands toward the warm coals. Even from behind, his tall, slim body looked slightly sinister.

"We have searched the hills and questioned the peasants who live in their shadow. There is no sign of the thief. Anyone who had knowledge of him would gladly have given it up to us when we were done with them."

He turned, crossing the room with his long, cat-like strides until he stood before Galerien. He seemed to loom over the desk, his face still half-hidden, despite the light of the chandelier. "But the girl is still alive. We tracked her to Hadar's palace, where servants told us of a slave woman with golden hair, newly arrived. The Nantal had sold her to Hadar only a few days before. She was being groomed for Nicholas Rostov."

Galerien slammed his fist down on the inlaid writing desk. "Why did you not take them in one blow?"

"I couldn't. Hadar had agreed only to a small force, should anything go wrong. If she had been sleeping in his bed, we would have dispensed with them both, but either Rostov has scruples or he is a eunuch. She was reputed to be quite beautiful."

"The witch was beautiful, too," murmured Galerien.

"At any rate, Hadar's man waited and watched outside the door. The girl sounded a warning and threw herself on Juseph. Of all the men lost in that attempt, I shall miss Juseph the most. He was a genius with a knife." He shook his head, a puzzled expression crossing his normally frozen features. "The girl has actually made me feel...something, if only annoyance."

"However," continued Laslow, settling into the brocade library chair Galerien silently pointed to, "I believe she has gone to Laurentia with Rostov. Whether he has taken her under his wing permanently or has merely given her safe passage is yet to be seen. I shall send men into Laurentia to ascertain if she lives beneath the king's protection."

Galerien clutched the edges of the inlaid desk. He thought he might actually crack off the piece of molding with the intensity of his grip. "You know my need, Laslow. The thief I hired escaped with Arkadia's secrets and its treasure. Find him and the Heart of Fire. Torture the location of the cliffs and the waterfall from him. At least a week before the twenty-first of December, the girl and the ruby must be mine."

"Why the twenty-first?" Laslow fixed him with a curious look.

"The witch once told me that the waterfall froze by that date, and that the cliffs were then visible to the world. Without the Heart of Fire to act as a key to the cliffs, Aestron or his council will seal them shut forever. I need the information and the key before the gates close. See to it, and smartly!"

Only with the power and wealth of Arkadia could he hope to take what ought to be his. Galerien closed his eyes and laid his head against the back of the chair. The skin covering the backs of his hands itched as though fire ants were feeding upon it.

"I must have it all before Napoleon leads his troops hence," he muttered. "I'll be a force to fear in this world." There was utter silence in the room, so profound as to make him believe that Laslow, spectre-like, had slipped away. He could hear the ticking of the French clock on the mantel, the hiss of coals on the grate.

"What is this madness?" Laslow's voice, cold, contemptuous, sliced through Galerien's thoughts.

"No madness. An order. From your king."

"I can guarantee you victory over Laurentia by spring, for your young men flock to our training camps, selling their souls for a chance to put food into their family's bellies. But there isn't enough time to train them for an all-out assault on Arkadia or any other country before the solstice. Aestron has powers that can render us helpless, even if we breach the cliffs protecting Arkadia."

Anatole waved his hand impatiently. "I never truly believed what the witch told me about Aestron's abilities, and besides, it was so many years ago. The man's old. He may be dead by now for all I know, and with him, whatever power he had. Get me the ruby. And bring the girl here. I wish to witness her death."

"I shall prepare my best men to invade Laurentia. By week's end they'll find the thief and bring me news of the girl," said the count.

"Good." Galerien waved his hand in a gesture of

dismissal.

The count gave him a look of utter contempt and a bow so perfunctory that from any other man, Galerien would have punished it with death. But he needed Laslow and his desperate martyrs until he satisfied the hunger that roiled in his belly—for Arkadia, for Laurentia, for respect.

***

In the Mage's palace, Jacob Augustus stared at the fading figures in the scrying glass, his breath coming so fast he had to concentrate on slowing his diaphragm's movements to their normal, unhurried state. He must not give way to emotion. Doing so was deadly, both for him and the Outlander enemy. When he felt more in control, he looked across the desk into his grandfather's eyes. He saw an ocean of calm, more than he ever thought he could manage, himself. And pain showed, too, beneath the serenity.

"I shall go into Laurentia and bring her home," he said quietly.

"No," said Emmanuel Aestron. He placed a velvet cloth over the glass and sat back in his chair. "Give her time to find the thief and return on her own. Perhaps she will find more than the ruby in the Outlander world."

Was his grandfather finally aging and slowly losing his excellent judgment? Jacob hastily put that fear away to concentrate on the problem facing them now.

"She has no Hill cloak. Even if she finds the thief and the Heart of Fire, she will never get past the animals that hunt her, or past filth like the Nantal and Hadar who will see her as a prize for some man's lust."

"Perhaps there are some who will protect her, even to their last breath."

"Outlanders?" Jacob gave a dry laugh. "They will happily rape her and bind her into slavery, but they won't lift a finger to help her."

His grandfather held him on a long, steady look. "Jacob, I do not make this decision lightly. You were too young to understand what happened all those years ago. Perhaps it is time you knew."

Jacob stared at Emmanuel in rapt attention. At last, he was going to learn about those terrible events that had ripped Sera's world apart.

"I shall never forgive myself," Emmanuel said with quiet agony. "I trusted that all was well with Marissa and Stephan. Their people loved them. The Brotherhood was a small group of fanatics no one took seriously. I thought it was safe for me to retreat to the summit of Mount Joy for the summer solstice, to rededicate and purify myself as I am required to do each year. In accordance with tradition, I took no Hill cloak to ease my journey, so, like any Outlander, I toiled up the mountain. After my fast and rituals, I journeyed homeward, becoming more and more uneasy with every step."

The look on his grandfather's face tore at Jacob's heart, but the old man continued in the same quiet tones.

"When I reached my study, I cast the scrying spell immediately. I was too late. My beloved daughter and her husband lay slain in their own blood. The men who had done this had already left the chamber. Then I heard a soft sound, a child's terrified whimper. I donned my Hill cloak and raised the hood. The journey to Beaureve only took a moment, but it was the longest, most tormented journey I have ever experienced. I had visions of the assassins returning to find Sera before I could reach her."

Emmanuel took a deep breath and shut his eyes for a long moment. "Luck was with me. I found Sera in the wardrobe. Your aunt Marissa must have hidden her seconds before the murderers broke into their chamber. I did not plan revenge—it is against our beliefs to take it, anyway. I wonder if I thought, at all. I simply grabbed Sera up, sheltered her within the folds of my cloak and brought her home to the Hills. She did not feel the journey nor anything else for days. She simply sat and stared out the window. When she finally spoke again, I wanted to go to the temple of Athena and swear to keep her safe in Arkadia forever."

Emmanuel's eyes fixed on Jacob in solemn intensity. "I could not do so. The Outlander world may be her fate. And I believe we must not act to keep her from it."

Moderation in all things, Jacob cautioned himself. He wanted to shout and smash his fist down on the desk, but forced himself to speak quietly, so the anger in his heart would not enter his voice. "Grandfather, Sera and I are closer than first cousins because you raised us as brother and sister. Even if love didn't prompt me to save my sister, she is my blood, and my responsibility. Do not make me leave her helpless in a world of such violence and danger."

Jacob had difficulty swallowing. Like Sera, he had been very young when he lost his parents to a plague that swept India. Like Sera's mother, they had gone into the Outlander world to do good. "Grandfather, both Sera's and my parents died because they left Arkadia, and for what?"

Sometimes, in the silence of the night, he still felt the hole in his heart from the loss of his parents, and on those nights, he had no philosophy. He also knew his grandfather's pain was overwhelming. After all, Emmanuel had lost his only children and their mates. First Jacob's father and mother, and then Aunt Marissa and Stephan, the Outlander king who married her. He had seen the lines of pain in his grandfather's face, the tears on his cheeks as he sacrificed at their memorial tombs. He knew how deeply Emmanuel mourned them.

Jacob disagreed mightily with Emmanuel's decision to give Sera time in the Outlander world, but his grandfather deserved the utmost deference. He walked to window and looked down at the Temple Square, the high spear of Athene catching the rays of the afternoon sun and reflecting them back to him in a spark of glory.

"Will you allow me to watch her in the scrying glass from time to time? That way, if she is in terrible danger, I can go to her."

Emmanuel nodded, his lined face kind. "We shall both watch together. And wish her only good."

Not enough, Jacob thought, but it would have to do. He dipped his head in acceptance and rose. "I shall go to the exercise ground," he said. Perhaps he could exercise away the tension due to his worries about his sister and find, in physical release, the serenity that eluded him now.

***

In an attempt to learn the city, Sera looked about her as they entered the tall wooden gates of Montanyard. The more she understood its layout, the more quickly she could escape it.

Word of Nicholas Rostov's return had obviously gone ahead, for the narrow streets of the capital's outer ring were thronging with people. Little houses—some of wood, some half-timbered—lined the narrow, cobblestone streets.

Brimming flower boxes and wooden shutters painted with
hearts and animal silhouettes decorated their leaded glass
windows.

There was a great deal of noise, most of it joyous
cheering. Women dressed in bright gowns and sparkling
white aprons leaned perilously far from second story
windows, throwing garlands or waving handkerchiefs.
Little girls, their braids trimmed with white, flower-like
bows, skipped unafraid, leading the horsemen into the
city. Nicholas Rostov seemed to spark a warm response
from his commoners. But as she looked at the king's face,
Sera saw a smile that strained a little, as though he was
faced with a rambunctious, affectionate puppy and didn't
quite know how to deal with it.

The streets broadened as they wound toward the city
center, crossing squares of elegant townhouses built of
golden stone and decorated with colonnades. When she
made her escape, she must go quickly through these
streets, for there were no narrow alleys to hide in.

Ladies of quality dressed in colorful silks and muslin
stood on the wrought iron balconies with men in superfine
jackets. They waved as the Outlander king rode by, and
Nicholas Rostov responded, but again with that air of
reserve and slight unease. At least he was no snob. He
seemed uncomfortable with rich and poor alike.

Several of the women stared at Sera with a speculative
look in their eyes. She held her chin high and stared back,
but beneath her outward appearance of disdain, she was
shaking and uncertain. She did not want these Outlanders
to judge her in the plain Hill gown she had insisted upon
wearing for travel, particularly when she was already aware
of their opinions when it came to her people.

The road widened into a large square before the palace,
an overwhelming building of the same golden stone
gleaming in the sunshine. Sera's heart sank. About the
palace was a high fence of black painted iron, with spikes
at the top and guards at their posts along the perimeter.
She scanned the palace, itself, to check possible entryways
and exits.

Between the giant pillars holding a roof topped with
statues, a rather plain young woman with brown hair and
eyes to match waited. She wore a white muslin dress with
a blue satin sash. At her side stood a stern, somber older

woman in a black gown. As they came into view, the girl's eyes lit up, and suddenly, she became beautiful. She was looking at Andre Lironsky, who rode to Sera's right. Lironsky made a soft sound. Sera's gaze flew to his face. He was staring at the young woman with a rapt look of wonderment.

Nicholas Rostov was also looking from his friend to the girl waiting so eagerly beneath the colonnades. But he was frowning.

"Andre," he clipped. "Please find a groom to see to Sera's horse while I greet my sister."

Andre bit his lip and nodded. He dismounted quickly and stood beside Wind Rider. "If you please, Miss Sera," he said, offering his hand. His handsome face was marked with strain.

She was moved to pity. "Thank you, sir," she said. "But if there is anyone here you wish to greet, kindly show me the way to the stable area, and I shall find my own way."

Andre swallowed hard. "It is a question of honor, Miss Sera, not one of wishing."

As she allowed Andre to help her down from Wind Rider, Sera looked over Andre's shoulder and saw the girl run forward to embrace Nicholas Rostov, and she heard the gentleness in his voice. Beyond them in the courtyard, she spied a large maple tree. Its leaves had already turned a bright, autumn red. Her heart sank as she looked at it, a living reminder that her time was inexorably slipping away.

Three

"Katherine." Nicholas smiled down at his sister and took her by the elbow, leading her up the grand stairway. Mademoiselle Toinette, the princess's governess, followed behind.

"Tell me what you've been up to. And what you have learned while I was gone."

As Katherine's face mottled with color, Nicholas mentally kicked himself. What she has learned. Good God! Surely, he could do better as a brother than give Katherine that old tired inquisition.

"Not as much as you would wish me to, dear Nikki," said Katherine, refusing to meet his eyes.

Nicholas tried to think how he could undo the damage he had already caused. That unbecoming blush always spoiled Katherine's looks when she felt self-conscious or ashamed. "I am certain you have been applying yourself," he said gently.

"I have tried, but I cannot master the pianoforte any better than when you left," said his sister. "I fear I fumble so with the keys, and that Bach piece is so very complicated. Mademoiselle has told me that I must give a little recital, but Nikki, I do so dread it! Must I?"

Nicholas felt the usual tug of emotions. He wanted Katherine to get over her terrible shyness, but at the same time, he wanted to protect her. What was the need, really, for her to give these performances she so dreaded? At the last one, the women of the court had applauded politely and then laughed at Katherine behind their fans. Even though he knew that soon he must decide whom she would marry, and that her future husband would expect her to show some aptitude for music and a great deal of dignity in front of his courtiers, he could not bear to expose Katherine to ridicule again.

"And how are your riding lessons coming along?" Nicholas asked, attempting to change the subject as they passed through the tall doors and into the grand entryway. Beneath the high dome, he paused and smiled at Mademoiselle Toinette, waving his hand to indicate dismissal. The woman bowed and turned into the left hallway, her black gown swishing along the marble floor.

Katherine hung her head. "Oh, Nikki, they are even worse. The new mare seems to throw her head up whenever I mount her, and I am so frightened that she'll bolt at any moment."

Even though Katherine's head was bent, Nicholas could see her lips tremble. "I am very sorry to be a disappointment," she whispered.

"Little bird, you are never a disappointment to me." Nicholas hugged his sister tightly. "You are kindness itself to everyone in the palace. They all love you, and..."

But that was it, of course! Sera would love Katherine, as well.

The woman certainly was a champion at holding a grudge. She had barely spoken to him on the long ride to Montanyard. But Katherine, if she were not overwhelmed by shyness, could soothe even the most obdurate soul into acceptance. She would make Sera happy here and, in the process, gain confidence herself.

"I need your help, Katherine," he said, telling her about how he had met the Hill woman, and why he had brought her to Montanyard.

"I'll be honest with you. There is the remote possibility that she is a spy. I cannot relax my suspicions until I'm certain of her innocence. But if she is innocent, she's a brave and honorable woman and deserves your friendship. You two are of an age, I believe, and Sera might become a friend to you. But she'll be very resentful for a while and will probably see our courtiers as arrogant snobs."

Katherine's tiny, ironic smile told him that she, too, had often thought the same.

"I know you'll see past the anger, and in a short time, you'll show Sera that she can be happy here. Will you do this for me?"

"Of course, Nikki! I'll have her sleep in the chamber next to mine. That way, we could talk late into the night. And she must have new gowns. I'll notify the dressmaker. Perhaps she could share my dancing lessons, as well. There is much to do!"

Katherine's face glowed. When she forgot herself, she was beautiful, thought Nicholas.

"Could you tell her now, Nikki? I would so love to begin."

Nicholas had no desire to brave that little lioness's

displeasure again. Besides, a king did not traipse after a Hill slave, no matter how unusual the circumstances.

"I need to see my ministers, but I shall send someone to tell her," said Nicholas.

"Nicholas." Katherine's soft voice held a faint reproof. "You're the only person Sera knows here. She will be unhappy and frightened by all the changes. Surely, you can spare a few minutes to tell her what her future will be."

Nicholas felt his shoulders slump. He had already been an ogre to his little sister. In all conscience, he ought to do something to please her. Thus, he couldn't rid himself yet of his obstreperous little burden.

***

Immediately after finding a groom for Wind Rider, Andre left Sera to attend his duties as king's minister. Sera refused the groom's offers of help. She wanted to be alone to compose her mind. The sight of that maple tree in the courtyard had jolted her. A week had already passed since Nicholas Rostov had brought her out of Hadar's palace! She tried to remember how it felt to be calm, and she concentrated on the small tasks at hand, bringing water and hay to the stallion, settling him comfortably in his stall. Then she wandered through the magnificent stables and across the yard that opened into a large landscaped park, looking for a way out. She noted in despair that, for as far as she could see, a very tall, thorny hedge bordered the park. She needed to explore the park, looking for a break in the hedge, a way to freedom.

She returned to the stable, walking past stalls paneled in smooth oak with shining brass hinges and door latches. Everything was spotlessly clean. Further along the corridor was a huge set of doors that opened into a colonnaded indoor arena.

Before she stepped into the arena, Sera sensed that something was wrong. Jangled impressions—pain, anger, and stubborn resistance—flowed to her through the dust motes dancing in the air above a gigantic training ring. The feelings came from the pretty mare that a very young groom lunged in circles on a lunge line. The mare's pure white coat was streaked with sweat and dirt. The groom shouted at her to make her break into a canter, but the mare set her hooves.

The boy shouted louder and cracked the whip behind her, at which point she took off at a desperate hard gallop, dragging the groom across the arena after her.

"Stop the mare." Sera had seen enough of both the lad's and the mare's increasing misery to know that the situation was becoming dangerous for both.

The boy scowled at her. "And who be you to tell me what to do here?" he panted. He gave a yank on the line, and the mare stopped dead, sides heaving and runnels of nervous sweat running down her flanks.

Where was the pain? Sera thought, easing close and running her hand along the mare's neck. The near fore hoof flashed into her mind, with a large stone lodging between the shoe and the frog.

"I own the chestnut stallion," said Sera. "If you let me lunge the mare, I shall give you a leg up on him within the week."

"The chestnut in the fourth stall on the far wing?" asked the boy with round eyes.

Sera nodded, holding out her hand.

The boy hesitated. "You swear you know what you're doin'? I need this job."

"I swear. Give me your hoof pick." The boy gave it over and Sera bent over the hoof, working the stone loose.

"Smart little girl, aren't you?" she whispered to the mare. "I would not have obeyed, either. But now, it will be easy for you, so no excuses."

Sera took the whip and the line from the boy. The mare stood where she was on the circle and, pawing the ground, eyed Sera.

"One bad habit at a time," said Sera, picking up the whip and rolling the line smaller as she closed the distance between herself and the mare.

"All right, my beauty," she said softly. She touched the back legs lightly with the whip. "Walk on," said Sera in a soothing tone. Expecting only more pain, the mare stood stubbornly, and Sera tapped her again, this time hard. The mare jumped forward, but met the light pressure of the line and slowed.

"Good girl," said Sera. "Walk." The little white horse moved forward in the circle, her ear pricked toward Sera.

"See how she listens?" Sera said to the boy, never taking her eyes from the horse. "Keep the tone quiet for the walk." It was this that she needed to combat the desperation beginning to choke her—this still, intent concentration in a simple task, and the comfort of using her one small gift. She had forgotten how she loved the work. The smell of horse sweat and sawdust on a warm autumn day brought it all back to her in a rush of feeling that stung inside her chest.

The mare walked herself cool. Her coat was beginning to dry, and her breathing had evened out. The boy stood close to her in the circle watching, really listening to the lesson.

"Now she has rounded up well." Sera called a halt to the lesson, praising the horse and scratching her behind the ears.

"If you would like, I shall come tomorrow and we can work again," she said as she gave the line to the boy. "Bring an apple for a reward." The lad nodded and tugged at his cap. "Thank 'ee miss. Just ask for Ned, and they'll direct you to me."

She turned as young Ned led the mare to the wash stall and saw Nicholas Rostov leaning against the arena wall, his arms crossed over his chest. The king looked elegant and commanding even in his dusty boots and open jacket. She wished he'd stop regarding her with such intense concentration, for he made her feel like a creature beneath a magnifying glass.

She attempted to brush the dirt and horse dander off the front of her frock, then gave up when it became apparent that most of the grime had settled into the light linen. He had obviously noticed her dishevelment, she thought crossly as she made her way across the sawdust. She could tell by the way his brows were raised in that slight air of disapproval.

Someone coughed, a furtive sound in the upper seats of the arena between colonnades. Sera looked up and noticed several men dressed in boots, rough linen shirts, and worn breeches. They made a quiet audience, lounging in the seats, watching her and Nicholas Rostov with bright, curious eyes.

As she drew closer, Nicholas gave her a grave look. "The mare you exercised so competently belongs to my sister Katherine," he said. "She would like to get to know you. She's even now making plans to put your chamber next to hers inside the palace. Would you like that?"

The resentment returned, leaving her feeling heated and bitter. "I am a slave," Sera said with a shrug. "I have no choice in the matter."

Nicholas Rostov sighed and looked down at her. "That's not true," he said. "You may do anything you wish within the confines of the palace. The position of a lady-in-waiting to the princess is a high honor, however. You need to learn the rules of court etiquette and the arts of fine needlework and dancing. You could even learn to play an instrument if you wished."

Sera felt herself bristling. "You needn't patronize me. I know what a lady-in-waiting does," she snapped.

His lips tightened. "What would you prefer, then? To apprentice to one of the cooks? I assure you, it would be hot and heavy work for one of your delicacy, but if you wish it, you may work all day in the kitchens and sleep by the fireplace at night. Unless you favor the laundry more." By now, Sera recognized that tone of silky sarcasm.

If he was angry, he might be honest about it, she thought while the irritation washed over her. "I wish to work here," she said, just to goad him further.

He frowned at her with thunder in his eyes. "As a stable hand?"

Suddenly, in a flash of understanding, she realized that the gambit she was using to fight him was something very necessary to her future. Wind Rider was here in the stable. If these men who now sat in the upper seats of the covered arena were at all like the stable hands in Arkadia, they would know all the news in Laurentia before anyone else in the palace, for the coach drivers and the soldiers came to the stables first. She could ascertain more about the thief and she could escape from Montanyard more easily if she worked here.

"Truly, Nicholas Rostov. If you watched me lunge the horse, you saw that I did it well. You say I am free to choose my occupation. Let me work here."

He frowned, staring down at her. He was no longer furious, she saw, for the look he gave her was troubled, almost concerned. "This is a rough place. The men might take liberties."

"If you only give me a chance, I shall prove myself to them all. In truth, I am uncomfortable at the very thought of entering your fine palace and of meeting the nobles of your court. They will scorn me, Nicholas Rostov, and you know they will. Think how you yourself regard a person from the Hills, and a slave, at that! I shall be happy here, and I'll work very hard."

Nicholas Rostov was looking at her with the same expression he used often—as though she were an irritating puzzle he had to solve.

"No one could ever scorn you, Sera. From the first moment I met you, you acted like a princess. If this is what you want, so be it. I'll command the grooms to treat you with respect."

Sera executed what she hoped was an acceptable curtsey despite the fact that her legs were trembling from relief. "Thank you, Nicholas Rostov," she said, keeping her eyes lowered while her heart leaped in triumph. In two days she would know enough about the stables and the countryside to execute her escape.

***

In the evening, Nicholas dictated the last dispatches to his secretary Holmes. He had spent two days mapping out Napoleon's progress through Russia and arguing with his ministers. One or two insisted that Britain had obviously proven an unreliable ally—that Nicholas should consider the alternative. The very outrageousness of the suggestion made Nicholas realize how bad the situation was. For a king of Laurentia to approach the French despot with hat in hand and plead for an alliance was tantamount to abandoning his country to the enemy. The hour was late, but he still had several dispatches to dictate to his secretary.

What to do? The answer was obvious. He must cement the alliance with Beaureve. Nicholas sent an emissary to Anatole Galerien requesting a meeting, and he began to consider what concessions he would have to make with trade and import taxes in order to sweeten the agreement.

He wished that Galerien's niece, Catherine Elizabeth Galerien, was well enough to leave her convent and finally marry him. Although Nicholas was far from being an eager bridegroom, the marriage, agreed upon by his father and her father, Beaureve's late king, would cement the alliance, making Laurentia stronger.

A knock on his study door interrupted his thoughts,

and he felt his irritation rise. He had left word that he was not to be disturbed.

"Enter," he called in none too pleasant a voice.

A guard who had the conscience to turn red-faced with embarrassment entered, dragging what looked like a very wet, very dirty ragamuffin across the study to stand defiantly before him.

He shook his head, scowling down at a bedraggled blonde braid and a pair of flashing blue eyes. Holmes made a choked noise in his throat. He dismissed the man with an impatient wave of his hand.

"We followed her out the gates of the city," said the guard. "Had it not been for your instructions, Sire, we would never have caught up with her, but the men waiting on the eastern road waylaid her. There was a bit of a scuffle, I'm afraid, and the lady unfortunately fell into a puddle. I beg pardon for the inconvenience, but you had commanded that we inform you immediately."

"No need to apologize, Lieutenant. You have all done well. Please leave us." He waited until the man had bowed his way out and shut the door before exposing Sera to the Rostov frown. She was in no mood to concede, he realized, when she squared her shoulders and glowered right back at him.

"You posted guards on me!"

"And you obviously justified my mistrust. You should have listened when I told you it would do no good to sneak away. Pray do not attempt such nonsense again."

Sera had the temerity to cross her arms over her bosom and turn her back on him. Her wet linen gown was provocatively plastered against her body, giving him a fine view of gently flaring hips and a nicely rounded backside. In immediate reaction, his loins tightened. His hands itched to lift that sodden skirt inch by inch and mold themselves to her slender thighs, warming the goose bumps he knew must have risen from the chill of the water. Then he remembered that every soldier he had posted to this task had caught a glimpse of those singular charms, and his anger surged again. Before he could stop himself, his arm snaked out and grabbed her shoulder, whirling her about.

"You have embarrassed yourself and the crown. Your behavior is more fitting for a two-year-old in a tantrum than a young lady. I expect better of you in the future, or your activities in the stable will end, and you'll become what every other ward of the king is in this country—a cosseted, protected young lady of irreproachable reputation."

Sera stared at him for a long moment, her brows furrowed above eyes narrowed to blue slits. She looked like a furious kitten getting ready to spit. For the first time in his life, Nicholas regretted his philosophical stance against beating women.

Sera drew herself up to her full height and gave him a frosty look. "You are in danger of becoming the greatest prig that ever lived," she said.

He let go of her arm and watched her lift her other hand to rub the soreness out of it. Shame and resentment warred within him.

"Perhaps," he said coldly. "But I am the prig controlling your life. Make your peace with that and we shall get on better."

She opened her mouth, seemed to think a moment, and closed it again. Foolish little brat not to realize he could see her thoughts flash right across her face. He reached out one hand, turned her toward the door, and gave her a little push.

"Tell my secretary to return immediately. Then go to your rooms and bathe that muck off. Oh, and take a cloak from the first guard you see in the hallway. You look like a dox—a woman of loose reputation—in that wet gown."

She had begun her procession toward the door with upheld head and an apparent air of nonchalance, but at this last, she stiffened, picked up her skirts, and ran the last few feet, slamming the door behind her. All Nicholas was left with was an empty ache, misspent anger and regret, and a trail of small, muddy footprints across the light blue Aubusson carpet.

***

The next day, Sera was saddling the white mare, when the young girl she had seen upon her arrival at the palace made her way slowly toward her. Immediately, because of her timid approach and her plain, worried face, she recognized the princess, Nicholas Rostov's sister.

"I hope…" The princess's strangled whisper faded away to nothing. She cleared her throat and tried again.

"My brother told me you would be here. I was hoping—that is I am afraid to ride out alone—a-and the riding master is so strict with me. I was hoping...Would you please..." The rest of it came in a rush. "Would you mind terribly if we rode together?"

Sera felt a sharp twinge of sympathy. The princess was painfully embarrassed. How could anyone say nay to her?

"I should like nothing better," she said.

"Thank you," said the princess, still flushed with embarrassment. "I forgot to introduce myself. Katherine Rostov," she said. "I-I mean that is my name." She curtsied to Sera.

A princess, bowing to a groom! Sera quickly covered her startled giggle by clearing her throat.

"That is my name, too," she said in an attempt to help Katherine relax.

The princess glanced up quickly. "I thought your name was Sera."

"Oh, that is a short name, a—what is it in your language? A pet name from a larger one."

"A nick-name," said Katherine looking interested. "How many names do you have? I have four—Katherine Mary Annalyse Rostov."

"So do I." Sera clamped her mouth shut. How could she have been so unguarded with an Outlander? The situation called for a quick change of subject. "Let me introduce you to my horse. He's become quite gentle now that he knows the grooms, and he loves treats. If we stop by the apple barrel, you can feed him."

Katherine was happy with the suggestion and seemed to forget all about their conversation. Sera sent Katherine off to get her mare and pressed her forehead against Wind Rider's nose.

"I was an arrogant fool to think I was worthy of this task," she whispered. The horse snuffled affectionately at her hair. "I know," she said looking into his large, kind eyes. "Worthy or not, I must get on with it. But I have been trying, Tzirah. I cannot get out by the gates. Someone will always stop us. I must find a place where we can jump our way out. Each day I have gone as far as I can in the park and checked the walls of this place, but they are too high for us."

Wind Rider just looked at her, a calm, accepting presence in the dark stable. She sighed. "Very well, I'll keep looking. Every day, I promise."

Katherine was already mounted when Sera led Wind Rider into the stable yard. The princess's face was ashen as the mare tried to skitter out from under her. Holding the reins with a death grip, Katherine gave Sera a look of desperation. Sera shook her head and quickly mounted. She trotted her stallion to the obstreperous mare's side.

"Give me the reins, Katherine," she said quietly and pried them from the princess's hands. "That's right. Hold on tight to the mane." With a sharp jerk that brought the mare's head up hard, Sera pulled the little white into Wind Rider's side.

"Walk," she said in a stern voice and tugged once. The mare fell into a walk, her head and neck relaxing into obedience.

"You just have to be firm with her," Sera said, turning to Katherine as she led the mare into the park's grassy expanse. The princess's head was bent, and what Sera could see of her face was a mottled, blotchy red.

"I wish you hadn't seen that," she whispered. "I wish I could at least lead my own horse out of the stable without showing you how badly I..."

Sera's laid her hand on top Katherine's. "I don't care how well you ride. Why should I?"

"Because it is expected that I do well, and instead, I am a laughable failure at it."

Sera shook her head. "I don't know how it is possible for any of your ladies to ride well in those ridiculous sidesaddles. Where can you hold on with your legs? How can you learn your balance? You'll notice that men do not ride with both legs on one side of the horse."

Katherine stared at Sera open-mouthed. Then she looked again, this time with a gleam of skepticism in her large, dark eyes. "You are riding sidesaddle as well as I," she said accusingly.

Sera grinned. "Only to that copse of trees. Come along. I'll show you."

Sera halted Wind Rider within the little wood and dismounted. "I hate these hard saddles," she said, working the girth free and setting the saddle on a fallen log. "I cannot feel the horse at all through it."

Katherine climbed down from her mare's back. "I don't want mine, either," she said, and began to pull the girth loose."

"You might hurt yourself."

"It won't be the first time," said Katherine grimly. The little mare began to sidle away from the princess.

"Oh, bother!" said Katherine.

Sera grabbed at the reins and tugged once, hard. The mare stood while Katherine fumbled with the girth buckles, disposed of the saddle, and climbed a fallen tree trunk she could use as a mounting block.

By the time Katherine, after several tries, had swung herself up on the mare's back, she was flushed with effort and sitting very tall. "Lead on, MacDuff," she told Sera, grinning.

Sera looked at her in puzzlement. "That is from the play by the Englishman—Shakespeare? But what does mounting a horse have to do with those Scots?"

"'Tis a jest," said Katherine.

"A jest?"

"Yes, a humorous, silly play on words to make one smile. A joke, and on myself, actually. After all, those Scots were strong and brave and certainly knew a horse's head from his hindquarters, and here I am finally doing something perhaps a little brave for the first time in my— don't you know what a jest is?"

Sera shook her head.

"You have no humor in the hills?" Katherine's eyes were wide with surprise.

"There is much happiness," said Sera, "but I have never heard of this hu-mor."

"I shall find you examples much better than my poor attempt, I promise. Now, show me how I am to ride this horse."

***

Later that night, Sera tugged at the hold the young guardsman had on her arm, but he refused to let her go. She had to run to keep up with him as he dragged her through the palace.

"I apologize for the inconvenience, Miss, but orders is orders, and I'm not to let you go until I deliver you to the king. Again."

In this, her third attempt to escape and her third

capture, she was beginning to recognize the statues on the way to Nicholas Rostov's study. The guard marched her past the Apollo Belvedere on the right pedestal and the small, blind Laocooin covered in writhing serpents on the left Chippendale table. Tentatively, he rapped at the door of the study. A deep voice called "Enter", and Sera found herself standing once again in the daunting glare of Nicholas Rostov's disapproval.

"Where did you find her this time?" He moved around his desk, put down his papers, and sniffed once. With a frown, he pulled a handkerchief from his sleeve and held it to his nose.

"Don't tell me, Edwards. Let me guess. She used the sewers."

"I'm afraid so, Sire. She was on her way to the woods behind Musgrove's stables, where, as I reported last night, she'd put the horse. We tried to rinse her off at Musgrove's, but the night was cool, and we thought it best to return her lest she take a chill."

"Well done, Edwards. Notify the kitchens that she will need a warm bath immediately."

The guard bowed. "If that is all, Your Majesty, I'll wait for her and return her to the stables. My tour isn't through for another hour."

"Whose is the midnight watch?" Nicholas Rostov asked.

"Bellows has it, Sire."

"When she smells presentable, return her to my study," said Nicholas Rostov with a slight curl of disdain to his mouth. "Bellows will accompany her back to the stables afterwards. You may take a well-deserved drink and tidy yourself as well."

The guard looked positively overwhelmed with gratitude. Sera rolled her eyes.

The clock chimed half past eleven o'clock when the young guard brought Sera back into Nicholas Rostov's study. She was wearing one of the head cook's long white nightgowns, belted with a worn stock tie to keep her from tripping over the voluminous hem, and a worn but clean blue cloak. Her hair was braided loosely and hung down her back.

"What took you so long?" Nicholas asked in a clipped voice. He'd begun by thinking of reasonable openings for this latest standoff between Sera and himself and ended, as the clock chimed the next hour, in getting angry all over again.

"Sire, I apologize. Cook, you see, is young Ned's mother, you know, the stable lad, and Miss Sera here, she helped Ned learn all sorts of things Master Raymond doesn't have time to tell him. When Cook learns she's in the kitchen, nothing would do but she must come down to see to the bathing. And then Cook wants to feed her, because Miss Sera missed her dinner, what with running away and all. Then Cook says Miss Sera's got to dry her hair before the fire or she'll catch her death. And that's why," the guard finished, breathless.

"Thank you, Edwards. You may go."

So. The stable boy and the cook fussed over Sera. And Katherine ran about the palace with a smile on her face. The guards, of course, treated her as though she were a princess, when all the while, she gave them extra duty following and capturing her. It seemed that Nicholas was the only one in the palace who found Sera a constant source of frustration.

Perhaps Andre was right. If he could take her to his bed, he might look at her as just another woman and not a siren so soft and warm that all he could think of was his overpowering need to get closer to her.

Sera braced herself, wondering when Nicholas would finally pronounce her fate. As the small ormolu clock on the mantle ticked the minutes away and he still refused to look at her, Sera's anxiety and resentment grew. She knew he must do this on purpose, just to set her on edge. He was perusing something of seeming major interest out the window, his hands clasped behind his back. Soon, he would turn, and she would suffer one of his lectures yet again. She was sick of them.

"If you ordered the guards who watch my every move to accompany me home, I would be safe in my Hills, and you would be rid of my inconvenient presence."

His back stiffened. "No."

"Just...no?" Suddenly, she felt she couldn't go on without crying, and she hated him for making her feel that way. She never cried. Did he think she enjoyed this contest—that she liked going down into the rank-smelling sewers populated by rats and snakes, and Zeus knew what other horrors? How could he do this—imprison her for no reason at all except her supposed safety? What game was he playing with her?

"I cannot spare the men." Still, he did not turn to look at her.

"You already spare the men to watch me. Dear Heaven, why won't you let me go?"

It always caught her off guard, his ability to wheel so quickly, so gracefully, like a large, sleek panther. He loomed over his desk, hands planted on each side of the papers, his eyes burning into her with an intensity that seared her to the very core.

"Tell me who you are. Tell me who your people are. What were you up to when the Nantal found you? Tell me why you know eight languages, and why your horse is of the finest blood stock I have ever encountered, and why you treat a king as an equal, or perhaps a not quite equal. Tell me all that, and I shall think about letting you go."

"It is nothing to you," she said, backing up and flinging a look over her shoulder toward the door, her means of escape from his infernal questions. Her movement made the long braid fly. It fell across her breast, and the small thread of hair that held it broke. Dry now, it began to separate into strands, catching the lamp light. Nicholas Rostov's face underwent a subtle change. The intensity was still there, but his gaze was fixed on that slow fanning out of her hair. His cheeks seemed to hollow, the planes and angles of his face seemed sharper. A slow flush deepened on his face.

Her breast rose and fell unevenly with her breath as he walked from behind the desk like a great cat stalking his victim. He loomed over her, large and inscrutable, radiating a force of will so dangerous and so seductive she feared he could bend her to his every wish if he gave it half a try. She couldn't seem to move, to breathe. He reached out a hand, lifting the length of her hair, seeming to weigh it in his hands.

"Nothing, you say. I wish it were that simple. There is something about you, Sera with no last name, no history, no family madly searching for you."

"Your hair," he said softly, his fingers slowly stroking the strands into a fall of gold that gave back the light of the lamp. "It almost pulses with life. Warm." He lifted the fall of hair to his face and breathed it in like perfume.

"Fresh and sweet, with no remaining trace of the sewers." He leaned close, holding her just by his light touch on her hair. Sera felt the warmth of his cheek, his breath a slow exhalation against the side of her neck, and she shivered. His lips moved, touching, and not quite touching, the hollow there, like the wings of a butterfly.

"Sweet," he whispered against her sensitive skin. She stood helpless, in thrall to that deep timbre of pleasure, the warmth enveloping her. "Soft mystery. Lady in peasant's garb."

She made a sound, helpless and wanting at the same time. He drew back a little. Slowly, the boundless depths of his eyes regained their usual focused intensity, and an expression, sudden and startled, crossed his face. He backed away, reddening.

"I...my apologies." He turned his back to her, shuffling papers on his desk. "Bellows," he called out in a rough voice.

The door opened. Nicholas Rostov turned. He was scowling again. "Take her back to the stables. If there is further trouble, notify Minister Lironsky."

Sergeant Bellows bowed smartly. "Very good, Sire," he said and led Sera from the study.

***

Nicholas sank into the chair behind the desk and put his head in his hands, groaning. She was killing him, very slowly and very painfully. The sensual dreams were bad enough, but midnight meetings with Sera close enough to catch that elusive, flowery scent were madness.

She'd had enough time to contact another agent. She hadn't. He was beginning to believe she was what she appeared to be—a victim of circumstance. He had enough proof of her incessant longing to return to those blasted savages in the Hills. Why the hell didn't he just send her back? She'd be happy. He'd be free of her.

But there was something about her. He had felt it from the start, when that damned prickle at the back of his neck warned him to take her and to watch her carefully. Something Laurentia needed from her, and needed at this particular time. He couldn't dump her back into the mountains whence she came. And he couldn't sit here, night after night, lusting after a Hill slave who acted like a queen, at least not until he knew the how and what and why of her.

Nicholas reached for the brandy decanter sitting on his desk and poured himself a bountiful glass. Downing the contents in three gulps, he called for a footman. "My carriage," he said shortly. Twenty minutes later, he alighted before the door of a large, well-appointed townhouse in the King's Crescent. The door opened and a maid curtseyed very low, the ribbons of her cap bobbing.

"My lady is above stairs," the maid said, taking his cloak, gloves and hat.

Nicholas bounded up the elegantly curved stairway to a sumptuously decorated boudoir. A tall, statuesque woman, a dramatic auburn beauty, rose from her dressing table and gracefully glided toward him, extending her hand.

"You honor me, Sire. Let me make you comfortable," she said in the dulcet tones that Nicholas occasionally found soothing. Tonight, so far, they were doing nothing to calm him.

"Good to see you, Elise," Nicholas said, turning away from her as she lifted his coat from his shoulders. He allowed her to loosen his cravat in that playful manner she assumed with him. But it suddenly felt so practiced, so artificial.

"Some refreshment, Majesty?" Elise swept to the table beside the bed and bent over a wine bottle. The candles on the table outlined her soft, luxuriant body beneath the lace peignoir. She crossed the room to him, offering the glass. The scent of musk and roses filled his nostrils. He took the glass, seated himself and crossed his legs, looking at her over the rim as she returned to the bed and lay upon it, languid and inviting.

She looked perfect, he thought. She looked too tall, too dark, too knowledgeable, too damned aware of every affect she made. He was sick of this loveless lovemaking. He wanted—damnation!

Nicholas put his wineglass on the table beside his chair and stood, straightening his waistcoat.

"Shall I call for food? Those cakes that you love, filled with poppy seed—I had some delivered today."

"No. Thank you. I just dropped by for a moment to..." What the hell could he say he'd come for? He took up his coat and his cravat, shrugging into the former and wrapping the latter haphazardly about his throat.

"Inquire about your welfare, Elise," he said. "It has been a long time since I paid you a visit. Unfortunate that I don't have time to stay tonight." He was out the door five minutes later, leaving not the first woman in a string of mistresses who probably found him more trouble than he was worth.

Back in his study, Nicholas stood at the bookcase, thoughts churning. What a fool he was, lusting like a stable boy after the milkmaid, incapable of taking his pleasure elsewhere. He had never thought of his future wedding to the sickly and perhaps weak-brained Beaurevian princess with pleasure, but now he pondered it with something close to dread. Kings cannot hope for happiness, he told himself impatiently, lifting his eyes to the bookcase.

His gaze fixed upon his collection of journals by intrepid travelers who had explored the wastelands and mountains of the known world. From boyhood on, they had excited his imagination. If he could have any freedom, it would be this—to travel, to see strange and wonderful sights no other man had seen. Idly, he picked up *A Road Well Taken* by Countess Elizabetta Volkonsky, a Russian eccentric who claimed to know more about the mysterious Hill People than anyone on earth.

He sat behind his desk and flipped through the pages, stopping at a chapter titled "Myths and Rumors". The countess, it appeared, set little stock in these stories, but the people who lived in the foothills of the Arkadian mountains told the tales faithfully to their children in each generation.

He skimmed through much of it—the powers of the mysterious Mage to heal the sick with just his touch, to bring the rain or the sunshine for needy farmers, to appear magically when his name was invoked in times of great peril. He skimmed another paragraph, his eyes beginning to water from a long day of reading dispatches and tense meetings. Suddenly, he started awake, rubbed his eyes, and re-read the paragraph.

The Mage, wrote the countess, is said to teach his power to his people, so together they have the ability to disarm their enemies. It is said that, from time immemorial, strange things have happened to armies that attempt to conquer Arkadia. Ghengis Khan's men found their arrows breaking and falling from their suddenly unstrung bows. Their horses fell into heaps, and the riders could not get them up again until the Khan commanded his trumpeter to sound retreat.

"Humbug," said Nicholas. But the prickle at the back of his neck was there again. The prickle told him to pay attention to a fairy tale.

He rubbed his eyes and put the book back on the shelf, shaking his head in self-disgust. How could he trust his instincts when every muscle and bone in his body screamed for that incorrigible little chit in the stable? Of course he would believe in any nonsense that would make Sera appear invaluable to Laurentia and, therefore, permit him to keep her.

Realistic politics, not fairy tales, would save Laurentia. Nicholas took up the brandy and a glass on the way out of his study. When he reached his bedchamber, Simmons, his valet, snapped to attention, and then stared, open-mouthed at him.

"Sire," Simmons muttered in a choked voice. "Your cravat!"

Nicholas glanced down at the trailing ends of the tie and waved him off for the first time in years. "Go to bed, Simmons. It's late," he said. The valet gave him a wounded look and left the room.

Nicholas pulled off his half boots, drew off his waistcoat and cravat and opened his shirt. Not even bothering to pull down the counterpane, he climbed into the great bed of state with a full glass of brandy and lay among the pillows. His groin ached, and his brain ferreted about, reshuffling information into possibilities and patterns.

Damn the little minx! Within three weeks, she had invaded his life, refused to stay where she was put, and literally created a stink. She seemed to be the one thing in his kingdom he couldn't control. Now, to his humiliation, he lay half-dressed in bed, drinking brandy and, no doubt, preparing to dream of a small, lush woman who could heal the sick, command the weather, and break an arrow with the force of her mind.

Four

After a sleepless night, Sera wished Nicholas Rostov in Hades. A more mystifying, infuriating, arrogant man had never lived before the king of Laurentia. The more he pushed, the more she wanted to push back. Until he came too close. Until his lips moved not a whisper away from her skin. Then she stood as though chained to the spot, in thrall to the very hint of his touch.

She churned with such extremity of emotion that she felt completely Outlander. How Grandfather would sigh at her helpless attraction to Nicholas Rostov. How Jacob would lecture!

With all this foolishness, she was no closer to either finding the thief or returning, shamed but safe, to Arkadia. She tried to concentrate on grooming the gentle bay gelding Master Raymond needed in half an hour, but her thoughts returned to the need to escape.

"Ho, my pretty, and where were you so late last evenin'?" Dawson's voice cut into her thoughts. A brawny hand landed on her shoulder. Sera shrugged hard, trying to dislodge it. The groom was getting to be a real nuisance.

Tall and muscular, handsome in a crude sort of way, Dawson thought the world of himself and very little of others. Too bluff, too hearty, and hiding a streak of maliciousness beneath a good-fellow bonhomie, he passed for a one-of-the-boys prankster among the others, but Sera saw what he was, and he knew it. Lately, he'd developed a new sort of torture for her—his unrelenting sexual pursuit.

The hand rubbed itself down her back. Sera gritted her teeth. "Get off with you, Dawson. You've enough to do today without bothering me."

"Prickly little piece, ain't you? I saw you returnin' with Sergeant Bellows in the middle of the night. It might int'rest you to know he's a wife and two kiddies at home. You might play closer to your fellows and forget your ambitions up at the palace."

"Leave me alone, Dawson, or I'll shout for Master Raymond, and you'll be out of a good paying job."

Dawson's hands clamped hard on her shoulders. "Try it, you little tart, and I'll tell him you threw yourself on me and begged me for it. Who's he going to believe—you, a slave and a Hill woman, or me, a man from his own city?"

Dawson bent close. She could smell rank sweat and the onions he'd eaten with his breakfast. She sighed, loathe to use any power that might brand her more of a threat than she already was.

"Let go, Dawson," she said one more time, but he clung, hurting her arms.

She concentrated, knowing where both his hands were, knowing where both his legs were. And turned in one fluid motion, using the force, letting it flow from her belly to her elbows, arms, and fists. In one lightening movement, she broke his hold, kicked solidly into his gut, and sent him sprawling in the dirt.

"Touch me again, and you'll get worse," she said and turned back to the horse she was grooming. As he gasped for air and crawled to his knees, she added, "Nobody saw this. I shall tell no one. I have no interest in humiliating you, Dawson. I simply wish you to leave me in peace."

She heard nothing behind her but the heavy tread of his feet as he shuffled away.

**

Nicholas rode the Russian border throughout the next days, securing it as well as he could against the French. Everywhere, he found homesteaders willing to take a stand and fight. He saw nobility in these simple men, and a certain skill with a pistol and muzzle-loader. It gave Nicholas an idea, which, on this crisp autumn afternoon, he was about to discuss with his generals. He awaited their arrival in the private dining chamber of a border tavern.

The generals trooped in, bowing and seating themselves where Nicholas indicated. His ensign, Carlsohnn ushered in a group of serving maids with blonde braids coiled about their heads. Their colorfully embroidered skirts and apron ties flew behind them as they hurried to the long table, carrying groaning trays. Within moments, the generals had emptied a large turreen of Russian borscht, plates of heavy, rich black bread, bowls of creamy yellow butter and gleaming black caviar. The maids refilled glasses of tea and Russian vodka as quickly as they emptied.

Nicholas smiled and leaned back in his chair, quietly surveying the men at table as the vodka and warm borscht relaxed them. Oblomov, grizzled and clever, was the key to the rest of them. An aristocrat and a brilliant tactician, Oblomov had begun his career before Nicholas was crowned. The other generals were stubbornly loyal to the old ways, but they would follow if Oblomov led.

Nicholas waited until they were well along into their fifth glass of vodka and watched Oblomov carefully. When his stocky shoulders slumped in relaxation, Nicholas knew the general's mind was both still lucid and at its greatest stage of openness to new ideas.

Nicholas drew himself erect in his chair. "I wish to enlist all the able bodied men on the borders into a citizen army. I'll need several of your finest trainers to drill them in the basic use of their weapons. Each of you must give me a list of your best infantry leaders. Yes, General Oblomov?" Nicholas recognized the general, bracing for reservations.

"You can't expect untrained men to form a unit in a matter of months. It takes time to make a good military man."

"Time is one thing we have not got," Nicholas said.

"But to learn the maneuvers, the basic commands, to work together, standing in line, facing the enemy..."

"I don't wish them to stand in line. These men have defended their homes and stock against the bears and wolves of the forests. They know how to use a weapon and re-load it."

"Sire," General Milensky, a tall, upright old campaigner of seventy said. "This is no bear we face. We need every seasoned veteran we have to fight the greatest armed force history has ever seen."

"As did the American colonists not so many years ago. Our borderers are the closest thing we have to the American colonists. I want them to stand behind trees, behind houses, on rooftops, just as the colonists did. Each French soldier they take out is one less for our troops to fight. And, as the British showed us in the Carolinas, facing a shadow army in the midst of heavy forest is frightening and demoralizing. We'll do as I command in this instance, gentlemen. Spare your men now to save them later."

The generals' mutterings died down as each man stared into the clear liquid in the glasses before them and thought.

Oblomov suddenly pounded his fist on the table. "By God, I like it. Simple, workable, and the Corsican will never see it coming. My compliments, to you, Sire." Oblomov stood and raised his glass. Milensky rose to stand beside him. One by one the others got to their feet and raised their glasses.

"Nicholas Alexander Andreyevitch Rostov," said Oblomov. "King Nicholas," replied the others, tossing back the vodka, and throwing their glasses against the fireplace mantle. At the sound of crashing glass, the serving maids returned with new tumblers.

Nicholas stood and raised his glass. The generals hastily refilled their replacements. "Laurentia!" said Nicholas with a broad smile, throwing back his head and swallowing the pure, stinging liquid.

"Laurentia!' shouted the generals and glass crashed against the fireplace again.

Nicholas gave a great, inward sigh of relief. He might never be the king his father could respect, but if he compensated for his physical flaw with his brain, perhaps he could make his people believe in him enough to save Laurentia.

Nicholas was so pleased by the meeting that he decided to return to Montanyard earlier than he'd anticipated. Laurentia needed strong allies as well as a citizen army. He should meet with Anatole Galerien of Beaureve soon. And he needed to check on any number of matters at home.

Sera, for instance, he thought as he arrived home. Distance had not lessened his strange obsession with the Hill woman. He had thought of her every day, worrying that she would escape in spite of his command to double the number of soldiers who guarded her. Katherine would know if she'd gotten into any trouble.

"Send for the princess, would you? I'll meet her in the blue drawing room," he told a welcoming footman who took his cloak and gloves. Two flights of stairs and a long corridor brought him to the comfortable, elegant room with light blue silk wall hangings and the Gainsborough portrait of his mother sitting on a chair, her arm about his shoulders as he leaned into her skirts. He must have been three when Gainsborough had come to court. Somehow, the artist had captured his mother's fresh beauty and the softness of her expression as she gazed down at her son.

Three years later, all that love had died with his mother.

"Nikki!" Katherine burst into the room, her face alight. "Oh, I am so glad you're finally home!" she cried, throwing herself into his arms. "How was your journey? Did you find the borders secure? Please, tell me everything."

"The journey was tedious, as it always is on the rutted October roads. And yes, the troops are diligent and alert at the borders—where they can be guarded. There are so many rough streams and so much forest cover, but we would know if an army attempted to cross."

Nicholas refrained from revealing his deeper fear—that in spite of the citizen militia, a small, well-armed cadre of terrorists could cross in the darkness at three or four points along the northern and eastern borders.

Nicholas turned again to his sister. "I plan to send Andre to Beaureve within the week in order to begin discussions with the regent."

"But Nikki! Andre has just returned. Surely, you will not send him away again until he has a chance to rest and..."

"Katherine," he said in a gentle voice. "You know that Andre must do his duty, as you must also do yours." He hated to see the pain in her eyes before she averted them.

But when she raised her face to him again, her eyes were clear and steady with purpose. "I know," she said in a quiet voice.

Nicholas took her hand and led her to a divan covered in blue and ivory brocade. Drawing her down to sit beside him, he put one arm about her thin shoulders and said, "Now, tell me everything that has happened during my absence."

"Well..." She was smiling now, all sunshine. "I'm learning to ride, Nikki, really ride. Sera teaches me every day. And my mare is much more willing."

"Sera—she's well?"

At least now he knew she was still in Montanyard.

"Oh, I think she's in fine health. Although I wish she would have taken the bedchamber next to mine when I offered it."

"She's still sleeping in the west wing of the stable? I thought you were going to convince her to move into the chamber we discussed."

"You needn't thunder, Nikki. She refused to move into

the palace, even after I begged her to."

"By God! We can't have that." Nicholas rose and began to pace. "Why, a lady who looks like—ahem, she can't sleep in such close proximity to the other grooms. I'll speak with her about this as soon as possible."

"But I may still ride with her, may I not?" Katherine's lips were trembling, Nicholas noticed. Damnation. If he didn't watch out, he'd reduce his sister to tears.

"Of course," he said to her. "I'd like to come with you. Then I'll have a chance to reason with her and convince her to return with us to the palace."

Katherine jumped from the couch. "You wouldn't wish to join us before the week is out, would you?" A look of alarm crossed her face.

Obviously, she and Sera had been up to no good in his absence. Nicholas carefully hid a grin. Never had Katherine acted so—like a girl. Nicholas had been looking forward to more dispatches and legal work before dining, but suddenly, all he wanted to do was to forget he was a king. It seemed that, for just an hour, he could simply be a brother to Katherine and a—a friend to Sera. It would be interesting to discover what possible mischief the two of them could have gotten into.

"I believe now would be an excellent time for a ride," he said evenly.

"Yes, of course. I-I'll go ahead and warn...let her know."

Nicholas whistled as he traveled the long corridor to his chamber. He had known that a friendship with Sera would be good for his sister.

***

"Sera! We're in for it, now!"

Sera tied the bandage she had just placed over the leg of a bay gelding and straightened slowly, forcing her weak muscles to hold her weight. The foolish horse had cut himself badly in pasture, and the healing had drained some of her strength.

Katherine must have run all the way from the palace, for she was panting and red-faced. "Nikki's home, and he's insisting upon riding with us. Now." She pulled Sera along through the barn and toward her room.

Nicholas Rostov—returned. As she followed Katherine into her chamber, Sera felt an odd tingle in the pit of her stomach, as though she had whirled in circles one too many times.

"Quick! Think of a reason why he can't ride with us today. Or for the next month. Hurry!"

"I don't understand. Why don't you want him to see how well you're doing?"

"Because I only ride well astride. He'll be horrified. No lady rides astride. You know that."

Sera shrugged. "If he is the man you keep telling me he is, then your brother will be impressed with your improvement, and not waste his time insisting you follow that foolhardy Outlander custom."

Katherine's mouth dropped open. "You're not the least bit afraid of my brother, are you?"

"What would he do to you? Beat you? Cut off your head?" Sera said.

"You don't know my brother. It could go far worse for me than capital punishment. Nikki can be quite impossible when he chooses to be. You just haven't seen it yet."

Sera's lips quirked. "I sincerely hope I have."

Katherine was searching the little room frantically. "You'll have to tell him you're not well. A sudden case of the grippe, or something."

Sera shook her head. "Katherine, I cannot lie."

"Oh, bother your scruples!" said Katherine glumly. "I'll simply have to lie to him, myself. Where is your mirror? Don't you dare tell me you haven't a mirror somewhere!" Frantically pinching her cheeks, Katherine leaned over the little bedside table and looked into the small looking glass Sera placed there for her.

"That's it," she said with satisfaction. "If I run all the way back to the palace, my cheeks will be on fire and I'll be breathless. A sudden case of something or other—palpitations, maybe. I must hurry before I'm caught out. Nikki is terribly clever, blast him." Katherine paused on her way to the door.

"You don't have to lie, Sera. Just don't say anything that will make him disapprove of me."

Sera gave her reassuring smile. "I promise."

***

Nicholas strolled toward the stable feeling the smile on his face widen into a grin. Something definitely was afoot. He knew immediately, of course, that Katherine's flushed face and breathlessness were self-induced. She'd barely had time to sprint back when he'd accosted her in the courtyard. He anticipated a miracle cure when she discovered that he had just requested the pastry chef serve iced gateaux with tea.

He was looking forward to his ride now more than ever. Katherine was one subject both he and Sera could discuss without making the issue a spitting contest between them. He entered the stable near the alcove where Sera's chamber lay. Momentarily adjusting his eyes to the darkness inside, he sought out her room.

He'd made it his business to know its location as soon as he had discovered she was still sleeping in the stable. Standing before the door, he placed his hand on it in a light, unconscious caress of the warm oak. Before he could knock, the door, not completely latched, swung open.

He saw Sera then. She sat straight-backed upon a chair, her loose linen gown flowing about her body. Sunlight from an open window poured down upon her like a stream as she plaited her long hair. Each strand seemed made of living gold. He stood in the shadowed aisle watching her, knowing that he had no right to spy like some obsessed degenerate skulking in shadows. But he was helpless to stop.

She must have felt his scrutiny, for she quickly tied the braid with a blue ribbon and glanced his way. The swiftness with which she rose to face him and the wary look on her face saddened him.

He cleared his throat. "Katherine has developed a most inconvenient case of the grippe," he told her, watching her glide toward him, her gown flowing against her in the sudden breeze. "I hope you'll take me as a substitute today."

Sera inclined her head. "I shall saddle your horse, Nicholas Rostov."

Why must she pretend to be a servant when everything about her screamed aristocrat, damnit? He took her arm to stop her from slipping past him and kept the irritation he felt from his voice. "The grooms will saddle my horse and yours, Sera. I hear he now tolerates others near him."

She looked down at her hands folded in front of her. "Very well," she said. "I'll go and ask them."

"I have already ordered it done."

Nicholas waited with Sera in the stable yard. She

looked everywhere but at him, and Nicholas quite clearly heard her sigh of relief when Ned and another of the grooms brought the horses forward. Her bright chestnut wore no saddle, at all. Nicholas moved to assist her in mounting, only to find her already sitting astride the chestnut with the reins in her hands. His eyes widened, but he said nothing before the others.

When they had left the yard far behind them, he walked his horse close to hers. "I suppose you've been teaching Katherine to ride like this," he said, his eyes glued to the sight of a trim, booted ankle peeking from beneath her skirts.

"She only does so in the privacy of the park, Nicholas Rostov. And only for as long as it takes her to learn balance. She plans to ride sidesaddle as soon as she's confident enough."

"Is she doing well?"

"Very well." The sun illuminated Sera's face and left him feeling tongue-tied as a young boy with his first dancing partner. Funny, when he was away from Sera, he never thought consciously of her beauty. He was too obsessed with visions of her body beneath his.

They rode on in silence for a few moments, until Nicholas made an inarticulate sound of frustration. "What does she think I'll do? Imprison her for riding bareback?"

Sera's voice was very soft. "She is afraid to disappoint you."

Nicholas ran his fingers through his hair. "Doesn't she know that I would do anything for her?"

"That is not the same thing at all. She wants your approval, not your protection."

Nicholas stared at Sera for a long moment. He had worked for so long to provide for everyone and make decisions that would keep them all safe. A fearsome question pricked him. Did he really know the first thing about Katherine or his people?

He shook his head. "Tell me, little magician, how you convinced my sister that she could ride that mare when one of the best riding masters in Europe could not."

The set of her shoulders relaxed, perhaps because of his compliment. Maybe she liked it when he didn't play the king.

"Oh, it was quite easy, actually," Sera said, slanting a

look at him from beneath her lashes. "I don't know how your women put up with those stiff things," she said. "How can you feel the movements of a horse beneath you in any saddle, for that matter?"

"You know," he said. "One of the best rides I've ever had was on one of the worst nights I can remember. I daresay you remember little of it, but your chestnut carried both of us for hours to the border and beyond. He has a canter that rolls like waves."

He watched her as she stretched her hands high to the sky in an age-old gesture of sensuality and freedom. "Wind Rider is magical. At home in the hills, I ride him every day. I need to, for my spirit is not as calm and reasoned as it should be. But Wind Rider does not care whether I am filled with storms. And when we are through with our gallop, I am peaceful again."

She smiled, seemingly unaware of what she was doing to him, how his body was beginning to throb.

"But Katherine only needed balance. After she learned the rhythm, we played tag in the clearing." Sera pointed ahead to a close meadow rimmed in the gold and brown colors of the oak trees. "Wind Rider is fast, but that little mare is even faster. She wheels and veers so quickly, I fell off twice trying to escape Katherine."

Nicholas pictured two young girls full of high spirits, madly circling their horses and sprinting after each other. "I wish I had been there to see it or even to play."

"You, Nicholas Rostov?"

"Do you think I'm such a stuffy curmudgeon that I won't even play a game of tag?" He used the full force of the Rostov frown, just to make her eyes flash.

"I think you'd lose on that great war horse of yours, that's what I think."

"Oh, you do, do you?" It was a direct challenge, and from the way she squared her shoulders, Sera obviously knew it.

"The one with the shortest arms gets the crop," she said, and leaned into him so quickly that the whip was out of his hands before he could fully grasp it. She galloped toward the meadow full tilt, her long braid bouncing against her back with every lift of the horse's haunches.

He watched her race away, and a longing that had nothing to do with lust churned deep inside him, almost making him ache. A simple game of tag. When had he last played a game of any kind? For five minutes, he could do so and the world wouldn't stop spinning on its axis. Just five minutes—

Nicholas's blood raced in his veins as he urged the horse on behind her. "One game, until the sun sinks just behind the mountain. Winner awarded one forfeit," he shouted after her. She halted her horse, grinning as the chestnut pranced beneath her.

"Agreed!" she called over her shoulder and wheeled the horse to the right, dashing to the narrow end of the clearing to wait, and then attack.

It took Nicholas longer than five minutes to learn Sera's strategy, and then he began to turn the tables on her. She was coming in closely, darting past as she aimed her crop to touch his shoulder, when the sun hit the rim of the mountain to the west.

Nicholas grabbed the end of the crop. Something glad and triumphant rose in his chest. "Done," he said, feeling the grin widen on his face. "I win by one point."

She sat the horse, flushed and vibrant, the light from the red-streaked sky still shining in her eyes. Her hand still held the other end of the crop, and her mouth made a disappointed little moue. Warm from effort and excitement, her skin glowed, and her hair curled in damp little tendrils about her temples. He could smell the scent of her, almost feel the creamy texture of the soft skin right above the prim collar of her gown. She looked just as she had in his dreams—sensual and enticing beyond a man's daytime imaginings.

"Winner claims the forfeit," he said, tugging gently on the crop. She was stubborn, just as he had hoped she'd be, keeping her hold on the crop out of sheer impudence. He tugged a little further and she swayed forward, laughing. She was close enough. Nicholas snaked out an arm, swept her off her mount and onto his lap.

Outraged, she opened her mouth to say something scathing, he was sure, but he held her hard against him, staring at her lips. She went still, watching him intently. Her breathing grew rapid, from fear or rising anticipation, he could not tell. Bending his head, he inhaled deeply, taking in the scent of horse and exertion, and the heady essence of Sera.

Her lips were soft as a sigh beneath his. He had imagined the taste of her for so many nights, and she was sweeter than he had dreamed. The whole world seemed hushed. There was nothing left in it but the two of them. The way she fit against him, the way her arms lifted, twining about his neck, the small sound of surrender deep in her throat—all of it flashed through his body, and he wanted closer.

He held a treasure to be savored slowly, and he controlled the rising heat. He teased her mouth with little kisses, tasting her sensual lower lip with his tongue. With a gasp of surprise, her lips parted. He took advantage, entered, and tasted the sweetness of her mouth with his tongue. He was certain it was new to her, for she froze at first, not understanding. In some deep, elemental way, he was glad of it, and plunged deeper, claiming her, branding her his. She caught fire at that, opening eagerly to him. A low hum of pleasure began deep in his throat.

It was sweet, the way she clung to him. When, hesitant, she touched her tongue to his of her own accord, he gave a groan of pure, passionate joy and tugged at the ribbon holding her braid. It fluttered to the ground. Loose, all the warm treasure of gold fell around his hand as he cupped the back of her neck. She arched against him, pliant beneath his onslaught, trusting, matching his hunger, and he was undone.

No woman had ever ignited at his touch the way she did. No woman had ever stoked the fire in him from a slow burn to the flash of heat that made him forget who he was, where he was…Good God!

Very slowly, very carefully, Nicholas raised his head to look at Sera. Her face was flushed, her eyes were dark with passion and hazed as though she were spellbound. He raised a hand that was barely steady and stroked the tumbled hair back from her face. Her lips were bee-stung with his kisses. Anyone in the stable would know whom she had been with and what she had done.

"It grows late," he said.

He saw the exact moment when she came back to reality. Even in the twilight, he could see her deep blush. "Yes. My—my horse." She slipped from his arms and to the ground. The air felt cold against his chest.

"We should return to the stable before they miss us."

Sera swung up on the chestnut's back. She raised her chin and nodded once, then took up the reins and started off ahead, her shoulders stiff.

Nicholas cursed himself for a randy bastard. There was no excuse for his actions. To take a woman whom he had sworn to protect when betrothed to another—he was ashamed of himself.

Nicholas knew how to get what he wanted. He knew the art of persuasion and the delicate threat of force. This miracle resting just a moment ago in his arms could be his. And if he pushed her to it, she would be the one to suffer guilt, remorse, and the appalled stares of his courtiers. He would only feel the libertine's dark satisfaction.

Nicholas made a decision. He would see her once more tonight, privately. He would promise, with the utmost gentleness and respect, that he would not trouble her with such overtures again. And he would demand that she move into the palace, where there would be sturdy locks on her chamber door to keep him and every other reprobate out.

***

Katherine knocked on the door to Sera's chamber later that evening. "What did my brother say this afternoon?"

Sera stared at her, a mass of confusion. She didn't wish to tell anyone what had happened with Nicholas in the park. She had not known that so serious a man could have a smile so sweet that it stung deep in her chest just to look at it. How could she tell the way his gray eyes went soft and amused right before he kissed her for the first time?

And the feelings, all jumbled and twanging inside her! She had wanted his kisses with an urgency that shocked her. Even more humiliating was Nicholas Rostov's behavior after he had kissed her until she was clinging to him, making those animal sounds deep in her throat.

The man simply froze against her, as though she were the wanton concubine he had originally thought her. It made her go red right now to remember his cold, clipped voice as she slipped to the ground. Blast him for trying to pretend it had never happened. Blast him for making her feel like the harlot she was not!

The worst of it was, she'd caused the whole humiliating mess. From the start of the ride, she had wanted to tease

Nicholas, to show him that she wasn't afraid of him. It was rather like tempting a tiger locked safely behind cage bars, and then finding that the beast had gotten loose— and that he was inside you.

She must not delay longer, losing her calm focus. She must find the way home.

She rubbed her eyes and heard Katherine's voice again.

"Are you well? You look feverish." Katherine looked at her with concern in her dark eyes.

"No, no, I'm fine," said Sera. "Now, to answer your question. Nicholas seemed very pleased that you were riding and enjoying it, and he does not care how you learn. Does that make you happier?" Sera started, shocked. Why was she calling this arrogant Outlander by his first name?

"Very much. He was so strange at tea. He said not one word to me, not even when I thanked him for the lovely cakes. He just started and then frowned vaguely at me, but that was all. After tea, he walked out onto the balcony and stared at the park. Then, still frowning, he bade me adieu and said he had to go to his study. When I asked him what he was going to do, he frowned again and said, 'Contemplate my sins, as any man of conscience would.'"

His sins? Hah! So he saw what happened between them as a sin!

"I am so afraid I disappointed Nicholas," said Katherine, folding her hands before her and staring down at them. "I should hate to think I failed at being a sister, as I have at so many other things."

"Whatever do you mean?" Sera stared at her in surprise.

"Oh, Sera. At least you could be as honest with me as you are with everyone else," Katherine said softly, fiddling with her skirt. Even though only one lamp lit her room, Sera could see the self-conscious flush rise to her cheeks. "I am clumsy and tongue-tied at a ball, small and plain, and generally as timid as a whipped puppy."

"But you are beautiful, Katherine."

Katherine looked at her very carefully, her eyes full of skepticism, then looked away.

"When you smile, when you forget yourself in another person, your eyes shine and your whole face lights up. And I am not the only person who believes this to be true."

Katherine's gaze swept to her face.

"When we arrived in Montanyard, Andre Lironsky rode beside me, watching you the whole time. He looked at you as though you were the most important thing in the whole world. He was like a man caught forever in a snare of dreams."

"Andre. You're telling me that Andre cares for me?" Katherine's face, suffused with joy, held a blazing beauty that brought the sting of tears to Sera's eyes.

"No. I'm saying he had the look of a man in love," said Sera softly.

Katherine hid her face in her hands for a long moment. When she raised her eyes to Sera again, they were luminous in the lamplight.

"I'm so very glad of it, and so sorry, as well. I have loved him all my life. He has a carefree, great heart, and he always makes me feel worthy and good. But to have him suffer even a little as I do. This I cannot bear."

"Why should either of you be unhappy a moment longer? He is a nobleman and a councilor to your brother. Katherine, I was taught about many of the Outlander customs. Surely, there have been love matches between royalty and the aristocracy before in your country."

Katherine nodded. "At times, yes. Our father and mother had such a marriage. I am certain that is why Papa was so cold and silent for all those years after her death. But when Laurentia is in need of alliances, marriages are the manner in which we form them. Now is such a time."

"Because of this Napoleon Bonaparte? All of Europe is battling this man."

"And he is winning," said Katherine.

"He is not always the victor. The island nation still fights him. I have learned about Trafalgar, and the war in Spain, too."

"Britain is far away. Nicholas sends representatives to persuade the prince regent to come to our aid if Napoleon attacks us. But the British are not very interested in a small country so close to the Russian border. Napoleon has hundreds of thousands of men, Sera. How are we to stand against him?

"We must align ourselves with our neighbors and pray that Great Britain will aid us eventually. That is why I'll never be able to wed Andre, no matter how much I love him.

"Still," Katherine smiled and squeezed Sera's hand. "It's a blessing to know that he cares for me. And a joy to have a friend who will tell me so."

After Katherine left her, Sera went to Wind Rider's stall. She curried him to a bright sheen and filled his bin with grain, deep in her own thoughts.

When Grandfather had shown her the palace at Montanyard through the scrying glass, Sera had not guessed that the proud, bejeweled ladies and gentlemen dancing at the winter balls might be hiding an inner grief. That is just what Katherine would be doing when she married a man she could never love, and loved a man she could never marry.

This world was too confusing and sorrow-laden. There were so many terrible tragedies in nature—death, famine, and flood. Why did people insist upon making the rest of life so difficult?

"Sera!" Young Ned, the groom, broke into her reverie. "Master Raymond says come to him, please, and help him poultice a horse's hoof. He says you are the best at healing he's ever seen."

Sera paled. If Master Raymond had noticed, soon others would, too, and they would begin to suspect. But what else could she do when she saw a horse in pain and had the means to take it away? Silently, she followed Ned.

In the brightly lit aisle way, the stable master, a wiry man of middle age, stood next to the afflicted horse, one arm draped casually over the big bay's back. Sera recognized Frederick, one of the ostlers who traveled between Montanyard and the border towns to the east, leaning against an oak wall and chewing upon a long stem of grass.

"There you are, my girl. I've got him soaked and the poultice made up. If Frederick and I hold his leg up, you'll have an easy time of it pasting that slop into the hoof."

One of the grooms held up a lantern as Sera bent over the horse's leg, feeling all around the hoof, homing in on the pain. There, to the right of the frog, she sensed the thick buildup of blood beneath horn, the throbbing of pressure unable to release itself. Placing her palm over the spot, she shut her eyes and willed the tingling warmth to flow from deep inside her, into and through the hoof. The blood beneath the hoof grew liquid and flowed back into the capillaries. The horse relaxed, his muzzle resting against her shoulder.

Frederick grunted as the big warm blood leaned heavy on his arm. "He got the bruise right over the mountain, near Selonia. I swear, that road gets worse and worse. The only part that's decent is the stretch right out of the city, beyond the palace woods. Some`un might have a word with the king and the council about the waste of good horse flesh unless that road gets repaired."

As she poulticed the horse, Sera hid her smile and let the ostler's words roll over her. Frederick was a complainer, but she liked him. As the grooms often said, he could talk to a post for hours. When he had finished with the latest list of grievances, he would doubtless begin to tell them all the news from the border.

"The nobs, now—they'll be worrit about the same thing when they bring those fancy carriage horses back over the mountain for the Season."

"When do they return?" Sera asked.

"Soon enough," said Frederick with a snort. "No doubt one of `em'll be sportin' a pretty fancy ruby. Eh, girl! Watch that poultice lands on the hoof, and not on me back. Now what you jerkin' so hard for?"

"I'm sorry," Sera said, beginning the bandaging. "I'll wash the shirt, Frederick. I wouldn't want to make more work for you."

"Hmph. That's all right, Sera." Frederick stood and stretched his back for a moment, leaving Master Raymond to hold the horse's hoof.

"As I was sayin'," he went on after he bent again to the horse, and Sera finished the wrapping. "The whole town's talkin' about this ruby. Never seen one so big, they say. A footman for Count Vasily comes to the inn where I'm stayin' fer a package, and he says he's seen it. Some merchant, a fancy, dark fella with a thick mustache, brought it to the estate. He was so important that he traveled in a fine coach with ten outriders—all armed to the teeth."

All the grooms had gathered around Frederick and were listening intently to the story. Sera straightened. She put her hand over her heart to stop its racing.

"So the merchant brings in this big silver case with him, and he opens it. Inside there's a black velvet cloth and a pouch that he opens. He spreads the cloth and shakes out the pouch, and..."

As Frederick drew out the story, Sera fought a terrible urge to push him on.

"...huge, beautiful gems fall out of the pouch and lie there, twinkling up at Count Vasily." said Frederick. "And all of `em perfect."

"Own up, Frederick," said the stable master. "No merchant has jewels that size. It's all a big tale, and the footman ought to know better."

"That en't the worst of it," said Frederick. "He's got this special pouch, the merchant has. An' when he opens this 'un, he draws out a ruby, big as a robin's egg, an' every way he moves it, it catches the light an' throws off fire sparkles like nobody's ever seen before."

"Horse manure!" Master Raymond shook his head. "Never happened, Frederick."

"They all believe it in Selonia." Frederick grew very red in the face. "The merchant's stayin' at a fancy inn there, with his hired guard."

"Tell us another, Frederick," a groom said while the others nodded. "True or false, they be good stories, eh?"

As Frederick, mollified, began another tale, Sera slipped from the gathering and made her way to her chamber. As soon as the door shut behind her, she slumped against it and took a deep, calming breath.

The merchant with the jewels fit the description of the thief. He was in Selonia with the Heart of Fire. And the Selonia road was just beyond the palace woods. At first light tomorrow, she must be gone from this place.

Restlessly, she paced the tiny room, trying to ignore the dull ache that seeped through her. She wanted to go home, she reminded herself. She needed to stop the portals between the two worlds from slamming shut. And she needed to feel the warmth of the Hill sun on her again, along with her people's loving acceptance. But she felt something tugging at her, wanting her here in this place.

She ran down the stairs and into the night. Flinging herself against a fence in a practice ring, she stared at the stars, shining so brightly, showing her way home.

She could make it back. She could be home in only a

few—

An arm snaked out about her waist, lifting her from the ground and pulling her back against a solid, very large male body.

"Dreamin' of the king, now, are you?" Dawson's hateful voice, hot in her ear, the stench of liquor heavy on his breath. "Was you out whorin' with him in the park today? I've never had a piece the king's had before. Should prove interestin', no?"

"Let me go!" She struggled, shoving with her elbows, her fists, but he had her from behind, and he used his weight and his strength to tow her backwards into the brush just beyond the stable. His gloved hand clamped over her mouth, cutting off the very air until she thought she'd faint.

He pulled her into a copse of trees and flung her to the ground. She flipped, sucked in her breath, and raised her voice in a piercing scream. With a savage oath, he was on her, covering her body. He stifled her scream with his mouth, his tongue shoving between her lips. His beefy grip on her throat bruised and choked her. Her lungs strained, burning for air. She bit down, hard, and he hauled back, slapping her face with such brute force that her head spun. She tasted blood. But her legs were free for a moment. She concentrated with all the force of her mind, found his groin and shoved her knee upward with all her strength. He screamed in agony. Dawson still had his hand on her throat, and it closed tighter, cutting the air completely from her lungs. Black dots swam in front of her eyes.

"You bastard!" Nicholas Rostov's voice growled, somewhere close.

Suddenly, Dawson's hand wrenched free of her throat and she gasped, wheezing. Nicholas Rostov stood above her, his fists curled about Dawson's collar as he flung the man about to face him.

"Stinking, perverted bastard."

Sera shivered at the deadly calm in Nicholas Rostov's voice. The full moon came out from behind a cloud. In its light, she saw how Dawson's eyes went wide with fear. His head moved from side to side like a cornered boar looking for freedom. Then he must have realized that the clearing was empty of witnesses, for he slowly raised his fists, circling Nicholas Rostov.

Nicholas Rostov turned to follow Dawson's movements, but he looked lazy, almost bored—and beneath that mien, implacable. She had forgotten how large he was. His shadow loomed over Dawson. The king stood stripped of all gentleness, all civilization. Only the elemental remained, and that was brutal. Animal. Deadly.

Nicholas Rostov lunged forward so quickly, Sera wasn't certain she had seen the movement. He grabbed Dawson by the throat—the throat! The man stumbled, gasping for air.

"You think to brutalize *her?* And that none will say you nay?" Nicholas Rostov's voice was whisper soft. A chill ran up Sera's neck. The king looked ready to kill.

Dawson whimpered. "It wasn't what it seemed. She wanted me bad. She's been trying to get me alone for days. Y'er a man. You know how it is with these women. Ride like men, act like 'em. She likes it rough. Women like her— they're askin' for it."

Nicholas Rostov smiled, a wolf's baring of teeth. He lowered his hand from Dawson's throat. "You've given me all I needed to know," he said softly. "Defend yourself."

Dawson put up his hands and swung. Nicholas Rostov deflected his fist as though it were as light as a butterfly. His right fist crashed into Dawson's jaw. Sera cringed at the crunching sound. Dawson spat blood and broken teeth and slowly straightened. He raised his fist again and swung.

The king moved left, lightning swift. The blow Dawson aimed at his jaw hit nothing but air. Dawson toppled forward, righting himself just in time to catch a slamming blow to his stomach. He doubled, racing sideways like a crab, but Nicholas Rostov appeared in front of him, lifting him with one arm. As Dawson struggled to get away from that grip of iron, the king dropped him back to his feet and hammered him on the face and on the belly, again and again. His breath came hard, but even. He could go on all day that way, Sera realized. Until the man was a bloody piece of meat lying dead on the forest floor.

"Stop! Oh, dear gods, stop." She couldn't keep the sob from her voice.

Other voices murmured in the dark night. Sera turned her head and realized they were not alone. Master

Raymond, Frederick, and all the grooms stood in a semi-circle around them. Some held lanterns, bringing more light to the clearing. They stared with startled, horrified faces at Dawson, now lying in a battered heap at Nicholas Rostov's feet.

"This is how you protect a lady?" The king's voice cut through each man. Sera could see that they all shook at his words.

Sergeant Bellows stepped forward out of the shadows. Someone must have run for him soon after the king appeared.

"Escort this offal to the prison for a month of confinement," Nicholas Rostov told him. "Afterward, we'll decide what to do about him."

"Very good, Sire," said Sergeant Bellows, and Dawson was led away, still whimpering.

The grooms, speechless, bowed low and disappeared into the darkness beyond the lantern light. Nicholas Rostov stood, fists clenched, jaw rigid. Sera rubbed her arms, trying to relieve their shaking.

"Why didn't you stop?" she said in a voice that croaked and saw the shudder that ripped through Nicholas's tall frame at the sound.

She took a breath and tried to clear her throat, but the hoarseness stayed with her. "To do violence like this will only spawn more violence," she said to him. "Let him go after a few days. Perhaps he will learn from it. And he did me no real harm."

Nicholas turned to her, his eyes radiating his outrage. Very lightly, he stroked her throat, and she flinched even at his careful touch. He took her face in his hands, lifting it so he could see her. He looked closely at her lip and pulled his handkerchief from his sleeve, gently dabbing at it. Then he held it before her face. The darkness of blood stained the white linen.

"You call this no real harm?" he asked her. "What would you have me do? Stand by and watch him rape you, asking, very politely, that he desist? Do you think he'll learn a thing from this? I wanted to kill him. Seeing him...seeing you..."

Sera shook her head. Denying, refusing to believe it was true, she backed away from him. She felt crushed by the ugliness, the brutality, the lack of choice. This was a world of horror.

Nicholas took Sera's arm and pulled her toward the stable, holding her with that same gentle touch. "Someone must see to your injuries, my lady," he said. His manner, his voice, had undergone a lightning swift transition. He was grave, and his eyes were so soft.

"I'll not insist that you move to the palace tonight. You're weary. You're sickened by what you have endured. The doctor will come within the hour. And tomorrow, you'll come to live where I can be certain of your safety and well-being."

"No. Please, Nicholas Rostov. I am well. I am happy here. Don't make me live in that prison."

He shook his head, stroking her hair back from her forehead with a hand that trembled a little. "I can't protect you here. And I can't let you go. Tomorrow morning, my...Sera. You must come to live with us. Where you belong."

The doctor came and went. The moon rose higher. Sera stared at it from her window. She couldn't bear it, not another day. Nicholas, so gentle one moment, so dangerous the next. The violence of his world reflected in his swift, terrible vengeance.

Outside her room were the contented sounds of sleeping horses. Occasionally, one snuffled and blew softly. She slipped from her room and crept down the stairway, making her way to Wind Rider's stall.

"I am here, Tzirah," she whispered to him in the Hill tongue, her language, reminding her of her life. She bridled Wind Rider as quickly as she could and led him into the park. Throwing herself on his back, she galloped him out, trying to break the pull of the lodestone holding her here.

Sera raced for miles to the very end and saw what she'd been looking for since she had come to this place— a break in the tall, thorny hedge that walled the grounds in. The broken hedge still stood at ten feet. Two thirds of the way up, wicked thorns spiked out at all angles. A horse and rider crashing through them would be torn to shreds. Sera halted Wind Rider and stared at it, her breath catching in her throat. Half Outlander that she was, she lacked the full power of the Hills, didn't she? Did she dare to risk them both?

There was no doubt that she must go now. There was

a way out and a destination. It did not matter how compelling a straight, tall, utterly unpredictable man with broad shoulders and beautiful gray eyes could be. It did not matter at all.

She took a deep breath, shut her eyes, and *willed* Wind Rider up. The stallion's powerful haunches gathered and sprang. In a burst of strength, they soared, arced and came down again on the other side. With barely more concussion than a four-foot jump would have taken, Wind Rider landed, and without breaking stride, galloped away to freedom.

Five

"They've sacked Selonia!" The first messenger arrived, shouting the news in the courtyard. Pandemonium hit the palace. Nicholas reestablished order as quickly as he could.

"Oblomov," he said to the grizzled general, whom he trusted to keep his head in the midst of a whirlwind. "Remain in Montanyard with most of the army. I'll lead four regiments to Selonia. Above all, we must keep the news of the raid quiet for as long as possible." He didn't need a nation in panic right now, and even less did he need his enemies to realize the Brotherhood had somehow slipped through his eastern border.

General Obomov bowed his gray head. "It'll take a few hours to put together the heavy weaponry and the supplies." The general left in quick step, followed by his aides.

As he called for his ministers, Nicholas could hear Oblomov's voice barking orders all the way down the hall.

A short time later, when Katherine burst into his chamber, her eyes full of fear, Nicholas was dressing for the journey and was suffering Simmons' ministrations on the knot in his brown stock tie.

"Sera's gone," she said. "Nobody has seen her since last night."

Nicholas froze, then pushed away from Simmons' hand. "Her room is empty?"

Katherine nodded. "Wind Rider is gone, as well."

"Damnation!" As anger pushed back the panic, Nicholas shoved his left foot into his riding boot and muttered. "Little fool. To think after what Dawson had done to her that she could survive out there alone on the road." Katherine handed him the right boot, and he pulled it on with more force than necessary.

"Of all the times to pull this stunt! How the hell did she get out? Does anyone know that, at least?" He flung himself out the door, striding down the hallway with long, quick steps.

"The guards say she never passed the palace or the city gates." Katherine ran to keep up with him. "Andre's waiting for you on the grounds before the palace."

Nicholas thought of the way Sera had looked at him after he'd beaten Dawson. She had thought he was some mad, ravening beast. He, too, had been shocked by his lack of control. But the world was full of more dangerous beasts. His stomach twisted in fear.

"I should let her persist in this mad scheme. With the Brotherhood loose on the land, not to mention your usual assortment of killers and rapists hiding behind every crossroads, she'll be dead or worse in a day." Nicholas had reached the grand staircase and was running down it two steps at a time.

"Nikki!" Katherine cried out to him in a voice that echoed all the way to the painted dome three stories above them. Impatient to be off, he turned and looked back at her standing on the landing. Her face was pale and her eyes haunted.

"Bring her home, Nikki. Please."

He nodded sharply and, not waiting for the footman's services, shoved his way out the high double doors.

In the courtyard, Andre was already mounted. "She didn't get out the gates. They're certain of it," he said holding out the reins of Nicholas's chestnut. Nicholas swung up into the saddle.

"That means she's loose in the park. She was horrified last night by the violence, the blood—she can't understand what kind of evil exists in this world. And I thought she might be a spy! She said once that when she was troubled, she rode. Andre, if she went out in the darkness, not knowing where the cliffs end out there beyond the paths..." His voice broke. "I shall never forgive myself."

Andre stared at him. Then his face softened with something akin to pity. "Katherine says she rides like a Valkyrie. That horse has sense, even if she doesn't. Come. It will take the army a while yet to assemble with the supplies. We have time to check the park."

"Take the outer perimeter. Just in case there's a way through that hedge that even the gardeners don't know about."

Andre nodded. "You'll take the park, itself?"

"Yes." If he found her, if she was...dead, he wanted to be alone if he had to face that possibility.

Nicholas took a deep breath. Fear would only get in the way. He followed the hoof prints made the night before by a large, well-shod horse cantering along the park road.

At one point, he heard Andre on the other side of the hedge and shouted to him. "I've found her trail. Keep up with me along the perimeter unless you hear a shot."

He got to the very end of the park before he saw it, and then he simply jumped off his horse and stared at the ground. Here, the hedge rose to ten feet, not its usual twelve. Still, not even a puissance rider and horse could take a jump that height. Yet six feet from the hedge, a good sized horse had gathered his haunches and taken off in a jump that wasn't possible. Thorny twigs scattered about meant that he had grazed the top of the hedge with his hooves.

"Andre!"

"Almost there." Andre's voice shouted back to him.

He heard the beat of hooves and the long slide to a stop outside the hedge. "Check the ground about six feet from the hedge," he called out.

There was silence for a moment. Then Andre's voice, slow and stunned. "I don't believe it."

"She landed there?"

"And kept galloping, it appears. How is it possible?"

Nicholas barked out a wild laugh. "Hill magic. What else?"

"Are you saying that Sera's a—a witch of some sort?" Andre's voice held just the hint of a hoot.

A witch...where had he heard rumors of witchcraft before? Who had been so branded? Somewhere, in the back of his memory, a shadowy picture of a woman rose, dark-haired and beautiful. Then that small flash of recognition was gone.

"Not a witch, exactly, but something—different. Something...powerful."

In spite of his fear for Sera, a soaring exultation welled up from that place he could never control where she was concerned. He would find her, by God, and he had his justification for keeping her. The woman could make a horse fly like Pegasus. What other wonders could she perform for Laurentia?

"Get back to the palace. I'm going after her."

Shortly thereafter, Nicholas sat a fresh mount in the courtyard, assigning a troop of men to accompany him and then turning to Andre, now re-mounted beside him.

"Lead the army along the road to Selonia. I'll ride ahead and meet you with our truant in tow when you arrive there tomorrow morning." *Please God,* he added silently.

Nicholas and his men followed Sera's tracks into the forest. Her trail was so clear an old man with cataracts could have followed it. He grew both more anxious and more certain of finding her.

As the hours passed, Nicholas galloped through the forest in a state of gnawing anxiety. Nightmare visions invaded his mind—all of them featuring Sera in tears. It was well after moonrise when they came upon a little camp in a mossy clearing beside a stream. Nicholas looked through the trees and saw Wind Rider grazing placidly.

He raised his hand to them. "Stay here. I don't want her frightened or disturbed."

The men nodded and dismounted, gathering brush to make a fire and settling in for the night. Nicholas walked silently into the clearing.

Wind Rider raised his head and widened his nostrils at Nicholas's approach, but he soon lowered it again, cocked his hind leg, and half closed his eyes. Nicholas spied a small, bundled figure lying still beneath a blanket. There was no fire to warm her, he noticed as he knelt beside the blanket. At least she had known enough not to light one, lest she attract the attention of any brigand in the area.

Sera slept, trusting as a child, in the midst of a forest filled with wild beasts and outlaws. She was breathing, Nicholas reminded himself as he bent over her. She was alive and safe.

Nicholas was afraid to touch her because he wanted to shake her until her teeth rattled, or kiss her until the crazy fear that had haunted him all day burst into fire, burning away all the turmoil. He drew the blanket down to get a good look at her before he wakened her. The overhanging branches swayed in the wind and the moon shone through, giving him light to see her face. She looked tired and worn, and he shook his head, feeling half his anger drain out of him like sand from a sieve.

He shook her shoulder far more gently than he had planned to. "Get up, Sera," he said low.

Her eyes remained shut. She raised her hand to his as it cupped her shoulder, lifted it and brought his palm to her lips. Rubbing against it, she breathed deeply, taking in his scent.

"Nicholas," she whispered. "I miss you already." Her voice had the soft slur of a dreamer half-waking.

Something cold and frozen melted inside him, filling him with a confusion of emotion he had no means to understand. His voice came out in a strangled, low moan. They had hours yet to meet the troops on the Selonia road, he reasoned. She was so tired. As he slid beneath the blanket, it occurred to Nicholas that he had never before actually slept with a woman. He had simply satisfied his lust and returned to his duties.

He settled Sera into the hollow of his hips, her back to him, the lush curve of her buttocks warm and soft against him. It was a good feeling, to have his arms wrapped about her, and the sweet touch of her body all along his. She fit him as though she had been made for him. He drew her closer against him, burying his face in the tender curve of her neck.

He smoothed back her hair breathing in the elusive flower scent. "Go back to sleep, Sera," he said. And lay beside her, keeping watch through the night.

***

Sera dreamed that Nicholas was kissing her—all over. Somehow, his hands were beneath her gown, caressing her breasts, teasing them into a fullness of inchoate need. Then his mouth was traveling in a slow, tantalizing line from the curve of her shoulder down. She could feel the light flicker of his tongue and the nibbling kisses along the path he was taking, heating her skin wherever he touched it, making her tense with anticipation. She liked it, lying with him, feeling the warmth of his breath hovering over her nipple. She made a sound in her throat, a helpless murmur, and arched upward, moving her hips as he gently kneaded her with his hands. She didn't want to wake up.

Slowly, in her dream, his taut warmth left her. Confused, she opened her eyes to find he was indeed there, but standing with his back to her, his body rigid in the gray light of dawn. She scrambled to her feet, still dream-befuddled and wary.

What had he done to her? Had it been real, or just a figment of imagination, a weakness in her character? Did she desire this man so much that his mere presence caused

her to dream such wicked things? Should she be outraged
with him or with herself?

"Don't run away from me again." He didn't turn. He
didn't move. He was a statue in the growing light, perfect,
immobile, his very essence marble-hard.

"Let me go," she said. "And I shan't have to run away."

"Tell me your secrets. How did you jump that hedge?
What more can you do? Tell me, and help me keep my
country safe. Then I'll let you go."

"I cannot." She wanted to scream with frustration, to
sit in a heap on the forest floor and just cry for loneliness
and grief. If she allowed it, one world would brand her a
witch, just as it had branded her mother. And the other
world, the one she protected with her silence, would see
her betrayal as the weakness of an emotion-laden child,
incapable of higher understanding.

He finally turned around, his dark eyes boring into
her as though he wanted to read her very soul. "Little fool.
Do you have any idea what could have happened to you?
Even a first time hunter could have followed the tracks
you made. It's time to face the sad and sorry truth, Sera.
You can't survive without protection."

He began to stride for the trees, leading Wind Rider
along with him. "My men await us just outside this copse.
Ten minutes, Sera. That's all the time you have for a
toilette."

She washed hurriedly at the stream, hearing the
snorts and rustles of horses, the unmistakable sounds of
men breaking camp. She realized with horror that she
had slept through the arrival of what sounded like an entire
regiment of soldiers.

Sera hurried toward the cavalry troop massed at the
edge of the copse. Nicholas was already mounted on his
own horse, holding Wind Rider firmly by the reins. She
took the reins from him and mounted, following Nicholas
out of the forest and onto the road.

They rode silently through the morning, the men
clustered about them for protection. Nicholas called a halt
at a crossroads and gave her a hunk of bread and a flask
of water.

When she was finished eating, he called to half the
men. "Take her to Montanyard."

"You don't understand," Sera said. "I have to go east,

to my home. Is that so terrible a crime?"

"Not someday, when the world is a safe and decent place. But you'll never survive such a journey alone, and I can't afford the men it would take to guard you beyond my borders. Especially now, when even the borders are no longer safe." He stared bleakly into the distance.

She hated the look on his face, the anger, and the weariness.

"Selonia was destroyed," he said.

"Dear Heaven." All that she had hoped, all that she had been running to, now shattered.

"You've never seen Selonia, have you? It was a lively summer town, full of theatres and assembly rooms and baths. The buildings were put to the torch two days ago."

"Who would do such a thing?" She thought of the people who worked in Selonia, the attendants who helped the wealthy take the waters, the maids and seamstresses and stonemasons who lived in Selonia. "Oh, Nicholas, how many were hurt?"

Nicholas turned his head at the low break in her voice. His expression softened at what he must have seen in her face. "Perhaps there's another way to convince you that your place lies here, helping me keep my country safe. Come with me, and you can see for yourself."

The men fell in beside them again, and they cantered down the eastern road.

***

Emmanuel Aestron walked through the Temple Square, acknowledging the respectful bows of the young men and women gathered to debate philosophy at the colonnade. He inhaled the sweetness of the wisteria vines curling about the Doric columns and festooning the marble trellis shading the students as they resumed their logical arguments. He passed the marketplace, nodding to the farmers whose stands brimmed with jeweled fruits and vegetables piled in artistic patterns of color and shape. The scent of fresh apples and autumn strawberries followed him as he wound through streets lined with perfectly proportioned marble buildings, their columns topped with friezes of Arkadia's heroes and Mages.

At the palaestra of Demosthenes, he turned in, pausing in a small courtyard. Two lads, just bathed after wrestling by the looks of their wet hair and fresh bruises, reclined on benches beneath a tree, sipping water. Seeing him, they both sprang to their feet and bowed.

"Hypocritas, how good to see you," he said to one of them, the son of a friend. "Is my grandson here?"

"Yes, my lord Emmanuel. He won his bout. Now he is in the bath. Shall I fetch him for you?" At his nod, the boy ran off and returned a moment later with Jacob Augustus, who outstripped him as he quickly crossed the courtyard, his towel hanging over one shoulder, a loincloth affixed to his hips for decency's sake.

Emmanuel could never look at Jacob Augustus without pride welling up from some deep place inside him. His body, as beautiful as it was, exemplified the perfection of his mind and his spirit. Strength and harmony encompassed it, a result of the work Emmanuel knew Jacob put into it. Tall and strong, his specialty was the pankration, the no-holds-barred wrestling that, for some reason, soothed Jacob's soul while disciplining bone and sinew. Since Sera had gone from Arkadia, Jacob had used this outlet more often than in the past.

"Walk with me," he told Jacob.

Jacob nodded and they strode into the bright sunlight of the street. "What news?" he asked his grandfather.

"She tried to escape. The king has found her again. He takes her to Selonia."

"Where she'll feel more sympathy for these Outlanders. Rostov is clever. He ties her to him, and to his world."

Hearing the bitterness in Jacob's voice, Emmanuel sighed, reaching within for forbearance. He knew he owed his grandson an explanation and didn't much relish the reaction he anticipated from Jacob. The boy would doubtless hate him for days before he understood the right reason that prompted his actions. Best to get it over with, he thought.

By now, they had left the city center and walked through a quiet neighborhood filled with houses. Emmanuel stopped at a bench beneath a willow at the edge of a public park. He sat and motioned for Jacob to do the same.

In the quiet, he could hear the buzzing of bees, and across the green, a group of girls and boys sat, concentrating in the stillness on brightly colored balls balanced in the air above them. Some of them had gotten their balls to spin. A tutor watched them carefully. In this way, the more gifted among them would be chosen to attend the academy, learning to expand their powers for the good of Arkadia's citizens.

He wanted to weep for Sera, all alone in a strange world, without the comfort of a mentor as the startling strength of her power began to evidence itself.

Emmanuel turned his attention to his grandson, who sat on the grass at his feet, plucking the blades one by one with his restless fingers. "You have a right to be angry with me, Jacob," he said. "It is my fault that Sera has gone to the Outlanders."

Jacob shrugged. "No Grandfather. You have reason to let her stay for a while."

"But it preys on you, that you must trust this Nicholas Rostov to keep her safe. I have to tell you why Jacob, and that I had more to do with Sera's flight than you believe."

Jacob sprang up before him, his blue eyes, so like Sera's narrowed. "What do you mean?"

Emmanuel remained seated, wishing calm, watching his grandson's face soften a bit, feeling his mind open again to him. "You know that Sera is not only Arkadian. She is the daughter of an Outlander king, and thus, the lawful heir to the throne of a troubled nation, should she wish to choose her heritage."

Jacob nodded, his gaze on Emmanuel's face.

"Your love for me has kept you from realizing the truth. Do you believe that I did not look into the soul of the Outlander Sera saved and asked us to heal? Do you think I did not know he lusted for riches, that he held honor cheap and would easily sacrifice it to get what he wanted? Do you really suppose that any thief could have stolen the Heart of Fire from its resting place if I had not wished it free?"

Jacob's burning gaze seared Emmanuel. "You arranged for her exile in the Outlander world, for her captivity, for the brutality and shame she has suffered and seen?"

Emmanuel's heart cracked beneath the weight of his grandson's outrage. "I did not foresee the Nantal burning her Hill cloak. But I knew that Nicholas Rostov would visit Hadar's palace." He stood and reached out for his grandson.

At the touch of Emmanuel's hand on his shoulder,

Jacob flung himself away, staring at him in fury. "You wished her to go to him as a *hetaera*?

"Jacob." Although his power was strong, Jacob could not withstand the compulsion of Emmanuel's voice. "It is in the worst of circumstances that the true nature of a man reveals itself. I wished to see what Nicholas Rostov was made of. And I wished for Sera to see it and choose her destiny freely."

"You cannot keep her safe. You cannot watch her every minute."

Emmanuel slowly sat again on the bench. "You know the Outlander tale of the Garden?" He motioned, and Jacob dropped to the bench beside him.

"From their holy book?"

"I was thinking of the story by their John Milton, that *Paradise Lost*," Emmanuel said. "You remember?"

Jacob nodded.

"Sera, like Adam and Eve, is gone from the Garden now. Danger is all around her, and greed and hatred. But she has something she never had here. She has free will. She has the right to grow up, like Adam and Eve, and the right to choose her destiny."

" 'And the world was all before them, where to choose Their place of rest, and Providence their guide,'" Jacob said slowly.

"Yes. Do you understand?"

Jacob gave Emmanuel a reluctant nod. "I understand. But I do not like it." He looked at Emmanuel, his face filled with misery. "Grandfather, if the time comes when I think I must, I shall challenge you on this and bring her back, myself."

***

Selonia was a charred ruin. From what Nicholas could see as he and Sera rode into the little city, the ravagers had burst upon the spa town and destroyed everything. This was a crime of madmen who used their foggy religious rationalizations as an excuse to terrorize the country and sap it of its will to resist. They had not only torched the Georgian assembly rooms and the beautiful villas of the wealthy. They had systematically razed the workers' small row houses.

People were everywhere, dull-eyed with shock, muttering or crying out amidst the blackened timbers of houses. The smell of charred wood and stone and the nauseating odor of burnt flesh clung to the air. Nicholas wanted to tear apart the men who had done this to his people, to slice each one of them into shreds. But they had disappeared into the terrain like vipers after a satanic feast. And he was left to pick up the pieces.

"Weakling. Unfit to be king," his father's voice whispered to him. Nicholas had no answer to the damning doubts. But fit or not, he was all Laurentia had.

So he left Sera at his temporary headquarters while he and Andre met with the mayor of Selonia and his council. Late into the night, the leaders of the town sat with him, giving their reports of the damage in property and human lives. He gave orders to a group of soldiers to scavenge the countryside for supplies and food. He delegated authority, requisitioned supplies, and made countless other decisions for hours. By the time he had finished all he could do for the evening, he was bone weary and still fighting his outrage against the Brotherhood.

He and Andre walked back to his headquarters through the empty streets of the city. He could smell the acrid smoke still smoldering from the ruins, see an occasional scavenger picking through the rubble that remained of his home.

"I don't know whether I can control the rage, Andre. I want to find them and kill each one of them—slowly. But someone is giving them the money for arms, someone who wants to weaken us and then conquer. If we don't find the man backing these terrorists soon, the country will suffer more of the same."

"Napoleon?" Andre asked.

"Perhaps. If he takes us first, he can easily plough through Jehanna. Beaureve will hold out for a while, but he'll have all the harvest from Laurentia and Jehanna to feed to his army."

Nicholas rubbed his tired eyes. "If I could get close to that devil and kill him in cold blood, I would in a minute, and sleep like a baby afterward. It would be justice," he said. "I wish I were one of the Hill folk. I could foist all of this baggage off on the Mage and go find a woman."

Sera, he thought. To go as deeply into her body as she could take him. To hide from this horror in the scent and heat of her.

Some time in the night, he had fallen asleep, only to awaken on top of her in the morning's gray dawn. His hands had been all over her, his mouth following. And he had wanted closer, wanted deep, wanted with an urgency that hit him like a wall of flame. He had rolled away from her to stand with his body clenched in heat and desire. Fight as he might against it, the never-ending lust simply grew stronger.

"You're too tired to do any more. Hell, I'm too tired to think, period." Andre rubbed his hands through his hair until the blond curls flew in total disarray.

They had reached the large tent set up for Nicholas. Andre gave him a rough squeeze on the shoulder and propelled him inside.

"Get something decent to eat and go to sleep. We'll know more what to do in the morning."

Nicholas had just entered when an aide rushed into the tent, followed by a breathless messenger, his face sweat streaked and dirty with dust from the road. The messenger knelt on one knee.

"Lieutenant Mirovsky, Sire," he gasped. "I come from Count Vorchov."

Vorchov—Laurentian Ambassador to Russia!

The messenger's face was a mask of fright. "Bonaparte has taken Moscow. The Russian troops under the command of Prince Kutuzov have retreated to the Kaluga road. What shall we do, Sire?" Mirovsky's gaze clung to Nicholas, as though he could magically halt Bonaparte's inexorable march toward Laurentia.

Well. One more nail in the coffin, he thought wearily. "Thank you, Lieutenant. First you will rest and bathe. In the morning, I'll send you back to Count Vorchov with instructions. You have my gratitude."

The lieutenant pressed his hand to his heart and rose. Bowing smartly, he followed the aide de camp out of the tent.

Napoleon would winter in Moscow. By spring, he would be on the road south. How would Nicholas protect his people against an overwhelming army when he couldn't save Selonia from a band of terrorists?

He sat down on a camp chair set up before his traveling desk and leaned on his elbows, his head in his hands. He sat there for what seemed a long time, dead and empty.

He heard a shift of canvas, and then felt the breeze on the back of his neck. Attempting to obliterate the impression of weakness he must have made when thus caught unaware, he straightened his back and looked over his shoulders, expecting his young aide de camp to be standing in the doorway.

Sera stood there with a tray. The lantern light formed a nimbus around her hair. Her eyes were a deep, soft blue as she looked at him. All of the life in her seemed to surge toward him in that look. It made him want to go to her and hold her without having to speak, forever. But he was frozen in shame.

She walked to the desk and set down the tray. Without a word, she pulled the other camp chair close to his and sat down. He could feel her shoulder, a light, warm solidity against his arm. He fisted his hands in his lap, digging his nails into the flesh of his palms. He would not break down in front of her now. He would not reveal what a fraud he was.

Out of the corner of his eye, he could see her profile as she stared straight ahead. Her hand settled on one of his, soothing it. It hurt to swallow. He shut his eyes, his teeth bared like an animal, fighting the need to let her see how much he needed this. Her fingers stroked, gentle, relentless against the resistance of his fist. His own hand betrayed him. With a sigh of defeat, he felt it tremble and open. She turned it, palm up. He squeezed his eyes tighter, only feeling the softness of her fingers as she laced them through his.

He shook his head, stiffening, mouth tight. He wouldn't crack. He wouldn't.

But he couldn't control the break in his voice. "A better king would have kept them safe."

Her voice was soft in the still air of the tent, her fingers magic, melting the frozen musculature as she lifted his hand and, turning it over, traced a gentle circle on the palm. "I saw a woman today at the children's center. She had lost two of her own children and was there to find her sister's babe. She had seen me ride in with you, Nicholas. She asked me to tell you, from all of them, how much hope your coming has brought with it. She said as long as you are their king, nothing will defeat them. She called you the hope of Laurentia. Nicholas, they love you here.

They know what you do for them."

So. They talked to Sera. While he hid from the people, sick with what his lack of foresight had wrought on Selonia. And *she* had spoken to his people, and they had trusted her.

And because of her, they trusted him.

Long ago, he had decided to keep secret his vulnerability—the illness and his regimen for fighting it. His decision had led to a distance, it seemed, between himself and his own people. Had Sera, within a few hours, brought his people back to him?

"They're fools to trust me," he said aloud on a laugh that was a groan. He dropped his eyes to their entwined hands, afraid to let her see the emptiness that must show on his face.

"You have to eat," she said finally. There. She had dismissed him. He slipped his hand from hers, and she poured a glass of red wine and gave it to him. "It is not very elegant, but the soldiers all say it is good."

He took a sip and very carefully placed the silver cup on the table before him. "It's good," he managed.

She came back to sit beside him, he noticed with relief. Lord, she'd been cold and stony this morning. Until he had told her about Selonia. Then this wellspring of compassion had broken through and changed her, utterly.

As if she had been following his thoughts, Sera touched his arm shyly. "The children, Nicholas. They need...oh, everything. I put them in one of the buildings that escaped most of the fire—St. Andrew's chapter house. No one has used it for several years, and there were still feather beds we could spread on the floor for the little ones. I asked the quartermaster for food."

"Briggs?" Nicholas was surprised into a laugh. "He's a stingy fellow. How did you ever manage?"

Sera blushed. " I promised him you would make sure the supplies were replaced."

Was she afraid he'd find her impertinent? She had such a pretty blush—pink and rosy from her down-turned lashes to her rounded chin.

"I would have told him the same thing," he said.

"I have hope that some of the parents are still alive. Do you know those animals went house to house and murdered the people in their beds? They always seem to leave the children alone, don't they? As though they expect them to die of want and misery.

"Do you know what it is like, to see your father and mother stabbed repeatedly by these vile demons?" she continued. "To hear their screams, to see the blood, everywhere. And then, when they're too weak to scream any longer, they just whimper, but you know they're still screaming inside. Oh, God! It is not human, what they have done to the children."

Sera clutched his forearm. Her face was white as a new fallen snow, and her eyes unseeing. She was telling him more than what had happened to these children, he knew. She was telling him something that had happened to her. Of a sudden, his own struggles faded in the light of Sera's pain.

He pried her hand off his arm, then grasped her elbows. "Tell me, Sera. Tell me what they did to you."

She gasped, struggled against him hard enough to push away. He saw her eyes before she turned her face from him. They were focused again and fearful. "I don't know what you are talking about," she said, jumping up and fiddling with the plates on the tray. "We are discussing the children, that is all."

"Yes," he said, careful to keep his tone neutral. "The children." She had shut the door, and he couldn't open it now with more questions. He could wait until she told him of her own free will.

When hell froze over.

Or he could find out through his own sources.

"I only meant, we cannot leave them to die. We have to help them all."

This at least, he could do. He nodded, stretching his legs in front of him in a deliberate pose of relaxation. "Every one of them, Sera. Just tell me what they need."

She recovered herself, writing out a list of supplies for the abbey, and she slowly became easy with him again. Later, she called for hot water so he could bathe.

The young ensigns who arrived with the hip bath bowed to him, and then Sera before they set it down according to her instructions.

"Very good, Mr. Evans. Thank you, Mr. Carlsohnn." Good Lord, she knew them by name already. The men tugged at their caps like besotted schoolboys and bowed their way out of the tent.

"Is there anything else you would like tonight, Nicholas?" she asked, foolish woman.

He smiled, keeping his lascivious thoughts to himself. "Thank you, no, Lady Sera."

She gave him a look of surprise from beneath her lashes. "Why call me that?"

"Because that's what you are. I'm not the only one to name you thus. All the men are speaking of Lady Sera. Should I be the only one not to recognize the obvious?"

"I am just a Hill woman and a slave." She gave him a wary look.

His fingers touched her cheek, then fell to his side. "You are not *just* anything. And I meant it. Thank you."

Sera nodded, a little uncertain motion, and swept out into the night.

She could be incredibly sweet when she wanted to be. He would assign Oblomov to her, for the streets weren't safe for a woman alone in times like these, and he knew instinctively Sera would go wherever someone needed her help.

He wished that she could stay with him. Would she have nightmares tonight? He wanted to be there to wake her and reassure her. He wanted to hold her in his arms again as he had last night, to keep her warm and safe.

He cursed softly. Andre had moved up the date for a meeting with Galerien, regent of Beaureve. Within a month, he would probably be wed to the blasted Beaurevian princess, the key to the alliance with Beaureve, which must be kept at all costs.

This time was all he could ever have with Sera. He had to fight the lust, and even more seductive, the need for her. Just to hold her through the night and cover her small, warm body with his. So he could sleep, and keep the nightmares at bay.

Six

The chapter house was in chaos. Children who had scarcely noticed their surroundings suddenly became hot tempered little savages, screaming at anyone who tried to discipline them into some kind of order.

Nurses and priests ran to Sera as soon as she walked through the door. If it were possible for the room to become any noisier, it did then.

"What are we going to do, Lady Sera?"

"We have no clean linens for the nursery."

"Those boys—they're running wild!"

She narrowed her eyes at the confusion of arms and legs in the center of the room—a group of boys pummeled each other over imagined insults. Well, if nobody else was offering solutions, she might as well come up with a few, herself.

Grabbing up a bucket of cold water in her hands, Sera charged into the melee. She dumped the water over the heads of the biggest four and watched them sputter and jump apart like dogs disturbed in the midst of a fight.

"I need you," she barked, while twelve and thirteen-year-olds rubbed their faces and pulled soaking hair out of their eyes. "Who knows the streets of Selonia the best?"

"I do," said the tallest boy.

"No, I do," yelled another, an urchin with bright red hair and an impish look.

"Fine," said Sera. "You can both prove your claim. You." She pointed to the older boy. "Take these three, and take the eastern half of the city. You are looking for any and all children who have nowhere to go."

"You." She pointed to the second boy. "Do the same with these three on the western side. I want you back by noon. I want your names and your parent's names before you go out, in case somebody comes looking for you. And I want your report before you go to the refectory to eat lunch."

The redhead rubbed his nose, over which were scattered a very nice sprinkling of freckles. The boy had a lean, hungry look to him, but his blue eyes were sharp and clear. "Nobody's looking for me," he said. "My mother's been dead for two years now." He paused, then raised his chin and looked her straight in the eye. "Never knew my father."

"All the same, I want your name and that of your family."

"Ivan," said the boy, patting his split lip with his fingertips. "Ivan Drominsky. S'pose now you don't want me to look for the others."

Sera raised her brows and fingered her own lip, still swollen from the backhanding Dawson had given her two nights before.

"Do you know the city better than the others?"

"Hell—beg pardon, my lady. Aye. I know it."

"Kindly bring your boys forward to give their names and then take them out. Remember, return to the chapter house by the time the town clock strikes twelve."

"I'll do that, my lady."

Sera found herself grinning as she watched him leave. She liked that scamp, Ivan. Liked his courage in giving her the truth of his parentage. Liked the clear, intelligent look he'd given her as he spoke.

She took a deep breath and walked on to the nursery. More chaos there, it seemed. Babies who had listlessly sucked warmed goat's milk yesterday were fussing on the harried priests' laps for their mother's breasts today. Frazzled priests and a few of the ladies, who had come to the shelter with vague pretensions to philanthropy, looked ready to throttle the infants.

Sera sighed with relief as one of the priests, a portly, balding man holding a baby in one arm, unpacked cloths to use for diapers with the other hand. The baby was blessedly quiet, and the priest seemed the only adult in the room with any sense. Sera reached for the infant and cuddled it close.

The priest turned to her and shouted over the cries of the other infants. "I'm Father Anselm, my dear. I take it you are the Lady Sera who put this place together yesterday."

"I am," she said, with a glance at babies. "They don't sound happy."

"They're having a hard time, but at least they're getting some nourishment."

"Why not send for wet nurses? Or better still, why not send for mothers who lost their babies in the raid?"

Father Anselm gave her a long, considering look and

nodded slowly.

Sera pondered that look, for she thought her suggestion perfectly logical. Perhaps the holy men of this country didn't want to hear about the earthier aspects of a woman's existence.

But all he said was, "Excellent idea. I'll see to it immediately." He left her holding the baby.

Father Anselm returned later with about twenty women, all hollow-eyed and expressionless. They entered the chapter house as though they didn't know where they were, or why they were there. It hurt to see them so lost.

"Come with me," Sera said. The women followed, looking neither right nor left. She didn't waste time explaining, but led them into the make-shift nursery. The women stood like statues, staring at the red-faced, writhing little bodies in the cribs.

"Oh, God in Heaven!" cried one of them. Tears streamed down her face as she ran to a crib and, with careful, practiced hands, lifted the little burden. The baby's legs pumped in a paroxysm of hungry rage, and his back arched against the woman's hands, but she held him safe, settled on a window seat and gathered him against her. The baby snuffled blindly and found what he needed.

Another woman went to a cradle, and another, and another. The room, as if by miracle, quieted. Nothing could be heard but the contented, soft sound of babies at the breast and a woman's occasional, fierce sob.

Father Anselm stood quietly beside Sera. "Our king may believe that he brought you to our country, but I know better, my dear. When there is great suffering, God sends his angels."

Sera shook her head, red with embarrassment. "I am no angel," she said.

Father Anselm's mouth curved in a kindly smile. "Not for many years yet, I hope. But when there is need in Laurentia, you will fill it."

***

Two days later, Sera sat in the cloister of the chapter house awaiting her chance to slip away. Almost everyone but the smallest children helped at this early morning hour with the rebuilding efforts in the city. Thanks to young Ivan Drominsky, she had a list of Selonia's inns.

Until yesterday, Lieutenant Oblomov's careful

attentiveness had made it impossible for her to search for the thief. Everywhere she walked, he followed. When she tried to evade him, he simply smiled and said, "I'm under orders to keep you safe, m'lady."

To keep me from escaping, she thought glumly.

So yesterday morning, she had asked Father Anselm to walk her back to camp every night. Then, she told young Oblomov that he could leave her each morning after depositing her in the orphanage. Of course, he didn't need to know that she would leave the orphanage at noon in search of the thief.

Sera rose and headed for the cloister gate. With her hand on the latch, she heard Father Anselm calling out behind her.

"Sera, come quickly!" The priest sounded winded and frightened.

The expression on his drawn face made Sera hurry to him. "What's happened?" she asked him, matching his running steps as they passed through the archways to the kitchen.

"Ivan's hurt," he said, mopping his brow as they entered. Ivan lay whimpering on the long wooden table in the center of the kitchen. Blood ran down his leg like a stream in flood. A pile of bandages and a bowl of clean water lay on a small table beside him.

"He fell on a broken windowpane. I told him not to forage through the ruins, but would he listen? Heavens, the doctor's on the western side of the city, and I must fetch him myself. Will you stay with him until I return with the doctor? He's bleeding heavily. I don't know, Sera," Father Anselm said in a low voice. "It looks very bad. Perhaps there's something you can do for him."

Fear gripped her—that she was unequal to the task, and that Ivan would suffer for it. "I've only worked with horses, Father. Do not expect much. But I'll try," Sera said.

"Do your best to stanch the blood flow," said Father Anselm. He ran off to find the doctor.

Ivan's freckles stood out on a thin little face that was as white as the bandages, and his eyes were wild with pain. "Didn't mean to, milady," he said in a reedy voice. "But it hurts something fierce, it does." He grabbed Sera's wrist.

"You helped the babies. Help me, please." Sera felt sick with apprehension. From the looks of it, the boy didn't have long. And the doctor was very far away.

Oh, gods! If only the gift flowed through her in full strength! All of her pity surged toward Ivan. He grew more waxen by the minute. She *had* to try. Tying a bandage around Ivan's leg just above the wound, Sera let the limited power she had rise within her.

"Sleep," she wished him.

Ivan's eyes blinked once, twice, and closed. His face smoothed of pain.

Sera examined the leg. The glass was still embedded, a long, wicked shard plunged into the skin. Ivan's pulse was weak and thready. She shut her eyes and thought clarity, thought peace, thought strength.

The light flooded her. Her heart pounded in a rhythm deep and steady, like the tolling of a bell, like the sighing of waves against the shore.

She bent to the work before her, washing the boy's leg and grasping the glass between steady fingers. She tugged, one pull, and the glass slid out, leaving a deep gash. She put her hands on the gash, delving into that place of calm, directing it outward and into the wound, as she did with the horses. The wound grew warm beneath her hands. The very air about them both vibrated, and she felt the surge of her own blood, her own life, rise through her and into Ivan from the tips of her fingers. And there was stillness to the room, as though time had stopped in its tracks, as though all life paused to listen. A pulsing peace encircled her and the child.

"All will be well," she said, from the lucid calm that cradled them.

Suddenly, it was over. Sounds from the street insinuated their way into the room, and the breeze piped about her skirts. The boy slept on, and she sagged against the table, drained, weary beyond belief. Her legs could just carry her to a plain wooden chair, and she collapsed into it.

Time must have passed, but she barely noticed it. Her legs were still limp as wet wool. Her heavy lids opened reluctantly to view her patient. Ivan slept peacefully. It might have been another hour before she had the strength to get up, and when she finally rose to her feet, she bandaged the boy's leg and cleaned up the blood.

Footsteps sounded in the corridor outside the kitchen. Sera looked up to see Father Anselm hurrying in with the doctor, who set down his bag and deftly unwrapped the bandage.

He looked from the leg to Father Anselm. "You brought me from a woman in labor for this? 'Tis but a scratch."

Father Anselm bent over Ivan's leg. "No. It couldn't be. He was bleeding copiously."

The doctor raised a skeptical brow. "Then I suggest you set up a shrine in this kitchen, because that boy's just had a miracle cure. On the other hand, perhaps you need a rest, Father. You have obviously been working much too hard."

"I saw it, I tell you."

The doctor waved his fingers impatiently. "Some other time we'll discuss this. I must return to Madame DuLac."

As the doctor's footsteps died away, Father Anselm stared at Sera. She turned away from him and busied herself with needless cleaning chores.

Out of the corner of her eye, she saw Father Anselm shake his head. "I'll not ask you a thing, my lady. Nor will I discuss this elsewhere. But I thank you for saving that boy's leg, and I hope someday you'll tell me how you did it."

Sera slipped from the kitchen as soon as she could, leaving Father Anselm to sit by Ivan until he awoke. As she left the orphanage, her stomach queasy from doubt and effort, she fretted.

Had the Gift finally awakened in all its fullness? How would she learn to control it without Grandfather's guidance? Would it be obvious to others here—like a second head suddenly sprouted? They would hate her if they knew. They would whisper, and the whispers would grow into shouts of hatred. In the end, they would kill her, just as they'd killed her mother. If the Gift remained a part of her, home was the only place where she could live in peace.

She hid her clenched hands in her apron. And felt the crackle of paper—her list of inns—her possible exit from this world of terror and misery. Stopping a woman passing by for directions, Sera set out for the hill leading to the northern end of the city.

She climbed, skirting fallen timbers and rocks until, halfway up, she paused and stared, bemused. Silhouetted against the sun, Nicholas stood speaking to a group of men. He mustn't see her and wonder and ask questions.

She slipped behind a copse of bushes. His back was to her, his long legs braced slightly apart, and he pointed at something in the distance. The light turned his thin linen shirt translucent. The play of muscle along his broad back and arms left her slightly breathless. Her gaze stroked his slim waist and hips.

The men clustered around him looked at him with absolute trust. Someone gave him a map. His head bent over it, and he spoke again. The men's faces cleared of worry.

Something hurt, deep in her chest. She would be leaving so soon. Seizing the stolen moment and holding it close, Sera committed his face, his beautiful, strong body, his lithe movements, to memory. Very soon, she would be home again. And life would no longer hold the promise of his presence. Carefully, silently, she backed away, and then she climbed up the long, steep hill.

The Blue Herron was situated high above the ruins. A stiff wind would have torn the inn's ramshackle shutters from the windows, and the building leaned precariously to one side. In the yard, drovers shouted crude invitations to women leaning from the upper story windows, the necklines of their gowns cut so low that their breasts were barely covered.

At Sera's approach, a man turned. "Eh, Darlin', wantin' a bit of coin, are you?" He came toward her, grinning and holding out his hand. "You look like a fine 'un, you do. Come away with me, luv, and I'll show you a good time and give you top price."

Sera's heart began to pound. The man looked at her as Dawson had. She forced herself not to back away and run.

"Leave 'er be, Tom," yelled another across the yard. "She's quality, she is."

"What's she doin' in a place like this, if she's an aristo, eh Cully?" the first replied.

"I'm looking for a man," said Sera, just barely holding her ground.

"See, Cully, what'd I tell ya'? An' I'm yer man, I am."

"No, you are not." Sera cleared her throat. "I am looking for a particular man. A merchant. Medium height, dark hair and beard, carrying a great many jewels. Have you seen him? I can offer a reward for any information."

"How much?" asked the big drover.

"Five Laurentian pounds sterling." She had that much in wages from Master Raymond. "Do you know of him?"

The drover scratched his head. "Little lady, I'm that tempted to say I do and take your money fer a tale I'd make up, but there's too much trouble in this town, and I'll not add to it. I'm that sorry, but I don't know of any merchant. We're just arrived yester'eve. None of these men will know him."

"Perhaps the women, or the innkeeper..." Sera looked up at the women in the windows, who were listening intently.

"The innkeeper, is that what you call him these days?" shouted a blonde with rouged lips and cheeks. The others all laughed.

"I might know of someone who knows of someone who knows where the merchant is," said the blonde. "Come back tomorrow, and bring your money. I'll have more news by then."

A short time later, Sera slipped back into the orphanage. At this moment, giddy with hope, she wanted to dance, to leap and skip. Tomorrow, she would surely find the thief and the ruby.

She had to calm herself, before anyone saw her in this state of exultation. Sitting down on a bench warmed by the sun, she shut her eyes and breathed deeply. When she opened them, she saw Father Anselm walking toward her. His face clouded in worry.

"Do you mind?" He motioned to the place beside her on the bench.

"No, please." Sera made room for him and he sat with a gusty sigh.

"Ivan Drominsky has fully recovered, but I suppose you expected that. He asked for you, and when I told him you had left the orphanage for a little while, he said you've been wandering the city alone, and not in the safer districts. Is that true?"

Sera froze in fear.

"I can see that it is," said Father Anselm quietly.

"Really, my dear, I must warn you that it's not safe for a woman to walk alone. Can't you ask young Oblomov to attend you on these journeys?"

Sera pressed her fists to her sides. "He has duties of his own."

In the silence, she could feel Father Anselm's gaze and held her breath, wishing him away before he asked for what she couldn't give—the truth.

"Please," she whispered. "Don't tell anyone else."

"I won't disclose your secrets unless you allow me to. But for your safety, please take Ivan and a few of the older boys with you, wherever you go. It will keep the young scamp occupied and out of the ruins. Will you do that, at least?"

The boys...Did she dare involve them? Did she have a choice?

"All right," she said.

Father Anselm patted her hand. "That's good. You have taken a weight off my mind, Sera." Then his gentle gaze held hers. "Please consider me a friend. I'll never fear you, my dear, nor condemn you for any unexplainable gifts you might have." He left her then, to sit, trembling, until she could force herself to walk back into the chapter house.

***

"There you are. Not working her too hard, are you Father?" Nicholas forced himself to walk toward Sera in an easy, relaxed stride when what he wanted to do was race to her and shake her for being late and not sending word tonight. How could he possibly get anything done when he worried about what perils she might face in the gutted ruins near the chapter house? Just yesterday, he'd heard that she'd searched through a condemned house for a child's favorite blanket.

She looked tired, and at the same time almost twitchy, with a kind of excess emotion tugging at her beneath the calm surface she attempted.

"I have kept an eye on her, sire," said Father Anselm. Nicholas gave him a grateful grin.

"But she is a stubborn little thing," Father Anselm continued. "I doubt she took the time to dine this afternoon."

"I was planning on it, Father," Sera said in protest.

"Other problems took precedence."

"As you see, your majesty." Father Anselm gave Nicholas a wry smile.

Nicholas nodded, seeing far too well. "Between the two of us, we'll keep her healthy," he said.

"I am perfectly fine," said Sera quickly.

"So I see." With Sera, a man had to pick his battles carefully. "Lieutenant Carlsohnn has already laid the table. Will you join us, Father?"

"No, thank you. I must return to the orphanage. Two of the boys got into a scrape, and I'm to judge their punishment. I shall see you on the morrow, my dear." He bowed to Sera, and then to Nicholas, and walked away, whistling.

She entered the tent ahead of Nicholas and took her seat at the small table. He sat across from her, studying her face while he told her about his day.

"The architect who will build the baths has a temperament. Have your ever met a man with artistic temperament? No, there are probably none where you come from.

"This man closes his eyes and says, 'I'm thinking.' Then he goes on to say ochre Ionic columns or Roman murals of mermaids and satyrs or something else that gives apoplexy to the entire city council. And then I am supposed to make aesthetic judgments on this project—I, who have no real interest in more than the rough engineering and problem solving. I'll be the first king deposed for his lack of artistic appreciation."

Sera looked down at her plate. For a moment, studying her down-turned face, Nicholas thought he saw guilt and fear flit across it.

"I must be losing my touch," said Nicholas. What foolish scheme was she hatching now, and why?

"I thought you were beginning to like my Outlander hu-mor," he said, accenting both syllables as she did. At his gentle teasing, she lowered her chin further, and her flush came all the way up to her forehead. The niggling worry turned to real anxiety.

"Is anything wrong, Sera?"

"No," she said.

Finally, Nicholas dropped his napkin beside his plate and leaned toward her. His fingers lifted her chin. He frowned, studying her face.

"You look weary. Haven't you been sleeping well?"

"You needn't interrogate me," she said with more asperity than he'd heard since he'd informed her that she must stay in Laurentia, with him.

The anxiety turned to dread. She was planning something—another escape. He was certain of it. "If you don't get more rest, perhaps you should return to Montanyard."

Sera's chin jerked. "Absolutely not. I'm fine, I tell you."

He raised a brow and gave her a long look. "Why aren't you sleeping?"

"I sleep well enough," she said and grabbed her fork, spearing the fillet and chewing rapidly to keep him from asking her more questions.

"Yes, I can see by the circles beneath your eyes. And your voracious appetite," he continued, eyeing her half-finished plate. "We shall have to order larger portions for you."

"That is another attempt at this Outlander hu-mor, no doubt," Sera said. She gave him a defiant look, but there was fear beneath it. And suddenly, tonight, he didn't want to fight. He just wanted what he always wanted from Sera. A little trust, so he could solve the seemingly overwhelming problems she carried with her.

"Well?"

"It's the children," she said, and he knew immediately from her quick, guilty glance, and the relief behind it, that it was not the real reason, but also, not quite a lie. "There are some who will never find families to take them in—boys too old and street-wise to be charming, girls not pretty enough. What will you do with them?"

"Wrong question. What will you do with them, Sera?"

"I?"

He nodded. "From the first day here, they belonged to you. Set up a school, an apprenticeship program—everything we've talked about. Tell me what you need, and I'll see that you get it."

"First Father Anselm and now you," she said with a sigh. "I shan't be here long enough to oversee such a project." So she thought. But he knew how she liked Ivan, scrappy, angry with the world, mischievous. He tugged at her, just as the other urchins did. She couldn't deny them.

He needed this to hold her here, with him.

So Nicholas simply gave her a knowing smile, and he called for Carlsohnn, who cleared the table and brought his writing desk. This was their pattern. Every evening after dinner, she wrote directives while he dictated. He would pace the small tent, then pause behind her to think as she bent over the writing desk. Idly, he would brush his fingers down the graceful nape of her bent neck and rub his thumb along the silken skin right beneath her hairline, pretending he wasn't holding his breath, waiting for her shiver of pleasure. He would lean over her to see how she'd written a phrase, his hands cupping her shoulders through the light wool of her gown, tormenting himself with the fresh, wildflower scent of her, wanting more, needing at least this.

"First the school, I think." He stood directly behind her and kneaded the knot of tension in her shoulders and neck. He felt triumph when she closed her eyes and arched her head back toward him. She was so close he could smell that elusive scent, see the rise and fall of her soft, rounded breasts beneath her gown with every heightened breath she took.

And all the while, growing warm and hard from her closeness, and the need that sprang from something elemental inside him, he kept his voice light as he dictated directives that would bind her even more to him and this land.

It was wrong, he knew, to have this overwhelming desire, to try to tempt her so she would stay forever. But here, in Selonia, they lived in a world apart. Couldn't they both forget their duty to others, if only for a while? Besides, his country needed her. She had to stay.

"The medical facilities," Sera suggested, dipping the quill into the inkwell during a pause, as Nicholas began to pace the small tent.

"It will need its own doctor, a good one. This is just the project that will bring Baron Summers out of retirement. He needs something more interesting than that ancient trout to keep him busy."

Sera stole a glance at his face, her face alight with their plans, with purpose. Like a greedy miser, he stored the memories—portraits of Sera in all her moods. And the odd sense of—what? Was this what they called joy?—that he felt on nights like this, when they joined their minds and hearts in common, hopeful plans.

"Are you weary?" Her soft voice twined around his thoughts.

"Not a bit."

She bent again to her writing, her lips curling in the beginning of a smile.

Sera, who haunted his dreams, even when she fled him. Sera, who gave him sweet ease from his grief and his guilt over Selonia. What would he do with her when it was time to leave this place and return to his obligations? How could he ever tear himself away from her?

***

The next afternoon, excitement jittered through Sera as she set off with the boys for the Blue Herron, the precious silver Laurentian pounds in the pocket of her gown.

Solemn with their new responsibility, the boys climbed in a protective circle around her to the inn. The courtyard was even busier than it had been the day before. Wagons stood about while drovers yelled and unhitched horses skittered left and right in the noise. The blonde woman who had been at the window yesterday called out to her and beckoned with her hand.

"He's inside," she said shortly. Sera entered the ramshackle building and stepped down a few rickety stairs into the main room. After the bright sunlight outside, this place was dim and gloomy. Years of soot from the fireplace stained the walls and ceiling. Old, scratched and marred tables and chairs with uneven legs filled the room. It smelled of sweat and sour ale. A burley man sat at one of the tables drinking ale. His clothing, once a bright red jacket and black trousers, looked grimy and soot-stained. His face had a hopeless, empty look to it.

"There's your man." The blonde woman pointed him out and left the room. Sera walked to the table, taking care to keep her clothing from brushing against the gritty furniture. The boys closed in around her, their eyes glancing left and right.

"Are you the man who knows of the merchant who was here last week?"

"The one with the ruby as big as half your palm? Aye, I be he."

Sera slid the coins across the table toward the man.

The man slid them back to her and gave her a look of despair. "Nay, mistress. I can't take your coin, for I no longer know where he's gone."

Sera's heart sank to her feet. "Can you direct me to someone who will know?" she asked.

The man shook his head slowly. "Nay. He hired us to guard him. There were ten of us, and later, ten more. We stayed at the best inn in town, The Pavillion. Never saw such a place. It was fine, it was. Until it burned the night the bastards came to Selonia and sacked it." The man stared down at his ale.

"I was the only one of the ten who made it out alive. The merchant? They didn't find his body, but nobody knows where he's gone. He just disappeared. Now all I want to do is go home and see my wife and children again. After I find work here, I'll save enough to get home. Just see if I don't." The man sat, staring at nothing, his hand lying listlessly on the table beside his ale.

The world turned gray as ashes. Sera bit her lip and looked down at the coins on the table. Then she looked at the man slumped before her. His face showed the defeat she felt. She gathered up the money and took the man's hand. Turning it over, she placed the coins in it and closed his fist around them.

"Here," she whispered. "Take it and go home."

"But mistress, I..."

"By the gods, man. Be grateful you can go home." Sera squeezed the man's shoulder and walked blindly out of the inn. The boys ran to catch up. She was vaguely aware of their presence through the gray mist that closed her in. She was vaguely aware, as well, of the children's games, the lessons going on in the makeshift classroom and the light slowly changing as she worked through the rest of the day.

But when the darkness came, she entered Nicholas's tent, and he was real.

"Sera?" he said softly.

She ran into his arms. "I am so tired," she said.

So easily he took her weight as she leaned into him. Tonight, she allowed herself to let go in this world of strangers and uncertainty. He smoothed her hair, lifted her into his arms, and strode to the cot. He sat holding her, stroking her back, murmuring against her hair that it would be all right, that he was there. He didn't even ask what was wrong. He just held her, deep into the night.

***

Sera woke in her cot. She was still dressed in her gown, but someone had removed her slippers. Nicholas must have carried her here some time in the night. She dragged herself into a sitting position and faced facts. The thief was but a chimera, now. But nobody knew for certain that he was dead. He might still be alive. Father Anselm had offered her help. That afternoon, she asked him for it.

"Yes, I have heard of the merchant and his treasure," said the priest. They were sitting in the chapter house garden, taking in the noon rays of sunshine with their meal.

"Is it important to you to know whether the man is dead or alive?" he asked.

"It is vital. And where he is if he is alive. Can you help me?"

"It may take some time, but I have several friends in the countryside. If anyone knows of this man, I'll send word of him to you."

"Thank you, Father. Thank you with all my heart." It was only after Father Anselm gently removed her hand from the sleeve of his cassock that Sera realized she had been clutching it as though it were a life line. Relief flooded her, that Father Anselm trusted her. She began to hope again.

That night, Nicholas told Sera that they could leave the city in the hands of its officials. She set out for the capital beside the king, surrounded by the divisions of cavalry. Still, she carried hope in her heart and purpose renewed.

It was not until Nicholas and she rode together through the gates of Montanyard that Sera learned the king had not forgotten her last escape attempt, or his decision regarding her quarters.

"When this war is over, I hope you'll take part in solving the problems of all Laurentia's orphans. In the meantime, your move into the palace will help you become acquainted with the people you will work with in the future."

Sera stared up at him, her eyes narrowing in the first stirring of fear and anger. "What do you mean, my move into the palace?"

"I've already ordered your room readied," he replied with a maddeningly calm smile. "It's quite lovely, actually. You'll like it. We'd do well to hurry, Sera. The modiste will be waiting for you now."

Sera had a difficult time keeping her voice from rising to a shout. "I have no need for new dresses. The horses do not care what I look like."

"Ah, but the courtiers do. Far more than is reasonable, in my opinion." Nicholas's voice was smooth as a boat gliding over quiet waters. "And since I expect you to be accepted as a member of my court, you'll have to dress the part. It's time for you to burn those plain gowns you seem so fond of." He gave her a slow, heated look that covered her from the top of her head to the tips of her toes.

"Did you think that I've forgotten what Dawson did to you? Did you suppose I would rescind my order? Learn this, if nothing else. Once given, my word is absolute. You are a lady to the bone, and as a lady, you will live."

Sera trembled with an overwhelming combination of fury and fear. If she could not get to Wind Rider, how would she ever get home? "You cannot keep me from the stables!"

"You may ride every day with Katherine or one of the guards." Nicholas looked different, now. His face was all sharp planes and angles—his brows straight, black slashes above eyes that burned down into hers. He looked too powerful, too dangerous, too male. He looked at her as though he owned her soul. Numbly, she shook her head, trying to shove back against the force he was exerting on her with just a look.

"If you have another brilliant plan to escape, forget it," he said in a controlled, low voice that made her shiver more than if he had shouted at her. "I'll know where you are at every moment." He leaned toward her, ostensibly removing a small branch from her shoulder where it had fallen sometime during the ride, but Sera knew he was using the moment, branding her with that light touch, just to let her know how closely he intended to guard her.

"I told you on the night when I came after you, Sera. You are mine, and I'll never let you escape. Get used to it."

Nicholas waved away the groom waiting to take his horse. He wheeled sharply and galloped off in the direction of the park, leaving Sera to dismount at the entry to the palace, trying to still her body's helpless shaking.

***

Nicholas found a secluded prospect in the park upon a rocky hill. He dismounted and sat blindly staring out at the river beyond. He wished he had never seen Sera, wished that he had her in his bed, at his table, by his side every waking hour of the day.

Wishes were useless, trapping a man in dreams that couldn't come true. Because of wishes, he held a woman against her will whom he could neither woo nor forget.

He faced reality. Selonia was over. The desperately needed alliance with Beaureve had him trapped. Even if he were free, his obsession with Sera threatened everything he had worked all his life to build.

His father had shown him what happened to a man who lost control of his emotions. Everyone in the kingdom had suffered because of it.

He would never do the same. Laurentia's fate depended upon it.

He knew the tightrope he walked every day, holding on to his health by strict self-control, never knowing when his body would betray him. So far, that control had protected Laurentia, for it kept the illness at bay. That control also meant that he very rarely made a mistake.

Until Sera. With Sera, he'd lost his edge, cared less about perfection and more about joy. Any more of this self-indulgent dreaming and he'd lose complete control.

Usually, he hid inside from winter, fenced and boxed rigorously, got his rest, and never overindulged in food, drink or sensuality. But now, he had visions of skating with Sera on a frozen pond, teaching her to drink champagne, and keeping her up all night with his lovemaking. With Sera, he forgot he wasn't...normal. He gritted his teeth. What folly! He might make himself sick for weeks and bring the country down with him. He remounted, and rode toward the palace. And halted the horse twenty feet from where he had begun.

"Bloody hell," he said aloud. Why had he ordered that Sera occupy the one chamber in the palace that was accessible to his?

The first hale from a guard galloping toward him startled him from his thoughts. "Oblomov," he said, recognizing the young lieutenant from Selonia. He and Carlsohnn were close friends and both had excellent heads on their shoulders, except in the presence of one impossibly beautiful Hill woman. They had followed Sera about in Selonia like adoring pups.

"What news?" Nicholas asked.

"Dawson, Sire—he's escaped."

The first chill of fear shot through Nicholas. "When?"

"Last night. He had a visitor, a woman. She must have slipped him a knife. He used it to kill the guard who brought him supper. The soldiers have been searching since midnight, but to no avail."

"Send out more men. Scour the forest where he'll go to ground. Go. Do it now."

Oblomov wheeled his horse and galloped back toward the palace. Nicholas took the path toward the stables at no less a pace. He didn't understand why his heart kept pounding like a hammer in his chest. Any sane man would cut and run given Dawson's options. But there was something about the way Dawson had looked at Sera. Nicholas had seen that look on the faces of the country folk when they set out milk and honey at night to keep the wood spirits from stealing their babes. It was raw fear of unknown, powerful forces—like witchcraft and magic. And a man like Dawson would wish to utterly defile and destroy what he feared.

***

Dawson raced through the forest, almost mad with exultation and terror. He had managed it—taken advantage of the confusion after the sacking of Selonia and escaped the dank, filthy pit they'd thrown him into. The young guard who had heard his moans in the night and his pleas for help lay dead, his throat slit. It was child's play, really, and even easier to steal a mount from the stables when half the grooms were at the borders with the army.

If he could just get to the eastern border and enter Beaureve without being stopped! He was so close. As he whipped the horse on, it crashed forward through bracken and vine. He was going to make it, he just knew—

A hand shot out, grabbing the reins. The horse shied,

rearing, and flung Dawson to the ground. He groaned, shook his head to clear it, and rose on one elbow. A sword at his throat, the point sticking in just enough to pierce the skin, stopped his movement, and he looked up in terror. A band of men surrounded him. He was too scared to turn his head and count them, but there were many, dressed completely in black against a gray dawn.

The Brotherhood! He'd be dead in less time than it took to swallow if he didn't think fast. His mind worked at a fever pitch. "Please," he said. "I have naught against you. I like what y'er doin'. Got my own beef against that bastard Nicholas. Truth to tell, I was lookin' fer you, hopin' to join with you against him. I'm good with a knife, and I can shoot straight. Just tell me who to kill, and I'll do it. Won't ask fer a pence, believe me. It'll be my pleasure."

The man with the sword at his throat paused a moment, looked over his head to another who stood opposite. They spoke, to Dawson's surprise, in Beaurevian, and he felt his bowels cramp. From what he heard, they normally never spoke. If they betrayed their nationality in front of him, he didn't have much of a chance, did he?

"I know the palace real well," he said through a dry throat. "Jest take me to the man in charge, and I'll tell him things that'll help him." The point of the sword at his throat dug in deeper.

"Think how mad he'll be if you lose this chance, eh?" he wheedled, driven by desperation. The sword withdrew, slowly. Dawson remembered to breathe.

"Come," the man standing above him said in Laurentian. They let him mount, which Dawson considered a hopeful sign. Then they shot out of the forest and across a field. For a few hours they traveled through rocky ways, until they came to a mountain valley. The leader rode ahead. The others made him dismount and watched him with cold and wary eyes. Dawson stood up and tried to look cocky until the dark stares of the men sent him skittering for a log. He sat, head down, trying to block out the gibbering terror that lodged in his brain.

At the sound of hoof beats, he jumped up. A rough hand pushed him down again. He groaned, landing on his knee against a sharp rock, but he remained kneeling, too terrified to even look up.

A shadow crept over him, chilling his flesh and making

it crawl. "You have information about the palace?" The sinister voice seemed to come from the grave.

"Aye. I worked there for many a day," he said and shifted, trying to ease his knee off the rock.

"Tell me why I should not kill you now," said the voice. He chanced a look at the speaker. A figure, cloaked and hooded in black seemingly without face or real substance, stood above him. For one mad moment, Dawson thought he looked at Death, himself. But a hand covered in flesh appeared from beneath the cloak.

"I can help you. I can tell you things about the palace, about the people who are closest to the king. You can use me, sir."

"I am interested in a girl," said the voice. "A new arrival. Do you know of her?"

"Aye! Aye, I do, sir. Sera, she's called. Worked in the stables, 'til the king took a liking to her." He thought of the thrashing, the humiliation, and his anger overrode his fear.

"Now I hear she's to settle in the palace. Nicholas, he wants to ride her. She's a pretty enough piece, and eager to spread her legs for him."

"Sera," said the voice. "Seraphina, perhaps."

"If you want her, sir, I could find her fer you. I'm probably the only one here who knows what she looks like, eh? And I'll do it, not fer a reward, but fer the pleasure of seeing that little whore brought low. Would you like fer me to bring her, sir?"

The hand holding the sword hesitated and dropped. Dawson shuddered in relief. The sweat poured down his back, and he prayed that his cramping bowels wouldn't give way. The specter motioned, and three men stepped forward.

"These men will accompany you. They will stick closer to you than your own skin. If you have not produced the girl by the month's end, they will kill you. Do you understand?"

Dawson nodded madly. "Aye, sir. You needn't worry, sir. I'll bring her back before the new moon."

Seven

"Sera!"

As she stared in devastation after Nicholas galloping toward the park, Sera heard Katherine's voice. Katherine ran down the stairway, her face flushed and wreathed with smiles. Reaching Wind Rider's side, she scratched his chin and looked up at Sera.

"I am so glad to see you. Nicholas sent a messenger to me immediately after he found you. I was so relieved." Katherine reached up a hand and squeezed Sera's as it gripped the reins. "You mustn't try to run away from us again. So many terrible things could have happened to you, and then how I would have suffered for you!"

A groom helped her down and bowed low. Reluctantly, she realized there was nothing else to do but walk into the palace's front entrance beside Katherine. She had never come this way before. Her ignominious visits had been in the dark of night, through the back stairways for yet another royal scolding. Now she climbed wide marble stairs and walked through a tall set of double doors intricately carved in bronze. Another imposing marble staircase led into an enormous hallway beneath a high, high dome.

It was an odd sort of palace. For all its glittering ormolu vases, its overly fussy inlaid furniture and its magnificent statues, it was beautiful in the way that a harmonious natural setting was beautiful. If Sera didn't consider it a prison, she would have felt almost comfortable in it.

"My grandfather had it built," said Katherine. "I've always loved it—the airiness and the sense that a family, not a monarch, lives here."

"Come," she said, as Sera lingered before a statue of Apollo with his lyre, thinking of home. "You must be fitted for gowns. Tomorrow, if you're not too weary from your journey, I'll show you the town."

Katherine stopped before a door on the second story and opened it.

Sera stepped inside and stared. "You use these chambers merely for sleeping?" she asked, shocked at the space around her.

"Of course. Nicholas insisted that this one be made ready for you. It was my grandmother's. Do you like the wallpaper? I used to count the species of birds when I was a little girl, but I never could count that high."

"This is not a room for someone like me," said Sera, looking at the bright colors on the wall, the pink silk curtains hanging from the high tester above the wide bed, the blue Aubusson carpet that covered the entire floor.

"Oh, but my lady, it is perfect for you. With your golden coloring, your delicate bone structure." A tall, slender modiste with graying curls bustled in, followed by three assistants, buried beneath the large bolts of cloth they carried. She bowed to Katherine as the princess walked toward the door.

"I'll see you later today," said Katherine, and shut the door behind her.

The modiste looked her up and down. "His majesty chose well—a charming setting for his beautiful jewel."

His beautiful jewel? "I am no one's beautiful anything," said Sera with a frown.

The modiste prattled on as though she had not even heard Sera. "Now, we have little time to lose. You must have the first gown ready to wear by this evening, and also a sleeping gown, one that will enhance your lovely bosom and those soft shoulders. I have chosen a sky blue for you tonight. It only needs the measuring to complete it, and we will make more each day. If you will shed that..." Staring at Sera's travel stained gown, the modiste sniffed and hurried her behind a screen set up at the end of the chamber.

Deftly, she unhooked the gown, leaving Sera only in her chemise. She stood behind the screen, hot with embarrassment, while the woman wielded a tape measure across her breasts, her hips, and down her legs, clucking in admiration all the time. Sera had stripped to a short tunic many times on the exercise field, but never in her life had she experienced anything so invasive.

"You are quite special, you know. The king has never gone so far as to house one like you in his palace."

Sera froze. "And just what do you mean by 'one like me', Madame?"

"An irresistibly beautiful young woman who has captured the imagination of the commoners and the passion of a king." The modiste nodded her head once in satisfaction. "Yes, that is exactly how I shall put it to

Monsieur Carlsohnn when I order the rest of your fabric."

"You will not discuss me with anyone, Madame, else I shall not wear one of your gowns, and if I am asked why not, I shall say it is because you are a foolish gossip." Sera controlled the urge to shake the woman.

The modiste seemed not the least bit fazed by her outburst. "I assure you, Lady Sera," she said cheerfully, "the courtiers gossip already. Now that I've seen you, I shall certainly express my own admiration of your beauty to all of them."

Sera heaved an exasperated sigh and simply gave up the battle. The woman chatted on about how careful Sera must be to dispose her favors upon only the most powerful and the richest of the nobles, for she would, of course, wish to influence the king in their favor only when liberally rewarded. "Take jewels, that's my advice. Coin is so déclassé," said the modiste as she pinned and tucked the dreadful silk nightgown that revealed far too much of Sera's breasts.

Sera felt her stomach lurch. One such as she. The king's mistress—that is what this woman meant, and everyone knew it.

The modiste finally quitted the room, taking Sera's only gown. She heard a sound at the door and skittered behind the screen again. As it opened, she peeked out. Servants entered with a hip bath that they placed before the fire and filled with hot, steaming water. They laid towels and a robe upon a wooden chest and left silently.

She scrubbed her body hard in the bath, trying to wash away more than the dust of the road. Her mind went round and round on the best way to escape Montanyard, but there were guards, and walls, and a king who could find her as easily as a mage could find the Hills in a hill cloak. She bowed her head, her hair trailing in the cooling water, feeling like a bird caught in a snare.

She shivered, reached for a towel and dried her body. Wrapping the robe about her, she walked to the tall windows and looked out at the park, longing for freedom and home. Her hand rested on the wall, with its brilliant paintings of birds and flowers. Idly, she traced the outline of a beautiful bright green bird in flight, stroking the spread wings, the rose colored throat, the jeweled eye. Her fingers paused. Her eyes widened.

"A nikos," she whispered, startled and amazed. "How? Who knew of this?"

A nikos, precious and symbolic—found in only one place in the world.

Arkadia.

Sera pressed her forehead against the cool pane of the window and quiet filled her soul. Surely, this was a sign that somehow, someday, she would go home again.

The next morning, she left the beautiful cage that was her chamber to meet Katherine in the palace's entry hall. The princess, dressed in her pelisse and muff, peered out the high window and frowned. "I don't know whether we can go today," she said. "Just look at those clouds. You can hear the wind. It's going to rain at any minute, and I'm not allowed to go out when the weather looks so threatening."

Sera looked up at the sky and over at Katherine's gloomy face. In some ways, the princess was as much a slave to her position as Sera had been in Hadar's palace.

She looked up at the sky again and wondered. If I truly had the Gift in all its power, would it be so bad to use it for Katherine? To give her a happy day, would it be wrong to ask the sun to come out and the clouds to disperse? What harm could it do?

"Come on sun," she whispered inside her heart, inwardly chuckling at her own foolishness. "Shine for Katherine."

The sky lightened. The clouds thinned. Wisps of blue showed through the gray, and then, like a triumphant conqueror, the sun burst through, warming the earth. Even the brisk wind quieted to a pleasant breeze.

Katherine turned to her laughing in delight. "Did you see that? It was almost as if the sun felt sorry for me. Hurry! If we get out of here now, nobody can call us back."

Katherine's face was aglow with more than crisp air and bright morning sunlight. "I want to thank you," she said in a confiding voice.

"For what?" Sera asked in guilty surprise. Could Katherine have guessed? For that matter, had she actually brought about the change in weather, or had she simply wished when the weather decided to change of its own accord? Fear gripped her. How could she learn what to control and what to set free when she had no one to ask?

"To thank you for so many things," Katherine said, bringing her back from her frightening thoughts. "Your friendship. The chance to talk to you about matters closest to my heart. For the courage you gave me to finally reveal myself to...to..."

"You didn't! Did you truly, Katherine?"

Katherine blushed, this time a rosy, feminine color that complemented her glowing dark eyes. "I did! I lured Andre into the garden last night, and I told him of my feelings for him, and he, well, he returns them, Sera. Really, to hear him, his ardor, his voice! He took my hand, and he kissed it. He knelt before me—can you believe it? Me!"

"Of course I believe it, goose. Anyone looking at him could see it in his eyes. That is wonderful news. I wish you happy, Katherine, with all my heart."

Katherine stared at her as though she had lost her wits. "But we cannot wed, you know that. Still, it's good to know one is loved in so delightfully thorough a manner."

"You should wed! When this war is over, everything will change for the best. Perhaps the Russians will defeat Bonaparte, and Nicholas will find and defeat the Brotherhood. It is possible, you know."

"Oh, my dear," said Katherine, and her beautiful, expressive eyes looked upon her with such compassion. "You are a dreamer, and I'm, well, I'm a Rostov. My future doesn't hold happiness, but duty."

Then, her lips curved in a mischievous grin. "So, let us be realists, Sera, and indulge ourselves where we may, in a shopping spree."

"A shopping what?"

"A spree. Where you don't care about economy—you just buy whatever you like and hang the cost." At Sera's blank stare, Katherine laughed.

"Don't tell me you've never done anything without considering the cost?"

"One thing," Sera said quietly. And that was why she was in this strange world.

But it was difficult to hold even a wisp of resentment with Katherine. The townspeople bowed and smiled at them as they walked toward the town, followed at a discreet distance by a palace footman. The princess insisted upon buying her an intricately embroidered blue shawl from

Kashmir, a pair of pink satin dancing slippers that were so pretty she did not even object, and a pair of white leather gloves that were soft as butter.

The drapers, silversmiths, cobblers, and confectioners Sera met that day made her feel more at home than the pinched-nosed courtiers she had passed on her way to Katherine's room. They welcomed her with the same familiar fondness they showed their princess. At Carlsohnn's, the fine fabric shop, Sera spied some lace in the back corner of the shop window. It would be perfect for Katherine. Sera bade her move ahead to the next shop, planning to buy some of it for her as a surprise.

"Aye, Lady Sera," said the draper unrolling the lace and cutting several yards of it, "it's convent made. Feel it, now. Ain't it lovely?"

Sera allowed that it was, indeed.

"Our boy, Billy Carlsohnn, was the ensign for his majesty, all the time you were in Selonia. And our cousin, Carrie, her youngster was the little girl you found at the orphanage for her. Oh! You're all they can talk about. We're that grateful, my lady."

The draper handed her a brown parcel wrapped with a length of string. "And if I might be so bold as to congratulate you, my lady, I believe I speak for all of us."

Sera ran to catch up with Katherine, who stood beside the heavily burdened footman in front of a small teashop with a blue and white sign above the door.

Katherine eyed the menu posted upon the window. "Oh, lovely! They have those little poppy seed cakes that you must try, and the cream filled tarts."

"Katherine," she said, holding her back with a hand on her arm. "Monsieur Carlsohnn wished to congratulate me on something. What was he talking about? Have you any idea?"

"About the new title and lands you own." Katherine wrinkled her nose. "Didn't Nikki explain it to you? You're the Countess Fremons now."

Sera shook her head. "I haven't seen him since we returned from Selonia." That was only yesterday. Why did she feel as though eons had passed since she'd been with him?

"What is this Countess Fremons nonsense?" she asked after Katherine led the way into the teashop and ordered for them.

"Oh, Nikki thought that you ought to have a title and land of your own. Fremons has been in our family for generations. It's a rich province, and you'll love the old castle. It was built several centuries ago, but just last year, Nikki had it renovated."

"Katherine, I cannot accept a gift like that."

Katherine's nose wrinkled in puzzlement. "Why not?"

Because your controlling brother didn't even bother to tell me himself, she thought. The waitress smiled and bobbed a curtsey as she set out the cakes and tea.

Sera tried to put the matter calmly for Katherine's sake. "Well, it's rather a... bribe, isn't it? For staying, I mean. I expect to go just as soon as I may." She looked carefully at Katherine. "You do realize that, don't you?"

Katherine shrugged and smiled. "Oh, I know that you wish to leave soon, but you wished to leave last week, and the week before that, and you're still here." She squeezed Sera's hand. "It's only fitting that you receive a title and land after all you have done for us."

"I have done nothing," said Sera, and the teacup rattled against the saucer when she put it down.

"Montanyard and Selonia do not agree. Nor do I. Now, try one of the gateaux—the one with the pink marzipan flower."

Nicholas gave her none of his time, but an outrageous title and land to go with it, did he? That underhanded, overbearing... Outlander! I am going home, she thought. Very soon. Just wait until I see him again—I'll tell him what I think of his titles.

***

Nicholas spent the time waiting for Sera to comply with his summons by attempting to work at his study desk. But he could barely concentrate on anything but the hands of the ormolu clock slowly rounding the hour. At the soft knock on his door, he jumped up from the chair, forced himself to stand quietly against the desk, and called for her enter.

She slipped inside, a graceful woman of almost otherworldly beauty, her cheeks pink and her eyes bright. "You wished to see me, Nicholas Rostov?" she asked him.

"Where the devil have you been? I hoped to see you an hour ago."

"I was in the town with Katherine. Are you angry because you thought I had already escaped?" Sera's face set in a stubborn expression, and Nicholas groaned inwardly.

Against his own good sense, he had called for her in order to, well, not quite apologize, but to try and make up a little for their last meeting. It wasn't well done of him to leave Sera alone without at least helping her to fit into palace life.

He took a calming breath and began again. "I wished to see how you're getting along, that's all. Do you like your chamber?"

She shrugged. "It is comfortable—as prisons go," she said.

He sighed. "I'm going to ignore that last, Sera, rather than go into the whys and wherefores of your stay in Laurentia. So you've been out in the town with Katherine. Did you enjoy yourself?"

"When I could forget. I do not wish a title and land, Nicholas Rostov. Please, take it back."

He shook his head. "You don't understand yet, Sera. Someday, you'll meet a man at court. Someone you'll wish to—to..." Oh, God, he had to stop stammering. He took another calming breath. "Someone you may marry. And in order to do that, you'll need both the title and the land."

All the color drained from her face, to then rush back again. Her eyes gave off blue sparks of fire. "You think I would ever align myself with an *Outlander*?"

He nodded. "If—if you loved him." Rushing on, getting it all said, was the whole reason for this meeting, he reminded himself sternly, even as he ground his teeth at the thought of Sera with anyone else.

"And you need to know all about the court if you're to make a proper match. So I've made a list of your activities for the next month or so." He grabbed up the paper and thrust it into her hands quickly so she would not suspect his own were a trifle unsteady.

She perused the list, a look of shock fading from her face, to be replaced by the disdainful thrust of her chin.

"A schedule. You've given me a schedule, like a schoolgirl. Do you think for one moment I shall keep to it?"

Merde! It was worse dealing with Sera than with a

hundred hostile ambassadors. He hated being devious and clever with her, when there had been only perfect harmony between them before. "If you wish access to the stables, yes. I think you'll meet with the masters listed and learn what you need to know from them."

Her eyes flashed in regal scorn, and for a moment, he wondered what idiocy made him think she needed to know anything more about being a noblewoman. His hand reached out for her, then fell to his side.

"I only want you to be happy here, Sera. It's the best I can do. Please, try to understand that."

"I understand perfectly, Nicholas Rostov," she said with ironic scorn. "You want me to turn into one of your ladies. I must embroider, dance, gossip, and learn the proper way to curtsey. And then my life will surely be meaningful and therefore quite happy, will it not?"

That had been how they'd left the matter. Except that Nicholas woke each morning with the feeling of a heavy weight pressing him down, and it had nothing to do with the future of Laurentia. It had everything to do with the one woman he could not stop thinking about, and lusting for, and wanting beside him—and how she'd looked at him when he threatened to refuse her the one joy she had in this palace she thought a prison.

Thus, by the king's command, Sera faced a battalion of embroidery masters, instructors in court etiquette, tutors in Laurentian history, and lastly, Monsieur Gallopet, the spindly legged, supercilious dance master, with whom Sera finally drew the line.

"Tell that monkey to leave me alone!" she said to Katherine one day in mid-week.

"But Sera, Nikki said—

"He never bothered to say anything to me about any of this. Do you realize that all his—his orders have been delivered by you? I shall not learn to caper and simper, even upon the command of the king."

"Oh, dear," said Katherine. "What shall I tell Nicholas?"

"Tell him I shall see him in Hades before I put up with that spider."

"I'll tell him nothing of the sort. As a matter of fact," said Katherine with a lift of her chin, "I'll tell him nothing at all."

"As you wish," muttered Sera.

She was strangling in this place.

***

That evening, the maid Annette helped her into a woolen dress of a soft rose color. "You dine en famille tonight," she announced. "And the king will be there."

The décolletage shocked Sera, who had only gone about in day dresses before tonight's command performance. "I cannot wear this," she said, coloring.

"Oh, my lady. It is charming and quite modest, I assure you." Annette fluffed out the sleeves, which came to her wrists, and turned her to the cheval glass. "You see? Barely any cleavage showing, at all. It is much more demure than your ball gowns."

Ugh. If she had to appear in anything lower than this neckline, she might as well stand in front of a house of ill repute holding a sign that read "for hire; hourly rates."

Why was she so tense? It was just dinner. Just Nicholas, who had dictated what her life should be and then avoided her forever.

The sky was dark by the time Sera followed a footman holding a branch of candelabrum down the long corridor, past other silent footmen in powdered wigs and satin. If she were stark naked, she wouldn't have felt any more exposed. The man opened a door into an elegantly appointed dining room. A small table was set beside a window overlooking a small garden.

Katherine and Andre, who had been standing close together, jumped apart as the door opened. Katherine colored prettily. Andre recovered first and bowed to Sera.

"Another lovely damsel. Whom shall I assist first?" he asked with a grin.

Sera smiled back at him. With Katherine's and Andre's joy fairly flaming on their faces, they would be good company tonight, making this meeting less awkward. Still, she would have preferred a larger buffer—say a dinner party for eighty.

"Katherine first, if you please," said Sera with a wry smile. "She has been a princess longer than I have been a lady."

Andre's hands rested possessively upon Katherine's shoulders as he helped her into her seat.

As he took his own, Sera leaned toward Katherine. "This gown is too low in front," she whispered.

"No," said Katherine peering at Sera's chest. "It is quite modest."

Nicholas walked into the room.

"Late again, Nikki," said Andre. "This makes the fifth time this week. Anything I should worry about?"

Sera turned to look at the king. She had a difficult time catching her breath. Nicholas in travel-stained clothing was a formidably attractive male, but in evening dress, he was splendid. His deep blue velvet coat and breeches fit his body so well that one saw everything—his wide shoulders, his slim waist and hips, his long, muscular legs. Elegance, strength, and symmetry together in one man. She looked down at her hands clasped before her, her stomach a tight ball of nerves.

"Nothing of note. A meeting that ran overlong with the Chancellor of the Exchequer."

Nicholas's curt nod settled into a frowning stare as he took his seat opposite Sera. He rose and rounded the table, taking off his dinner jacket, then dropped it over Sera's shoulders. "That gown is not proper to be worn publicly," he said.

"I told you," Sera muttered to Katherine. She wished she could crawl back to her room. Nicholas returned to his chair. He kept his eyes on the wine the footman poured for him.

"Nonsense, Nikki," Katherine said. "The gown is charming. Mine is cut a good deal lower."

"Then perhaps you should both use a different mantuamaker. Kindly see to it tomorrow."

"I shall do no such thing! Nicholas, what has gotten into you? You've never complained about my gowns before, and Sera's are perfectly proper. Are you threatening some form of social isolation for us?"

Nicholas stared at Katherine in what looked like blank shock. Sera wondered if she had ever openly questioned her brother's judgment before.

"When a kitten turns into a little tiger, it's wise to let her have her way," said Andre with a sidelong glance at Katherine.

After a moment, Nicholas inclined his head in a gesture of defeat. "Very well. Let Sera be a slave to these immodest fashions," he said. "And hope the men of the aristocracy have some self-restraint."

So she was nothing to Nicholas but a Hill slave who had embarrassed him yet again. She wanted to clutch the heavy dinner jacket around her and run back to her room.

Nicholas motioned to a footman standing unobtrusively against a wall, and the man reappeared within moments with the first course.

As Katherine, obviously emboldened by Andre's admiration, teased and laughed with him, Nicholas lapsed into a stiff silence. He looked at the salmon on his plate as though it were the most fascinating of objects.

Sera cautiously watched Nicholas out of the corner of her eye. He leaned back in his chair, dangling his wineglass by the rim. His face was as remote and formal as it had been when he first refused to look at her in the palace of Iman Hadar. He looked as though he had never been young and never laughed.

"What are you thinking, sitting so aloof in your corner?" Katherine asked him.

It had taken an act of will for Sera not to ask that question. It would have flowed from her so naturally in Selonia. She needed a good, swift kick.

"I'm wondering about the Brotherhood, and about Napoleon, and how the French are waging a bloody clever internal campaign against us, and how I wish to h—beg pardon—to heaven we could crack their code."

"Why are you certain Napoleon is behind the Brotherhood?"

The words were out of her mouth before she could call them back. Nicholas looked at Sera as though she were a foolish child allowed to sup with adults who had more important matters to discuss. He raised his hand and began counting reasons off on his fingers. "Bonaparte is conquering Russia. Laurentia borders Russia on the south with well-built roads to all of Europe. We are a wealthy state. Our people are ripe for the winds of liberalism—actually, they lead the rest of Europe in that philosophy. The country is ready made for Napoleon's brand of reform."

Sera raised her brows in what she hoped gave an impression of cool superiority. "If I were king, I should not forget Ockham's Razor before I ruled out other possibilities."

"What?" Nicholas looked at her as though she had just stepped out of a madhouse.

"William of Ockham," said Sera, in a voice that sounded pedantic to her own ears. "Reduce things to their bare essence by shaving away facts that do not impact upon the situation."

"I know what the devil Ocham's Razor is, Countess." Nicholas gave her a look that might have downed a bird at thirty paces.

"Excellent," she said through gritted teeth.

"I wouldn't wish to discuss subjects that might confuse you." "Would you care to enlighten us upon the bare essence of our problem?" At Nicholas's icy sarcasm, Katherine squirmed in her seat, but Sera was too angry to be cowed.

"The Brotherhood attacked you in Jehanna. Jehanna is southeast of Laurentia. Napoleon and his army are northwest of Laurentia."

"Foolish woman." Nicholas said. "Iman Hadar is far too old and soft to mount such a devious campaign."

Sera wanted to punch him in the stomach. "Goat-brained Outlander." She allowed herself that pleasure, at least. "There is another to the east of Laurentia, younger, more evil, and devious enough to destroy the devil, himself."

"Galerien?" Nicholas looked at her—really looked at her. Then he shrugged, neatly relegating the unruly Hill child to the nursery again. "You speak from a natural antipathy, but your theory has no factual basis. I realize Galerien harasses the Hill people. However, Galerien, although an unpopular king, is a long time ally."

Sera waited for more, but Nicholas only began to spoon Russian caviar and sour cream upon his salmon. He's only an Outlander, and therefore, a dolt, she fumed. Why do I even care to warn a man who ignores me and patronizes me and rudely demonstrates that he barely suffers my presence?

Sera remained silent through coffee and brandy. When Nicholas rose and bowed formally to her, holding out his hand, she stood without accepting it, and preceded him out the door.

"The Season begins soon," he said, walking beside her down the long hallway. "You will make your debut at the opening ball."

Sera had eaten little at supper. Now, she felt the effects

of the wine she had drunk. "I don't wish to mix with your court. I don't wish to be here, at all."

"You will do quite well here. As long as you make an honest attempt to understand the expectations of society." She hated the new tone of voice he took with her. As though he were ages older and far wiser. "You have a quick mind, Sera, and a great deal of natural grace. With help and instruction, you'll fit very nicely at court. Katherine and you will do very well together."

"And that is my new position, is it?" Sera shook with some very nasty emotion she had never felt before, but it was tearing her insides apart. "I am now a sham countess, and the Princess Katherine's friend." *And nothing to you,* she added silently.

"That is exactly your position. Any woman of your former status would be delighted with this advancement. And as I shall be quite busy in the next months, it is natural that you and Katherine utilize the time to become close companions."

Sera looked straight at him. If her eyes were blazing or tear-filled, she could not care less that he saw. "Firstly, you may be ashamed of my 'former status', but I believe the shame of it belongs to the Nantal and Iman Hadar. Secondly, nothing is natural with you, Outlander. That is your saddest problem."

When she heard a shattering crash behind her, she was too furious to look behind her to see what it was. Instead, she threw the dinner jacket at him. And to her own consternation, she picked up her skirts and ran all the way down the long hallway, past the perfect figures of stolen gods and heroes, past stone-faced guards who looked straight through her, into the empty place of artifice they had chosen to call her chamber.

"I hate you, I hate you, I hate you," she said in a voice low and harsh to her own ears. Her fists clenched at her sides. She wanted to scream. She wanted to break something. She wanted to—

She whirled, her gaze blazing, and stared into the fireplace, where kindling and wood for a fire had been laid in wait for the maid to light at Sera's return. A curl of smoke rose from the kindling, and then the wood burst into flame. Pushed aside by the force of her anger, the iron fire tools beside the mantle crashed to the floor, clanging against each other as they rolled.

The door flew open. Annette raced into the room, then slid to a stop in front of Sera. "Oh, my lady, I heard the noise and came as soon as I..." She turned, her attention caught by the heat coming from the fireplace.

"But what is this?" she said, replacing the fire tools in their stand beside the mantle. "You should have rung for me," she said as she added another log to the blazing pile. "You should not try to light the fire, yourself. It is not seemly."

"No," said Sera, sitting down on her bed before her knees gave out from trembling in the sick aftershock of realization. She had started the fire with her mind! "I should not try that again."

***

Nicholas automatically caught the jacket and leaned against the corridor door, staring at nothing as his mind churned. He hadn't meant to hurt her, damnit. What right did she have to show him everything she was feeling? Had she no defenses at all? What could he do but what he was doing already?

She tied him up in knots. Why did she have to wear a gown like that tonight, so he could see the creamy swell of her breasts just above the taut wool? Little fool! Couldn't she see he was hanging on to his honor and hers by a thread? The thought of other men eyeing her, dancing with her, seducing her, sent him into a paroxysm of jealousy.

Beautiful little fool. He ought to send her back to her hills, and be free of this damnable lust. Perhaps that was the best way—for both of them.

But then, she was not such a little fool, was she? Ockham's Razor, indeed. Was Sera's theory worth investigating? He pushed off away from the wall, still deep in thought. Galerien had been an ally for a very long time.

He glanced across the hall at a Chippendale table placed beneath a high, arched window. Shards of a Chinese vase, Ming Dynasty, he believed, lay scattered on the floor beneath it. He crossed the hall, hunkered down and picked up a shard, staring at it. A breeze no doubt had swept it to the floor. He stood up and examined the window behind the table, expecting to find it open.

It was shut. The night beyond was clear and calm. No gust of wind had pushed the vase off the table.

He looked down the hall in the direction Sera had fled. Was it possible? Could she have done it in anger? In hurt? In frustration equal to his own? If she had the power to break an object with her mind, was that mind also capable of superior understanding, concerning, for instance, Galerien and Beaureve? She spoke the language, after all.

He remembered that prickle at the back of his neck, warning him to take her with him for the good of his people. In these terrible times, what country could afford to lose an advisor whose mind was quick and cool, whose power could send a vase crashing to the floor? What king could ignore her?

He couldn't send her home now. The feeling of relief that coursed through him made him despise himself. Unbridled lust was for the weak. He had a country to lead.

He looked at the broken vase again and shook his head. Some servant, dusting in hurry, had placed the vase too close to the edge, no doubt. Still, a man ought to investigate every possibility, even what seemed remote at a given time.

He went to his study and called for Lieutenant Carlsohnn. It was cobwebs and moon dust, in all probability. Nonetheless, he would send discreet agents across the border. It would give him something to think about. Something besides how much he ached each night, burning for Sera, knowing she was just below him, and all he had to do was walk the secret stairway to her chamber, and like the lowest libertine on the face of the earth, take what he craved before he succumbed to a lifetime of duty and regret.

Eight

Sera did not see Nicholas again for rest of the week. Immediately after what she thought of as the disastrous dinner, he sequestered himself in his chambers. It was for the best, she knew. She had never feared a man more than she feared Nicholas Rostov, the catalyst to an outburst of magic so overpowering, it set wood ablaze and flung iron to the floor.

Too late, the Gift she had longed for all her life, the proof she was a true Arkadian, flowed forth. But she was alone here, without the comfort and the aid of a mentor. And she didn't know how to control the power.

Why now? Somehow, it was all tied up with Nicholas. And Katherine, and Andre, and Selonia, and the merchants of Montanyard, and the palace guards, and Ivan and Ned, the stable boy, and...Her heart was full to bursting with all the feelings these people evoked. This world so full of violence and beauty stirred things inside her she'd never felt at home. It was as though she were a butterfly emerging from a cocoon, and her senses were painfully alive to everything around her. Was this what Grandfather called the painful process of growing? If so, she prayed it wouldn't last very long.

She should stay away from Nicholas until she found calm. She should try to forget whatever strange and terrible longing he stirred in her. It was hopeless, after all.

But where was he? Andre would know. Sera finally found Andre in the library and questioned him as to Nicholas's whereabouts.

"Don't worry yourself, Sera. He'll be fine in a few days."

"What do you mean?" she asked, beginning to feel sick. Had she hurt him, too, that night when she'd been so angry? "Is he ill?"

"Almost well again, actually. Nothing serious this time."

"This time?" Now she was alarmed.

Andre shifted uncomfortably on his feet. "A lung problem. He's...susceptible if he becomes overtired, or chilled, or...overexcited. Now, Sera, he'll be quite all right. As I said, it didn't become a problem this time."

She was at the door in a wink, but Andre was right

behind her, holding the door shut with one hand outstretched over her shoulder. "He won't thank you for going to him, Sera. Don't worry. He knows how to take care of himself."

The days grew shorter. Nicholas, apparently recovered, thank the gods, was far too busy ruling the country to request Sera's company. She went from fearing for his life to wishing she could give him a piece of her mind, and then leave this blasted prison before she burned the place down.

"Sera." She heard Katherine's voice from the corridor. Sera ran to unlatch the door.

"Hullo. Are you feeling quite the thing? I haven't seen you for two days." Katherine looked worried and more lonely than normal.

"I am quite well, thank you. I was simply...out of sorts."

"It's the chill, and the constant rain. I'm glum, too. Since we can't go outside, would you like to explore the palace?" Katherine looked so wistful, she hadn't the heart to say no.

"Of course."

"Oh, good." Katherine took her arm and walked the corridors with her, showing her room after room of treasure—robes of fine silk and ceremonial swords from the east, porcelain from England and Germany, teak wood and gold from the Americas.

"Those are my ancestors," Katherine said as they strolled through the long gallery. Kings in full court dress, with swords at their sides and scepters in their hands stared down at Sera with a haughty resemblance to Nicholas in his most dictatorial moments.

"Goodness," she said, not knowing what else to say.

The queens were no better. Proud and stiff, they dominated the paintings without actually inhabiting them.

"They make me feel rather small, actually," said Katherine, shivering. "Come, let us go into the blue room. I'll show you my favorite portrait."

They walked back to the family quarters and entered a lovely room Sera had never seen before. She looked up at the woman so informally posed with a small boy at her knee.

Katherine stood before the portrait, looking at it with undisguised yearning. "My mother," she said. "She looks...warm, doesn't she?"

"She looks very kind," said Sera. "What was she like?"

"I don't know anything about her," said Katherine. "She died giving birth to me."

"But your father—didn't he tell you about her?"

Katherine bit her lip and refused to meet Sera's gaze. "My father never spoke to me at all. Well, of course," she went on, her words hurried, "he was very busy. He barely had time to oversee Nikki's education, much less pay attention to me."

"But surely Nicholas would have told you all he remembered."

Katherine sighed. "I have asked him once or twice, but he says he was too young. He remembers nothing of note."

"I see," said Sera. What a family! If she could, she would have gone straight to the grave and dragged the old king out of it to give him a piece of her mind. As it was, there was only Nicholas to harangue. If she ever saw him again.

***

A letter came from Father Anselm the next day. Sera raced down the corridor, caught the startled eye of a footman, and slowed her steps to a much resented ladylike pace to the library, deserted at this time of day. Once within its privacy, she broke the seal of the letter and eagerly read through his news of the boys and Selonia to the passage that made her heart leap in her chest.

You asked me to send news of the merchant who visited Selonia just before the terrible attack. A man bearing his likeness was seen in the village of Vurst not twenty miles from here. He travels east to Montanyard, but is so mysterious about his plans that no one knows for certain when he should arrive in the capital or what route he will take. From a word or two that he dropped to the farmer with whom he stayed, I would surmise that he will reach Montanyard within a fortnight or so. If I hear anything more, I shall certainly apprise you of it.

A fortnight! She still could get home with days to spare before the cliff walls closed. Now, she had a choice to make. She could leave and run the risk of capture and death without ever finding the thief, or she could remain in Montanyard and wait for him. She clenched her fists. The thief would come. She might find the ruby before she escaped to find her way home again.

There was always the chance that the thief would arrive at the capital early. Her mind began to whir, planning ways to anticipate his entrance into the city. As long as she took someone with her, she could roam all the countryside east of Montanyard, and no one would stop her. She could pretend to visit the ladies' necessary in the inns and instead question the innkeepers.

She did not have to sit like a coddled child while fate played out her last chance. By the gods, she would free herself from the foolish extremes of emotion buffeting her heart. She would go home, learn to use her power wisely, and forget all about Nicholas Rostov.

***

Nicholas stepped into the library. A fire burned in the hearth, dispelling the chill of the corridor. How he hated the coming of winter, particularly after the close call he'd had last week. He walked toward the marble mantle, holding out his hands to the warm blaze.

And stopped short to see Sera sitting before the fire staring into the coals. Her hair glowed like a halo above the high collar of a gold velvet gown. His fine plans to keep her at a distance melted like dew in sunlight. It was all he could do not to raise her from her chair and tug her into his arms. He parted his lips, as though he might breathe in the taste of her in the elusive perfume he could just discern from across the small room. She was so deep in thought she hadn't even heard him.

Nicholas's honor was losing ground to his baser instincts. He turned to go, and at that moment, she looked up at him, blue eyes coming back into focus from a long distance. She slipped a piece of paper into the pocket of her gown. Was it a letter from some besotted nobleman? He frowned, reminding himself that it was none of his business who courted her.

"Please excuse me," he said and bowed slightly. "I didn't mean to startle you." His voice sounded stiff and cold to his own ears. He turned again to go.

His hand was on the door latch when she spoke. "You might have your secretary give me your daily schedule so I may stay entirely out of your way."

He turned and leaned against the door, assuming a

casual stance. "Why such sarcasm, Countess? I have not been avoiding you."

"And why turn your face from reality, king?" Her voice rang, silver, mocking. "I accept this latest development in our non-friendship. Surely, you can do the same."

He crossed to the fire, facing her, his shoulder leaning on the mantle. "Very well. I am the king. My duty dictates that I have no...intimate friendships."

She remained seated, refusing to rise and acknowledge him as king. No, she sat in the brocade library chair as though it were a throne, back straight, her feet tucked beneath the folds of her golden skirt. Covered from head to toe, she glimmered. Like a queen or an angel.

And like a queen, she waved a hand in an unmistakably dismissive gesture. "I take your meaning, Nicholas Rostov. I am aware that it is not your way to take companionship from a woman, even one with whom you might have an...intimate friendship. But tell me. Does your duty deny you a sister?"

"Of course not." He grew heated that she should, in a typical feminine maneuver, switch tactics on him and accuse him, not of ignoring her, but Katherine. "I give my sister attention, the best instructors, and companions like yourself with whom she may be at ease."

"And what of yourself have you given her?"

"I care about her," he said, stung.

"Enough to tell her of her mother?" Her voice was soft.

"Mother?" Something sore and painful closed in on itself. "Mother died when I was six. I barely remember her."

"Katherine knows nothing about her at all. I have studied the Gainsborough painting. She was very beautiful, and she had a look about her that reminded me of—well, she looked very kind." Her voice went on, a soft, relentless challenge to the very core of his control.

"Your father hated Katherine, didn't he? She has told me he never recognized her existence. He must have blamed her for your mother's death. For that, and many other reasons, Katherine needs to know that her mother would have loved her." With a swirl of gold, Sera rose and gave him a parody of the deep court curtsey used by petitioners to their king.

She walked to the door, proud, chin up, and turned to

face him across the room when she reached it. "If you please, Nicholas Rostov, permit yourself—within the parameters of your heavy duties—a sister."

He turned his back to her and got very busy poking at the fire. And didn't put down the poker until he heard the quiet click of the door shutting behind her.

He lay awake for a long time that night, his hands stacked behind his head, staring at the tester above his bed, red velvet in the red light of the fire. In the morning he sought Katherine.

"Walk with me," he said. The day was overcast, but warmer. Katherine got her gloves and umbrella and walked beside him, out the doors of the palace and into the wide lane entering the park.

"Our mother," he began, "was happier than I had ever seen her when she knew she was carrying you."

***

Nicholas dressed quickly for the supper party Katherine had planned for his last night at home. Sera would attend, along with enough of a crowd to ensure that he did not throw her on the table, fling her skirts up, and force himself upon her—at least until dessert. He had fought the battle against his damnable lust for weeks, and all he had for his success was a wicked temper and a sense of intense emptiness. Well, at least he would see her, if he could crane his neck far enough to catch a glimpse of her down the length of the table.

He hurried to the Egyptian salon, a fantasia that his mother had decorated with pillars, small, bright figures, and ancient vases, long before the craze hit England. Katherine stood before the fire, resplendent in a tiara and a blue satin gown trimmed with silver lace. The color of the lace somehow brought out the cool silver in her eyes.

He fingered the lace at the elbow of Katherine's sleeve. "Very pretty."

She looked up at him with pleased surprise. "You think so? Sera gave it to me, just for this gown."

He wondered what it would be like, to have the freedom to give and receive—presents, thoughts, emotions—with Sera. And he was jealous of his own sister.

"I'm glad we're alone for a moment, Nikki. I wanted to thank you for telling me about our mother yesterday. But I also wanted to ask you something." Katherine stared down at her folded hands. "What was our father like before she died?"

Unbidden, a memory sprang to mind. He was very young—five, perhaps. He was in the garden with his mother, and he heard a voice call out to them. His father's voice, deep and eager, from the balcony off the first floor drawing room.

What a hero he'd looked, tall and young, laughing as he leaped over the rail onto the grass below, sweeping his mother up into his arms, covering her face with kisses. He'd grinned down at Nicholas, lifted him to his shoulders, and Nicholas had felt like a conqueror, riding so high above the ground, safe and loved.

"He was a good king. A good father. He had a lot of friends then," he told Katherine.

"But not after," she said in a quiet, wistful voice.

"No. I think love was very bad for him. It destroyed him inside and, worse, endangered Laurentia. Oh, he knew how to act the king. But he neglected his friends. He neglected...his children. He didn't pay attention to details. When he died, our defenses were inadequate, and our allies no longer reliable."

Nicholas shook his head and frowned. "Love isn't for kings. He should have known that."

The room slowly began to fill and he took his place, grave and cool as his father had been, murmuring the correct phrases to the noblemen and their wives who bowed and passed on to accept a glass of wine from a footman.

"Lady Tranevale, how good to see you," he said to a stout old dragon festooned in diamonds. The old biddy kept her purse strings notoriously tight.

"Delighted, your majesty," she said with a curtsey.

"And now that you are here for the Season, perhaps you would be so kind as to join my sister's committee for the orphans of Selonia." Nicholas perused Lady Tranevale's plump face for signs of rebellion and employed the Rostov frown when he found them.

Lady Tranevale froze in the midst of her refusal and gulped. "I shall certainly speak to the princess concerning these unfortunates."

"This evening, if you will," said Nicholas, smoothing his voice free of inflection.

"This evening." Lady Tranevale huffed away.

Good, thought Nicholas. She had no choice but to give, and generously, to St. Andrews orphanage. It was not much, but at least he could do this for Sera.

As though his thoughts had summoned her, she appeared in the doorway. He tried to stifle the shock of need and pleasure running through him at the sight of her. She shone from head to toe. Her hair was gathered up in soft loops, emphasizing her graceful neck. Her white gown, a simple, flowing silk etched with blue ribbon, dipped seductively above her breasts and clung to her hips, swaying when she walked. She wore no jewelry. A ribbon of blue enclosed her throat. He could still feel the texture of her skin there, its vulnerability, its warmth.

"Your Majesty." Another courtier bowed. He went through the motions, accepting the undeserved compliments for his "rescue" of Selonia. It was all so ridiculous. If he had been wise or diligent enough, Selonia would not have burned to the ground.

The dinner party swirled about him. They dispensed with the stewed trout and began in earnest upon the saddle of lamb when Nicholas felt he had divulged his expectations for agrarian reform quite enough with the finance minister seated to his left. He stole a glance at Sera seated several seats down the table from him. Immediately, he wished he had not.

The son of the English Ambassador, that young fop, Darlington, whose blond good looks and carefully assumed romantic air set Nicholas's teeth on edge, sat on Sera's left. He hung on her every word, and she wasn't even speaking to him. She was deep in conversation with venerable Lord Elder, to her right.

Nicholas watched Darlington with narrowed eyes. The bastard's avid gaze traveled to the spot just at the back of Sera's neck where it curved into her gleaming shoulders. Wandering further south, Darlington's gaze clung to the swell of Sera's breasts above her bodice. Damnit, he'd told Katherine to get rid of those gowns.

Darlington took advantage of what must have been a break in Sera's conversation with Elder. Whatever he said caused a blush of softest pink to suffuse Sera's neck and cheeks, and lower, lower, turning her skin from the purity of cool marble to radiant incandescence. Galatea, come to life. Darlington raised his glass to her in a slow, meaningful manner.

Nicholas clenched the napkin in his fist. Profligate swine!

"Your Majesty, won't you tell us about your plans for the Season? Rumor has it that the opening ball will be even more magnificent than last year's."

"I do not know, Lady Chandler. You must ask the princess about the arrangements, as she is responsible for the preparations."

"Such a heavy obligation for one so young. Perhaps I can help. I should be happy to do anything for your family, Sire. Or you." Lady Chandler slanted him a look and smiled seductively.

My God, thought Nicholas. Propositioned like a customer at a bawdy house—at my own table. What next?

Next came the lobster curry and more dreary conversation. Further down the table, Darlington smiled and pointed to Sera's plate. Sera raised her fork to her mouth. Surprise and undisguised pleasure lit her face. Nicholas clamped his jaw together. She'd just tasted something new to her, and Darlington would take the credit, explain it all, when it should be him.

Sera, for her part, took another bite of lobster and turned again to Lord Elder, escaping the pressure of Lord Darlington's attentions. She liked the old fellow on her right—liked his straight-backed, upright posture, the clean silver hair brushed to a shine, his stark black evening suit and snowy white linen. He seemed a forerunner of what Nicholas might become if only he developed some humanity.

Lord Elder was the only person present who, without a hint of snobbery, recognized her as a newcomer and had been telling her about Laurentian customs. He had just gotten round to betrothal practices.

"Laurentian swains do not gift their ladies with a betrothal ring. I suspect the custom began when the first possessive bridegroom-to-be wished to make it known beyond a shadow of a doubt that he claimed the lady he—forgive me, my dear...desired. Consequently, he bought not a ring, but a necklace, and as fine a one as he could afford. The custom prevails to this day."

"Does not the poor gentleman receive some token of his future wife's esteem?" she asked as Lord Elder motioned to the footman to refill Sera's glass.

"Oh, indeed, m'dear," he said. "The lady gives the gentleman a ring. If possible, the ring is old, treasured over the years by her family. If this is not possible, she makes a great show of visiting the jeweler's shop and selecting a fine ring on the morning after she has received the necklace. Her buying spree is more likely to spread news than would posting the banns, although we also do that, on the first Sunday after the exchange of gifts."

"Lady Sera." Lord Darlington leaned too close to her— again. She could feel his breath against her back, and inwardly wished him to the nether regions.

"And if the lady wishes to refuse the gentleman's kind offer?" she asked pointedly, staring as coolly as she could at Darlington until he reddened, sat back in his chair, and turned to the woman on his left.

"Ah, well, then. The gentleman need not be publicly embarrassed by her refusal. If the answer is yes, then the lady has worn the necklace and given her token for all to see. If it is no, then no one knows except the couple involved. Unless the lady is no lady, but a preening, self-centered wench. And then, the entire town has two interesting bits of gossip. Firstly, they discuss the poor gentleman's broken heart, and then they discuss his lack of taste in choosing a mate."

At last, sweet wine appeared at the table. From what the etiquette master had droned to Sera, she would be free in a short while to leave this table and, after another interminable hour, to return to her chambers.

With a swift nod of his head, Nicholas signaled to Katherine, who rose, followed by all the ladies at table. Sera followed the others, loathe to enter the sitting room, but knowing she must. Katherine took up a Chippendale chair close to the fire. Women surrounded her, and from where Sera stood against a window, partially hidden by shadows, she could hear their compliments upon the dinner.

"I think he's absolutely magnificent." A cloying voice cut into her thoughts. The woman Sera had noticed at Nicholas's side during dinner—the one who had all but sat in his lap—stopped beside an elderly lady hefting a great load of jewelry. They stood in front of her hiding place, speaking in low tones.

"Oh, no, my dear." The old lady wagged a finger at the younger one. "This is not a man to romanticize."

"But he is so—masculine. So powerful."

"Bah! He has no heart, only a stiff-necked conscience that he imposes upon the rest of us until we must shriek with boredom. He is cold as ice. My dear, rumor has it that his mistress must make an appointment with his secretary in order to see him at all. No, the king is not the man with whom to form a liason."

Sera reacted in the most illogical manner. She wanted to rail at the tart who wished to become Nicholas Rostov's mistress, and she wanted to defend him at the same time from the older virago's insults. If she chose to scold the former, she would cause a terrible scene. She froze, remembering her anger after the family dinner and its consequences.

Much better to cause only a little disturbance. She stepped out of the shadows.

"Your king has very few flaws," she said, enjoying the play of shock and affronted embarrassment on the older woman's face. "I would not count lack of feeling among them. Certainly, in his care and support of his subjects, Nicholas Rostov has demonstrated his noble heart."

Before the women could form a reply, Sera inclined her head a fraction of an inch just as fussy Monsieur Pettit had taught her to do with those courtiers who were below her. The barely concealed insult made the old lady's face turn a nasty shade of red. So, she had made an enemy. At least she'd not sent her whirling toward the ceiling.

Sera moved beyond them, willing her hands not to shake. But their voices rose, and she heard every word, just as, doubtless, she was meant to.

"Who was *that*?" the younger woman said in a stage whisper.

"Nobody," said the older. "A waif from the hills, an ex-slave. There were rumors that he wanted her, but no one has seen them together for weeks. She is only one of his good works, a charity case masquerading as a lady."

Sera continued across the sitting room. Schoolgirl lessons in an alien culture, a court of rakish fops and wasp-tongued women, and a monarch who turned from warm and caring to cold and disapproving for no reason at all. Why should she care what they thought of her?

She would ask one of the guards to take her riding tomorrow afternoon in the country east of Montanyard. Perhaps she'd just ask Darlington to accompany her. He'd be easier to fool. Perhaps she would bring water and food with her in her saddlebags, just in case she found the merchant. And then, she would race away on Wind Rider with the Heart of Fire. Yes, she would leave these Outlanders to the world they deserved.

***

Nicholas searched out Sera the next morning. She was not in her room, but a maidservant informed him that she was walking in the gardens. One of the gardeners pointed out the route she had taken down one of the brick paths. He followed the path until he came to an old walled garden. She was kneeling among the neglected roses, digging in the dirt with bare hands.

"Sera." His voice sounded too stern, he knew.

Sera put aside her spade and rose to her feet slowly facing him, worrying her lower lip with her teeth.

"We have servants to do that," he said. He wanted her happy and cosseted, not on her knees and breaking her nails over some silly weeds.

"I needed—they are alive. It soothes me to do something productive."

"Come here," he said, and it was no longer a command, but a plea.

Her lower lip jutted out in a stubborn moue, but she came forward until she stood before him, hiding her dirty hands behind her back.

"I have to go away for a few days. I want your promise that you will remain safely within the walls of Montanyard until I return. Will you, Sera?"

"I cannot give you that promise," she whispered and backed up a pace.

His hands clamped about her arms, pulling her forward until she was a hair's breadth from him. "If you can't, I shall take you with me. Which will it be—here or at Anatole Galerien's palace in Beaureve?

She seemed to turn to stone beneath his hold. "You go to Galerien?"

"He offers a closer alliance. I must go to hear what concessions he thinks to wring out of me for it."

She shook her head, her eyes full of fear. "He is an evil

man. Don't trust him, Nicholas."

"Don't worry." He loved it when she said his name in that soft voice. She was worried. About him. Her clear gaze held nothing of the coldness that had existed between them for weeks. He bent his head closer and smelled fresh earth and warm sunlight, and the natural perfume of her body. "I trust nobody. But Galerien needs Laurentia as much as I need Beaureve."

"I wish you wouldn't go." Her voice shook.

"Why are you afraid of Galerien, Sera?" A fine tremor wracked her body. She was silent for a long moment.

Then she lifted her hands, grabbing his arms. "He hates my people and has sent men to seek us out and destroy us all. If you must have this meeting, take a large army with you, Nicholas. I beg you. Don't discount my words. Galerien is a dangerous man." An unruly gilded lock fell over her forehead.

Nicholas gently drew it back, placing it behind her ear. Her muscles were still rigid. He could feel the tension all through her. He felt a perfect bastard, asking her to make a choice between a man who must give her nightmares and remaining in Montanyard. Then there was Dawson's escape. Should he frighten her further by telling her about it? He couldn't seem to think straight. Here she was, almost in his arms, rubbing her hands all over his chest and tantalizing him to the point of combustion without seeming to realize what she was doing.

A possibility came to him—perhaps she liked to touch him. He tried very hard to keep a grin of delight from breaking through and concentrated on her fears, instead, for they might get him what he needed—a promise from her to remain where he knew she would be safe.

"You would be unhappy to come within a hundred miles of Galerien, wouldn't you?" he asked her.

"Yes." She sounded so forlorn. Instinctively protective, he pulled her closer.

"Will you stay until I return?" Rather than demand, he asked her.

"I cannot promise you anything." She gave him that stubborn pout that was both an aggravation and a catalyst for lust.

A fierce heat blazed through him—frustration with her refusal to trust him, the hot need of his body and something more elemental that he refused to scrutinize. The fire surged through his veins, pulsing hot, burning away logic and caution. His hands seemed to work on their own, shaking her slightly.

"You will stay here for your safety and because there is something you give my country that I cannot."

Her eyes widened, uncomprehending.

"You are unaware of what they say about you in the market place, in the small towns? Word spread westward from Selonia. Already, the common people take hope because of you. They think you are some kind of gift, some good luck charm that can protect them from the evil threatening Laurentia. It's a superstition I shall use as long as I may.

"Only for a few days, Sera," he said. "Say you will stay for my people."

She paused, apparently deep in concentration, as though she were measuring something of the utmost importance—maybe just time. Abruptly, she nodded. "All right."

He let out the breath he hadn't known he was holding. "So. Here you will stay, where my guards can keep you safe. Don't suppose for an instant that a weak fop like Darlington is capable of protecting you." After weeks of frustration, the heat took hold and fanned itself into a possessive blaze of frustration.

She gave him a blank look. "Darlington? What has he got to do with this?"

"He was all over you last night. At dinner and later, when we joined you. Making sure you were seated near the fire. Laughing with you, complimenting you. Leaning over you in the most proprietary manner. Did he escort you to your door? Did he do this to you?"

Before she could protest, Nicholas pulled her roughly to him. He kissed her. Hard. This was what he had ached for. This was why he had wanted to throw Darlington out the nearest window.

"Just this one last time," he murmured against her lips. Before he sacrificed everything for Laurentia.He dominated her with his will, with his force, molding her lips to his. He could feel the exact moment when she softened in his arms, when she met his kiss with equal ardor, when her lips opened beneath his tongue. She tasted honey sweet. Gentling his assault, he reveled in the warm welcome of her mouth, of her body bent to him, her breasts pressed to his chest. His hand splayed across the curve of her back, pulling her up, rubbing the demanding heat in his groin against her hips. She made a low moan, and he molded the contour of her breast with his other hand, kneading gently.

The tight bud of her nipple peaked beneath the thin wool of her gown. He weighed the soft swell of her breast, lifting it in his hand, rubbing against the budding nipple with his thumb. She moaned low in her throat and arched to his teasing fingers. What incredible pleasure to touch her so intimately, hearing from the helpless sound she made that she had no defense against his passion. He wanted to take her now, naked in the soft, green grass, her body warm from the sun and the heat he was building in her.

He wanted—what he couldn't have. He froze, coming back to himself with furious self-loathing. And made the mistake of looking at her.

Her face was flushed, her blue eyes cloudy with passion. Slowly, he pulled his hand away from the curve of her breast and set her back on her feet.

"I—I have acted abominably. I'm so sorry," he said, almost stammering the words.

Her soft, unfocused gaze snapped into clarity, and she looked as though she would like to see him drawn and quartered.

"Say whatever you wish to others, Nicholas Rostov, but do not lie to me. You are not sorry, and neither am I." She reached up and fisted her hands in his hair, tugging his face down toward hers.

She kissed him—a sweet, hot, open-mouthed kiss, her tongue playing with his as he'd taught her just a moment ago. He groaned, pulled her closer, and plunged his tongue deep, reveling in the taste of her. She moved her hands down against his chest and gave a little shove, causing him to lift his face.

She looked at him for a moment and her face softened. She patted his cheek, her smile warm and giving.

"There," she said. Without another word, she turned and walked away, as regal as a queen.

***

Sera stood at her window watching the king and his men ride out. The soldiers were resplendent in their red tunics and blue breeches. Every buckle and spur gleamed in the afternoon sun. The whole scene looked like some brave pageant from a history lesson in the scrying glass, but their destination in Beaureve boded ill. Her fear rose, for all these brave men and the king riding so tall and proud before them.

Nicholas cared, at least a little for her. And he wanted her. She had felt the very real evidence of his desire. She didn't understand him a bit, but she couldn't carry anger against him any more.

Katherine stood beside her holding her hand, staring at the king's first minister who rode beside him, his hair an untamed mop of bright curls beneath his hat. She and Sera watched until the last soldier trotted out of sight, and the last sword hilt caught the glint of a sunbeam.

"Thank you," Katherine said.

"You are always thanking me. Whatever for this time?" laughed Sera.

"It is easier to watch them go with someone who understands."

Guards passed, courtiers hurried by behind them. "Come," said Sera. "Let's ride, so we can talk openly." Far better to talk with Katherine than Darlington, she thought and laughed. She wanted the wind in her face, the free flow of Wind Rider's haunches beneath her. Since she had walked from the garden, her spirit hadn't been at ease. She was worried about Nicholas and giddy with a tenuous hope she refused to examine too closely.

The park was still beautiful, for the trees were graceful even bare of leaves. The hemlock and the holly grew lush here in late October. She felt better in the clear, chill air.

Pulling up after a brisk race with Katherine, she said, "I believe you must tell Nicholas that you will not be a pawn in the game of power. Tell him you love Andre. Tell him you will do better for Laurentia if you remain here, happy and useful to him and your people."

Katherine gave her a sad smile. "How could I ask him for that which he denies himself?"

Sera shook her head slowly. "I don't understand."

"Don't you know? Nicholas is betrothed," Katherine said.

Sera worked very hard to keep her face expressionless. Very hard. "Betrothed," she said, and her voice sounded far away, as though it were coming from underwater. "To—to whom is he betrothed?"

"The princess Catherine Elizabeth of Beaureve. Anatole Galerien's niece. Galerien is really just the regent of the country until the princess weds." Katherine's dark gaze, always eloquent, spoke pity.

Sera ducked her head. She didn't want pity. "How long has he been..."

"Betrothed?" Katherine said gently. "Since he was six, I believe. My father took him to Beaureve to sign the betrothal papers. King Stephan and his queen were still alive. It was quite a ceremony, apparently. Nicholas told me about it just the other day. When they returned, I was born, and my mother was—well, dead."

"Why hasn't he married this princess? Surely, she is old enough to wed," Sera said, her heart pounding.

"She is not well," Katherine said. "She lingers at the convent where she has been at school all these years. Perhaps at this meeting, Nikki and Galerien will agree on a date, and then the wedding will take place."

"I see." The wind blew chill through the bare branched trees. "The night is upon us," she said to Katherine, taking care to keep her voice calm. "It is time we returned to the palace."

Sera sat awake long into the night. A storm raged outside the palace, but it was nothing to what raged in Sera's mind and heart. Her stomach hurt. She couldn't stop shaking, walking the floor of her pink and blue cage, trying to deal with the outrage and sick misery swirling through her. She had given her word to a scoundrel who kissed her and then went off to make a marriage with someone else, even if that someone else was really her.

The room was too confining. She took up a candle and slipped out into the hall. The guard near the door bowed, but she brushed past him, walking the stairway, her flame guttering in a sudden gust of wind. Up she went until she entered the long hall, past the disapproving, ghostly portraits, until she came to the last, a likeness of Nicholas.

Tall and straight he stood, his sword belted at his side, his eyes meeting hers in a young face cold, but seemingly honorable—what irony. "I owe you nothing," she whispered. "Tell me, why shouldn't I ride out of here tomorrow? What do I care if Napoleon or Galerien topples you from your blasted throne? What do I care if the cliffs close out your world forever?"

Suddenly, it was all too much. She put the candlestick beside her on the floor and sank down, drawing her knees up to her chin. "But there's not just you to consider, is there? I gave my word, thinking of Katherine and Father Anselm and the orphanage, and all the shopkeepers, and young Ned. You knew that, you counted on it, you reprobate. Even if the thief comes, even if I retrieve the Heart of Fire, I'm stuck here. Until you return with some sham princess probably trained to kill you while you sleep. It would serve you right, Nicholas, to marry a traitorous fraud."

Sera began to laugh. She covered her mouth, trying to stem the hysteria. The last thing she needed was for someone to hear and see her like this, alone at midnight, slumped on the floor of the long, dark hall, laughing like a lunatic while lightning slashed through the sky outside the high windows. But it was the final irony.

This stupid Outlander king who alternately wooed and ignored her was betrothed—to *her*. Sera—Catherine Elizabeth Seraphina Galerien, daughter of King Stephan and Queen Marissa, had fled Beaureve immediately after the Brotherhood slaughtered her parents. While Nicholas wasted his time in a cold, calculated attempt to build alliances, the elusive princess of Beaureve took shelter beneath his very roof from the beasts that still stalked her.

In her extremity, Sera did not perceive what was happening around her until it became shockingly evident. The rumbling sound crashing in on her ears brought her head up sharply into consciousness of her surroundings. The long gallery walls began to shake. The floor beneath her moved like a wave. Portraits swayed and danced on the walls, their heavy gilt frames ringing against the stone. The windows rippled, stressed by some cataclysmic force that beat against them from within the gallery.

Dear gods, was the force coming from her? Sera, her heart beating a tattoo of horror, shut her eyes. With all her will, she wished *calm*, wished *serenity*, wished *understanding.* She pictured her grandfather, his blue eyes deep with understanding, his calm seeping through her. She whispered to him, asking for his help.

The rumble died. The walls stood still. The oak floor boards settled into place beneath her. The storm abated. The rain no longer lashed at the windows but fell quietly to soak into the ground below.

Shouts sounded outside the gallery. Boots clapped against the wooden floorboards. She looked up to find a protective circle of guards bending over her.

"My lady, are you all right?"

She nodded, still too upset to speak.

"Thank heavens. We heard the noise," he said. "We thought the gallery might be caving in on you." The guard held out his hand and helped her up.

Another picked up the candlestick. He looked about him, eyes wide with surprise. "It appears to be unharmed."

"I am relieved," she managed to say.

Exhausted, she let them escort her down the stairs and to her chamber. The guard handed her the taper in front of the door.

"Please have the workmen check the gallery tomorrow," she told him, pulling her wrapper tightly about her. "Just in case there is a weakness in the structure you cannot see." *As there is in me,* she thought.

"Of course, my lady," he said, saluting her as she slipped into her room.

Her last thought before she fell into bed was that she had managed, for once, to control the Gift before it did irreparable damage. Whenever she felt these terrible, deep emotions, she would think of Grandfather and imagine him beside her, listening and accepting her, no matter what the truth in her heart might be. But the power was growing, and she had no assurance that next time, she would be able to restrain it.

For the sake of Laurentia and her people, she had to go home.

In the morning, Sera awoke with a pounding head. The sky was leaden with roiling clouds. She had promised not to leave, but she had not given her word to stop the search for the thief. The young soldier who always accompanied her when she left the city met her at the stable. He was a likeable youth, with round blue eyes and a snub nose. The guard waved them through the palace gate.

"Perhaps we could ride by the river today," she said to the soldier. The thief might travel the river, she thought. The youth nodded and fell in behind her. Usually, he was talkative and entertaining with his stories of his large family. But today, he seemed to know that she wanted time to herself, and with the gentle understanding she had never expected in a man trained to kill, he gave it to her.

At the edge of the city lay a river valley with lush fields and hedges to jump. Sera took the main road downward through the valley. Wood smoke rose from farmhouse chimneys, the yards and fences neatly kept. She felt the lonely twinge of jealousy the traveler feels for the native when home and kin are far away. She sank so deep into melancholy that she didn't even hear the thundering of a team of horses as a carriage approached from behind and nearly overtook her.

A shot rang out from behind. Sera pulled Wind Rider to the left of the road and glanced backward. To her horror, her young guard listed to one side, a stream of bright blood running from his shoulder. He dropped from the saddle to the road.

The driver gave a shout and swerved around the fallen soldier. Horses reared in their traces and men jumped from the carriage as it thundered to a halt a few feet in front of her. Sera pulled sharply at Wind Rider to gallop him toward the fields where the men couldn't pursue them.

Rough hands grabbed at the reins and caught at her, hauling her from the saddle. She flailed at the arms that held her in a grip of iron and stared up at Dawson's malevolent grin. She struggled wildly, but a huge hand came from behind carrying a handkerchief that smelled sickeningly sweet.

"Nay, Mistress Fancy, 'yer coming with us," Dawson crooned. "Too bad I can't have my pleasure with 'ye first, but there's someone wants you bad enough to give me plenty for 'ye. Perhaps later, when he's taken some of the starch out of 'ye and 'yer worth naught else to him. Perhaps then me 'n you'll have our fun, eh, Sera?"

Oh, gods, she thought in despair. And then the darkness overtook her, and she was lost.

Nine

Two miles from the border with Beaureve, a rider approached the train of soldiers and diplomats traveling with Nicholas. The king took one look at his dusty cloak and weary eyes and ordered a halt.

"Carlsohnn, " he said. "What news?"

Carlsohnn, grim-faced, saluted in the saddle and handed Nicholas a leather case. "I have found the Brotherhood base," he said. "Twenty miles east, well within Beaureve, in the foothills of the Arkadian mountains. The maps, the description of their numbers, their artillery and supplies are in the case."

"I see." Galerien, the bastard. Nicholas motioned Andre and his ministers forward. "We must plan our strategy." He turned to the weary, young shopkeeper's son who had brought him the precious truth.

"Thank you, William Carlsohnn, Baron of Alsynia."

Carlsohnn gave him a dazed look. "Majesty," he whispered. "This is unnecessary."

"You may have saved all of Laurentia, my lord. You are fit to rule some of it," said Nicholas. "Sit, take your rest, and then return to your family."

"My king, if you proceed to Beaureve, I would remain by your side. This man is treacherous. You may have need of every soldier here."

Nicholas clasped the young man's dusty shoulder. He had not thought that men such as Carlsohnn would care enough to risk their lives twice for him. It warmed a place in him where there had been only cool purpose.

Carlsohnn bowed and went off to clean the dust from his uniform. When Nicholas alerted his ministers to Carlsohnn's news, shock and outrage appeared on faces, old and young.

"What shall we do?" Andre asked.

"Proceed. Buy a bit of time. Sleep light and armed at the traitor's palace. And get out of there sooner than we thought to."

"Nicholas, there's the threat of poison."

"He doesn't need poison to take Laurentia. He has the Brotherhood. But just in case..." Nicholas smiled grimly and called an ensign to him.

"Get me a dog, small enough to fit into one's pocket. I don't care how ugly the mutt, as long as it is well trained and obedient," he said. "I've no desire to be found out for a fraud."

And so they went on, and soon they passed through the ancient arched gateway of the grim town of Constanza, which Nicholas remembered from his childhood as a cheerful, busy lake town. The stalls in the market offered only a few drab bits of garden produce—moldy cabbages, sad looking carrots, a few worm-eaten apples. The citizens, who were once prosperous, looked as desolate as people in the midst of a terrible famine.

"What has happened here?" Nicholas wondered in a soft voice.

Andre, riding beside him, shook his head. "I don't understand this. Beaureve's treasury has great wealth."

On the far side of town, the palace rose, now more a fortress than a summer home. Shards of broken glass jutted up from the tops of the surrounding walls. Nicholas stared at the guards at the front gate, armed to the teeth with sword and pistols. The place looked as though an outlaw king lived inside.

As they entered, Nicholas saw luxury to rival an eastern potentate's great palace. The hallway sparkled with the light of thousands of candles, reflected in the high sheen of gilt and silver. Andre and his guards checked Nicholas's room for security, as he shed his jacket and handed it to his valet.

Andre made a questioning sound. Nicholas caught him looking at the flowing linen of his shirt. It showed the dirt marks left by Sera's small hands.

"What?" he asked Andre.

"Been doing a bit of gardening, old boy?" Andre's tone was much too amused.

He attempted a look of disinterest. "I found Sera digging in the dirt. What of it?"

"And you didn't change afterward? How long have I known you, Nikki?"

Nicholas exhaled in an exasperated huff.

"Right. I've known you all my life. You hate being dirty for any longer than you can help. You could easily have changed that shirt before we left. Perhaps in future you might persuade the lady to give you a favor more in fitting with your sensibilities than half the kitchen garden. A silk scarf with a bit of her perfume might do, a glove that her tiny hand had graced, a—

"Shut up, Andre." Nicholas's whole face felt as though it were on fire. "It wasn't a kitchen garden. It was a rose garden."

"I see," said Andre with a wicked grin. "Well, that makes all the difference, doesn't it?"

"Go find someone else to devil," said Nicholas.

"Too pleasant to watch you stew, old man," he said, his hand on the door to the outer corridor. "By the way, we're to meet with Galerien in an hour."

Nicholas bathed and changed into full court dress for the state banquet. He stood before the mirror, wearing a long, white embroidered waistcoat, a blue velvet coat and knee breeches and silver buckles on his shoes. By God, he hated walking into a battlefield with nothing but a ceremonial sword by his side.

Galerien and his ministers were waiting for him at the end of a sumptuous dining room where silver chandeliers hung overhead, glittering in the light from a hundred candles. The long banquet table was set in heavy gold plate and fine crystal for eighty. Nicholas took his place beside Galerien to acknowledge the officials, and then took a moment to speak to his host before approaching the table.

At forty-five, the regent was still a handsome man, slender and straight backed. His dark hair was clipped short and streaked with gray, but his face was ruddy and his smile quite charming. Galerien's cloth of gold coat over maroon velvet knee breeches made him look like some oriental pasha.

"Rostov! How good of you to come," he said with a hearty, deep laugh. He took Nicholas into his arms to give him the kiss of peace, the snake. A furious yipping and snarling erupted. Galerien backed up a few steps and stared open-mouthed at Nicholas's coat pocket. Nicholas smiled apologetically and pulled a tiny lap dog from the pocket. The little cur growled ferociously and bared his teeth at Galerien.

"Sorry, Anatole. Mischa's invaluable to me. Here, why don't you get him used to your scent, and then he'll be as friendly as a puppy."

Galerien looked askance at the snarling little animal

who resembled a rat more than any canine Nicholas had ever seen. "Perhaps another time," he said faintly.

"Very well. One can't be too careful these days, what with the Brotherhood at our doorstep, and treachery abroad. Mischa is my taster." Nicholas petted the cur, who bared his teeth at Galerien again.

"This dog has a stomach so delicate, he'll become ill a moment after swallowing any poison. Clever little mutt, isn't he?"

Nicholas dumped Mischa back into his pocket and sighed, inclining his head toward the Laurentian troops just entering the great state dining room. "If Mischa here meets with an unfortunate attack upon his digestive tract, my guards will kill the man responsible." To Nicholas's satisfaction, Galerien blanched.

"Now, Anatole, tell me how you have been dealing with the terrorist threat that hangs over both our heads." He clapped Galerien on the back and walked beside him to the head of the long banquet table.

As the ministers bowed, Galerien gestured to the seat on his right, cautiously marking the position of the lapdog, which Nicholas proceeded to bring out of his pocket and place on his lap.

The china and crystal appeared almost at once, with an extra plate and bowl for Mischa. Through the turtle soup, the roast pheasant stuffed with truffles from France, the ices and gateaux, and the toasts, Nicholas fed the dog. Galerien, a smooth and convincing talker, was unusually silent through the meal.

In a quiet moment over brandy, Nicholas pondered the interesting fact that the Brotherhood had begun its nefarious work against Galerien's older brother, the popular and kindly King Stephan and his beautiful queen, Marissa.

Only their daughter, poor Catherine Elizabeth, survived. For the last two years, Nicholas had begun to suspect that the hidden princess was either a lunatic or a mental deficient. But he had thought himself trapped.

Until now. Amidst the muffled clatter of silver and plate, the realization struck him, almost taking his breath. The voices of the ministers receded. He was free to choose his own bride.

Nicholas felt the kick of his heart as it accelerated. He

pictured Sera, veiled and in white, walking the abbey's aisle toward him, and all the people rising as she passed. He kept back the smile that tugged at his mouth. Happiness spread through him until he wanted to burst with it, to shout to the ministers, and Galerien, and his own men.

"To Nicholas Alexander Andreyevitch Rostov," Galerien was saying. The ministers stood, lifting their goblets, and drank.

Nicholas quickly gathered his thoughts. He rose and gave what he hoped was an appropriate toast in return. He slid through it automatically while wondering why Galerien had called him here and when the despot would see fit to tell him. Galerien turned to him directly after the toast.

"Nicholas Alexander," the king said easily. "If you will be good enough to join me in my library for a private discussion after our repast."

"Delighted," murmured Nicholas. At last.

Surrounded by his first editions, Galerien was even more self-congratulatory than he was in the midst of his opulence. He sat behind his inlaid desk puffing on a cigar and swirling the brandy about in his glass.

When he pushed a small miniature forward for Nicholas's perusal, Nicholas thought it must be a portrait of his sequestered betrothed. In his present mood, which veered from cold fury to deepest relief, Nicholas felt a tug of sympathy for the princess he no longer had to marry. He'd help her if he could. Right after he knocked her uncle off the throne of Beaureve.

But the offered miniature was a portrait of Galerien, himself. Nicholas looked up from the portrait and gave Galerien a questioning glance.

Galerien waved a negligent hand. "I am sorry to tell you that there can be no match for you and my niece, Catherine Elizabeth. I have received distressing reports. She may be dead within the week." Galerien looked anything but distressed by the news.

"I shall speak plainly to you. Between these cursed religious fanatics and Napoleon's troops so close to our borders, our cause must be one. I am aware that your sister is of marriageable age." Galerien blew several smoke rings and sipped his brandy.

"As you know, Nicholas, I am merely regent of

Beaureve. My niece's impending death will cause uncertainty throughout the land. And because poor Catherine Elizabeth will die without issue..." Galerien let the thought hang in the air.

"Within days, I'll be king, with a responsibility to ensure the Galerien line. As you know, my late wife and I were not blessed with offspring, a veritable necessity for any monarch. Whereas your family has always been... fruitful, shall we say? Yes, your sister will be a fine wife, a treasured bride." Galerien carefully brushed an ash off the end of his cigar and steepled his fingers, looking at Nicholas over them. His eyes sparkled with greedy anticipation.

"I see," said Nicholas. Was Catherine Elizabeth truly dying, or did Galerien plan to hurry her demise? His hands itched, and he pictured them wrapped around Galerien's throat. "This is a matter I must take up with the council, of course, and with the princess," he managed to say smoothly. "You will have your answer in due time."

*And if you think, you snake's spawn, that I would let you touch my sister...*Nicholas kept his face still in that polite mask.

"Kindly do not make me wait too long, my dear Nicholas Alexander," said Galerien, executing his tight-lipped parody of a smile. "For the sake of both our countries."

"In due time, Anatole Dimitri," said Nicholas, rising and bowing smartly. "As I have told you."

"I shall wait as long as I can," said Galerien, also rising. He held out his hand, and Nicholas took it.

The back of his neck gave a warning prickle. There was danger here—deadly danger to Katherine and Laurentia. He had to find a way out. If only he could drop the pretense, challenge Galerien now, and get the whole thing over by dawn tomorrow. But kings did not duel with other kings. They simply went home and prepared to sacrifice thousands of lives in a war that could destroy both kingdoms, leaving only bare bones for Napoleon's soldiers to pick.

***

The next morning, Nicholas rose before the sun and rode out with his troops. Galerien, hastily roused, appeared at the balcony above the courtyard in his dressing gown.

"Why such haste, my dear Nicholas Rostov? Our meetings were to last three days!"

"Ah, my very dear friend and ally, this matter we discussed is of utmost importance. I must return and meet with my full council as soon as possible. You understand, I am sure."

"Of course, of course," said Galerien. Greed and cunning replaced the suspicion in his eyes.

The day was blustery and overcast, but they made good time toward the border and crossed it shortly before noon. Nicholas breathed a little easier for being back in Laurentia, but he was still wary of surprise attack. At a check to rest the horses, he informed his ministers of last night's meeting with Galerien and revealed his plans to attack the Brotherhood base.

"And," he said quietly. "All of what we've discussed must be kept absolutely quiet. I want none but young Carlsohnn, you men, and the generals to know of our plans."

Sera had known all about Galerien, he thought as they mounted up again. What conflict lay between her and the double-dealing regent?

In the far distance, a black carriage resembling a heavy mail coach with six horses rumbled towards them. Andre glanced at Nicholas, and he nodded. After what Carlsohnn had learned, anything attempting to cross their border would be searched. The men fanned out on the road, making passage impossible for a carriage and team. As the coach rolled closer, Nicholas could make out three men, heavily muffled, sitting atop. He spoke a few words to the captain of the guard, who saluted and urged his men forward. The horses were almost upon them when the captain shouted, "Halt, in the name of the king!"

The driver muttered and halted his horses.

"Step down," said the captain. "Reveal your faces!"

The driver slowly lowered his muffler to reveal a heavily bearded face and climbed from the box atop the coach. The other two outriders slipped silently down from the coach and raised their hands in the air.

"'Tis naught, my lord," said the driver standing casually against the coach. "Just a gentleman an' his lady off for a private matter, is all." Nicholas rode slowly forward and stared at the driver. Bearded as he was, he could have been any number of men. But Nicholas had heard that rough burr, almost a cur's growl once before, at a time so deeply etched in his memory that he would have recognized that particular voice anywhere.

Dawson! His blood froze in his veins.

"Open the door," he said to the soldier nearest him.

Dawson pulled a pistol and shouted a warning. The other two drew their own weapons. Dawson aimed and pulled the trigger. A soldier's arm shoved Nicholas to the side. The shot whizzed past Nicholas's head, just as a knife sailed through the air and sliced through Dawson's throat. Dawson, gagging, clutched at the knife and dropped to the ground. Nicholas's pistol smoked in his hand, as did Andre's. The other two men lay dead at Dawson's side.

Nicholas looked to his left for the man who had saved his life. Carlsohnn's hand, the one that had shoved him and then thrown the knife, was shaking, but his mouth was curved in a beatific grin.

"It's all right," Carlsohnn said. "It's all right." The lieutenant let out a gusty sigh of relief.

Nicholas's heart was going like a trip hammer. He dismounted at a run and flung open the carriage door. He tore the blanket from the small, limp bundle on the floor.

"Sera," he said. His hands were clammy, and his stomach clenched. But she was breathing, and even as he pulled her against his chest, her eyelids began to flutter.

"Ooh," she moaned.

"Sweetheart, hold still," he said, working at the ropes tying her hands and feet. "I'll have you up in a moment."

"I think I am going to be sick."

"Hold on just a moment. There. Lean on me and let it go."

He held her head until the nausea passed and then wiped her face with a handkerchief. "Be a good girl and lie down for a moment, here, up on the seat."

She curled up and moaned again, her head on his lap. A soldier came with water, and Nicholas gave her a sip.

"Better? Good. That must have been nasty stuff they drugged you with."

"Awful. Nicholas." She tugged his sleeve, pressing against him. "I didn't run away. There was a young soldier who rode with me. He has a mother and ten brothers and sisters. They shot him. You have to help him."

He signaled two of the men, and they galloped ahead to look for the soldier. "Of course you didn't run away.

You gave me your word. No, give it a few moments until you get your head on straight. Then I want to hear what happened. You can tell me on the way home. We'll travel in the coach, together."

Sera was still so pale. It made him sick with worry. Had Dawson—but no, he couldn't think about that, or he'd go mad. But had they given her too much of the drug? People died from chloroform in the hospital.

"I want to get out of here," she said. "It's awful. It smells of that stuff."

"All right. Tell me when you can stand, and I'll take you up before me on the horse."

"Now."

"Slowly. That's right, down to the ground. I'll mount first. No, let Andre lift you up to me. Captain! Another cloak. There, nice and snug." He tucked it around her, pulled her back against him, and gave the signal. As they moved forward on the road home, he found he was shaking all over.

***

"It is well. He has found her!" To the shock and consternation of the guests seated around a small room in the Mage's palace, Jacob Augustus threw open the doors with a crash. The sound echoed off the entryway and down the broad halls of marble. He stopped, ashamed of his outburst. In his relief, he'd raced downstairs from the watchtower wherein lay the scrying glass and burst into a feast his grandfather gave in honor of the festival of Hermes. Even a child of ten knew one did not dishonor the god with such a careless loss of dignity.

"How good of you to come, Jacob," his grandfather said smoothly, indicating the couch beside him. "My grandson had pressing personal business elsewhere," he told the notables in the dining chamber, "but we shall not pause from our discussion to talk about it." A servant appeared from nowhere. Reaching up, he carefully placed a myrtle wreath on Jacob's hair.

Emmanuel's face was serene, but Jacob, looking closely, saw joy light it, like a lamp in early evening before the sun has set. "Please, dine with us and tell us what you think. Myron has suggested that we add Euripides to the program of plays for the Dionysia this Spring."

Jacob composed himself and reclined against the

pillows at the head of the couch. A servant silently poured a cup of wine mixed with water and handed it to him. Another unobtrusively placed a plate of roasted lamb and a bowl of yogurt and honey on the small enameled table by the couch. He sipped the wine and took that instant to calm himself.

"My apologies, sir," he said to his grandfather, "and to all our guests. In this year of Outlander turmoil, I should think *The Trojan Women* most instructive. Long ago, the fate of those women brought tears to the eyes of hardened soldiers. Today," he added with a meaningful look at Emmanuel, "it will remind us of why we were sent to Arkadia, why we were instructed to remain separate, and what we have learned since."

Emmanuel took the dig with a forbearance that made Jacob ashamed of himself. Who was he to instruct his grandfather?

The talk of the festival went on around the room. "Jacob, give us the tale of the Delian Twins," his grandfather said. Jacob wondered if Emmanuel could see into his mind and knew his failing, or that he simply wished to make Jacob happier and, therefore, calm within himself. He rose and took the harp from the bard sitting in the corner of the banquet room. After a few moments of tuning, he began the old song of the twins coming into their strength, Artemis the Huntress, and Phoebus Apollo, golden, far-shooting lord of the bow, all truth and light.

He loved this story. First, because he was dedicated to Apollo and never tired of stories about the god. Secondly, because the music was sweeter than most of the bard songs that tradition allowed, and thus, he could raise his voice and revel in the lyrical beauty of the notes.

It confused and humbled him that this secret temptation should so overwhelm him. He would be Mage someday and responsible for carrying out all the laws of Arkadia. They, of course, included the ban on music that only aroused the senses without uplifting the soul. Indeed, he'd so lost himself in the hunger for music that he had learned to read the classical scores of the Outlanders, turning to them with a desperation like that of a man enslaved to drink or women. He'd felt an undeniable longing to hear their instruments. In secret, he memorized their notes and their harmonies.

Worse yet, when alone on the practice field with javelin or discus, he would silently imagine himself singing the notes of their composers and throw to the rhythm. It seemed that in this temptation only, his soul was capable of duplicity and evil. Even now, lost in the spell of the old music that he was permitted to sing and play, he held the last notes too long, surely a sin of pride. In spite of the appreciative murmurs from the diners, he could look at no one as he gave the lyre back to the bard.

As he returned to his couch, the talk turned to the Dionysia, the games and the plays, and the hope that this year's prizes would go to playwrights worthy of the old masters.

Drusus Antiocus, making a small motion to Jacob, spoke quietly from the couch to his left. "It has come to my attention that Thalia, the daughter of Leonides Palos, has come of age. My son Lysander is in need of a bride. He had been set to ask for your sister Seraphina some time back, before this regrettable business regarding the Heart of Fire. It would have been a good match—the Aestron Gift combined with our skill at mathematics and telepathy."

He gave Jacob a questioning look. "Shall I speak to Leonides or shall I wait?"

Jacob nodded, signaling his understanding. He'd grown up with Lysander Antiocus, respected his friend for the strong, kind man he'd become, and admired Lysander's calm demeanor and good sense. The women considered him handsome, as well. He would make a worthy bridegroom for Sera. He wondered if Drusus came to him because he sensed that Jacob wanted his sister back now. Whereas Grandfather would insist that she remain in that hellhole they called the rest of the world.

It would not go on much longer. Jacob would see to that. "Sera will return soon. My sister would bring honor to your family, Drusus. And I would be honored to give her to my friend Lysander. I shall tell him so, myself."

***

After meeting with his council, Nicholas sent word to Katherine that he wished to see her before luncheon.

She took one look at his face and said, "Do quit fretting. Sera's fine. And no, Dawson didn't touch her other than to hold her still while the others drugged her. She has a headache, of course, but the doctor promises she'll be fine by tomorrow. When Wind Rider came back to the stables alone, I think we all went a bit mad with worry. Thank the good God that you came home early enough to catch them."

"We have to discuss something else, Katherine." He threw the miniature of Galerien down on a small table before her. She grew white as a ghost and turned toward the window.

"Is this to be my husband?" she asked.

"No. I would sooner marry you to a stoat. But Katherine, I need time to rid Laurentia of the Brotherhood's threat. I won't bother you with all the details, but for the meantime, please, accept this betrothal, knowing that I shall break it as soon as I can."

She looked at him, her smile tremulous. "Am I to send a shy but pleasing letter to Galerien, thanking him for this honor?"

He nodded, feeling like the lowest worm on the face of the earth. "Just for a little while, Katya. If you could play him, t'would make a difference, I think."

"I shall compose something fitting by this evening. Do you not think that he will be satisfied to receive it by return messenger?"

"I do. I should like to propose a meeting between you and Galerien here, for a month or two from now. That will keep him quiet, I believe." He couldn't look at her.

"Nikki. The British—will they help us against Napoleon?"

He shook his head. "I don't know."

Nicholas didn't even hear Katherine's approach. Her footsteps were muffled by the thick carpet. It was only when he felt her take his hand that he raised his head.

She gave him such a look. He wanted to shout to her to hit him, or to run away, but not to fix her dark eyes on him with such love and trust when he couldn't give her any comfort or reassurance.

"You have done all you can do, Nikki. Don't waste this time in guilt. Take what you can from it. I certainly plan to do so. And if the angels are with us—who knows? Maybe both of us will be happy for the rest of our lives, no?"

When had his little sister grown up? She was right, Nicholas thought. His troops, posted now at the border with Beaureve, would repel Galerien's army. Plans to attack the Brotherhood base were well under way. There was nothing left to do but wait, and hope.

He felt an odd lightening of spirit. For the first time, he was no longer fighting shadows. He might be dead this time next year, but in the interim, he would take what he wanted and give back as much of himself as he could.

Nicholas left his sister and strolled the long hallway to his chamber. A footman's normally impassive gaze whipped to Nicholas's face. It was only then that Nicholas realized he was whistling a rather bawdy tune he had learned at a tavern on the docks of London when he was a student.

***

In the few days since he had rescued her from Dawson, Sera found herself once again totally confused by Nicholas's behavior toward her. On the first morning, he appeared at her chamber door several times, inquiring after her health to the most minute details—how much of her breakfast she'd eaten, how well rested she was, if she'd risen from her bed.

Not completely satisfied with the answers, he'd come into the room to see for himself, bringing Katherine and Andre along.

"An unfortunate necessity, for propriety's sake," he'd told her with a charmingly wicked grin—the reprobate. She'd steeled herself then and managed a cool, impersonal mien. He hadn't seemed to notice. Instead, he'd questioned her closely about the headache, a lingering result of the drug, insisted that she not get up again that day, and checked what food Cook prepared for her. A few days ago, she would have melted at his fussing, but she was on her guard with him now, too. Perhaps guilt motivated his actions.

She waited for the announcement of his betrothal to the false princess, but it did not come. And she wondered what unfortunate young woman Galerien had placed in that role.

Today, fully recovered from the effects of her abduction, Sera faced the trial of her final ball gown fittings. She realized immediately that Madame Sophie's propensity for outrageous gossip remained the same, and Sera took advantage of it. "Tell me, Madame Sophie, what do you know about the princess Catherine Elizabeth Galerien?"

"Oh, my dear child, you have nothing to fear. She is very sick—some say she is a little *fou,* you understand.

Her uncle has sequestered her for so many years that there must be something very grave about her problems. No, you will not be usurped by that poor little thing."

"Where is she? Does anyone visit her? Do some of the lords of Laurentia carry messages from the king to this princess?"

"No, no. She never receives anyone."

Perhaps there isn't a sham princess, at all, Sera thought as the modiste prattled on.

"Once the marriage is consummated, and the heir assured, I believe the king will return to you with the eagerness of a new lover."

"Kindly say no more." Sera went hot with indignation at Madame Sophie's insinuation.

"Ah, my dear, you are such an innocent." The modiste shook her head and patted Sera's shoulder. "You must look at your situation as the way of the world. Mistresses have a power over men that wives only rarely possess. And you already have that power over the king. All the people watched you return to town, myself among them. We worried, you see. You were half-conscious at the time and so pale.

"But it was the king who surprised us, nay, shocked us that day. For he rode with you in his arms, my dear. And he held you as though he would never let you go. Did you not realize?" she asked.

Sera grew hot with confusion and a thrill that sent her perfidious heart soaring. "That day is rather blank in most places."

"Ah. Understandable. But so it was. You have nothing to worry about from the little sickly princess. You will have no rivals for this king's love."

Sera felt worse, really, than she had when Dawson drugged her. The tawdriness of it all—a mistress waiting alone while the man she loved bedded his wife for a child! And then, apparently, they all expected that she would take him back to her bed, as though nothing had happened.

Annette knocked at the door and entered holding a blue gown across her forearm. "I hope you are almost done, here, Madame. I have orders to ready Lady Sera for the afternoon."

"Ah oui, I am finished." The modiste dropped a curtsey to Sera. "My dear lady, it is always a pleasure to serve you. Be aware that we Laurentians have a great fondness for you."

"You must hurry, my lady." Annette laid the dress across the bed and opened the door yet another time, to admit several serving men carrying a large copper tub and buckets of hot water.

Sera splashed and scrubbed as quickly as she could. Where was she going, and why hadn't anyone bothered to tell her?

The maid helped her into the day dress she'd brought—a light blue woolen gown with a matching cloak lined in sable.

"There, my lady," she said as she buttoned a pair of white kidskin gloves over Sera's wrist, "you'll be warm enough now to walk about."

The maid arranged Sera's hair in a complicated, upswept mass of curls as she sat before a vanity mirror and stared at the stranger she was becoming. As Annette slipped a tall sable hat over the coiffure and handed her a muff of the same fur, Sera felt like a goose being carefully stuffed for a gourmet's dinner.

It was already cold enough to wear a fur hat, thought Sera.

Time was passing inexorably. Another two weeks would bring snow to the mountains, and after that, the waterfall would freeze. She couldn't ask Nicholas for help. She had sworn the same oath of secrecy that every Hillman swore, and there was no recourse but to stay until the thief arrived. Where in heaven's name was he?

Her stomach knotted. *If he does not come soon,* she promised herself, *I shall set off at once for the Hills.*

"There," said the maid, smoothing the fur-lined cloak about her shoulders. "You'll not catch cold if I can help it."

"But where am I to go?" asked Sera in confusion.

"Why, to the grand staircase. The king will meet you there. Did he not tell you?"

"No one tells me anything, Annette." Sera picked up her skirts and walked down the long corridor.

Nicholas was standing at the foot of the great stairway, his elbow braced negligently upon the newel post as he watched her descend the stairs. He wore a brown superfine jacket that emphasized his wide shoulders and slim waist.

His cravat was tied in a complex fashion, and the emerald in the stock pin at his throat glittered in the light from the high dome. He looked elegant and easy in his overwhelming palace.

"Hurry up, or we won't have time for tea." His deep voice echoed all the way up the staircase. Sera kept on walking, feeling the heat rise in her cheeks.

She forced herself to look calmly at Nicholas, daring him to rid himself of that lazy, sensual smile.

He seemed entirely different from the unpredictable stranger who occasionally spun her senses in five different directions. He looked both younger and more frightening. A dark lock had slipped from his normally neatly parted hair and hung over his forehead. His gray eyes glittered with a restless heat beneath the cool depths, like a fire banked beneath ashes. As he straightened away from the newel post, he seemed suddenly alive with a fixed purpose, an intention concentrated upward, at her.

Even covered by the cloak, she felt exposed. He looked at her as though he knew all of her. Just seeing him again had her quivering in fear and confused her enough to make her clumsy. With a sinking in her stomach, Sera pictured herself slipping and sliding down this grand staircase, to the shock of powdered footmen who lined it like life-sized lead soldiers in blue and gold satin.

She was trembling when she finally reached the bottom stair. Nicholas did a strange thing. He bent over her gloved hand, blocking her from view of the servants. Turning her palm upward, he placed the gentlest of kisses on the sensitive spot just between the glove and the sleeve of her jacket.

As her pulse leaped, Sera felt his lips curve against it, and she quailed beneath the realization that he knew just what he was doing to her. She wondered how she would ever hide herself successfully from him. She thought of the modiste's and Lady Tranevale's original speculations and called herself a fool.

Nicholas straightened and took her hand, laying it upon his arm. In a light voice he said, "Young ladies who get abducted must learn to defend themselves. Come."

To learn what? Violence? "No." Sera shook her head vehemently.

"Yes," Nikki said gently and drew her inexorably to the

door.

Sera thought she might freeze on the spot. She felt the cold hit her face as soon as she walked outside.

Behind the palace stood a target. A manservant appeared from nowhere with a brace of pistols and offered them to the king. Nicholas chose one and gave it to her.

"This firearm does not resemble a dead rabbit," he said, carefully extracting the weapon dangling awkwardly from her fingertips and repositioning it in her hand. "That's better. Lift your hand and take aim. Brace your hand on your left arm. Even in the best of circumstances, these things are known to shoot wide of the mark, and we can't have that, can we?"

"No." She handed the weapon back to him, looking at it with revulsion.

"What do you mean, no?"

"I cannot learn to kill another human being. Ever."

"You're not going out hunting, sweetheart," Nicholas said in a gentle voice. "This is for your own protection."

She shook her head. "Not even to save my life. It goes against everything I was taught, all I believe in. Can you not understand?"

"I understand that I almost lost you. They could have killed you, Sera. They would have. And then I—I..." A look of anguish flashed across his face, hollowing out the curve beneath his high cheekbones, and then it was gone.

"All right. We'll call this target practice. I am only interested in making you a wicked expert at hitting that bull's eye in the middle there. All the other targets will never dream of attacking you. All right?"

"No," she whispered, but a small smile tugged at her lips, betraying her.

"Sera." He lifted her chin with his forefinger and looked at her, all serious and beautiful, and she was lost. "If Katherine were threatened by a wolf, would you shoot to wound, not to kill? It could happen, you know. Game has been scarce recently. Have you heard the wolves howling near the city? You ride with Katherine every day. Would you let her die if you could protect her? You wouldn't need to kill anything if you shot well enough to only wound."

Sera thought hard. "If I could heal the wolf afterwards, I would do so," she said.

His voice was soft as eiderdown. "But you would have

to be very good with a pistol to give the wolf a chance, wouldn't you?"

She bit her lip and nodded.

"Then I suggest you begin to practice, for Katherine's sake as well as the wolf's."

Nicholas's eyes were so full of trust. He seemed to be giving her everything he held dear, knowing she would protect it. And she, on the other hand, plotted every day to leave as soon as the thief came and she had the ruby.

Against her conscience and her upbringing, she took the offensive thing in her hand.

Nicholas's manner slowly changed. His concentration, always overwhelming, was focused solely on her in the most business-like fashion. He taught her to load her own weapon, powder, ball, and rod, again and again, so she wouldn't forget. It felt like she aimed a thousand times, and she found she had an uncanny instinct for hitting the target. In another life, she thought, she might have been a cold-blooded killer.

Finally, as her arm grew heavy and sore, Nicholas said, "Enough. Any more and I'll have to give you an army commission. Come. I wish to show you the abbey."

As she approached the courtyard, Sera caught sight of Katherine and Andre. "Are they going with us?" she asked, smiling and waving to them.

Nicholas leaned near. "Chaperones. Every well-bred lady needs them." His breath was a warm caress against her cheek. He took her hand again and tucked it into the crook of his arm. "I wanted your first real experience of the abbey to be with me. Rather selfish of me, I admit, but then, I am the one with the most to gain should you decide you like it here better than any other place in this world."

She hated his ease while she fought so hard against her own conflict—the need to go, the desire to forget that he was impossible and the worst sort of womanizer.

"I have to go home, Nicholas. Very soon."

"No," he said with a low growl. "I told you. Look around you. The people love you. They need you."

She understood quite well. He kept her for his country, not for himself.

"Don't you like it here at all?" he asked in a voice velvet soft.

She wanted to say yes, she liked it when he was close,

and kind, and seemed as though he needed her and valued her somewhere beyond the worth of an occasional mistress. "I am certain that, if you took me back to my grandfather, he would agree to help you with Laurentia's problems."

"How could he possibly help Laurentia?" She heard the barely disguised frustration in his voice and reacted blindly.

"He knows a great deal more than you do, Outlander." She stopped herself, appalled that, in her lack of control, she'd revealed more than she should.

Nicholas's gaze sharpened. He looked at her as though she were a butterfly of rare interest, one he would anesthetize and stick on a pin. "What kind of knowledge, Sera? Is he the Mage, perchance?"

"What would you know about the Mage?" she asked, stalling.

"Yes or no, Sera? Is he the Mage?" Nicholas's voice was soft, but beneath that very softness lay his inexorable will, and she shivered as she felt his hand clasp her wrist. "Don't attempt to misguide me. Yes or no?"

She felt sick inside. She could not lie, and she could not give him the information he sought. "Take me back to the hills and ask him, yourself," she said at last, but faintly.

He sighed and let go of her wrist. She rubbed at it, and he reddened. "Enough. I—I'm sorry. I don't wish to hurt you. But I have a country to protect. Whenever we're together, I want to probe and delve and worry you into giving up all your secrets."

"If people wanted to share their secrets, they wouldn't be secrets," she said, staring down at her toes.

"Yes. And we all have them, don't we?"

"Especially you, Nicholas Rostov." She thought of the sham princess whom he would marry.

"Especially me." He took her arm again, gave her a smile of such unalloyed charm that she did not know quite how to react. Her eyes narrowed in suspicion.

He laughed, raising his hands in surrender. "I promise, no more questions. Or, if you prefer, later, when we're alone, you may ask me as many or more questions than I have asked you. And unlike you, my dear, I shall attempt to answer them all."

Sera nodded. Oh, she'd ask him all right. She took a deep breath and raised her chin. If this was to be a truce

of sorts, she would walk with him into the central square
to stand before the soaring walls of Montanyard Abbey.
And by her calm, dignified behavior, he would never know
that he had the least effect upon her, at all.

Katherine and Andre, who had strolled slowly behind
them, now caught up.

"Nikki," said Katherine, "some baron's daughter, just
come to court, accosted me with a purse full of money and
a request that I introduce her to you. The lady certainly
believes she is pretty enough to catch your eye, Nicholas."

"I hope you warned her that bribery is against the law,"
said Nicholas. His gray eyes turned hard as slate.

Katherine smiled at Sera. "He's quite fierce about those
who wish to curry favor."

"I see."

What Sera saw was another aristocrat eager to take
Nicholas to her bed. And if Nicholas didn't want this one,
she was certain he'd find another. Which was fine with
Sera.

She hated Nicholas Rostov. No, she couldn't afford such
a violent emotion. She just pitied him because he was
Outlander and an unenlightened womanizer.

As they neared the abbey, Sera stared at its airy arches
and flying buttresses dominating the square. Nicholas held
the door for her. She slipped inside, hoping the soaring
vaulted ceiling and hushed corridors might soothe her.

Sera took off her gloves in order to keep her hands
from wringing together as she worried. Why couldn't she
stop thinking about this Outlander king and his sham
marriage?

Why hadn't Grandfather fetched her? Why had he left
her alone to deal with the burgeoning power of the Gift?
He need only look into the scrying glass, and he could find
her and come for her. Although he had never said one
harsh word to her, perhaps now he was very angry. A huge
lump rose in her throat. Would he allow her back into
Arkadia if she returned without the Heart of Fire?

She sank onto a bench and bowed her head, biting
her lower lip. Nicholas sat down beside her, so close to
her that she could feel the warmth and the tensile strength
of his arm and shoulder. She resisted the desire to lean
into that strength. Instead, she took a deep breath and
closed her eyes, calming herself in the cool quietude of the

prayer house.

Nicholas's solid shoulder just touched hers. She could feel every breath he took. How did it help her that he could be there, both accepting and ignoring her at the same time? She glanced at him beneath her lashes. He didn't look back. She watched his mouth curve upward, just a little. Then he took her hand, and his fingers laced through hers. The touch of his skin against her ungloved hand was electric, warm support and wicked enticement. She had to break the spell. Now.

She slid her hand from his grasp. He glanced at her, his brows raised in question. She rose abruptly, and without a word, he stood. When she moved, he walked beside her, matching his easy strides to her own. Seemingly ignoring her rejection, Nicholas pointed out the statues of the saints and the virgin, and the rose window at the western end of the transept, glowing with all the colors of the rainbow, until they reached the tall doors of the prayer house.

Once out on the street, he continued in the role of amiable host and tour guide. "The abbey has the finest acoustics in Europe and Russia."

"Perhaps Notre Dame has better, Nikki," volunteered Katherine, walking behind them with Andre.

"Never."

"Acoustics for what?" Sera asked him.

"Concerts, of course. Masses. Music." Nicholas looked at her closely. "Have you never heard a concert?"

Sera shook her head. "We do not have this music. It releases—dangerous emotion."

Nicholas looked at her sharply. "What sorts of dangerous emotions?"

"Those that confuse the soul and keep it from right reason," she said in a tone that implied that every school child ought to know this.

Nicholas felt the slight chill at the back of his neck, and the fine hairs rose there. His senses sang faintly, like strings of a harp when a wind passed through them. He vaguely recalled reading something to the effect when he was a schoolboy. What was it? Oh, he wanted to know everything about her. A lifetime would never be enough.

"Your majesty! Lady Sera!" Mrs. Torville called from the door of her teashop. "How good of you to come." She ushered them in, past the usual number of intellectuals, aristocrats, and gluttons who filled the little shop to capacity. They made their way to a rather private alcove where Mrs. Torville had laid a table for them.

The woman was a plump and beaming testament to her own delicious pastries. "I am glad to see you better, Lady Sera," she said. Sera gave her a startled look. "All of us know of your latest mishap, my lady, and of His Majesty's gallant rescue. I've got some blueberry tarts made special, to help you put the roses back in your cheeks. I call them the Lady Seras."

Andre and Katherine caught up with them, greeting Mrs. Torville fondly. Nicholas helped Sera into her chair, pushing away the twinge of disappointment. He had counted on their total involvement with each other to keep them in the dim recesses of the abbey long enough to give him some time alone with Sera.

At least at this small table, Sera sat close beside him to his right, and he could feel the warmth of her body and scent the elusive perfume she wore. But she did not seem to be in a very receptive mood. She stared at her teacup and merely pushed the tart around on her plate.

Nicholas refrained from raking his fingers through his hair in frustration. How did one speak to a brooding female, anyway? One discussed the activities of the day, he supposed. It certainly wouldn't do to begin with the shooting lesson.

"Montanyard Abbey is said to rival Notre Dame and Westminster Abbey in its architecture," he began, sounding every bit the pedant to his own ears. "It has been the scene of every royal wedding in the last six centuries." She froze and kept her eyes resolutely on her untouched plate.

"Didn't you like the Abbey?" he asked, hurt by her disapproval.

"It was quite beautiful," she said indifferently.

"Perhaps you would like to attend Sunday services there. We have a chapel in the palace, of course, but it is quite majestic in the abbey, and all the people of Montanyard..." *Will see us and know that I am courting you in all seriousness.*

"I shall not worship in your prayer house," she said, pursing her lips like a disapproving governess.

"You need not worship, but to see it with all the candles

lit and—"

"No. Your religion is nothing but lies. It says not to kill, but you hand me a pistol and teach me to do so, and still you may go to your prayer house whenever you like, and you all live that way. Why, you will marry your Beaurevian princess in that prayer house, and then you will take a mistress, even—even though you will promise to cleave to no other."

Katherine looked up from her private conversation with Andre. Her mouth dropped open. Sera was sure her shrew's voice must have carried through the crowded teashop, titillating and shocking aristocrats and commoners alike.

Nicholas threw a sharp glance Katherine's way. She turned beet red. And Nicholas, unaccountably, smiled at Sera, his face lit with what looked like tender amusement. No, it must only be amusement.

"I shall never take a mistress when I am wed, Sera. I promise you that. Stay and finish your tea," he said to Katherine and Andre. "I believe Lady Sera and I have something to discuss."

"I see I am no longer a gentle lady in need of chaperones," Sera said. By the gods, he was turning her into a snappish prune.

"Enough." Nicholas's voice was very soft, but dangerous.

She clamped her mouth shut, but shot him a searing glance. Nicholas took her hand firmly in his and pulled her to her feet. He planted it on his arm as they walked back to the palace. Occasionally, the folds of Sera's skirt flowed against the buckskin of his breeches, and she was terribly conscious of his long, muscular legs. He was close enough that she felt his solid warmth, even through the fur of her cloak. The shadows stretched across the square. One day almost gone. One of the last. She fought the sadness, reminded herself that the man beside her was a—what did they call these womanizers who tempt one woman while betrothed to another? A rake. She pulled her hand free of his arm.

He merely wrapped his fingers round her wrist and carried her hand back to his arm, holding it there when she tried to tug it away.

His voice was soft, impersonal. "I hoped today would go differently for us."

"What did you expect, that I would be like all your other mistresses?" She felt absurdly close to tears.

"You are not like anyone, and there have been precious few 'other mistresses'. I expected to have a happy day showing you my favorite places in Montanyard, so you could see why I love it, and, I hoped, come to love it yourself someday soon.

"But what I wished," he continued, "well, that is a different story. I wished to take you to your chamber, rather earlier than now. I thought I would close the door behind us. We would be alone, of course. That would be when I could tell you that I may marry where I wish, rather than where I was promised. Then I would kiss you until we both turned blue for want of breath."

She gasped, a sharp intake of breath. Had he just said what she thought he'd said? And why was he telling her? And what had he learned in Beaureve?

Her hand trembled beneath his fingers. They were up the palace's outer stairway, now. Two footmen bowed as they held the great double doors open. Nicholas nodded once and continued up the stairway, his eyes fixed straight ahead of him.

"Next, I tormented myself with visions. How I would touch you all over," he continued, his quiet voice beginning to strain. "I would tease you with my hands, my mouth, until you begged me to give you what you needed. But I didn't wish to do so immediately. I thought I would prefer to start all over again, making it last until we're both mad with it, and then—"

"Hush." She didn't dare look up at him. Her face was flaming. She could feel its heat.

Nicholas slanted a glance at her from beneath thick, dusky lashes. "I believe you ought to know that I am suffering mightily here. There is something about telling a woman just what one wants to do with her, to her, that makes one mad to do it."

She was suffering, as well. His sensuous words sent her into paroxysms of embarrassment and desire. They stood at the door of her chamber.

Nicholas didn't give her time to think. He merely opened the door, pushed her gently inside before him, and followed, shutting the door and turning the key in the lock.

Ten

Sera retreated to the window, staring out, looking anywhere but at Nicholas as he casually rested his back against the door. She didn't dare look at him. She knew what she'd see. A king, a sorcerer of mesmerizing power. Beauty, strength and vulnerability, wicked temptation and drugging kisses. All in an Outlander who said he was free to choose his bride.

She and Nicholas were a mistake, a chance meeting of two worlds that could never exist together. What an ironic joke. The gods must surely be laughing.

"I knew you would fit in this room," he said. His voice had gone deeper, thicker. "All pink and gold. Your skin, the gold in your hair—I've pictured you in here for so many nights. I know how you'll look lying in that big bed, with your hair fanning out in a halo on the pillow, and your neck arched as I kiss that tender little place right behind your ear—the one that makes you shiver in my arms. You'll like that, won't you, Sera?"

"No. I should not like it at all." Sera shut her eyes against the images his words created. He was saying all the wrong things, calculated words of seduction, and still, to her shame, she was growing taut and heated as his voice wove that deep enchantment. She barely heard his footsteps on the deep plush of the carpet as he came closer to her. His hand brushed down her cheek to that spot he had made intensely sensitive merely by naming it.

She kept her eyes tightly shut, but she didn't move away. She stood there, helpless, hating herself. He gave a deep murmur of pleasure. She felt his heat as he bent closer, still holding her only with a caress of his fingers. The warm, solid wall of his chest was only a hair's breadth away. Blindly, she reached out and grabbed his arm, afraid of the weakness in her own legs. His strength alone held her up, and his breath played warm against her ear, making her shiver with anticipation.

"See? I told you you'd like it." His voice was velvet soft as his lips found the spot directly beneath her ear.

"Mmmm." He nibbled delicately, as though she were a rare treat to be savored, and she clutched his arms with both hands, making those same sounds she had heard herself make with him in a dream.

"Don't fight it. Please, just let me—just once let me—" he whispered, soothing and inciting her to a hot, empty ache with his teasing kisses.

"This is wrong." Her voice was as insubstantial as a frayed autumn leaf. "You are a king. I am a Hill woman, a slave. We can have none of this."

He eased himself back, smoothed her hair and tilted her chin. "Open your eyes, Sera," he said, his voice tight and controlled, while she trembled, fearful of coming apart completely.

She looked at him, held by his thumb and forefinger, and by the spell he managed to weave around her.

He rubbed his thumb gently down her neck, settling where the blood beat heavy and strong.

"I have fought against this, using that kind of parochial logic." His smile held irony. "It keeps growing, this—need. Fool that I was, I thought it madness to want you like this, but if so, you share it with me. Both the desire and the fear."

She pushed against his chest, staring at the floor, shaking her head. He shook her shoulder once, gently. "Look at me," he said through gritted teeth.

Her eyes sprang open.

"Don't bother to deny what you feel. Your face and your body give you away. You want me as much as I want you. You have a beautiful sensuality, Sera. Your response is honest and precious to me.

"I want to watch you come alive to pleasure, one discovery at a time. I want to know every sweet secret of your body. I would take a very long time at it. There are so many places where you'll be incredibly responsive."

"Let me go," she said, choking on the words. She was shaking with her shame, hating herself for giving him this much.

"You are free to go any time you wish. I'll do nothing to you that you don't want, Sera. Indeed, I plan to leave you eager for more than I'll give you," he said in that deep, velvet voice.

She whirled about, her back to him, refusing to look at him, so beautiful with his dark power.

"When you're finally willing to accept the truth, you'll come to me. Look at the walls of the chamber very carefully.

There's a door in the wall, just over there." He pulled her to him and pointed over her shoulder. Sera's back was pressed against the solidity of his chest, her hips against the very evident strength of his arousal. She gave a start of shock. Nicholas braced his legs and pressed forward, holding her tightly against his hard heat with the curve of his arm.

She heard a rumble of frustration and amusement from deep in his chest. "You're not the only one of us burning from a simple kiss. Now, pay attention. Do you see the door, there, built so cleverly that you wouldn't normally see it?"

Sera looked. There, indeed, barely visible in the candlelight was the shadow of a door, covered as the rest of the room was in wainscoting and wallpaper.

"When your body is ready for me, push the beak of the green bird with the red throat on the wall to the right of it. The door to my chamber will always be open. The passageway will lead you to me."

"I do not wish to become your mistress."

His hands grasped her shoulders and then trailed down her arms, soothing her as if she were a fractious child, and he rubbed his cheek against her hair.

"Mistress?" There was surprise in his voice. She supposed he had not thought beyond today to the consequences of such a choice. "This was not a room for a mistress," he said. "My grandfather had it built for my grandmother, a Russian princess. Like you, she was a very beautiful woman. Actually, there was a vague feeling— within the family only, of course—that she had a rather unconventional upbringing. Grandfather was smitten with her from the first moment he saw her until the day of his death.

"Tradition decrees that the king and queen occupy separate chambers. But grandfather wanted his wife in his bed every night, and he wanted easy access to her. Thus the door. Only Vanbrugh, the architect, and the workmen knew and every one of them kept the secret. He was a very popular king, you see, as well as a clever one.

"I was lucky. He decided to tell me about it when I was but a young boy. Obviously, the story stirred my imagination."

"I shan't use it," said Sera, but her voice sounded weak

to her.

He turned her to face him, holding her lightly with both big hands on her shoulders. He smiled and gave her a wicked glance from beneath the dark fringe of his lashes. She fought the desire to put her hands on his wide shoulders and take another kiss.

"As I said, I was lucky to learn of it. We'll see if my luck holds out."

He left her, then, to think and worry over what to do. Marriage was impossible.

Oh, she cared little for what the courtiers or the townspeople thought, but she cared about herself, and him, now. She feared that Nicholas had the power to possess her until she was a helpless child, forgetting what she owed her people as long as he held her body in thrall. She thought of her mother, and the terrible consequences of the choice she had made. She thought of the hatred and avarice of the court, and what it would do to Nicholas, as well as her.

It didn't matter that he was beautiful and stern in a way that moved her soul. It didn't matter that his need for her, in spite of his reluctance to depend upon anybody, had been elemental, that at times he seemed to be another person in her presence, one who shed his cold remoteness and teased and laughed. He was of this place, where enough greed and resentment and self-hatred lived to taint even the gift of his body. She must leave, before she gave him the power to bring them both down.

Where was the thief?

**

In the cold, dread hour of midnight on All Hallow's Eve, a tall figure, wrapped in black from head to toe, stepped out of the fog-swirled light of a street lamp and into the shadows. Several other figures, all of them garbed similarly, gathered beside the spectral presence in the little town of Barkley, which stood between Selonia and Montanyard.

"You have done well," said the tall man in a voice that carried its own empty echoes. "To have infiltrated so far without detection considering the patrols, is proof of our superiority to this upstart king and his line."

"Our lives and our souls belong to you, Count Laslow," said the man who commanded the rest of the group.

Laslow looked around him proudly. These were the first to enter Laurentia, the ones who were responsible for the victory at Selonia. Those of the True Faith would sing of that victory for centuries.

"I am pleased," he said. "But Galerien grows restless. What news of the thief?"

The commander of the squadron shook his head. "He has gone to ground, most assuredly somewhere close. We believe he is making his way to Montanyard and will then attempt to head north to Russia, losing himself in the confusion of Napoleon's march south. "We surmise that the thief will creep into Montanyard within the month. He must sell the ruby before he leaves the country, for the Russians are not in the mood to buy, and the thief must have enough coin to bribe his way into Europe. As he must make his move before the snows begin, he will come to roost in Montanyard in approximately fifteen to twenty days."

"Very good," the spectre said. "I do not care about this thief, myself, but in order to prepare for our final push into Laurentia, we need Galerien's payment. He has promised us enough arms and cannon to guarantee victory if we deliver the ruby to him before the first of December."

The count looked long and hard at each man present. "I need your absolute loyalty, your sworn promise that you will succeed or perish in this attempt."

"You have it, my lord," said each man in turn, bowing low.

"Good. One more thing. The princess Catherine Elizabeth. Galerien had assumed she was already dead when he met with Rostov. After learning of Dawson's failed abduction attempt, he was apoplectic with rage. Now, he wants her death even more than he wants the ruby. If we can provide this for him, he will pay more. A great deal more. Enough to take Jehanna next."

He paused. When he spoke, his voice was just a whisper. "Find her. And when you do, kill her, and bring me her head. Galerien wants proof.

"When we have done all this, we shall return to our base and amass our legions. Laurentia will be ours, and the Rostovs will be but a shameful memory from Satan's time. Now go, and do what you are sworn to do."

The figures bowed low and crept into the night. Count

Laslow departed the empty square, unaware of another figure that suddenly stepped into the light amidst the swirling fog.

A tall, blond, broad shouldered man in a gray cloak lifted his hood about his head and disappeared.

***

"So now you see," Lysander said to the young men and women gathered on benches in the colonnade, "if we wish, we could defy gravity to such an extent that we could cause a machine to rise beyond the earth."

Jacob paused to watch his friend instruct the youths, aware of the other philosophers and their pupils gathered in small groups throughout the area. Lysander was already making a name for himself among them, and many fathers in the City sent their daughters and sons to him, for when he questioned a youth, he opened his eyes to truth, the way Socrates had in the long-ago days before the City destroyed him.

"To what purpose, Lysander?" asked an older man who wore his beard like the Spartans, without mustache. Demetrius Thasos was a vain man for all his ascetic appearance, a philosopher with a small following at best, and a desire to bring Lysander down to his own level by slick sophistry. Jacob leaned against a pillar and watched, knowing he'd not be necessary as an advocate for his friend. Lysander could take care of himself.

Lysander smiled. "Well you should ask, Demetrius. First, one must accept that we are a people to whom armed conflict is anathema. But this is what the Outlanders use, and will continue to use, until they have destroyed much of this earth. Before that happens, we shall leave, to found a new world beyond the stars. It is not too soon for our mathematicians and our scientists to ponder how we can devise machines in order to depart."

"Machines, in which we shall take our statues, our building materials, and our people?"

"We shall not leave our people behind, nor the means to feed and house them," Lysander said.

"These machines must be huge, indeed, to house people, tools, horses, and livestock of all kinds."

Lysander smiled. "And the statues sacred to the City." All eyes turned to look up at the Temple Square and the great Athene within her open sanctuary.

"And what will power the machine, Lysander?" the sophist asked.

Lysander's gaze crossed the Colonnade, to rest upon a group of tailors seated cross-legged on the ground. Each one sewed a nondescript cloak of gray, woven by the guild of weavers in the City. He then motioned to three boys, running along the exercise ground beyond the colonnade. Above their heads, beautiful, brightly colored kites designed in the Chinese manner, a dragon, a lion, and a bluebird, raced in the wind, attached to each boy only by the strength of his Gift. Children raced after them cheering.

One of the boys narrowed his eyes, and his kite rose higher than the others. Another, not to be outdone, swept his up to the same height, where it somersaulted, its tail a glorious, circling plume. The children laughed and clapped their hands. His two friends laughed as well, naming him the victor. Their concentration broke, and the kites drifted down into their hands.

"We shall carry our own power, Demetrius. Together, all of us aboard will lift the starship and sail it." Dismissing his opponent, Lysander turned again to his pupils, who worked now with stylus and parchment in the old way of the scribes.

"We are the beginning," he said. "We shall not see the culmination. But we shall chart the course." The youths and maidens looked at him as though he were a god.

But Lysander did not have an ounce of hubris, Jacob knew. He was a visionary, a brilliant man, a gift to Arkadia. He would care for his wife without invoking those turbulent emotions the Outlander king invoked in his sister. With a man like Lysander, a woman would have the help she needed learning to control her Gift.

He waited until Lysander dismissed his pupils, then joined him. "Come," he said. "Shall we drink together and talk?"

At these formal words, Lysander looked at him closely, and then he slowly smiled. They walked in silence toward the tables outside the tavern beside the baths. A servant brought wine and water, which Jacob Augustus, as host, mixed. He gave a cup to Lysander and raised his own.

"To Seraphina," he said quietly.

The raised cup paused before it reached Lysander's lips. "You will bring her home soon?" he asked, his gaze intent.

"I will," Jacob told him.

And Lysander replied in the age-old words of the marriage proposal. "Jacob, I ask you and the Mage permission to tell Seraphina that the earth rejoices in her beauty."

***

After a restless night full of strange dreams, Sera awoke to the Princess Katherine's knock on her chamber door.

"Your presence is requested at ten o'clock this evening. At the ball." Katherine paused at what must have been Sera's blank look. "Nikki told me he explained it all to you—the opening ball, etcetera, etcetera."

"Oh," said Sera, glumly shrugging into a dressing gown. "That ball."

"Indeed, that ball." Katherine gave her a half smile of sympathy. "Nikki will be in conference until the ball, and you are to rest."

"Doesn't your brother ever get tired of telling us what to do?"

"It is a king's way, to rule." Katherine gave her a smile. "I hope you will take tea with me beforehand. You'll need nourishment to get through the evening."

"I should like that," said Sera. "But afterwards...I am sure that my presence will not be noticed at this ball. Nicholas will entertain his friends, and you will be quite busy overseeing the chefs and the musicians."

She did not want to see Nicholas again so soon, particularly when he was dressed in the magnificent formal dress of his office, standing with arrogant ease among his friends, every inch a monarch. Why couldn't he wear his linen shirt and the fawn colored breeches that hugged his hips all the time? Why couldn't he be what he looked like then—a strong, upright, comely male of indeterminate station whom she wished she could love and bring home to live with her in Arkadia?

"Nikki most specifically instructed me to tell you that you have the requisite costume, the requisite élan, and the requisite command of the king. You are to make your debut tonight, Sera. I'm afraid we're both stuck." Katherine patted her hand.

"Your brother oversteps himself."

"Nikki only pushes when he honestly feels he must.

He realizes that I have no confidence. Thus he makes me endure these evenings, in the hopes that familiarity with his courtiers will at least breed a bit of contempt, and I shall feel that much better about myself in the obvious comparison with others. However, thus far I have only wished myself back in the peace of the convent, where the nuns did not care a whit for my lack thereof."

"But you have made a joke, Katherine. A play on words, no? And I caught it. Perhaps you are not so lacking in wit, and I am not so hopelessly hu-morless, after all."

Katherine's smile made her face glow with an incandescence that far outdid mere beauty. "Do you know, Sera? I've never had a friend before. 'Tis a wondrous lovely feeling to laugh at my sorry predicament with a friend."

Tea was a hurried affair, which Katherine and Sera ate from trays in the princess's rooms. Maids scurried past them as they ate, carrying petticoats and gowns and slippers for Katherine to choose from. They tried to talk of silly, everyday things—how and when they would ride the next morning, how in spring Sera's garden would bloom with the bulbs she had planted two weeks ago. It was only when the footmen appeared with the large copper tub that Sera turned to Katherine in a panic.

"I do not wish to go," she said, grasping her friend's hand.

"We'll be together," said Katherine. "It won't be so terrible. After all, what can happen?"

***

Nicholas took the last sip of brandy he was to get for the next two hours and crushed out the cigar he shouldn't have been smoking. The weather had been miserably cold recently. His chest already felt tight, and his throat had been sore for a few days. Any other time, he'd be skulking in his chambers with a mustard plaster on his chest. But he was here now, indulging in drink and tobacco in order to welcome his old friend from England, Lord Robert Grey.

Nicholas had spent the last days outside exercising with the cavalry. For the sake of their morale, the soldiers must see him working with them. He'd need to get away very soon to hide in some warm dacha until his breathing came easy again. The times were too perilous for him to succumb to pneumonia. Still, tonight, he must show himself to his court, to reassure the nobility and his generals that their king was hale and hearty.

And now he had to deal with England's message. Robert stood tall and straight-backed, looking out the window of the library. It was just like Robert, with his sense of honor, to come himself with the bad news rather than send a messenger.

Nicholas crossed the room to stand beside him. He stared down at the torch lit courtyard. Servants in livery milled about, opening carriage doors and helping ladies down from them. Like the last days, this night was unusually cold for November. All of the women entering the palace and most of the men, as well, were muffled up to their ears in fur lined cloaks.

"I hate the cold," Nicholas said glumly.

"I am sorrier than I can tell you, my friend. And furious with politics and the self-serving attitude of my government," said Robert.

"It's no matter, Rob. I knew this would probably be the outcome of your petition. Self-interest will guide England just as it guides Laurentia. But I'm prodigiously grateful that you came yourself to tell me of it."

"Nikki, if it's any consolation, the men and I are ready to fight with you."

"What? Your old outfit from the Spanish campaign?"

"We took a vote before I left home. All of us owe you our lives, man. 'Tis the least we can do to help out a bit here."

"You are very kind, Rob. Convey my heartfelt thanks to all of the men of the forty-seventh," Nicholas said, knowing full well he would never allow the regiment to fight for Laurentia. Aside from the obvious cloud of treason looming over Rob's horizon should he and the others fight for a country not allied to England, there was the very real concern that Rob's wife was carrying again and close to her confinement.

Nicholas rubbed his forehead between thumb and finger. Napoleon's troops moved south of Moscow. The march could turn into a rout or an organized attack on Laurentia.

Word of another attack, this one on a small village between Selonia and Montanyard, meant that the terrorists had traveled west a good hundred miles without detection. Nicholas must step up the plans for the raid on the terrorist

base. He had to do something. His people were in an agony
of fear.

"You did the best you could for us, Rob. Come. We
must open this damned ball."

Nicholas crossed the room to go directly to the
ballroom, pausing to leave his glass on the desk. "There's
someone I wish you to meet. A lady not of the mold you
would usually expect at a ball such as this one. Her name
is Sera."

"Sera Who?"

"This lady will not reveal her family name," said
Nicholas. "Actually," he looked at Rob, waiting to gauge
his reaction, "there is a good deal the lady will not share
with me. I'm having the devil of a time convincing her to
trust me. Odd, isn't it, when I'm the most trustworthy of
fellows?"

Robert laughed and clapped him on the back. "Perhaps
she senses a more dangerous side to you than do the rest
of us. I shall be very happy to meet this Sera. I take it she
has not stirred your interest because she is a master of
dead languages, or a philosopher."

Nicholas idly turned the pages of an illustrated volume
by William Blake. "Actually, she is quite fluent in several
languages, and her grasp of philosophy is rather strong,
but no, that's not a fraction of what interests me."

Nicholas wondered just how closely he could hold Sera
tonight in the waltz and still keep her reputation safe from
any further speculation by his snide courtiers. Certainly
not as closely as he wished to. He closed the volume of
poetry with a thump and gave Robert what he hoped passed
for a nonchalant smile.

"You'll see her tonight, when she makes her debut."

                                    ***

Sera slipped into her room and shook out her cloak. It
had been a risk, indeed, to sneak out into the night already
dressed for the ball and comb the inns within the perimeter
of Montanyard for any word of the thief. She knew by now
what harm could come to her. But the ball had caused
enough commotion within the palace to allow a brief
escape. This had been the first night in ever so long when
the guards were too busy to notice her.

No one had heard of the thief yet, and time was running
out. The first snow was only a day or two away. Although

the night was clear, she could already scent moisture on the air. She must visit Monsieur Carlshonn again quite soon. The draper might well have heard news from the inns amidst the shops in the city center.

Sera glanced into the cheval glass, smoothed down her hair and fluffed out her gown. Compared to the river wharves and the smoky taverns she had visited tonight, the ballroom should not hold much terror for her. But she found she was as nervous as a child attempting her first examination before the council of elders. She took a deep breath and lifted her chin. The sooner begun, the sooner done, she told herself as she swept into the corridor and down the long stairway toward the noise and gaiety at the end of the hallway.

The huge ballroom glittered. The mirrors along the wall and the windows opposite reflected the brilliant light from crystal and gilt chandeliers. The noise and the heat were overwhelming. Women in brilliant silks and brocades drifted past Sera, their throats gleaming with the dazzling light of their jeweled necklaces. The gentlemen were as showy in brocaded and embroidered waistcoats in every color of the rainbow, and bright evening jackets to match.

Sera stood amidst this gaily bedecked crowd in an ice blue silk gown that bared her shoulders indecently, a dance card that she did not plan to fill, and a fan she could only use like a novice dangling from her gloved wrist. Women glanced coldly at her. Men adjusted their quizzing glasses and perused her person. Sera pondered the earliest possible moment she could retire to the privacy of her room.

She was Nicholas' prisoner in flowing silk and kidskin, when she could be safe from all the turmoil and the agitation of his world. But when he kissed her as he had yesterday, she forgot everything else—even the sinking panic that she might never see her grandfather again. The only thing she wanted was more of his kisses, and his wonderful hands that knew secrets about her she hadn't even guessed.

"Princess Katherine. You look to be in fine form tonight. And your companion, m'dear? Would you be so kind?" An outrageously showy male wearing a pink velvet coat and peacock blue knee breeches on his skinny frame approached them, almost shouting above the murmurs of the crowd. Immediately upon reaching Katherine's side, he raised his quizzing glass and stared through it at Sera. The foppish gentleman bent over Sera's hand and actually put his mouth against her glove. Sera concentrated on the pale, shining bald spot in the middle of his crown.

"M'dear Lady Sera," the man, whom Katherine now introduced as Lord Effenby, Viscount Berington, intoned. "Such beauty, such grace. Might I interest you in a stroll about the room before His Majesty opens the ball?"

She was filled with embarrassed confusion as to how to refuse such an offer, but Effenby still held her hand tightly in his, and it seemed to her that this was not one of Laurentia's social niceties that she must endure. "I thank you, sir," she said staring at Lord Effenby's weak chin. "But I shall remain beside the princess."

"Perhaps you will honor me with the first dance." Effenby lowered his voice so that only Sera could hear him and a hint of malice as he continued. "I should enjoy hearing of your travails in the summer palace of Iman Hadar, m'dear. Several versions of your adventures circulate throughout our set. Perhaps you will give me the details, and I shall pass them on to the rest of the company assembled here."

She raised her eyes and gave Effenby a long, considering look. Surprisingly, Effenby paled, then flushed, as though he had been caught by a bishop with his hand in the charity box.

"I do not care to dance with you, my lord. Nor to converse with you any further."

"Oh, I say. Bit of a purse-lips, aren't you? Promised to actually lead you about, and give you entrée into our set, and you'd turn your nose up at it? What a wonder, to set yourself so high, when all of us know where you've been." Effenby walked off huffing.

Chinless, balding, self-righteous, bigoted, libertine! Sera fought the urge to run after him and give him a sharp tongue-lashing. Effenby slithered across the room, to pause before a group of gaudy ladies. One of them was the old woman covered in diamonds from Sera's other disastrous evening with the court. Effanby looked back at her with a smirk, and then returned his attention to the circle surrounding him. Whatever bon mots he passed along to them must have been quite entertaining, for Sera heard their burst of laughter from where she stood. She leaned toward Katherine, who was just ending a conversation with a rather lovely blonde in silver. The lady curtsied and strolled away with barely a glance at Sera.

"How much longer?" whispered Sera.

"We've been here scarce ten minutes, I think. At least another two hours," hissed Katherine.

Nicholas stood across the room receiving the last guests. His dark blue velvet coat and white silk knee breeches were a stark contrast to most of the colorfully dressed men in the room, and his comparatively austere costume only served to make him look more regal. This was his world, where he both ruled and felt entirely at home. She shrank into herself a little.

She had been so certain that Arkadia would be her home forever. She had never prepared herself to deal with this opulence, this conscious mixture of cruelty and politesse, unless one could call glimpses of this life through a scrying glass preparation. Nicholas walked among these people with power and grace, his height making him visible above the heads of men who surrounded him. He smiled with such ease at those who so clearly accepted his right to tell them what to do.

From somewhere behind a screen came a sweet sound of what must be music. She could not tell what the instruments were, but from her furtive studies after hours at the academy, she thought they might be stringed instruments. They played in a rhythmic fashion that seemed to imitate the beating of her heart. It rather took her breath away, this strange blending of separate tones into a harmonious whole, all lightness and gaiety together in that single beat that made one wish to nod along. Throughout the ballroom, men bowed to women, who curtsied back.

Sera watched Nicholas lead the ball off with an elderly woman with white hair. She wore an emerald gown and walked with the upright grace of a queen. A tall, muscular man with a kind expression on his face appeared in front of Katherine and, with a smile to Sera, took Katherine's hand with a bow. They proceeded down the row at a stately pace, Nicholas and his partner first. The lady turned in the dance with Nicholas, broke hands, joined together with Katherine and her tall, upright partner to form a group of four. Sera could barely take her eyes from them all. Even

Katherine, who blushed unbecomingly, knew all the steps of the dance. They were so graceful. Their movements and the music itself made her wish she had accepted Monsieur Gallopet's lessons.

The dance went on for a very long time. Sera retreated to a corner of the ballroom near a large door that led into a room with a banquet table holding a large punch bowl and refreshments. In the obscurity of her corner, she savored the orchestra's strange, fanciful sounds and watched the couples. Several of them had little to do for quite a while, it seemed, and used the opportunity to speak to each other. She began to see exactly how Monsieur Petit had meant her to use the thing hanging so limply from her wrist, for several ladies snapped their fans open and fluttered them in front of their faces, laughing behind the framed silk and lace. One playfully hit her partner upon the shoulder. Had the man done something or said something to deserve the little slap, or was the woman engaging in some kind of game?

The music finally ended, and the dancers executed deep bows and curtsies to each other. Sera looked for Katherine and spotted her halfway across the large ballroom with Andre. For once, he had managed to arrange his blonde curls into some kind of order. As he bent over Katherine, a look of such naked joy filled his face that Sera felt herself grow lighter at the sight. She remained in her corner, intent upon not disturbing their happiness.

Surely she must have stood in this ballroom at least two hours—the requisite amount of time she was to obey the command of the king. Pushing away from her haven, she began the careful task of slipping away, only to feel a gentle but firm hand on her arm.

"There you are." Nicholas was beside her. She had a confused desire to break free and at the same time to lean into his strength. She took a deep breath of his scent, woodland and soap and his own light, musky warmth, as he bent to take her hand and raise it to his lips. The crowd about them went silent for an instant, and then resumed conversation. She felt much like a tortoise rolled onto its back, helpless to move, exposed to the pokes and prods of small, cruel boys. She stared at her toes, avoiding the avid eyes she felt fixed upon the two of them.

"May I present Lord Grey, Duke of Ayres?"

"Lady Sera, I am so very happy to make your acquaintance." Lord Grey bowed over her hand. He was the same man who had danced with Katherine.

Sera accomplished a passable curtsey and studied Lord Grey. He had strong, patrician features, dark hair, and a kind smile.

Lord Grey suffered her scrutiny for a moment or two. The smile never left his face. "I wonder, my lady, if you realize that your eyes are rather frightening. They seem to see straight through a person and calmly judge the soul that lies within. I would think that, if you wished to, you could make this entire ballroom quail before you."

"I do not much wish to look at any of them," said Sera in a voice that sounded thin and whispery to her ears. "I have never known any people such as these before."

"I understand perfectly," said Lord Grey. "But beneath all the feathers and gilt, they are really very much like any others—most of them frightened to death of being found out for frauds." He perused a group of courtiers ahead of them and slightly to the left.

She heard Nicholas' smothered laugh.

"You think they are all as uncomfortable as I?" Sera stifled a sigh. "At least they all seem to know the correct steps of the dances, whereas I—"

Nicholas' voice held amusement. "Rob's right, you know. Appearances are all in this crush. Simply assume a bored manner, and the world will scurry about attempting to engage your interest."

She broke off at the sound of what must be the highest stringed instruments—what were they? The violins or the violas, she wondered irritably. Again, she felt like groaning inwardly—frustration and regret at the years she had wasted fearing this world too much to learn about it. And why, oh why, had she refused dancing lessons when they had been offered?

Nicholas gave her such a look—intensity mingled with a kind of reckless happiness. He executed a bow and took her hand. All Sera heard over the music were his last words.

"...the pleasure of this waltz, my lady?"

She realized with dread that Nicholas was pulling her steadily to the center of the polished floor. "No, no," she said, but the music was too loud. She shook her head, trying to dig in her heels, but his strength was more than she could withstand and the floor was slippery. She could only follow quickly or fall.

As they walked to the center of the ballroom, Sera noticed Lord Effenby and the old woman with all the diamonds scowling in her direction. They made a rather ridiculous couple, for Effenby was so spindly and the old woman so stout.

"La! I'll not dance, Effenby. Not while that Hill person is upon the floor. 'Tis a travesty," she heard the woman say.

"Don't fret, dear lady Tranevale. I'll have that man bring us a treat. Ho, you there!" Effenby called to a footman passing by. "Some claret and blanc-mange. Bring it at once." Effanby offered his arm to Lady Tranevale and followed behind Sera and Nicholas.

"Let's dance in close proximity to the woman until our repast arrives. Doubtless, she'll disgrace herself in some manner, and I shall want a good view of the show."

Knowing Effenby's prediction was about to come true, Sera blanched.

Nicholas must have overheard. His frown was as dark as a thundercloud. But Effanby was too busy settling Lady Tranevale before him, and the matron was too filled with her own self-importance to realize she'd been overheard.

He pulled her into his arms, and she felt his hand, steady and warm, on the small of her back. "My great-great grandfather would have stripped them both of their land and titles. I've half a mind to do so, myself."

Sera did not know where to place her hands. She glanced at other couples with her heart in her clumsy feet and shook her head with a kind of wordless misery. They were all looking at her and the king. The buzz of conjecture and speculation rose as the orchestra struck up the waltz and, because she and Nicholas just stood there, drifted into silence.

"I can't, I can't," she finally whispered, her cheeks flaming, feeling the disapproval that filled the room.

Nicholas pulled her closer. "Of course you can, love. Just feel the beat of the music and follow me."

"You don't understand. Those lessons you assigned me—I never had them."

Nicholas froze for the passing of one slow breath. Then he smiled, and with such tender humor. She wondered confusedly why it didn't seem to matter to him that beneath the scrutiny of his whole court, her body had turned to lead.

"Didn't like M. Gallopet, did you? Want to learn from me?"

"I'll disgrace you," she said to the top button of his waistcoat.

"No. You'll like it, I promise. Now, look at me and don't stop. The first thing we're going to do is think of a lovely revenge for Lord Effenby and Lady Tranevale. What will it be?"

Sera looked into Nicholas's eyes. At the twinkle of humor in them, her lips curved upward. "I wish to see them both with blanc-mange and claret—on their heads."

"Excellent! Keep that picture in your mind, and your eyes on mine, and follow." Nicholas nodded to the musicians, and they began to play again.

The music filled Sera and made her want to move with him.

"One, two, three," whispered Nicholas, and they were off, at first simply gliding forward and then backward to the beat of the music, and Sera had a delightful sense of flight and freedom within the rhythm of the waltz. Nicholas felt so warm and solid. She wanted to dance forever in the intimate hold of his strong arms.

"See? I knew you'd like it. Now for a few spins." And she was whirling, giddy and filled with music beneath the brilliantly glowing candelabra. She laughed and threw her head back. But suddenly, her foot caught on the hem of her dress.

Sera tripped, first over her own feet, and next on the long, trailing skirt. Nicholas caught her as she fell forward almost to her knees, clutching at his sleeves.

A few of the couples noticed and began to stare. At that moment, a footman made his way through the dancers carrying a tray of blanc-mange and claret. Aware of the sudden interest among the dancers in a particular spot, he stared straight at what they were looking at—Sera and the king. In doing so, he bumped into one whirling couple, stumbled, and lurched forward just as Lady Tranevale and Lord Effenby danced into his path.

Lady Tranevale clutched at Lord Effenby for balance and, straining against a force too powerful for his meager frame, Lord Effenby tottered. Lady Tranevale went down in a heap, Effenby followed, and the unlucky footman lost the tray. The entire ballroom, including the orchestra, froze, fascinated, as crystal goblets of claret and Limoges plates of blanc-mange sailed through the air, landing directly on Effenby's and Lady Tranevale's heads. A sticky trail of custard and sweet wine ran down their hair and into their faces like lava.

As footmen hurried to help them up, Nicholas stared speculatively. Then his lips quivered with repressed mirth. "Bull's eye," he whispered, escorting Sera off the floor.

Sera was horrified, and far more frightened than she had been that day she'd made fire, or when she'd caused a long gallery to tremble. Then, fury and hurt had roiled through her, and helpless against them, she'd let them loose on the world. She'd learned to control that force by calming herself, or calling forth her beloved Grandfather's image, to speak aloud her misery.

But now, merely a thoughtless wish had slipped out of her mouth, and the result was a cruel revenge because she still knew next to nothing about the power of the Gift bubbling through her blood! *Be careful what you wish for,* people said. Too late, she realized that an Aestron must never lightly wish for anything. "Might I be excused?" she asked him, trying in vain to keep the childish quaver from her voice.

"What is it, love? Surely you're not upset because two nasty idiots got what they deserved? Only their pride got hurt."

She couldn't think with Nicholas near. The half-conscious salute he gave her with his ironically raised brow indicated that he surmised she was responsible for this terrible accident. How could he still treat her so kindly?

"Let me escort you, my lady," said Nicholas. His voice was filled with concern, and it pierced her like a lance, to her very heart. He should be angry with her, furious, actually. If, for a moment, anyone else supposed the incident of the blanc-mange was anything but coincidence, she would be burned at the stake.

"Please, Nicholas, give me leave to retire," she said looking at his snowy cravat.

"You have my leave," he said on a helpless note.

Sera turned and walked from the ballroom floor, not

looking about her at the murmuring courtiers. Once out the large double doors, she fled, her steps echoing all the way down the corridor and up the stairs, until she slammed the door of her own room behind her.

She knew Effenby and Lady Tranevale were not alone in their opinion of her. Many called her a slave, a harlot, and an ignorant Hill woman. And their king had brought her to his palace, had given her an empty title, had heaped gowns and slippers upon her, and bade her come to the ball.

She had disgraced him and lowered him in the estimation of his people. She could hear the rumors beginning now.

"Clumsy, stupid Hill slave," they'd say.

"The king's witch," they'd eventually whisper, as the unruly Gift continued to evidence itself at embarrassing moments.

She needed help. She couldn't wait much longer for the thief. She had to go home.

***

After the waltz, it was necessary for Nicholas to remain in the ballroom, pretending that it was a perfectly ordinary event for a young lady to begin her dancing lessons at her first ball. He should be grateful to Effenby and Lady Tranevale for providing a spectacular distraction.

Had Sera's wish brought about their humiliation? Astounding if it were true. No, she couldn't have done it. Then he remembered the vase outside the family dining room that cracked the night she'd thrown his jacket in his face, and the way her horse had jumped that hedge. But again, he had the distinct feeling that she was shocked when the claret and blanc-mange began to fly. Silently, he cursed. Neither science nor logic could help him with this mystery.

How much magic did she have inside her? Would he ever understand the half of her? He realized with a start that he was far more concerned by the stark look of shame on her face after she had tripped than he was about what powers she actually had, and how they could help Laurentia.

Nicholas plastered an easy smile upon his face until he felt he could slip off to Sera without arousing undue speculation.

He had been a fool to put her into a situation that caused her pain. He vaguely remembered Sera saying that she had never heard opera or classical music. He had not once thought that there was some odd philosophical or religious aversion to music and dance among her people. He should have checked her progress with Gallopet before exposing her to ridicule.

After an hour of idle pleasantries, Nicholas went in search of Sera. Her room was empty. A rush of terror came over him. He looked out the window at the darkened park and saw the hard sheen of frost reflected in the full moon's light. Flinging the wardrobe open, he went slack with relief. Her gowns were still folded neatly on the wide shelves. Her ball gown was nowhere to be seen, which meant that she had not yet changed from it. Even in her present state of misery, Sera would have had the presence of mind to find a more suitable traveling costume before trying to escape.

But where to find her? He took the stairs to the wing opening out into the park. At the open doorway, he paused, examining the grass. The moon was bright enough to show the little indentations where small feet in satin slippers had crushed it down. He followed the footprints. It soon became clear that they were headed for the mews.

Nicholas opened the stable door and slipped inside. A lantern hung from a hook on the wall outside Wind Rider's stall, bathing the oaken walls in gold. He peeked into the stall. Sera sat in the straw between the chestnut's legs, her ball gown flowing about his feet. A bundle was propped against one corner, and she wore her blue woolen cloak. Her head was bowed, her forehead resting against Wind Rider's forelegs. The horse stood still as a statue. She was talking to Wind Rider, sad little words in the Hill tongue. Nicholas made out some the phrases: "hate me", and "want to go home", and "not safe" seemed to be her favorites.

He sank down beside her, his back against the wall and rested his arm on his knee. "Thinking of taking a little trip?" He tried to keep his voice as casual as he could, under the circumstances.

She kept her head bowed, presenting the definitive picture of dejection. "I don't have a cloak," she said in a small voice.

He was wise enough not to remind her that she was, in fact, wearing quite a warm cloak, hooded and lined with sable. One that he envied on this godforsaken cold night, when even in a stable warmed by the horses' huge bodies, a man's breath almost froze in the air. He shivered, looked about for a horse blanket and grabbed one from a rack outside the stall. He wrapped it around his shoulders. Sera still had her head bent. Restless fingers pleated her cloak.

He decided to take the initiative. He didn't relish sitting here till morning waiting for Sera to tell him what was making her so miserable.

"Do you hate music? Is that why you can't dance?" he asked her.

"We aren't allowed to have music like yours," she said, and he realized she must be shaken, indeed, to give him this much of an answer.

He took advantage while he could. "Why not?"

"It encourages the emotions to...wreak havoc upon the soul. We have bards who sing their stories, but only with certain harmonics and certain rhythms."

"Are you allowed to attend the theatre?" he asked carefully.

"I read about this theatre. The place where people pretend to be what they are not?"

"Sounds more like a description of my court," said Nicholas. "But yes, that is the theatre."

"Well, then, no. Long ago, actors and dramatic composers were not permitted at home. Now, at the festivals, we may watch the great tragedians, because they speak truth to the soul."

Nicholas tamped down his excitement. He'd have to tread carefully so he didn't frighten her into silence. "Who decides what is permitted?"

She gave a shrug. "Oh, the rules were decided eons ago, but if there is a problem, the Guardians and the Mage reach a decision."

He kept his tone nonchalant. "Through dialogue?"

She nodded, glanced sideways at him with forlorn hope in her eyes. "Nicholas, could you spare just a few men? To take me as far as the Arkadian mountains? I should be perfectly safe from there."

He put his arm about her, aware that he was holding her against him very hard. "I'm afraid not, sweetheart. After this is all over, I'll take you, myself. I should like to meet your grandfather. I want to tell him how much I honor and respect you. Do you think he would accept a meeting?"

She shrugged. "I want to go home, Nicholas," she said in a woebegone voice.

"I would miss you, Sera. Very much. Do you think you might miss me a little?" He turned her to face him and stroked her cheek.

Without seeming conscious of it, she leaned her face into his hand, rubbing against it like a kitten. "Yes, but I still want to go."

"Then I'll take you. Once the war is over."

"By then it will be too late," she said.

"Why?"

She leaned her head on his shoulder and gave a long, empty sigh. "I cannot tell you."

Nicholas pulled Sera closer still, rubbing his hand up and down her back in soothing repetition. But part of him was stung by her silence upon a matter of utmost importance to her, a matter that worried her, and one he could doubtless help her solve. It felt too much like rejection.

"Foolish woman," he whispered, rocking her gently. "Someday you'll let me take care of you."

Nicholas managed to get Sera back to her room without a rebellion. That was a good thing, for his mind was far too filled with questions and possible answers to manage the clever opponent Sera could be if she chose to oppose him.

He immediately went to his library to search out a dog-eared copy of Plato's *Republic*, which he had read as a boy of thirteen. Good God! It was all there—the exhortations against music that did not accompany poetry, the definition of permissible poetry as that which must describe only high character. And the description of the perfect state—one ruled by the intellectual elite and the philosopher king.

Nicholas wanted to shout with elation. The Hill people, whom Europe scorned as barbarians, were members of a secret, neo-Platonic society, based on reason and order and the search for truth. Hiding in plain view from the rest of the world. Untainted by greed, brutality, war. And, he would wager against any odds after matching wits with Sera, a society that upheld the equality of women in all matters.

***

The following afternoon, Sera was just changing into another of the confusing number of Outlander gowns she had to wear daily when she heard an impatient rap on her door. Nicholas flung himself into the room before she could even call out. She clutched the top of the tea gown together at the neck—at least she thought, given that the time was half past four, that this one was called a tea gown.

"Go away before somebody sees us," she hissed, pointing to the open door behind him.

Nicholas shut the door with a decided bang. "Not now, they won't." He sounded a bit hoarse, and his face was ruddy with cold and excitement as he crossed the room in his powerful stride.

"Here, let me do that," he said impatiently. His fingers brushed her skin as he fastened the tiny buttons with knowledgeable skill.

"Ooh, you are freezing cold." Sera shivered, half from the feel of his chilled fingers on her flesh, half from something else.

"It's bloody winter outside, or haven't you noticed?" he said, grinning. "Here, put on your cloak, and a bonnet, as well." He pulled the Russian sable down over her ears.

"The mercury's dipped so low, we've hit a record for November." He pulled her gloves over her hands as though she were a sluggish three-year-old, and shoved a muff into her arms. "Hurry up, now. We can't be late."

"But where are we going?" she asked, breathless from running across the great hall in an attempt to catch up with him.

"To the Abbey. Come on. We'll take the carriage."

She ran the last bit across the stones of the courtyard, and a groom helped her up into the great black carriage with the royal crest shining upon it. As it began to roll away from the palace, she said, "But Nicholas, what is it?"

"A surprise, and one I sincerely hope you'll like. You did imply last night that you don't hate music?"

"I like your music—the little I've heard."

"Good. I should hate to think I've made two damnably foolish blunders in less than twenty-four hours." Nicholas grinned, and Sera lost herself in thinking about how warm his eyes had become, and how young and handsome he looked.

"Here we are." The coach swayed to a stop. Nicholas

had the door open before the groom could open it for them. He waved the groom away, jumped down and held his hand out for Sera. Low in a cloudless blue sky, the sun blazed coldly through air sparkling with the promise of another frosty night. Sera put out her gloved hand. Nicholas ignored it and clasped her waist, lifting her down. When he had her on the ground, he tugged her along through the high arched wooden doors of Montanyard Abbey.

"Ah, we're in time," Nicholas said. The abbey's empty rows of chairs formed a silent guard. Millions of candles glowed beneath the vaulted ceilings. Sera walked down the rows of empty seats, trying to push her fur hat up farther from where it sat over her left eye, a result of Nicholas's enthusiasm and impatience. Nicholas stopped her in the center of the front row and motioned to a chair. When she was seated, he took the seat beside her.

"Music," he whispered to her. "For a prayer house."

Nicholas nodded to a man who stood a distance from them in the chantry. The man bowed low and tapped a stick on a podium in front of him.

He raised his hands and held them still in the silence. With one downbeat, then up, she heard it. Strings, again, but not the light, airy strings of last night's orchestra. These were somber, dark, solemn, rising in a four beat cadence to the steady thrum of her pulse as she was held, transfixed, upon the music.

Then suddenly women's voices, rising step by step along a scale, followed and darkened by the men's voices beneath them. *Kyrie eleison. Lord, have mercy upon us.* The voices rose, filling the abbey, repeating the cry. She was wrapped in the music, rocked inside it, helpless against its power.

The strings changed, softened their minor tone. A single voice soared above the rest. The modulation of pure, sweet sound filled her with ineffable longing. The voice went low— the range between its upper and lower notes seemed impossibly broad, even to Sera's untrained ear. Then it soared high again, bright, clear, against the very vaults of heaven. *Christe eleison. Christ have mercy upon us.* The women took up the chorus again, the men beneath them, flowing like timeless waters through a silent valley.

A short silence, and the voices rose in an exultant Gloria, thrusting her spirit against the barriers of the prayer house. She was bursting with it—the music, the candle flame, Nicholas beside her. It was too much. She wanted to cover her ears. She wanted to listen forever.

That sweet, strong voice burst into song again, playfully rising in a *Laudamus Te,* warbling, then deepening on those impossibly low tones, then rising upward again in clarion trills. Sera had never heard anything so beautiful in her life than this voice that dipped then soared higher than her soul had ever hoped to fly. *We praise Thee, we bless Thee, we worship Thee, we glorify Thee.* Such rapture, such exultant force.

Nicholas was looking at her. She could vaguely feel his eyes. He might have tapped her on the arm—she wasn't certain. Suddenly, his hands were on each side of her head, turning it toward the huge stained glass windows. Light blazed through them from the setting sun, filling them with piercing radiance. She rose and went toward the light, standing inside a rainbow of color.

The celestial music flowed over her. She raised her arms in her own silent hymn of praise. She might die of joy. The poets at home would understand just what this music, this blazing, sun pierced art, gave to the words of the mass. *We give thanks to Thee for Thy great glory.*

Time slowed, became as nothing. Had she been listening for a moment or a day? *I believe in one God, the Father Almighty, Maker of heaven and earth, and of all things visible and invisible.*

And finally, the choir filling her with the beautiful Hosannas.

The windows gave a last, brilliant blaze of color and slowly faded. The candles were a soft glow against the abbey's darkness. As she came to herself, she saw Nicholas slowly rise.

Nicholas felt as though everything was happening in slow motion, but in reality, he was at Sera's side only an instant after the last chord faded against the vaulted ceiling. His gaze centered on the play of emotions so clearly visible on her face. He pulled his handkerchief from his sleeve and mopped her cheeks. Strange, he had never seen her cry before, but now, the tears streamed unchecked and unnoticed.

The silence of the abbey stole over them. He felt a great satisfaction. She liked it—there was no doubt he had finally given her something she liked. He handed her the handkerchief. She dabbed at her eyes and blew her nose, and made all sorts of adjustments on her person, straightening her skirts, patting her hair into place beneath the Russian fur. She looked longingly at the chantry.

"Could we speak to them?" she asked.

"They would be delighted. Come." He felt himself expand like a balloon with pride. Sera's instincts were impeccable. He had chosen wisely, indeed.

She won over the choirmaster immediately, and the members of the choir were grinning from ear to ear.

Sera curtsied low before them. "To create such beauty is to achieve perfection. There is no greater goal on earth, and you have reached it."

"It is Mozart who created such perfection, Lady Sera," said the choirmaster. His eyes went very bright.

Nicholas took Sera's hand, resting it upon his arm. He gave his thanks to the flushed and beaming choirmaster. "It has been a long night and day," he told Sera. "Time for you to be home."

She walked beside him, her head bent, down candle lit aisles, past the statues of Saints and Madonnas, and through the high doors into the cold, clear evening air. Stars hung in the firmament, benevolent little lanterns in the dark dome of the sky. Sera climbed into the carriage and sat opposite Nicholas, her gloved hands clasping and unclasping upon her lap. Just as she lifted her face to look at him, the carriage rolled past a street lamp. She was incandescent as flame, her eyes the color of midnight. She stared at him with those huge eyes, her lips trembling on a smile, and then, abruptly, she flung herself across the carriage.

His arms caught her and held her close. His hands clasped the small of her back and the nape of her neck, where her hair hung in truant curls below the Russian fur hat. She kissed him madly, his eyes, his cheeks, the spot at the corner of his mouth that curved upward in what he knew must be a very foolish smile.

"Thank you, thank you. I wish I could think of a way to thank you properly. That you would give me such a gift! I shall never forget it, no matter where I am, or what happens."

He pushed down the shiver of apprehension her words

engendered. "Nothing's going to happen," he said in a voice that sounded rough to his own ears. "We shall be together forever, that's all." He held her cradled against his shoulder and looked into her face. The passing lantern light shot through the window, limning her lips, the soft contours of her cheeks, but her eyes were in shadow and unreadable. "It's fate, Sera," he said more fiercely than he had intended in his sudden apprehension. "Get used to it."

She raised her hand and laid it along the line of his jaw, and he tried very hard to unclench his teeth. "You are a romantic after all, Nicholas Rostov," she said. But her voice was sad.

He forced himself to smile, to lighten his tone. "If you wish to thank me, ride with me tomorrow. The day promises fine, and we shan't have many more like it."

"All right," she said and laid her head on his shoulder.

Good, thought Nicholas. He'd planned to get away, to rest and heal inside a warm, cozy place.

Like a bed, with a fine down quilt and Sera naked beside him.

He knew just where he would take her—to his hunting box a few hours outside Montanyard. And just how long he would keep her there. Sera might think that she was going to leave him, but he knew otherwise. And when she had been in his bed for at least a week, when she was limp from his lovemaking and completely tuned to his will, he would bring her back and call the Bishop into the palace for a wedding ceremony. With the world going to hell in a hand basket, he was justified in taking what he could.

Hell, if the generals found out where they'd been before the wedding, they'd applaud him. War was coming. The sooner he got her with an heir, the better for Laurentia.

He would notify the servants to provision the lodge tonight. And he would inform Andre of his plans, in case he was needed before he wished to return. When the carriage rolled to a stop before the palace, he sent Sera directly to her chambers where she would, he hoped, have a nourishing dinner and fall asleep immediately. If he had anything to do with it, she'd need every bit of rest she could get in preparation for the days to come.

Eleven

"What a glorious day," Sera said. She sat Wind Rider's easy canter alongside Nicholas's bay as they rode northeast from Montanyard. They had been out in the wind for two hours, but the sun was bright and warm. Nicholas said they'd reach their destination in another hour.

"Where are we going?" she asked.

Nicholas simply gave her a mysterious smile. "Someplace where we don't have to deal with the court. Good enough?"

"Better than good," she said. Only a few clouds laced the sky. Sera felt just like Wind Rider, who every once in a while kicked up his heels in a happy buck.

"This wind is making me hungry. Let's stop for tea," Nicholas said. He pushed an unruly lock of hair back from his forehead and glanced at her sidelong. In his warm houndstooth jacket cut in the English style and his simple brown woolen stock tie, he looked every inch the carefree, youthful aristocrat out for a country hack. He had tied his cloak behind his saddle, and he had insisted that Sera take one, as well.

Sera glanced up. Even as they spoke, more clouds had appeared in the sky. The wind gusted, and a cloud covered the sun. She shivered, looking forward to warming herself with food and her cloak.

"Is there a full English tea in the mysterious package you have in your saddlebag? How clever of you, especially when I could roast your lovely bay right now and eat him whole."

"A woman with an appetite—what a pleasure. And no, my dear Sera, this is not horseflesh, but the ambrosia of the gods," said Nicholas.

"Madame Torvell's wonderful tarts? Oh, bliss." Sera immediately squeezed Wind Rider into a halt. "This looks just the place, do you not think?"

"Glutton! This spot is completely open to the wind. If we stop here, any ploughboy coming home from the fields would see us. I could never steal a kiss from such a location."

Sera slanted him a look from beneath her lashes.

Nicholas was looking at her with a dark intensity that

made her stomach go fluttery. He looked as though he were hungry enough to eat *her*.

Playing at love was a heady thing. Those stolen kisses in the carriage had made her feel as though she had just taken a leap off a mountainside. She tried to remember caution, but it was too late for that. Whenever she was near Nicholas, a thrum of excitement vibrated through her blood. She squeezed Wind Rider into a gallop and threw her head back, drinking in the cold wind.

Nicholas gave chase. She could hear his deep laughter behind her. And then a sharp crack through the air, beneath the sound of hoof beat and wind. Another report, and then another, and the acrid smell of gunpowder came to her from behind. Nicholas had pulled even with her. "Run!" he shouted over the wind.

And she did, bent over Wind Rider's neck, his mane whipping against her face, the wind and her own fear spurring her on. Nicholas was beside her, pointing to the left, and Wind Rider swerved, narrowly missing a tree as they raced up the hillside, behind a cover of dull gray and evergreen brush.

The bitter wind buffeted her body with brutal force, and ice stung her cheeks. She looked up past the wind-blown branches at a lowering sky. Clouds coiled and roiled like sea serpents ready to strike. The sleet began in earnest,

Sera glanced over her shoulder once. She saw the haunts of her nightmares, black garbed from head to toe, gaining on Nicholas and her as they climbed the hill. She could hear the labored breath of Nicholas's horse behind her.

"Leave me and make for the top," shouted Nicholas. "Beyond is a road that will take you to a hunting box. Stay there. Somebody will come within a week."

Sera shook her head and kept going at Nicholas's slower pace.

"Damn it, woman. Leave me. That horse of yours is good for hours."

"I'm staying with you. I like the odds better," said Sera, controlling the tremor that shook her inside and threatened to spread to her lips. She gave him what she hoped was a brave smile.

Nicholas gave a growl of frustration. "Little fool! Stop being a damned heroine."

"You're stuck with me," said Sera. "So decide how to save us."

"Over there." Nicholas pointed to the left. "There's a deer blind behind those oaks. Hurry!"

She raced Wind Rider ahead. The blind appeared. She rode Wind Rider past it and found a post behind some trees and brush, but she didn't tie him to it. Instead, she slipped the saddle and bridle from the horse. If something happened to her, those snakes wouldn't be able to catch him. But they were following. They would find them.

They would kill Nicholas. Her heart almost cracked at the thought of all that beauty of mind and body, all that exuberant energy, draining with the bright flow of his blood into the ground. Her breath hitched in a sob as she realized what a precious place this alien world was because Nicholas was a part of it. Dear gods, she couldn't let him die.

She had to do something. She had to hide him.

Her soul opened, with an outpouring so great, she felt she must shout with the power of it. From deep within, from a lore passed down through generations—a lore she hadn't known existed, the words welled up inside her. She raised her arms high to the sky. In the ancient, formal language known only by the Mages, she cried out. *"Boreas of the North Wind, I charge you, in the secret name granted you by the gods! Anaisis, master of the storm! I charge you by the Gift surging in my blood! Come to me. Unsheathe your power. Give all unto my hand to work my will upon this place."*

The sleet fell harder, needles of ice that froze her cheeks. She wished snow, a blizzard of it, and the sleet grew light and softened into great flakes. The wind whipped them, swirling about her in a blinding haze of white.

Then Nicholas's strong hand was on her arm, pulling her back into the blind. As she checked the road below them for signs of the villains, he handed her something cold and heavy. She smelled oil and gunpowder. She didn't need to look down to know what she held.

Death.

Nicholas grabbed her hand. "This is no time for debate. And don't even think of having a fit of vapors. You'll shoot the damned thing, if you must, to save your life. Do you hear me?"

She nodded once. Her stomach made a queasy turn. *If the time comes,* she tried to reassure herself. *Not* when.

"Load this one while I shoot the other." Nicholas arranged the killing tools on the rock beside her. *Powder, shot, rod.* She despaired that she would forget, would kill them both simply because she was too much of a goose to remember correctly when it counted. The vermin were climbing now, their own horses stumbling on the uneven rock.

Nicholas grabbed her shoulder with his free hand and pulled her to him. She stared up into his eyes, slate-dark and intense, and he gave her a ferocious grin. Surprisingly, it gave her a shred of hope.

"You can do it," he whispered, and his lips covered hers in a fierce, hot kiss.

Sera heard the Brotherhood bastards curse as they climbed closer to the hiding place. There were too many of them.

"Hold this one until I ask for it," said Nicholas softly. "There's a good girl." He was kneeling on one knee, his pistol propped on his free arm. Except for the grim set of his mouth, he looked as calm as he had two nights ago in his ballroom.

The shot exploded with an ear-splitting reverberation. One of the men below slumped and fell. A horse reared on the steep mountain road and fell backwards, taking the rider down with him. Sera heard the crazed fear in the man's shout and then the snap of bone as the horse landed. The horse's body twitched, and she heard a moaning from beneath it. The others dismounted and fanned out, looking for places to hide. They skittered, black robed vermin slipping through the swirling white.

"Now," said Nicholas, his voice as calm as a summer sky. He handed her the pistol, still smoking. As she worked feverishly to load it, he aimed the other and fired again, and another man dropped from his horse, crying out in pain.

Powder, rod, shot, rod, thought Sera, working over the pistols as they were handed to her, handing them back again. She could not count the dead and dying. Even with animals like these, she couldn't think about their deaths. But Nicholas had fired several times, and he had given a satisfied grunt every time but one.

She could still see blurred movement through the slanting white curtain of snow. For once, that awful, unremitting black of the Brotherhood served to their disadvantage, for against the snow, they made easier targets for Nicholas. But one ran up to the blind, so close she could see the battle madness in his eyes. He gave a victorious shout and raised his pistol. Nicholas shot again. Sera watched in horror at the blood blossoming on the man's chest. With a groan, he dropped to his knees and then lay bleeding on the snow.

She bent to her work, choking back the nausea. *Load, pack, load, pack.* She could do it. Nicholas took careful aim at another fanatic who raced for the blind, screaming imprecations.

Sera caught a furtive movement to her left. Another was coming on Nicholas's blind side. His eyes—oh, his eyes—glittered with that madness that haunted her dreams.

It happened too fast for Sera to shout a warning. The terrorist raised his arm and aimed at Nicholas's back. Sera shoved Nicholas aside and aimed, squeezing the trigger. The malevolent gleam drained from the man's eyes, replaced by a look of surprise. He slumped and fell backwards in the snow.

"Oh, gods." Sera dropped the pistol.

Nicholas turned. "They're on the run."

Sera crept on hands and knees to the still body. A red stain spread from beneath it and tainted the snow's purity. His eyes were still open.

She stared, unable to turn away from his final question. "Why did you kill me?" his eyes asked. With shaking hands, she pulled the black mask down to his chin.

He was a boy, perhaps sixteen, with just enough blonde down on his cheeks to make an acceptable beard. He had a mother and a father somewhere, waiting for him to come home.

"Oh, gods, why wasn't I strong enough to hold him back?" She couldn't stop shaking. "What have I done? What have I done?"

"Sera." Nicholas's hands gripped her shoulders hard, making her rise. Hastily, he re-saddled and bridled Wind Rider. "We have to get out of here. They'll come back any minute and take us if we don't. All right? That's it, up on your horse, now. Here. Take my cloak. Put it over your own. You've had quite a shock. No, don't give it back to me. I don't need it."

Nicholas led her out of the blind, past the dead bodies littered in the snow. Sera gagged and clutched at Wind Rider's mane like a novice rider. The snow fell faster, almost a blizzard against a pewter sky. She followed Nicholas blindly, numb and cold in spite of the protective cloaks.

***

Jacob Augustus stared at his grandfather across the swirling surface of the scrying glass.

"They're safe for now," said Emmanuel. "The blizzard will shield them from the remainder of those beasts."

Jacob shook his head in frustration. "But she didn't know how to hide them forever. Untutored, she can't hope to use her power to its full extent." He was sick with regret that he'd left Sera alone to deal with all the changes inside her and all the terror around her. "Changing the elements didn't keep her safe from killing, Grandfather. She'll bear a heavy burden for that. And now, he'll get her lost in the snow."

"Not Rostov. He'll sniff his way to safety, even through a blizzard." Emmanuel lowered his head. "I had hoped that she would find what she needed out there. But I refused to ponder the horrors they work upon each other."

Jacob took a deep breath and calmed his mind. He thought past the last terrifying moments but came to the same conclusion he always had. "By all that's holy," he said. "Let me go to her now, before they destroy her entirely."

***

Sera held on as Wind Rider followed Nicholas through the blinding snow. The wind howled about her, sniggering and pulling at the heavy folds of the cloaks. Nicholas said nothing. Occasionally she heard him cough, a dry, hollow sound against the wind and the blowing snow. She had no idea how long they rode, only that she felt as though she were in Hades, wandering forever in the dim half night, never to be allowed to reach the isle of the blessed.

What have I done? If she shut her eyes, she could see that boy's face.

She was only half-aware when Nicholas halted his horse and helped her down.

"Go inside. I'll see to the horses. He gently pushed her toward a door.

There was light beyond the door, and a dying warmth. Nicholas would be cold when he returned, she realized dully. There was a great deal of wood stacked by a large fireplace at the end of the room. She piled logs upon the dying coals, glad that someone had started this fire. The Gift had exhausted her too much to start it as she had that day in her chamber.

Her cloaks grew heavy and sodden as the snow on them melted. She hung them to dry on chairs before the fire.

He came into the room several moments later. "Are you all right?" he asked, and then coughed again. "I'll do," she said, rising from her knees slowly. Her limbs trembled from the strain.

"You're shivering," she said, coming close and laying a hand on his forehead. "And hot. Is there a bedchamber in this place?"

"Several." He sounded slightly breathless. "Let's get you into the most comfortable one."

She followed him up the stairs, grabbing hold of the banister, like an old woman with arthritic legs. The gift had drained her, taking her strength with it. He led her into a beautifully furnished chamber where another fire was dying on the grate. As she added wood from the basket beside the mantle, Sera heard a loud thump.

Nicholas lay on the Turkish carpet, looking stunned. "Damn," he said hoarsely. "Damn, damn, damn."

"What happened? What is it?" She moved to his side, using her depleted strength to help him up.

"Oh, Christus," he said with a weak laugh, "of all the times..."

"Get out of these clothes," she said. Fear spurred her as she caught up a towel hung on a shaving stand and began rubbing his wet hair. Nicholas sat slumped on the side of the bed fumbling with the knot in his cravat. She lightly slapped his hands away and slipped the knot loose. His jacket and shirt were soaked through. So were his breeches from thigh to knee. By the time she got his clothes off and began to rub him down, he was shuddering.

"God, I'm cold," he whispered through chattering teeth.

"You've caught a chill," she said.

"Brandy." He coughed again, a racking, loose sound that seemed to tear at his insides.

"Absolutely not. Some soup, anything liquid. But no spirits."

"Damnit, woman, I'm cold. Get the brandy or I'll get it myself." He struggled to his feet and stood swaying like a drunkard. He seemed completely unaware that he was naked.

"The floor's cold. Where are my boots?" Nicholas looked down to find them and suddenly stumbled. "Oh, God," he groaned and sank back onto the bed. He struggled with the quilt. Sera pulled it up to his chin and sat beside him on the bed.

"Go away," he said.

"No. You have a nasty cough, and you're warm. I think you have a fever."

Nicholas turned his head away. In the firelight, she could still make out the pain on his face. "For God's sake, go away, Sera."

"Why?"

A tremor wracked him. "I can't bear for you to see me like this."

The shame in his voice made her want to take him in her arms and tell him he was quite brave and strong enough, but he would never believe her, not now. Instead, she busied herself about the room, dipping a cloth into the bowl and bathing him limb by limb, finding supplies in the kitchen and bringing tea and soup, and making him drink.

But these were things any Outlander could do. If only she could summon it, the Gift might heal him now. What if he got worse? She couldn't think about it. She sat in the wingback chair beside the fire, watching him, and praying. Soon, she couldn't even do that. In spite of her will, her eyelids drooped, and fell, and she slid into oblivion.

In the silent hour past midnight Nicholas slept fitfully. In late morning, he woke again, his breath hitching. Sera, awake for only a little time, brought him a posset she'd heated by the fire.

"Drink," she said.

He took a sip, then a long swallow. "That's good on my throat. What's in it?"

"Tea with honey, brandy, and a bit of laudanum."

"Drugging me, are you? Planning to have your way with me?" His smile faded. "Sorry. I had no right, even joking. Not now."

She didn't know what to do, what to say, when this black mood came on him. She had barely the strength to hold the drink. She had never felt this weary after using the Gift. When would it return? she asked herself in desperation.

He looked at her through fever heavy eyes. "How long have you been taking care of my needs?"

"Just through the one night." She had awakened several times during the night and seen to him, then collapsed back onto the chair, to sleep again.

"How much have you...had to do? Don't tell me. All of it, right?"

She knew he was thinking of the chamber pot. "You'd do the same for me," she said. "Stop being so silly. Even kings are human." She closed her eyes, felt for the power within her and found nothing.

Nicholas woke four hours later, fitfully tossing and moaning. Sera gave him more to drink and bathed his body again. He muttered and groaned as she lifted him to bathe his chest. He was barely able to lift his head. She sat down beside him and took his hand. It was frightening to see he didn't even have energy for pride any more.

"Shh," she said, smoothing his hair from his brow. She gave him a bit of the drug-laced tea. "I'll tell you a story from the Hills if you'll lie very still and try to sleep."

"All right," he rasped, tearing her heart.

"Once upon a time, a brave, handsome king rode into the Hills in midwinter and got lost there. He wandered through snow and sleet until he came to a waterfall that had frozen solid, a filagree of spume and ice. He was too cold, too weary to go any farther. He slipped from his horse, slapped it on the croup with his last strength, and lay down to die.

"But luck was with him, for a beautiful woman, the princess of a hidden world saw him through a magical glass in her study, and she called her father to her side.

"'See the Outlander, Father. He is a fine, handsome man, and I pity him. Bring him inside. Make him warm.'

"So her father took pity on the Outlander, for his daughter's sake, and brought him into the hidden land, where it was warm and the air smelled of blossoms, and they healed him. The first thing the king saw when he awoke was the beautiful princess, and he fell in love with her immediately.

"He began to court her, telling her of his fine palace and the wonders of his country. She was wary, not of the king, but of the Outlanders he ruled. But he spoke of his people with such love that she knew she would rather risk the dangers of his world to remain at his side than live in the safety of her home without him. So when spring came to the world outside the hidden kingdom, the king mounted a great stallion—a wedding gift from the princess's father. The princess mounted before him and they traveled down the mountains into the king's country. And all the people rejoiced that their king, whom they had thought dead, was home again."

"Then what happened?" asked Nicholas.

"Reality," said Sera. There was no need to tell him more. "Now go to sleep." She laid her head on the bed and closed her eyes, trying to find the Gift. It hid still from her, somewhere so deep within, she couldn't reach it. The fear became a palpable thing, clawing at her, mocking her impotence. She reached out for Nicholas, as though touching him would keep him from leaving her and crossing over to the Land of the Dead.

By mid-morning the next day, Nicholas's fever still raged. Sera stared down at his face. There were gaunt hollows beneath his eyes. His cheekbones showed prominently above the black stubble of his beard. She put her ear to his chest and heard the sounds she dreaded. His lungs made fine, crackling noises. When she tapped his chest, it gave back dull thuds.

"Nicholas, it's the pneumonia," she said to him. Nicholas didn't answer. He was unconscious.

"What am I to do? What am I to do?" Sera whispered. Oh, she couldn't bear it if he died. She searched deep inside, desperation adding some strength to that illusive essence men call the soul.

Fear shook her. She wasn't good at this yet. With great effort, she could mend an artery and slashed skin. But to heal a man so compromised!

She set her will and sent it deeper. The Gift responded, but it was weakened still from the battle with the

Brotherhood. She wasn't Grandfather. She didn't have the power of all the elders working in tandem. There was only her.

What would life be if Nicholas was gone from her? What foolish fear held her back from giving everything to save him? That she wouldn't succeed? If it cost her own life, she couldn't give him up without a struggle.

"At least we're alone," she told him, listening to his harsh breathing. "Nobody can accuse me of witchcraft here, can they?"

She disrobed until only her fine linen shift remained. The fire would blaze for a long time, she thought. She did not know how long it would take, or what the outcome would be. Her heart pounded in her chest so hard it hurt to swallow and to breathe. It didn't matter what happened. She couldn't let him die without a fight.

She slipped into bed beside Nicholas and took him into her arms. Gathering him as close as she could, she shut her eyes and put her arms around him. Downward she journeyed, through the bronchial tubes, into the lungs themselves. The infection pulsed and throbbed. Sera put her hands against his back, right above it, and let the peace possess her, maybe for an instant, maybe for an eternity.

The warmth welled up inside her, all golden and flowing into her hands. She pressed gently and let the light flow from her, along the path she directed past burning skin and lax muscle. Into the virulent mass it speared. She held on, sending the light sailing outward and into him on the current of her will, and saw beneath her closed lids the last of the fluid drain and the lungs heave and take their first easy breath.

After what seemed like eons, the glow dimmed and she felt again, this time the cool skin, the quiet rise and fall of Nicholas's back. He was sleeping, a healthful, healing sleep. Her limbs were heavy, almost paralyzed with the weariness of centuries. Beneath her heavy lids, color played, light red reflecting the fire. She snuggled closer to Nicholas. It took almost more energy than she possessed just to smile.

"I love you," she whispered and let the darkness take her.

***

Nicholas didn't want to open his eyes. He was so comfortable. There was only a bit of chill on the tip of his nose, but everything else was deliciously warm. His lungs felt better than they had these three weeks. He took a deep, satisfied breath and buried his nose against warm, scented hair. Sera. He felt Sera's arms wrapped tightly around him. Even in her sleep, she held him here with her.

He opened one eye. It was growing dark outside the window. The blizzard still raged, thank God, sheltering them from the Brotherhood fiends. The chill he felt on his nose was the room cooling rapidly. He glanced at the fireplace; it held only dying coals.

He slid from beneath the covers and threw on a robe hanging in the armoire in the opposite corner. Hastily, he made up the fire until it was a cheerful blaze, warming the room. Sera lay still in the great bed, her breath the even inhalation of deep sleep.

She must be exhausted after all she'd been through...when? Yesterday? Whereas he felt fit enough to traipse through the woods, hunting bear and pheasant to bring her for dinner. He walked to the bed and stroked Sera's shoulder through the thick, warm fall of her hair.

"What the devil did you do to me?" he asked her dreaming form, not really expecting an answer. Yet.

Nicholas bathed. He frowned at the sight he saw in the mirror, all wild hair and long, dark stubble. Hastily, he got out his razor. At least when Sera awoke she would see the old Nicholas, clean and groomed. A little too late for all this now, he thought, and cringed at the realization that she must have nursed him and cleaned up after him when he lay helpless as a babe.

Sera stirred in the big bed, rubbed her eyes and rolled over on her side, promptly burrowing deeper to go to sleep again. Nicholas wasn't having any of it. He wanted answers, and he wanted her too sleepy to be clever about the truth. He crawled into bed and rolled her over to face him. Then he shook her shoulder lightly.

"Wake up, Sera."

"Mm-mm. Too tired."

"Just a few questions and then you can sleep again."

"What?" She opened her eyes and stared at him owlishly, but the lids slipped shut again almost immediately.

He shook her shoulder again. "What did you do to me?"

"When you were sick?" she mumbled.

"Uh-huh. What did you do?"

She opened her eyes again, like a drunk trying to focus. "Set you to rights."

"What?" His bark of laughter seemed to jar her awake a little more.

"I set you to rights, Nicholas. Now let me sleep." She tried to roll away, but he wouldn't let her.

"How?"

"I put my hands on you."

"You healed me with your hands," he said flatly. He couldn't believe it.

"You were dying, Nicholas. I couldn't have that, could I?" She gave a yawn. "I'm so tired."

"All right, love. Go back to sleep."

Sera rolled over and tucked her hand beneath her cheek. She fell asleep in an instant. Nicholas kissed her forehead and tucked the quilt around her. "Little magician," he whispered. "I'm not done with you yet."

Nicholas descended the stairs and went straight to the stable. The snow was beginning to let up a bit as he trod a path to the stable and saw to the horses' care. When he returned, he deposited his saddlebags inside the front door and then carried wood in from the neat stack beside the outer wall of the hunting box.

His stomach chose that moment to make itself heard—loudly. He was ravenous. It took little time to prepare a tray of salted ham, cheese, and rich brown bread from the pantry. As he pulled the cork on a fine Pinot Noir, he remembered Mrs. Torville's sweets and added one to the tray. Slinging a saddlebag over his shoulder, he carried the picnic upstairs to the master bedroom, where he could watch over Sera until she awoke.

After lighting a brace of candles, he settled into a comfortable library chair and opened one of the books he had brought in his saddlebag, the old, battered copy of Plato's *Republic*. He munched a sandwich and read with a great deal of interest what had bored him silly in the classroom.

He read for hours in the cozy room, waiting eagerly for Sera to awaken. Night wore on. Sera stirred, shifted and sat up. Her eyes were large in a pale, drawn face. Whatever she had done to him last night had taken a toll.

"Hullo." Nicholas smiled at her and put down the book. He had looked at her dozens of times while she slept, trying to still the heat that surged in his blood for her. Now that she was awake, he had a difficult time meeting her eyes.

"I've been thinking you might like some privacy. There are gowns and those frilly things women wear in the armoire and warm water for bathing in the pitcher. Take your time. I'll wait for you downstairs. Dinner's not very elegant, but hearty, nonetheless."

He took the tray and the books downstairs with him. He waited nervously for her below, wondering which inevitable change in Sera's attitude would destroy him more—embarrassment at having seen him at his worst, or pity for his frailty.

She evidently made a quick toilette, for she appeared on the stairway twenty minutes later. "What is this place?" she asked him, taking in the fine furnishings, the elegant paneled walls, the tiled Russian stove warming the room even more than did the fireplace.

"My hunting box.

"She cast him a wary look. "Why are my gowns in the armoire?"

There was no way out of it, now. He looked at her, rosy and scrubbed like an innocent schoolgirl, her hair giving off a halo of warm light against the candle glow. He thought of the mess he must have been for—what was it, two long days and nights? She knew it all now, everything about his wretched body—his terrible, flawed lungs, the weakness that betrayed him and her in a situation fraught with danger.

"I...um...I'm afraid I wanted you all to myself for a few days. I had the place stocked and our clothing brought here. Aren't you glad to have them?" he asked as smoothly as he could.

She refused to be turned from the immediate subject. "Do you mean that you wished to take me to your bed, Nicholas?"

Direct, as always. Hell.

"Yes. But of course, I would not expect such a thing now. Not after you saw me succumb."

She came so close he could catch the scent of her, the damnably arousing perfume of flowers in a spring meadow.

"Succumb? You speak of pneumonia as if it were drink or gambling. 'Tis not a vice."

"Isn't it?" He turned away from her, filled with shame and a sense of loss. His voice sounded loud in his own ears. "To be so puny that one cannot even take care of his own needs? If I had been vigilant, given it enough time and rest before I brought you here, it never would have overcome me. But I was an impatient fool. You needn't worry. After what you've seen of me, I'll not ask you to share my bed, nor—"

Her light slap between his shoulder blades brought him up short. "I swear I shall go mad from your absurd self-flagellation," Sera muttered.

"Sera, how do you think I feel?" he ground out, turning and taking her shoulders, shaking them a little. "If they had come last night or the night before, I would have lain there like a slug while they took you. You think I can look at myself in the mirror knowing I was worthless? God! I resembled an overgrown infant more than a man, and you saw it all."

Her eyes flared with hot anger, surprising him. "Fool! Fool, to think I would care about any of that. What would you have had me do? Let you die because you're not fit? What is 'fit'? To be a man like your father, who would not even speak to his daughter? Who must have tormented you so that you feel you must be perfect always?"

She broke away from him and walked to the fire, hugging herself, a forlorn, stiff silhouette against the glow. "I don't think I can bear this nonsense," she whispered, more to herself than to him.

Suddenly, she whirled on him. "Nicholas, do you think that only you are allowed to feel shame? I couldn't keep you safe. I couldn't hide us well enough. And so they got through."

She took a shaky breath. "I killed a man," she said in a low voice. "Had he been aiming at me, I would not have done it. But he was about to shoot you. Nicholas, do you have any idea what you mean to me? That I would *kill* for you? So don't tell me how you're not 'fit'. Don't think me so stupid as to want you strong and beautiful every minute of your life. Just take me in your arms and help me get through the night."

Sera hid her face in her hands and sobbed as though

her world had blown up about her.

He shuddered at the sounds, holding tightly to his own control. "You'll regret it in the morning," he said shutting his eyes. But her sobs battered at him.

"By all the gods, stop being so damned noble!"

Pride and shame were no match against Sera's need. He came to her and opened his arms. She flung herself against him, clinging while he covered her eyes, her cheeks, her mouth with kisses. "Hush now. It's over. Sera, don't cry. I can make you forget. We'll help each other forget."

He lifted her in his arms. She leaned her head on his shoulder, giving herself up to him, accepting him. She was light as he carried her up the stairway and into the bedroom. Small and precious in the middle of the big bed when he laid her down.

He slipped off her shoes, pausing to stroke his hand up the arch of her foot, hearing her swift, indrawn breath. And then he sank into the mattress beside her. Her blue eyes, dark and fearless in the light of the candelabrum, looked straight at him and into him. No darkness could dim the radiance of her hair. He pulled the pins from it and spread it in a golden cloud on the pillow.

Combing his fingers through the silken veil, he tamped down the surge of heat in his groin. "I've imagined you this way for so long—from the first, I think. Just like this."

She said not a word, just lay there waiting for him, breaking his heart with the trust in her eyes. There was no sound but the hiss of the logs on the fire. The world, with all its condemnation, lay outside this room, outside this bed. But here, there was a haven, where there was no weakness that couldn't be forgiven, no need that couldn't be fulfilled.

He reminded himself to go slowly, but he had wanted her for so long. He feared to lose control. Direct as always, Sera unbuttoned his shirt and began to stroke his chest, learning him. Her touch was like a brand, searing his skin. He had to push her hands away and imprison them both with one of his. It had to be special for her.

"No. This is going to last," he said. He rose on one elbow and stroked the fall of gold on the pillow. "I want to see you. I want to make you feel everything."

"Yes," she told him.

Yes. To her it was all so simple. She cared about him.

Him. Not his wealth, not his power, not his failings.

Outside the window, the blizzard ruled. He had all night to make her forget everything but this room, and him.

Sera looked up into Nicholas's face as he leaned over her in the bed. His eyes, dear gods, his gray eyes, beneath the straight brows, had deepened to the color of slate. His lids were heavy, the dark, fringed lashes hiding his thoughts when she wanted to know everything. Then he gave her a look so heated her heart skittered into a faster beat. She pushed, and the soft linen of his shirt fell open, revealing a strong throat and broad chest, both darker than the white cloth and lightly furred with hair. His skin gleamed gold in the light of the fire. How could he not see how strong he was, how beautiful? She lifted her face to his neck and kissed the hollow of his throat. He gasped as her tongue found heat and soap and clean male— Nicholas's taste filled her, and she found it delicious.

"Let me pleasure you," he whispered, a deep rumble that made her catch her breath. "Let me show you how it can feel, how you can feel." His hand supported the back of her neck. He planted teasing kisses on her cheek, her chin, tasting the corner of her mouth with his tongue, his kisses light and sweet, a wicked, knowing seduction below her ear. His mouth covered hers in a searing kiss, and her lips parted helplessly beneath a deep exploration that left her mindless of anything but his strength, his mastery. After a long time, he broke the kiss. She gave a soft cry of disappointment. And felt his breath, the warmth of it.

"Take off your gown, sweetheart. I have to see you."

"All right." His hands helped her with the tiny buttons she couldn't open because she was trembling, torn between desire and a sudden, wrenching self-consciousness. In the harem, he had thrown his cloak at her and ordered her to cover herself. Did he find her ugly then? Would he find her ugly now?

She sat up and slowly lowered the bodice of her gown. He had risen to his knees, and his hands closed beneath her elbows, lifting her higher, until she, too was kneeling facing him on the bed. When he tugged at the gown, it slid down her torso and gathered about her hips in folds of soft wool. Sera shut her eyes against the possibility of his disappointment. Nicholas said nothing. He only slipped his hands down her shoulders, easing off the sleeves of the thin linen shift to follow the gown. She knelt there, exposed, hot with blushes in the fire lit room. She peeked at him, trying to determine his reaction. Pride alone kept her back straight as his eyes slowly perused her body with intense concentration. His eyes closed as he took a deep, shuddering breath.

Sera gave a whimper of defeat and grabbed the gown up again. Nicholas's eyes sprang open. "No," he said, pulling the dress down and then sliding his hands down the outline of her body.

"Why did you shut your eyes?" No more lies, even if it hurt to hear the truth.

"I had to stop wanting—Sera, it'll scare you."

Curiosity and fear warred as she took in the heat in his eyes. "What?"

He touched her then, a slow stroke of his forefinger from shoulder to collarbone and down, over the swell of her breast, circling once, and then rubbing with his thumb, and not once did he look away. His gaze locked upon her as though she were the only precious thing left in the world. And she—she couldn't hide what that soft abrasion did to her. Her body thrust forward against his hands. Her face, no doubt, reflected her every wanton response.

Slate darkness in candlelight, his gaze held her captive while he rubbed the nipple between thumb and forefinger. Sparks of heat shot to her belly, and farther down. She had a difficult time holding on to thought.

He watched her with a fearsome stillness. How could she reveal how wild, how lost she was to the heat he engendered with his clever hands? He would be appalled. Certainly, any Hillman would expect more dignity from his mate.

But desire overwhelmed her. She turned her head away, losing herself in fiery spurts of pleasure from that lascivious stroking.

"Look at me." His voice was a warm whisper against her ear, carrying her up on a spiral of urgency. She dared a glance into his eyes. Burning, intent, they left her helpless and imprisoned. His beautiful lips curved in a smile that knew all about her.

Oh, yes, he knew. Knew he had enslaved her at last. Knew she had no thought of making him stop—that she could not bear it if he stopped.

"We were discussing what I want to do," Nicholas reminded her, lifting her breasts with his hands, staring intently at the tight buds of her nipples.

"Yes," she said again, grasping at the spider web threads of his words.

"The same thing I wanted when I saw you for the first time at Iman Hadar's palace." He cleared his throat. "To come into you, as deep and hard as I could." The words came out in a low growl. His face looked different, leaner, strained, as though he were in pain. His gray gaze held her, a brigand's gleam in shadow.

"Oh." She raised her hand to his chest, to the springy hair and the solid muscle there, so different from her softness.

"No. Don't touch me...yet." He covered her hand with his own and brought it back to her lap, lingering there with his own hand, brushing through the wool, against the juncture of thigh and that private place, igniting hot fire where all the feeling centered.

"Just 'oh'?" His lips quirked. "Where's the bold Sera who challenged me?"

"Trying to touch you. I don't understand. What is this 'no'?"

"If you touch me, it'll be over before it begins." He gave a low laugh that turned into a groan and took her face in his hands. "One time, Sera, just once, trust me to do something without your help."

So soft were his lips as they molded her mouth. His body bent over her, finally close enough to touch, but he wouldn't let her touch him. He held on to her hands, pressing them to her sides while his tongue tasted and his teeth nibbled at her lower lip.

Sera arched her body and rubbed her breasts against his chest, feeling the soft tickle of his hair against her nipples. She was aching for more where he had touched her so lightly. He tumbled her back on the sheets, tasting her mouth, groaning when her lips parted for him.

Following her down, he covered her body with his, and she felt his thigh, long and muscled between her legs, and him, full and hard against her. No more teasing kisses now. His tongue plunged into her mouth in the rhythm his body took, pushing against her, urging her to move against him in the same beat. It was heavy, his body's demand, and sweet, too, the way he cupped her breast, stroking with his fingers, following with his mouth. His tongue curled around the nipple, and she cried out, rising up to him.

He'd freed her arms. She threaded her fingers through his hair. Oh, it was soft and thick and warm with life. The very bone of his skull felt smooth, finely wrought and solid beneath her fingers. She couldn't think, she could only feel the tug of his mouth as he suckled at her nipple, his heat pumping against her, so strong and eager and alive that she felt only joyous desire. Alive, she thought dimly. They were both of them alive.

Her hands fluttered from his hair down the strong, corded neck. She fumbled with his shirt and tried to tug it off over his wide shoulders.

Nicholas felt Sera's haste, and he wanted it, wanted her eager, and no more barriers between them. Rolling to the side of the bed, he sat up and pulled the shirt over his head, ripping stitches in his haste. He was so hard and swollen, he feared he'd never peel his breeches from his hips. He rose and made the mistake of facing Sera. She stared at him with wide eyes.

God—he had to get them off before her eagerness gave way to virginal fear. He turned his back to her, ripped a seam at the ankle and shoved with his feet. He lunged back into bed, hiking the sheet over his nakedness before he rolled to face her. *Don't stop, don't stop* he thought.

She was biting her lip. "You are... rather larger than the statues," she said in a voice that trembled just a little.

"Sweetheart, I won't do anything you don't want me to," he whispered just before he kissed her. And prayed he wouldn't be damned as a liar.

Miraculously, she relaxed against him with a sigh, and his tongue swept in to taste her sweetness. She moved restlessly beneath him, and he knew she wanted his hands on her, thank God. He stroked the soft swell of her breasts and studied her face. His touch—his kiss—brought the haze of passion back to her eyes.

"Your skin—it's softer than velvet." He traced the perfectly rounded contours of her breasts with his fingers, saw the flush cover them—pink on gold, like the opening petals of a blushing rose. He tasted her and drove her with lips, teeth and tongue, pushing her up into the vortex.

He wanted her need to match his own.

He had begun this thinking he could redeem himself a little. To help her forget. That had lasted for about a minute. Now, he couldn't stop, even if the world ended. In the worst way, he wanted to postpone the act until she writhed beneath him, screaming with pleasure. And in the worst way, he wanted to spread her wide and seat himself to the hilt inside her tight heat.

"Off," he said, grabbing gown and shift at her waist as he nipped kisses at the underswell of her breast. With one quick tug, he had it at her knees, and with another, completely off and onto the floor. Nothing impeded his view of long, slender legs, tiny waist, and rounded hips.

"Beautiful," he breathed. His hand cupped her, stroked through the curls between her legs. She shut her eyes and rolled her head away from him, moaning and trying to hide from his gaze at the same time. Not enough—it was imperative that she recognize him.

"Look at me," he demanded again, and she opened her eyes, her vision focusing on the intensity of his gaze. "Watch what I do to you. I am the one making you feel this, Sera. I am your first lover. Your only." He lowered his head, tracing his tongue down to her belly. The warmth in the room and her own heat gave off her secret scent. He breathed it deeply and rubbed his face against her belly, feeling the smooth satin of her skin against his cheek.

She didn't fight his progress. No, she helped him, lifting against his mouth, her hands on his shoulders, kneading, making small, helpless cries. He settled between her legs, brushing his mouth against the soft curls.

"Gold here, too," he said. "Such a beautiful part of you."

Sera entered a place where every feeling was magnified until it was almost too strong to bear. Oh, the sound of his deep sigh, and then the tickle of his fingers as he parted her, stroking once up the cleft, showing her the pearly drop of moisture on the tip of his finger, outlining her lips with it, and then rising to kiss her, his tongue tasting. Oh, the way he lowered his head again to that heated core and used his tongue, holding her still with his strong hands, commanding her on a rasp of breath not to move when she was mad to thrust up against him, to demand more.

And how he entered her—one finger, then two, burning

and pressure, his fingers thrusting, his thumb circling where his mouth had been, his lips covering her nipple and suckling in rhythm. She cried out in ecstasy. He made a deep, hungry sound, as though he wanted to possess her, to know her so intimately, that surely this was more than simple lust. His head lowered to her breasts and burrowed in the valley between, and she heard his smothered groan, felt his breath, his warm weight, and all the while, his fingers stole reason from her. She could hear herself coming apart, sobbing to him to give her release from this wonderful, maddening pleasure.

He lifted his head from her breasts. His eyes snapped open, riveting her with his gaze. "Let it happen," he ground out. "Let it come."

Frightened by the enormity of the urgent spiral building and building, she reached out helplessly for him, her anchor in the storm that buffeted her body. She rolled her hips, lifting to take his fingers deeper, and he stroked her until her legs trembled.

"Now," he said, and the lightning burst through her, again and again, throwing her into space with its force.

Suddenly, he reared over her. She hung on a pinnacle of sensation and felt his hard heat at the juncture of her thighs, felt him thrust slowly, inexorably, into her, felt the pain mixing with the pleasure. She hurt, but she wanted this entry, this hot, complete possession.

His lips nibbled at her, soft kisses on her lids, her face, her mouth. And all the while he pressed into her, past a place of pain where she cried out. When he was deep inside her, filling her completely, he held himself still above her, taking his weight on his elbows with a tensing of his biceps and a grimace, as though he felt the same pain. She waited, caught in that net of feeling, wishing he would tell her what to do. And he lowered his face and kissed her hard, almost bruising her mouth. He lifted his head and held her gaze with his. Finality and a joyous triumph leaped into his eyes.

"You're mine, now. You belong to me."

She looked at him, helpless, but his dusky lashes swept down to hide his eyes, and he lowered his head to her shoulder, biting her lightly, stallion to her mare. She gave to him, raised her arms and put them around his shoulders as far as she could reach. That motion released him. He began to move inside her, thrust and retreat. There wasn't much pain, now, but an ache, a tension, and she moved restlessly against him, trying to help him, to keep him deep at the height of his thrust.

He must have sensed it, this new emptiness she wanted filled. Perhaps he was beyond anything but the demand of his body, because he put his hands beneath the small of her back and pulled her up against him with every thrust, quickening the rhythm, his breathing harsh in her ear. His hands slid lower, kneading and lifting her buttocks. She wanted release from this overwhelming lust. She could hear his rasping breath, her own sobs. He raised himself away from her just a little, still moving inside her. He watched her reactions with such an expression on his beautiful face. She felt completely naked, far beyond shame or self-protection.

She trusted him. She did. And in that instant of recognition, she gave him what he wanted. With a cry of surrender, never shutting her eyes, she let him see the earthquake burst free and lift her out of herself. He groaned deep in his throat and thrust one last time, his back arched, his face drawn in pain or ecstasy, she could not tell. He held there above her, and a shudder wracked his body. He was as high and deep as he could go inside her. She shut her eyes, sighing, and felt his gift, the vital, surging warmth of his seed.

Nicholas gave a ragged sigh and lowered himself until his body covered her from head to toe. Still joined, he rolled to his back, taking her with him. She could feel heat, the beaded moisture where her cheek lay against his chest, and lower, where she was slick from lovemaking and him. He said not a word, but lay with his limbs relaxed, his heartbeat slower now, and steady against her ear. She stared at the fire shadows dancing on the wall and despaired.

Everything was changed. She was no longer Sera, the Mage's granddaughter, or Sera the captive, or Sera, the combative friend of a king. All of those Seras had wanted one thing above all—to go home. But dear gods, how could she ever leave him now?

Twelve

Nicholas awoke to the sounds of muffled hoofbeats. "Sera!" he said as he leaped from the bed and grabbed the pistol he'd placed on the bedside table the night before. But she only muttered and pulled a pillow over her head.

Nicholas peered through the window. The snow had abated, giving him a good view of the riders who rounded the corner of the barn. They wore the resplendent red tunics and navy breeches of Laurentia's cavalry. Andre rode at the head of the full troop, his face drawn and pale with worry. Dismounting with a few of the officers, he tried the front door, which Nicholas had locked. Andre produced a key and slipped it into the lock.

Nicholas grabbed his trousers. As he lifted a leg to put them on, he saw that his thighs were stained with Sera's blood. He looked at the bed. Sera still slept beneath the quilts. What with his illness, and last night...well, he must have worn her out. Nicholas knew he ought to waylay the men at the foot of the stairs. But an idea occurred to him that would get him exactly what he wanted. His Rostov mind seized upon it, quickly turned it this way and that to look for flaws, and found none.

Sera was the most stubborn woman he'd ever known. He needed an incident that would clearly illustrate their situation to her and the obvious solution to it. And here it was, climbing the stairs.

He tried to keep the grin from his face as he tumbled back into bed and took Sera in his arms, slipping the quilt down just enough for the men bursting into the room to have an excellent view of one pink, naked little shoulder.

The noise of the door almost flying off its hinges brought Sera awake in his arms with a jerk. She struggled to sit up, but Nicholas held her fast against him, keeping the quilt well over her breasts.

"What is the meaning of this invasion?" he thundered at the gape-jawed men who stood around the bed.

"Sire, our apologies," stuttered Captain Oblomov, the soldier who had followed Sera about in Selonia. His face wore the look of a man who wanted to cry. He bowed stiffly, first to Nicholas and then to Sera, who finally grasped her situation and burrowed deeper beneath the quilts. The men followed Oblomov's example and retreated from the room, almost falling over themselves in their hurry.

Andre, giving Nicholas a fierce look, was the last to leave.

"They're gone," said Nicholas as he went in search of Sera. He found her halfway down the great bed. "Come out," he coaxed, gently tugging her up against him. "You'll suffocate under there."

She batted his hands away, but he was insistent and stronger than she. When she finally surfaced, he took her into his arms and held her there for a long moment.

"I've ruined you," she said dully.

He did grin, then. "I think it's the other way around, love."

She shook her head against his chest. "Not with your court, it isn't." He hated the bleakness in her voice. She actually believed that nonsense.

"Most members of my court are full of praise for you. However, it's also true that I've ruined your reputation, not mine. I'm afraid there's only one solution, Sera."

She looked so trusting, worrying her lower lip and staring up at him, that he had a real pang of conscience— for approximately an instant.

"You'll have to marry me, sweetheart. I believe it will take a few days to make all the arrangements. Obviously, we cannot wait much longer. The gossips will have quite enough on their plates when this gets out."

"Couldn't we simply ask the men who entered the room not to speak of this?" She sat up in the bed, not even aware in her agitation that the quilt had dropped to her waist. Her nipples tightened in the room's cold air.

Nicholas pried his gaze off her breasts. "I'm afraid it's too late for that." He put both his arms around her and leaned toward the window beside the bed. Safely shielded by his back, she could peek out and see an entire regiment of cavalry shaking their heads and muttering.

"I believe they all want to call me out for this," said Nicholas, feeling extraordinarily cheerful.

"No."

"Well, of course they can't actually do so, but their faces, love. They're positively grim."

"No, I won't marry you."

"What do you mean, 'no'?"

"I won't do it to you, Nicholas. Many powerful nobles already doubt your good sense in making me your friend. If you marry me, they will begin to ridicule you. A few will whisper that I bewitched you. Then someone will hear about your illness and call me a witch in all seriousness. And then you will no longer be safe from your own people. Believe me, I know what I'm talking about." She scurried out of the bed and grabbed her shift, pulling it over her head.

"How can you think for one minute that my people would react to you—to me—that way?"

"Don't treat this lightly, Nicholas. It has happened before to kings who were just as kind and just as clever." She finished buttoning her gown as she spoke and bent to the floor to slip on stockings and shoes. She threw him a dressing gown and went to the door.

"Hurry," she said. "I shall wait in the next chamber while you dress and go below to speak to them. Perhaps they will accept your taking me as a mistress, Nicholas. But they will never accept me as their queen."

"Damn!" Nicholas muttered as the door quietly shut behind Sera. It took but a moment for him to dress and take the stairs. He had not expected this amount of resistance. It was evident that she wanted him as much as he wanted her. And she cared about him, damnit. She did. How long would it take to change her mind?

***

After their return to the palace, Andre poked his head into Nicholas's study late in the day. Nicholas glanced up from the book of jewelry illustrations he was perusing. "Where is Sera? Still hiding?"

Andre shot him another of the black looks he'd been giving him all morning during the ride back to the palace. "She won't even let Katherine in to see her. How could you do it?"

"Oh, do let off, Andre. Even if she'd been sleeping in another bedroom, she would still have been utterly ruined. I simply wanted to clarify the issue for her."

Andre let out a whistle. "My God. You're going to marry her."

"On Saturday next, to be precise. I've seen to most of the arrangements." At Andre's grunt, he looked up quickly. "You don't disapprove of the match, do you? The people love her. She has an extraordinary gift, Andre. What she did for me was truly—well, she'll be Laurentia's secret weapon."

He grinned, full of satisfaction over the outcome of their adventure.

Andre frowned. "It's just that, well, I assumed that you would be more...I don't quite know how to say this, but it appears that you're approaching your wedding without a whit of sentiment."

Nicholas raised his brows in surprise. "Obviously, I desire Sera. I respect her. Laurentia needs her." He glanced down at his book again, then slowly raised his gaze to Andre's perplexed face. "You don't expect me to blather some poetic nonsense about love, do you?"

"Something on that order might be nice for Sera to hear," Andre said.

"I wouldn't insult her with such a lie. Kings can't love. Why, what if something happened to her, and I fell apart? What would become of Laurentia?"

Andre gave him a long look. "Sounds to me like you're scared, Nikki."

"Nonsense!" He realized he was shouting. Clamping his mouth shut, he motioned Andre toward the desk, and pointed to the book. "But the necklace," he said, keeping his voice calm and cool. "I can't seem to find what I want in the Jewel Tower. And I want it before the opening ball."

Andre, apparently reluctant to accept the change of subject, sighed loudly enough to almost ruffle the book's pages. "There's a merchant just come to town yesterday. A jewel merchant reputed to have the most beautiful ruby in the world. He's made discreet inquiries at the palace. Shall I arrange an interview?"

"A ruby, eh? Yes, that might do. Something better than those cold, lifeless diamonds. I'd be grateful for your help, Andre. In the matter of the necklace, and in other things as well...Listen to this: 'It follows from what we have just said that, if we are to keep our flock at the highest pitch of excellence, there should be as many unions of the best of both sexes, and as few of the inferior, as possible, and that only the offspring of the better unions should be kept.'"

"What is that?" Andre picked up the book and flipped through it. With a laugh, he dropped it into Nicholas's hands again. "Plato? On the getting of children? Perhaps I should have paid more attention to my Greek translations."

"It sounds as though he was proposing some kind of superior race—one slowly developed through time. And what do you make of this?" Nicholas picked up another bound volume, this one in Latin, and translated, "*An Historical and Mythical Study of The Ancients.*

"*'After Alexander the Great utterly destroyed the city of Thebes, the Council of Athens convened, for they saw the end to their democracy.*

"*So they sent out a colony of citizens, youths graced with mental and physical acuity—and maidens of high virtue and beauty, athletes, craftsmen, sculptors, philosophers. To these they gave the laws and the great works of the city. Their duty was to disappear from mankind, to form a perfect society in which greed, brutality, and all manner of baseness was seen no more. These men and women were never heard from again.'* "

Nicholas closed the book and stretched his legs in front of him, slumping back in his chair. "Would you think it lunacy to believe that there might be a superior race of people hiding in plain view of the world? That they have managed to eradicate 'all manner of baseness' from their society?"

Andre raised his brows and gave a shrug. "Perhaps it's possible," he said slowly.

"It certainly would answer a lot of questions about Sera's silence on the subject of her upbringing."

"A master race, you're thinking? Is it possible? Is it even ethical?"

"Whatever the ethics of the plan, the result is a rather naïve master race—one that knew nothing of 'all manner of baseness', judging from my reluctant betrothed. Well, perhaps I am dead wrong about this. By the way, my rejection of the marriage-alliance position includes my sister, Andre. You'll have to be patient and discreet until we've vanquished Galerien, but I wanted you to know my mind in this. In case you're interested."

It was good to see Andre's smile as he jumped to his feet and left the study. Almost as good as imagining Katherine's reaction to his revelation, which, judging from Andre's alacrity, ought to happen in a few minutes, thought

Nicholas.

He settled into his chair and picked up the old volume of Plato again. What a shame he didn't have a council to decree that Sera arrive in the abbey on Saturday dressed like a bride. Just how the hell did a man get a supremely stubborn woman to marry him?

Nicholas was still pondering the question late that night. He lay in his big state bed, staring at the green velvet tester with the golden crown above his head. Sera hadn't appeared at dinner, even though he'd sent her a no-nonsense invitation that Katherine had slipped beneath her door. He was beginning to worry. Had he pushed too hard?

How long would it take Sera to accept her fate? He hoped he'd gotten her with child. It would certainly simplify matters. He sighed, looking at the door in the wall that he opened every night after his valet left him in peace.

And there she was. Her hair flowed down her back in lustrous waves the way he liked it best. Her bare feet peeked out from beneath the folds of the dressing gown she wore.

Nicholas rose swiftly and came to her, taking her in his arms, closing his eyes in relief. She was so soft, and she smelled so good. She rubbed her cheek against his bare chest, and he made a low sound of satisfaction.

"Aren't you cold?" she asked, and Nicholas suddenly remembered that he wore nothing but his trousers.

"Not now." He smiled into her hair. "Come to bed."

She nodded and slipped her arms around his neck like a trusting child. He swung her up in his arms and crossed the chilly floor to the bed.

"I have to tell you something," she said as he laid her on the mattress.

"All right." Suddenly, he was afraid. With a few well-meaning words, she could shatter him. He stalled for time, changing the subject as he joined her on the bed. "Your feet are frozen. Why didn't you wear your slippers?"

"I didn't know I was going to come until I was halfway up the stairs. I couldn't sleep, and I wanted you, and, well, then it all seemed simple."

He rubbed the shapely little blocks of ice and made them warm again.

"Oh, that feels lovely."

"Come under the covers. I'll make you warm all over."
He kissed her cheek, right at the tender spot below her
ear, and trailed kisses down her neck, wondering what
accident of fate had placed this precious gift within his
keeping.

"When you do that I can't think," she said, rubbing
up against him.

"Good." He opened the tie at her waist and slipped the
dressing gown down her shoulders, following its slide with
his lips. He didn't want her objections to the marriage,
not now, when her limbs opened to embrace him. He fought
for a modicum of control. It was important to resist the
urge to drown in the depths of that tenderness she offered
with such generosity. It was she, not he, who needed to
be convinced they belonged together. "Let's keep you that
way," he said, and bent to her, reveling in the challenge.

Afterwards, he braced his arms to either side of her,
breathing so hard he thought his lungs might burst of it.
He was pleased to see she was doing the same. When he
found the energy to move, he rolled onto his side and drew
her close, one arm clasped possessively around her.

When had he become so entwined with Sera that a
mere distance of inches would leave him bereft? He
frowned. Tomorrow, he would think about it. Right now,
she felt too good to let her go.

Sera lay beside him, her head upon his shoulder. She
contemplated the tester for some time, and then, on a
sigh, she rolled to face him.

"It is very strong, this feeling, isn't it?"

"Yes." He stroked the damp, golden curls back from
her face, dropped his hand to her waist and traveled up
the arch of her back.

"What is it that happens between us, Nicholas? Is this
what mating is like always?"

"No. There is satisfaction, but not this wrenching
completion."

"I have to tell you something."

"Even now?" What could compel her that was stronger
than what had just happened between them? He tried to
push back the worry, but it nagged like a petulant shrew.

"Especially now." She paused to take a deep breath. "I
love you. It's been growing inside, since Selonia, I think
and then in the hunting box, when I was so afraid for

you...I'm so filled with what I feel. I thought I must burst if I didn't tell you."

His hand stilled. He thought the whole earth might have done the same.

Her face was radiant in the firelight, and in her eyes—those deep, dark pools a man could drown in—her soul shone. "I don't need for you to love me back, Nicholas. And I want to stay with you for as long as you'll have me. I hope it makes you happy."

Her face, tremulous and luminescent in the light of the candles, humbled him. He had never seen anything the like of her naked joy, except perhaps...

A vision rose, of a palace and people everywhere, grown men and women in fine clothing. He was a small boy, brought to Beaureve by his father to sign the betrothal papers and stand, solemn and straight beside the cradle of the little princess. Her mother, the queen, had looked at her father and said, "I love you, Stephan." Just that, but the look on her face as she said it, the same incandescent joy that had shone there had made something in him quiver with an intense yearning to someday have what they shared. As the years passed, he had forgotten those words, that look, except in dreams that became only a warm blur upon waking.

"I love you," the queen had said—Sera had said.

"Oh, God." He took her face in his hands and traced the contour of her cheeks, thought that if the curls springing from her temples were black as a raven's wing, and not gold...

And knew the secret of Sera, and who she was, at last. Catherine Elizabeth Seraphina Galerien, daughter of King Stephan and Marissa, the queen from the Hills that some called witch. His little lost princess of Beaureve. His betrothed.

He bent to her and shut his eyes against the salty sting. He laid his kisses on her cheeks, her mouth, and rested her head against his throat so she wouldn't see that he knew.

She was deathly afraid of Anatole Galerien.

Her uncle.

The stories for all these years of the sickly princess languishing in a convent were Galerien's lies. And he had believed them, not caring, as long as Laurentia was served by an alliance his father had continued with Beaureve after King Stephan's death.

A deep sorrow rose in Nicholas, for all the lonely nights she must have spent in Laurentia, fearful and isolated with her secrets, while an Outlander king kept her imprisoned for his own designs. Sera might believe she loved him, but she didn't trust him to keep her safe. Of course, after seeing him so ill, how could she believe he was capable of protecting her? He didn't believe it, himself.

Nicholas rocked Sera in his arms, soothing her with his hands, rubbing them up and down her back. She loved him, did she? It was wonderful. It moved him like nothing else had in his life. He wished he could tell her he loved her, too. But not now.

A king couldn't afford to love.

He couldn't let love weaken him at time like this. He had to rid his country of the Brotherhood, and then go after Galerien. He had to make his country safe, to keep Sera safe. Then she'd know, at least, that she could trust him. In the meantime, he would use every Rostov trick in the book to bind her to him. "Someday, Sera..." he whispered.

Maybe someday, he could permit himself to love her.

His hand covered her breast. Her eyes flew open, but he gave her a teasing smile and fondled her nipple. When he took it in his mouth, she gasped and shut her eyes, undulating like silk ribbon in a soft breeze.

He teased her until she was mad with it. Until she said "Please." Oh, yes. He would hold her with this.

***

Well before the sun streamed through his window next morning, Nicholas carried Sera down the stairway and laid her on her bed. He shut the door in the wall behind him and thought about how much easier life would be when she was his wife. He would make a new edict so she didn't have to sleep anywhere but in his bed.

He spent the early morning finalizing plans for an attack on the Brotherhood base with his aides and Andre. He put young Oblomov in charge of the troops, and he gave Carlsohnn permission to draw up a plan of attack based on what he had learned spying out the base.

"We won't fail you, Sire," said Oblomov. Since learning of the upcoming marriage, both had served him with renewed enthusiasm.

They were so eager and so young, thought Nicholas, until he realized with a start that both men were a year older than he. He glanced at the paperwork and decisions that had piled up during the last few days. Well, perhaps he had always felt old, until now. Nicholas called his secretary into the room and turned to Andre, who stood by his side as the others left.

"Sera will need a new gown for her wedding. I want her to choose the fabric. Perhaps it will give her some small feeling of control over what is happening to her. She likes Carlsohnn's father. Would you mind accompanying her and Katherine into the city this morning with a few of the guards? I don't want her alone for a moment outside the palace with those jackals so near Montanyard."

"Of course." Andre gave him a grateful smile. "I want all the time I can get with Katherine."

Nicholas tried to work but found his thoughts straying back to the night before. A tidal wave of happiness washed over him, taking him with it. Sera said she loved him. She promised to stay with him. Shaking himself mentally, Nicholas returned to his task with renewed concentration, reviewing the plans for attack on the Brotherhood base.

A discreet knock on the door jolted him out of his thoughts. A footman ushered in a small, thin shadow of a man with a scraggly brown beard and amber eyes, tugging at the hat in his hand. The fellow was dressed in a bedraggled velvet coat and frayed lace. He glanced unsteadily, furtively, from one corner of the study to another, with the look of a hunted outlaw.

"The merchant, Sire." The footman bowed and closed the door behind him.

"Something to drink on this cold afternoon?" asked Nicholas.

"Aye. Spirits, if you please."

Nicholas poured brandy, never ceasing until he reached the top of the glass. He pushed the glass across the desk until it reached the other side.

The merchant lifted the glass. His hands were trembling so much that the brandy slopped over the sides.

"Would you care to sit?" Nicholas asked gently.

"That's very kind of ye'," said the merchant, lowering

himself into a deep cushioned chair. He picked up the glass and tried again, this time making the distance to his mouth and swallowing a deep draught of brandy. "Oh, my that is good," he sighed.

"I understand you're in possession of a rather unusual stone," said Nicholas in an encouraging voice.

"Aye, that I am. I'll be honest with yer majesty. I must leave this country fast. There are those who look for me that I dursn't meet again. The ruby's all I have left to trade, for I've been paying those that'll shield me for months now. T'was more in the manner of a reward I left for them to find, mind ye, than payment up front. They're kind, your people, and I was bringin' them danger.

"I'll not lie to you," he went on. "I must be off across the border today if I'm to live healthy. I need money to cross and to make my way west through Russia what with all those Frogs and the Russian army, too. I hope ye'll like the stone enough to buy it. That's all." The merchant had trouble with the knots on the pouch holding the jewel.

"May I?" Nicholas held out his hand. The merchant nodded and dropped the pouch into his palm.

Nicholas drew out the ruby and laid it on the desk. He looked at it for a long time.

"Yes," he said, pulling a brace of candles closer as he stared into the fiery depths of the stone. It was mesmerizing, changing constantly, giving off sparks of rosy light almost like living fire. It tugged at his heart with a mystical power. He had never looked at anything inanimate before and given a judgment to it other than to say, "This is beautiful," or "This is unpleasing."

But the stone had a soul.

"It is exactly what I wish," Nicholas said. "How much do you want for it?"

The merchant named a sum, and Nicholas immediately wrote out a bank draft. "You know," he said, handing the draft to the merchant. "You're welcome here for as long as you wish to stay. I could get you out of Laurentia in two weeks with a diplomatic mission heavily surrounded by a troop of cavalry."

The merchant tugged at his hat again. "That's kind of you, Sire, but I can't risk it. If ye don't mind, I'll let myself out and gather my things together at the inn." He deposited the bank draft deep into the pocket of his coat. Nicholas rose.

"I'll tell the guards to admit you again should you change your mind."

"Thank ye, Sire. It's very good to me you've been, and all your people. I don't deserve it, but I'll not forget it, either."

"Good luck to you, man," said Nicholas.

"I fear my luck has run out," said the merchant with a hollow laugh. "But ye can always hope." The man bowed his way out of the study.

Nicholas opened his hand. The ruby lay warm against his palm. Had he been fanciful, he would have thought the haunted merchant unfit to carry this stone. But the ruby would grace Sera's throat now. Who better than Sera to wear a jewel that aroused such joy?

Nicholas called for Monsieur Laliche, the court jeweler. "I need this by tonight. Surround the stone with diamonds," he said. "But don't cut away even the smallest amount of it. It's perfect just as it is."

***

When Andre proposed their shopping trip for her bridal gown, Sera panicked. "I don't want to," she said in a voice that wavered like a child's. Where was Nicholas? She needed to remind him of all the reasons why he shouldn't marry her.

"Every bride needs a wedding gown," Katherine insisted. "Come along. We need to get to Carlsohnn's and then return again for your first fitting."

Edmund Carlsohnn did not make it any easier for Sera. He had already heard through the capital's intricate grapevine that she and the king were to marry very soon. By the time they reached his shop, yards of white lace and creamy silks and brocades lay upon the cutting table at the back of the shop, and Monsieur Carlsohnn stood behind it with a delighted expression on his face, rubbing his hands together.

"I cannot tell you what an honor—Lady Sera, our good wishes for joy and happiness. All of us in town, we're ever so pleased."

Sera, helpless against such kindness, could only give her thanks in what she hoped was a gracious tone of voice. She stood at the cutting table, leaving all the decisions to Andre and Katherine. Everything was moving too quickly, and she was filled with such uncertainty.

She vaguely heard the sound of the shop's bell behind her and turned her head to see who had entered. A man shut the door, his back to her, a gray cloak covering his broad shoulders. Then he turned, and she saw his long blond braid hanging well below his shoulders. He fingered a piece of silk laid on the front counter and Sera froze. The man looked directly into her eyes.

Jacob Augustus had come at last. She wanted to run to him, throw her arms around him, and ask him a million questions. But Jacob gave a swift glance sideways at her two companions and their guards. He bent again to the material, his dear, calm face perusing the frivolous ribbons as though they were the most important things in the world.

Jacob looked up a moment later and held her gaze. He nodded once and turned, leaving the shop. The bell trilled, the only proof that Jacob had, indeed, been there. She knew he'd be able to find her. She need only get away. Her hands trembled as she lifted the brocade to touch its delicate flowered pattern.

"This will do nicely, I think," she said. Her voice sounded breathless to her own ears. Andre gave her a strange look, but she was too filled with new joy, new worries, to care. "And the lace for the veil. That will be lovely. Shall we return to the palace? It's a beautiful day, and I haven't ridden for such a long time."

"But I thought we'd stop at Mrs. Torville's," protested Katherine. "I purposely ate only a piece of toast for breakfast, anticipating a cream puff. Could you not put off the ride until later this afternoon?"

"I have an excellent idea," said Sera, mad with the need to see Jacob again. "Why not send me back to the palace in a carriage? Then you and Andre can go on for pastry."

"That will not do at all," said Andre quite firmly. "I shall accompany you both to the palace. Then perhaps Katherine and I will return to town."

"Thank you so much, Monsieur Carlsohnn," Sera said, gathering her reticule and gloves. "We must leave, now. Ready, Katherine? Here, let me help you with your cloak." Her fingers managed the buttons, even shaking a little.

She walked beside Katherine wishing they had taken

the carriage, hating the time passing before she could see Jacob again. She cursed the Outlander rules that made her run back to her room and change into a riding habit before she could mount Wind Rider and head into the park to find him.

The park, on this bleak December day, was deserted. As Sera rode up the gentle rise far from the stables, she saw Jacob Augustus standing beside Lightning, his mount, a few hundred feet ahead. She didn't have to nudge Wind Rider forward. He whinnied once at the bay horse that had been his companion and sped toward him in a pounding gallop. They surged up the rise where Jacob waited and Sera came to a halt before him, jumping from Wind Rider and throwing her arms about his neck.

"Oh, I have despaired of ever seeing you again. How is it that only now you've come? Did you know where I was from the beginning?"

"Grandfather wouldn't let me come until those vermin attacked you."

Sera lowered her eyes. "Does he hate me, then, for being such a fool?"

Jacob hugged her again. "No, of course not. He will explain everything to you as soon as I get you home."

"Home? But I—I can't go home, Jacob."

He looked at her as though she'd suddenly sprouted two heads. "You cannot be happy here, Sera. They are so stupid, so venal. Why, I have been here for less than a day, and I cannot breathe in their foul city."

"It is better than many others, Jacob, and Nicholas will only make it better as time goes on," she said, stung by his criticism. "Nicholas is such a good man. You would like him. Grandfather would like him. Come, you must meet him. We can help him so much."

Jacob gave her a piercing look. "You have allowed yourself to become...involved with this Outlander king, haven't you?"

She squared her shoulders. "I love him, Jacob."

"Love. An Outlander word. Oh, gods, it's as bad as it was with your mother."

Why was everything going so badly? She had been so happy, and now Jacob was growing angry and shocked by her new loyalties, as well. "Do not be so certain we Arkadians know everything. There are things we have lost in order to keep harmony amongst ourselves," Sera said quietly.

Jacob gave her an impatient look and said, "We have no time to quarrel. The thief has come to Montanyard. If you wish to keep the cliffs open, we must find his lodgings and go to him. Together, we can persuade him to give us the Heart of Fire."

"Yes," she said. "Oh, Jacob, if the cliffs will stay open, I can return. I can bring Nicholas and Katherine. You would see then that there are good things about these Outlanders."

He gave her an abrupt nod. "The city is filled with frivolous, demanding aristocrats who come and go through the palace gate. Return your horse to the stable and slip away. I shall meet you beyond the gate, and we shall go to his inn to retrieve the ruby."

"Yes," she said and mounted Wind Rider, turning one last time to plead with him. "Jacob, come now to the palace with me. You could meet them, help them. Please."

He shook his head. "My only concern is to bring you home safe. If that means retrieving the Heart of Fire with you, I shall do so. But that is all. I plan to leave the Outlanders to their tantrums and their self-destruction, Sera. And you will wish to do the same, after you have been back with your people and used right reason again."

***

Anatole Galerien paced in his study. His hands were on fire, his stomach was tied in so many knots that he could no longer eat or drink without pain. The door swung open gently, and Count Laslow stood before him, only his eyes visible above the black cape. Laslow seemed more and more a specter, but the king no longer cared with what kind of man he dealt. He was too furious at the cursed luck of his enemies.

"Why didn't you bring me the girl's head? It was a simple matter, from the dispatches I have read."

Laslow inclined his head. "A blizzard sprang up in the midst of the battle."

"What battle?" screamed Galerien. "There were two of them against ten of yours—isn't that correct?"

"Rostov carried firearms. He picked my men off as they attacked. And then no one could see a thing. The two men left almost froze to death, but luck was with them. They chanced upon a farmhouse and disposed of the family living there."

"So they ate and drank while Rostov and the girl returned to the palace."

"They were surrounded by a squadron of cavalry. But the thief has arrived in Montanyard. Tonight is the eve of a palace ball ushering in the Christmas Season. With all the confusion, my men have had no trouble slipping into Montanyard. Even as we speak, they are at the thief's inn. You'll have the ruby and the location of the cliffs into Arkadia shortly. You can deal with the other two after you have conquered Arkadia. Unless, of course, you wish to end your association with us?"

Something about the rasp of Laslow's hollow voice gave Galerien pause. He had fed this band of cutthroats until they were an army. Should they turn against him, he would never sleep safe in his bed again.

"No. Bring me the ruby, and I'll make you my representative on the throne of Laurentia, just as I promised."

"Very well." Laslow bowed and turned to go.

"Count." Galerian said, and Laslow turned again to face him.

"In a few days, you are to stage an all-out attack on Laurentia while I take the army to Arkadia. Gather your men together at the base. Begin to plan the details."

"No," Laslow said. "There's a chance that the base has been discovered. I must diversify our troops, not call them together in one place."

Galerien knew that the time had come to use the secret weapon he held over the count. "I have a list with the names of every man you have recruited. If you don't obey me, I shall rid myself of every member of your organization, and his family, as well. Think carefully. Which will it be? A little courage now will gain you a throne."

Laslow's eyes were cold as ice. Galerien fought against the shudder that threatened to course through him, standing tall and narrowing his own eyes into a look that meant instant death.

"Very well," said Laslow. "Beware that you don't lose all in the winning of this point."

***

Sera crept up the dark, narrow stairway of the Black

Bear after Jacob. The old inn, surrounded by warehouses and businesses now empty at this late hour, was located near the posting house at the northwestern outskirts of Montanyard.

"Which way?" she whispered as they reached the third floor's uneven landing.

"To the left. The second door down."

"But the innkeeper told you this man was as thin as a wraith. That does not sound like the thief."

"He has been running for the last three months. Constant terror and uneven meals can change a man."

They stood before the door. Sera took a deep breath. All the last months had led to this, finally.

Jacob pushed the door open and walked into the darkened room. Sera followed at his heels, only to bang into his back when he suddenly stopped short. She peered over his shoulder and stared in horror at the scene before her. The thief was strapped to a chair, covered in blood from wounds all over his body. Jacob turned and herded her out the door.

"Gods, who would do such a thing to him?" she whispered, gagging. "His eyes, oh heavens, did you see? They cut out his eyes."

"I know, I know." Jacob had his arm around her, holding her upright. "From the look of it, they enjoyed their work. Will you be all right here? I am going back in to see what else I can find."

"I'll come with you," she said, afraid to remain in the dark, narrow hall. "If they are hiding behind some doorway, if they return..."

"No," said Jacob. "They have been gone for several hours. Wait for me here. I do not wish you to enter this room again."

Jacob shut the door after him. She stood alone in the gloom, growing more fretful as the minutes ticked by. Finally, the door opened and Jacob ushered her down the stairway and out the front door.

The cold air hit them. Jacob took a deep, angry breath, like a man in need of cleansing his lungs. "So many against one man. He must have stolen something here—from a nobleman, or perhaps a member of the royal family. Is this how your king conducts an interrogation?"

She felt her spine stiffen. "Nicholas would never treat

another human being that way, not even his worst enemy. It was the Brotherhood. They have infiltrated Laurentia all the way to Montanyard. We must help him, Jacob."

"You are a little fool, Sera." Jacob steered her into an alcove where there was some small shelter from the biting wind. "Face facts. You put Arkadia in danger when you brought the thief past the cliffs. You rode out into this carnage alone, unschooled in the arts that would keep you safe. Do you think we can trust this Rostov with our secrets any more than we could trust Galerien?"

"He is nothing like Galerien!"

"Look at you, clothed in lace and furs yet shivering in the freezing wind. You have lived with this corruption for so long, your judgment is clouded." Jacob's eyes burned into her soul. "Your oath on it, Sera. Not a word to Rostov or any other Outlander. About the Heart of Fire, about Arkadia, about me. Do you understand me? On your sacred honor, not a word."

Sera shook her head numbly. "You cannot know what you ask, or you would never ask it."

Jacob's face was stern and implacable. "The oath, Sera, for the good of your country."

The blood seemed to seep from her veins, leaving her insubstantial as a dead leaf hanging by a thread from a bare branch. She took a deep breath. "By the gods and the sacred One they represent, I shall never break trust in these matters even under threat of death, imprisonment, or loss of all that is dear to me." The formal words that had kept Arkadia safe in times of upheaval came out in a bare whisper.

Jacob nodded, and his expression softened. "You will come with me tomorrow, safe and warm in a plain gray Hill cloak."

"I cannot leave them." She felt her soul rip itself in two and almost cried out with the pain of it.

"Listen to me. The Heart of Fire is gone. In little more than a week, the cliffs will close for good. I shall not argue this matter longer. Tomorrow morning I return to Arkadia, and you will go with me. Otherwise, you'll never see home again."

"Jacob." She clung to his hand. "If I go, I shall never see Nicholas again. You have to understand, to tell Grandfather."

Jacob drew her back into the streets filled with merchants closing their shops and hurrying home, heads lowered against the wind.

He walked beside her through this crowd of humanity until they reached the square leading up to the palace. Drawing her aside beneath an archway where they couldn't be seen, he said, "I shall come to the palace tomorrow at dawn. I shall wait beneath your window. Come to me then, Sera."

She nodded stiffly and hurried across the square and past the gate. She ran up the stairway and through the great doors, into the light and the warmth of Nicholas's home.

***

Someone rapped sharply on his chamber door an hour before the ball's opening. As Nicholas finished fastening a ruby stickpin into his white cravat, Simson, the valet, opened the door and Andre burst in. Simson returned to his side with the long brocade court vest.

With a sharp look at Andre, Nicholas took it from him. "Thank you, Simson. That will be all." The valet bowed and slipped quietly out the door.

"Nicholas, I must speak to you at once." Andre's face was red and his hair looked even more windblown than usual. He had obviously just ridden hard from wherever he had been. "You do remember our conversation about the possibility of a superior society."

"Of course."

"It's true. I've just run into one of them, and the experience was not pleasant."

Andre opened the door and called to a footman. "Brandy and two glasses. Hurry, man." Nicholas sat down slowly and motioned Andre to a chair. The footman arrived and poured both glasses. Andre took his at a gulp, motioned for more, and dismissed the servant.

"You'd know him right away. A veritable colossus of a man, and absolutely perfect in form and feature. I swear to you, he could have posed for those damned statues in the hall. Long blonde hair in a que over one shoulder—very broad shoulders, indeed. Tall, taller than you. And as beautiful as Sera. His eyes are the same dramatic blue as hers."

Nicholas raised the glass to his lips and swallowed

the burning liquid down. "What was he doing here?"

"Looking for Sera. He came into the draper's and stood there for a minute. They looked at each other, and then he left. Afterwards, Sera was almost giddy with excitement and eager to be off. I followed her as soon as I got her and Katherine back to the palace. She rode out to the bluffs, halfway into the park. He was waiting."

"And then?" Nicholas felt the dread rise in him. He poured another brandy. Andre took the bottle and filled his own glass.

"I came close enough to watch them. I hid in the brush." Andre looked away. "She—she embraced him."

Nicholas tightened his hand on the glass until his knuckles turned white.

"They talked, got into some kind of argument, I think, but one of those very civilized ones, where there's no shouting. I couldn't hear a word of it. Then Sera rode away."

"She didn't embrace him again? Or did she..." He choked on the word. "Did she kiss him?"

"No. He watched her go. She returned her horse to the stables and slipped past the guards into Montanyard, where she met the man before." Andre cleared his throat and stared down at his dusty boots. "They went to an inn together," he said woodenly.

Nicholas felt something icy and sharp slice through his belly. "How long..." He swallowed hard. "How long did they stay?"

"Barely fifteen minutes. She looked white as a sheet when she came out, and the man's face was grim. They hurried back to the palace. I followed, and I got close enough to hear their plans when they paused at the stone wall beside the gates. He plans to meet her tomorrow. At dawn. Then she left him and glided back inside the gate without attracting notice."

"I trailed the man back to the cliffs and made myself known to him. God, you should have seen the look on his face. A bit of amusement, a lot of contempt.

"'What do you want with the king's betrothed?' I said. He just smiled, a sort of flicker of the lips and the brows, as though he was considering whether to lower himself and reply.

"He looked me over from head to toe the way one does

an unruly child. 'Let the king try to wed her,' he said. I drew my sword, Nicholas. I thought to protect her, to protect you. And he laughed. He actually laughed at me.

"'Such a pity about you Outlanders,' he said. 'Violence is always the first choice, is it not?'"

Andre shivered and rose to stand by the fire, rubbing his shoulders and arms.

"And then?" Nicholas demanded.

"Somehow, I—I dropped my sword. My arm went numb, and my fingers must have opened. The sword just slipped out of my hands." Andre's hand trembled as he looked at it. "Then he raised the hood of his cloak. And he disappeared. I swear by all that's holy. He disappeared."

Nicholas took a long swallow of brandy and rose, staring at the fire. "Whatever she did with this man, she'll tell me about... eventually."

"Unless she leaves with him first."

The glass crashed into the fireplace. "She won't leave me! She gave me her word." He closed his eyes and gathered himself together. "She's never gone back on her word. Never."

Andre's eyes flicked to the silver jeweler's case sitting on Nicholas's desk. "Don't give her the ruby tonight." Andre's mouth, usually so apt to smile, was set, stubborn.

Nicholas grabbed up the case, holding it so tightly that the edges pressed painfully into his palm. Fifteen minutes. Enough time for the man to—to...

He'd said it, himself. What was love without trust? She had said she loved him. He had to at least try to trust her.

"I see no reason to alter my plans."

"Postpone the wedding for a week or two. You want to be sure of her."

No, no, no. Nicholas's heart beat out the rhythm in his chest. "No matter what you believe, Andre, I know she is faithful. In two days, she'll be my wife."

Thirteen

In a turmoil of gnawing anxiety, Sera bathed and dressed. She tried very hard to keep the horrifying image of the dead thief out of her mind, but it kept returning and, with it, Jacob's warnings.

But Jacob was not using right reason. Nicholas would never brutalize another man.

Except for Dawson, something whispered in her mind. Dawson's face had been battered and bloodied at the end of the fight between the two of them.

She clenched her hands together, straining against the niggling doubt that Jacob had placed in her mind. Dawson's case was different. Nicholas had gone a little mad seeing Dawson in the process of raping her. It was understandable, even though no Hillman would react with such violence. But a Hillman would have other means at his disposal to stop violence. All the Outlanders had by way of defense was more violence.

She went to her window and looked out at the stars, seeking peace. Her fan's staccato rhythm tapping against her hand told her she had not found it. A soft knock sounded at the door to the secret stairway, and it slid open. Then Nicholas stood behind her, pulling her against him. She let go of all thought, all struggle, and felt only his warmth, the strong arms encompassing her, the rise and fall of his chest at her back. She leaned back and let herself relax against him.

After a long moment, she turned in his arms and looked up at him, hoping for reassurance in the form of a kiss. He did not disappoint her. It was soft and sweet, as though he, too, had decided to savor every moment and leave thought until the morrow.

"You look very beautiful tonight. This gown..." His fingers slid over her shoulders above cream-colored silk and lace, and her whole body responded blindly. It had been thus for her since their return from Nicholas's hunting box. She walked about in a haze of heightened sensuality, remembering the secret, wicked things he did to her in the dark, where no one could see. Now all he had to do was touch her, and her body readied for him. She was in thrall to Nicholas like the most bespelled lady in a fairy tale.

She didn't want to think about Jacob now.

She concentrated on Nicholas's smile. Oh, his smile made his whole face change. Everyone said that Andre was the handsome one, the golden, careless Adonis. But Nicholas was beautiful, in the way the paintings of Renaissance princes were beautiful. Dark, brilliant, passionate.

He held out a silver jewelry box wrapped with a gold ribbon. "Open it," he said.

She held the box in her hand, and Jacob's words came back to her, wringing her heart. "*Look at you, dressed in lace and furs....*" If he could see her now, ready to don jewels as well, he would turn away from her in sorrow.

She fumbled with the ribbon, and Nicholas took the box from her hand.

"Come." He led her to a mirror.

"Shut your eyes," he said, and she heard both gaiety and something slightly fevered in his voice.

A chain slipped round her neck and a heavy jewel hung against her collarbone. Nicholas's hands were warm and gentle at the back of her neck as he fit the clasp together.

"Now open them," he said.

She opened her eyes and stared at the woman in the mirror. That woman wore a necklace of fine craftsmanship, a chain of ruby flowers and diamond leaves from which hung a single, priceless jewel circled by diamonds.

The key to a kingdom of riches and magic.

The Heart of Fire.

The murdered thief's treasure.

"Where did you get this?" she whispered in a voice so thin she didn't even recognize it as her own. She had to hold her hands together to keep them from fluttering like parchment in the wind.

His eyes held only confusion at her question. Above the turmoil rushing through her brain, Sera realized that this was not the reaction he had hoped from her.

"A merchant asked for an audience while we were gone. I saw him this morning, and he showed me the ruby." His fingers lifted the stone, and he looked into its depths, smiling. "It's warm, ever changing, brilliant and alive. It reminded me of you."

He slanted a shy look at her. His eyes couldn't hide

the vulnerability, the worry and, above all, the innocence that lay within their gray depths. "The jeweler has been working on it all day. I know it's not the custom for your people to wear such things, but I thought...I wanted you to have something good enough. Do you care for it a little?"

He stood there, something endearingly hesitant about the way he looked at her. She took a deep breath, the first she'd taken since that unworthy suspicion entered her mind. He would never torture and murder a man, she thought.

He only hoped to give me a treasure.

And, she realized with sudden shock, to make good his promise and quiet the cruel speculation and lascivious gossip. He had given her a necklace so valuable that none would doubt he meant to make her his wife. That calculating Rostov brain, hard at work again.

She wanted to laugh—a high, wild, hysterical bout of relief. Yet her heart wrenched at the irony of it all. The Heart of Fire, the very key to her freedom, was now the lodestone that would bind her to this man, and this world, forever. She stood on tiptoes, threw her arms around his neck, and, as it was all she could reach, brushed kisses on his chin. Nicholas gave a faint, relieved exhalation, like a man who wanted to believe his luck but could not quite do so. He lowered his head and covered her lips with his.

Sera threw all of her love into the kiss and felt his joyous response, the warm mingling of breath and spirit as his mouth played over hers. He deepened the kiss, and as his tongue slipped into her mouth and tasted her, she accepted his claim on her soul and lost herself in him. Her body opened and hungered as she clung to him, forgetting the expectant courtiers gathering at this moment. The passion he aroused was so sharp and deep and joyful.

When at last he lifted his head, he was smiling, and his face was young and beautiful. "You do like it!" he said.

"More than you can imagine." Her path was clear now, and if fear and violence were the price to pay for this deep a love, then so be it. She would never doubt—she would never fear—Nicholas again.

He traced the curve of her cheek with his fingers, and she leaned into the palm of his hand.

"Sera." Nicholas looked at her most gravely. He seemed about to ask her something of serious import, but then he took a deep breath. Fast as quicksilver, his expression lightened, and his lips quirked. "Have you been working with Monsieur Gallopet as I begged you?"

She smiled up at him. "Once I give a promise, Nicholas, I never break it. I have seen that effete, self-promoting humbug of a dance master every day since we returned to Laurentia."

"Have you learned the steps of the Quadrille?"

She gave him a grimmace. "Each and every one."

"Excellent." He held out his hand to her. "Then, my most diligent lady, may I have the honor of the first dance?"

Nicholas wished to open the ball with her as his partner, as sure a sign as the ruby around her neck that she was his betrothed. She felt the heat rise to her cheeks, and a giddy excitement filled her. She gave him a deep, graceful curtsey. "Most gladly, my king."

Leave caution behind, she challenged herself. You are no longer alone.

***

Late in the night, Nicholas took the stairway to Sera's room smiling. He was right to take the risk and trust her. She had made him so proud and happy this evening. She glowed with an inner fire that warmed everyone who saw her, and when she looked at him he knew she burned for him, alone.

To see all of the courtiers bow deeply as soon as he entered with Sera on his arm had been a singular satisfaction, for they bowed not only to him, but to the woman who wore his necklace.

He had set about the rumor that Sera had saved his life in the Brotherhood's ambush, and the nobility had been suitably impressed. Although he wanted to disclose his illness and the fact that she had nursed him back to health, Sera had refused to allow it. She had a terrible fear of Outlander mistrust, and no wonder, given what her mother had endured.

All of it made sense now—her inexplicable abilities, her fears, her nightmares, even her extraordinary beauty. He was filled with excitement and dreams. Someday, when he rid his country of the Brotherhood's evil incursions, Sera might trust him enough to tell him everything. Above all, he wanted to go to the Hills with her, to meet the Mage, to learn everything he could about this land of mystery. If the Mage found him worthy, he might help find a way to keep his country safe from the French.

He paused in the open doorway to her chamber. She stood facing him. Above the graceful curve of her shoulders, the necklace at her throat glittered in the light of the candelabrum. But what held the eye was the ruby, its facets giving off living fire like a beating heart. The ruby was Sera—deep, passionate, resonating with life.

He walked into the room and pulled her into his arms. He bent his head to her neck and placed a kiss on the creamy skin above the necklace.

"You danced most gracefully," he murmured, breathing in her sweetness, and beneath that the sudden, intoxicating scent of desire. His body responded immediately. He became rock hard, straining to take her without preliminaries.

"Mmm," she said, arching against him and making it worse. "In spite of Monsieur Gallopet."

"You simply decided to accept your fate, sweetheart. Was it so bad to waltz in my arms, after all?" he asked, trying to concentrate on the conversation.

"Only when I thought of what I would vastly prefer to be doing." Sera slowly untied his neck cloth and unbuttoned his shirt. Her hands slipped inside, moving restlessly over his chest, her fingers smooth and enticing on his heated skin.

"And what might that be? A ride across the park, perhaps?" He was dying.

She pulled the shirt free. When she began to open the first button on his trousers, he put his hand over hers to stop her. He was so hot, so hard, that he feared he would humiliate himself and lose all control.

"No," she said. "I thought of doing just what I am doing now while you held me in the waltz. Didn't you realize that your touch could leave me this impatient?"

She reached out to him again.

He didn't want it quick and hot. "Oh, no, my lady. From the moment I saw you in my necklace tonight, I conjured other plans for the evening." Nicholas lifted her in his arms and carried her high against his heart, taking the stairs to his room swiftly. The candles glowed, lighting the room just enough to allow him to see every inch of her.

Sera's arms circled his neck. He slowly lowered her, letting her slide against him, feeling the crush of her breasts against his bare chest, the soft curve of her hips against his erection as she stood in his arms. He carefully brought her arms down from his neck and held them out on either side of her, framing her body with his hands, sliding them along her sides, molding her hips.

"Stand very still," he whispered against her ear and felt her shiver in reaction.

Lifting his head, he noted the changes already apparent—the pink nipples pointed and erect through the creamy silk of her gown, the swelling of her round breasts. He pulled down the silk and the lace, lifting each breast free of the gown.

"Little goddess. Do you think you might have Cretan ancestry somewhere in your past?" he asked, brushing his hands up the underside of her breasts, lifting them. He drove himself mad with this slow, sensual perusal, but the mist of passion in her eyes, her quick, uneven breaths, were worth the denial he forced on himself.

"Nicholas," she whispered. She sounded tormented with anticipation. Good. He lowered his head, and while he lifted and stroked her, he blew his breath on the nipple. She cried out, arching her back.

"Shh," he said, and opened his mouth, taking the nipple and suckling it with measured, gentle movements of tongue and lips and teeth. She nearly collapsed against him.

"How I adore a passionate woman," he said on a low laugh. He held her upright in the curve of his left arm. The fingers of his right hand slid upward to the ribbon beneath her breast, and he slowly pulled it free. The gown fell to her hips, and then the floor, followed by lacy corset and petticoat.

He gently propelled her backwards, out of the pool of silk and lace, until she stood before the room's blue velvet covered wall. He wanted her clothed only in her white silk stockings and garters and dancing slippers. The betrothal necklace flashed and glittered on her neck. She was panting as she watched his gaze linger over her. She leaned against the wall while her whole body trembled. She made no move to cover her breasts or the silken mound at the soft juncture of her thighs.

He knelt and lifted each slipper from her foot, kissing the delicate, high arch before he put her foot down to the floor again. She gasped as his hands swept upward. His fingers stroked the soft skin at the back of her knees and higher up her thighs in infinite slowness. She moaned when his hands closed on her buttocks, stroking, then pulling her forward, towards his mouth. He looked up at her, imprisoned as she was by his hands, his body. He smiled, and watched her eyes widen. He blew on those glinting curls.

"Open your legs, love. I want to see you." With one hand, Nicholas stroked between her thighs, moving her legs apart, while he arched her toward him with the other hand until her hips were close to him. He rubbed his face against her belly. The scent of her arousal came to his nostrils, inflaming him. Freeing her, Nicholas brought his other hand forward. Her own passion held her prisoner. He stroked the apex of her thighs and gently pushed them even farther apart. Slowly, carefully, he parted the plump petals enclosing all the secret places of her body and breathed deeply.

"You're so beautiful here," he said. She arched her hips forward, straining closer, but he wanted her even wilder before he touched her.

"There are drops of moisture on your curls, sweetheart. They shine like pearls. You're swollen, and flushed a lovely pink, and sheened in that moisture. You smell delicious. I wonder if you taste as good." He blew gently on her soft, swollen folds.

"Nicholas," she whispered, helpless and aching.

"I'll do this to you every night, Sera. For the rest of our lives, I'll stroke you here in all your secret places. And I'll kiss you and run my tongue over that sweet, swollen nubbin right here...." He stroked her once and watched her jerk her hips.

"Nicholas," she said plaintively.

"Do you think you should like that, darling?"

"Nicholas!" She moved her hips again in that helpless, passionate, age-old sign of urgency.

"All right," he said, fiercely satisfied. He plunged his tongue into the soft, swollen depths of her and stroked her again and again, bringing her up relentlessly, until she moaned. Her head rolled back and forth against the wall, and her fingers curled into his hair. She held him close to that place, so lost in her need that she was without self-consciousness or shame. It humbled him that she could give everything of herself without holding back.

And with that thought, the lust rose hot and strong, obliterating all thought but one. He couldn't wait another moment, not even to carry her to the bed. The surging need overpowered him. Somewhere, the thought came to him that even tonight, as a result of this magnificent lust she aroused, his child might be conceived.

It was too much. He groaned and turned her to the wall. Pressing against her softness, he struggled for control and found he'd lost it.

"I can't wait," he said. His heart beat like that of a runner who saw the finish line and sprinted for it. He pulled her down onto the rug and cradled her against him, breathing fast.

"Sera, I won't hurt you. Trust me. Trust me." His voice sounded hoarse and straining. What was he asking her to give him—her complete faith when she realized what he wanted from her now, or some promise for the future? He positioned her, drawing her up on her knees with her back to him. Tearing at the buttons of his trousers, he freed himself and smoothed his hands over her buttocks.

She trembled, whether from passion or sudden fear, he could not tell. His member thrust forward, jerking with heat. With gritted teeth, he pushed down the pressing need. Instead, he bent over her, and nuzzled against the back of her neck. His hand reached round and cradled her belly, stroking that place he'd just kissed, until she sobbed and rolled her hips.

It was her passionate response that undid him time and again. His body blazed with hot urgency. He pulled her hips up. She rested her head against her bent arm. The very sight of her vulnerability, her body stretched, open and glistening, drove him over the edge. He made a sound deep in his throat, guttural, elemental. And plunged into her. He stroked deep, hard, as his fingers played upon her in the same quick rhythm.

He felt her body gather, taut and straining, and then the explosion within her, the trembling earthquake that stroked him as she screamed, muffling the sound against her arm. He gave a deep shout of release, and with one last plunge, he touched her womb. He felt himself shatter into a million pieces and, pulsing strongly, poured his seed deep within her body.

She was his. She was his. She was his. Forever.

***

Sera awoke in the gray hour before dawn. Nicholas slept at her back, his arm flung over her, his hand resting on her breast. She turned in his arms and looked at his face. He murmured something in his sleep, and his mouth curved upward just a little. A lock of his dark hair lay over his forehead. He looked young and happy, and it made her smile.

She fingered the necklace about her throat and slowly slipped out of the big bed. She knew what she had to do, and although it gave her great pain, she wouldn't hesitate to do it. Whether he had said so or not, Nicholas loved her. If she couldn't tell him why she had to do this, he would understand and forgive her, just as he had accepted her secretiveness before.

Taking up her gown and underclothing, Sera crept down the stairway to her room and dressed in a simple green wool gown. Then she wrapped the ermine lined cloak about her and took a back stairway down to a door beneath her room. It was a chill morning, with the scent of snow in the air. The fog swirled about her, settling in waves of wet cold on her face and bare hands. The distant trees in the park appeared to be indistinct shadows, as though this world was growing dim and unreal. Sera shivered.

Jacob came to her, appearing out of the fog like a shadow as he drew down the hood of his cloak, and then he solidified, and became real. She threw herself into his arms, already feeling the sorrow of imminent separation. He held her with the same sorrow and intensity, until she drew back and carefully, as though she were learning him by heart, caressed his face—forehead, eyes, cheeks, lips.

"You cannot mean to stay," he said, his voice tight.

Sera's mouth trembled as she tried to smile at him. "I cannot leave, but look, I bring you a gift." She lifted her hands to the clasp of the necklace and opened it.

"Gods!" Jacob stared at the necklace as she held it out to him, heavy with the weight of the jewel. Even in the gloom, it beat with a thousand pulses of light. "Where did you find it?"

Sera heard herself give a laugh that ended on a sob. "It is my betrothal gift, Jacob. Treat it carefully and someday return the necklace to me."

"Your betrothal—but Sera, this proves Rostov's a beast—a murderer and a thief. You absolutely cannot stay with him. You would not be that stupid, much less that immoral."

She shook her head again and again, knowing that she must convince Jacob of Nicholas's innocence. "The thief came to him in the palace. He needed money to escape the Brotherhood. Nicholas told me all about it, and if you could have seen the look on his face, you would know that he had nothing to do with the murder. All he wanted was to wed me, Jacob. That is his only crime."

"He lives in a world of criminals. If you remain with him, you condemn yourself to the same fate."

"Jacob, you believe that goodness exists only in the Hills. It is true that we are peaceful and powerful, and all in our world is based upon reason. But there are things we have given up, Jacob—things that enrich life beyond what you can imagine."

She had to stop for a moment to control the catch in her breath. She rubbed her cheeks and realized they were wet with more than fog. "I have seen such love here. A leader protects his people by constantly putting himself in danger. A grieving mother takes a dead woman's child to her bosom."

"And, Jacob, how they strive to understand the Divine, to reflect it in their own souls. If you could hear their music, Jacob. It would make the gods weep."

She shook her head. "They are flawed, more so than we. They search and struggle against their own demons and those imposed upon them by evil men. But they reach such heights of glory. And they love with all their strength. I could not leave them. In truth, I am more Outlander than Arkadian."

Jacob bent his head and took her own in his hands, until they stood, foreheads touching. "How will we deal with this, to lose you forever?"

"It needn't be that way, Jacob. That is why you carry home my gift. Convince Grandfather to use it and keep the cliffs from closing forever on us. Perhaps someday, he will allow me to come home again."

Jacob nodded and slipped the necklace into his tunic. He held out a folded square of gray material. "Take this. You may need it, Sera. There is war to come and perhaps famine after. Keep it."

She shook her head, backing away from him. "I cannot use it, Jacob—it is too dangerous. I am never certain I can control this new power I have. And besides, I am to be their queen. I could never leave while they suffer."

Jacob shoved the cloak into her hands. "Grandfather says your gift has grown very strong. You will know how to use it when the time comes. Take it, Sera. If just to please me one last time. I cannot leave unless I know you have the means to come home."

Sera nodded, blinking against the blur in her eyes. She needed to see him, to memorize his face. "Give this to Grandfather from me," she whispered, knelt before him and lifted Jacob's hands to her lips. He raised her up again, pulled her close and then stepped back, touching her cheek lightly.

"Farewell, and fare well, sister, most beloved friend. The gods keep you in their hearts."

"The gods go with you, dearest Jacob."

He tried to smile and then closed his eyes for a moment. Gathering himself, he turned his back and walked two paces. Then he lifted the hood of his cloak and simply... was no more.

Nicholas stood at the window of Sera's chamber and watched the Hillman disappear. Sera stood below him, her shoulders shaking in wracking sobs. But Nicholas felt only a dull, empty pain. It was much, he reasoned, like an amputee must feel, when laudanum took effect and he could almost believe that his arm was still there.

He had not been able to hear them, but he could see plainly enough with his own eyes. She embraced that golden stranger. She knelt and kissed his hands as though she worshipped him. She gave him her betrothal necklace. Her betrothal necklace, as though it were his right to have it! That had pierced him with such a flaming spear of agony, he thought he might howl and expire on the spot.

Andre was right. The Hillman—that incarnation of Hercules—was a superior specimen of the damned master race he sprang from. Certainly Nicholas looked a sad second to him. The comparison was laughable, really.

There was no doubt from her tears, her embraces, that Sera loved this better man.

"Once I give a promise, I never break it," she had said. She had made a promise to Nicholas, and she would be true to it. She loved the Hillman, but she'd sent him away.

That powerful bastard wouldn't give her up so easily. Nicholas knew that, because he himself would do anything to manipulate, or coerce, or seduce Sera into staying with him.

He rang the bell for a footman. He wanted answers—all of them, by God! He deserved them, and he was going to get them.

***

A few minutes after the footman had found her, Sera slipped into Nicholas's study. He stood by the window, his back turned to her. She had a strange surge of fear, a sense of déjà vu. It was very much like the beginning, when she was escorted, dirty and rebellious, to hear the king's displeasure at her escape attempt.

"Shut the door behind you." Nicholas's soft voice cut through her thoughts like a whip. She tried to quell the rising dread as the footman did so. He had never sounded so dangerous, so cold.

In one of those impossibly quick movements that still surprised her, he turned. His eyes blazed in a face absolutely drained of color. He looked like a man who had just escaped the rack and, now armed, faced his torturer.

"You met a man at dawn. You embraced him. You knelt to him. You kissed his hands. You gave him my *betrothal gift*, damn you! And now you're going to tell me why."

She looked into his beloved, tormented face and raised her hand in a plea—for this not to be happening, for some softening in the icy fire of his gaze—but he just stood there, his hands curling and uncurling into fists. She wondered wildly whether he would hurt her. He certainly looked as though he would like to. "I cannot tell you."

He was on her before she could even cry out, his hands gripping her shoulders, shaking her hard once, twice, and then he shoved her away from him and covered his face with his hands. "God! You make me into a beast."

He lowered his hands, and she backed away until she stood against the wall. His burning eyes pinned her there. She could feel the silk of the wall covering against her back, the only thing in the room that had any softness to it at all.

"You don't trust me enough to tell me who that damnable god was and why you loved him so much that you'd give him my necklace. You put me through hell, and all because you don't trust me. What is it? Do you think I can't keep your secrets safe?" He took a jagged breath. "Or is it that I can't keep you safe, Sera?" His voice was desolate and dry as a desert.

She stood there, her back clinging to the wall like a brand, while her thoughts whirled madly. She shook her head back and forth and shut her eyes. "You cannot keep me safe, Nicholas. Not in this world. There is disease and violence, and no one can protect me from those."

His laugh was a harsh groan. "Considering the number of times you saved my hide, I should think you'd occasionally want me to return the compliment."

"You rescued me from Hadar. From Dawson twice. Why do you torment yourself?" She hated his bleak humor, knowing that it hid a self-condemnation that went soul deep. "I cannot tell you who the man was. I cannot tell you why I gave him the necklace. I cannot tell you anything that you want to know, and still, I ask you to trust me. You say that I do not trust you, but on this you must trust me. Trust me when I tell you that I love you, Nicholas, for it is holy truth. Trust me that I stay here because my happiness is here, with you."

Expressions chased over his face—misery, fury, cynicism warring with hope. She hung on his gaze, willing him to believe her. He turned away from her, shaking his head.

"How can I trust you if you won't give me answers?" he asked softly.

A sharp rap on the door jolted her from the wall. "Nikki!" Andre swept into the room with Carlsohnn and young Oblomov before the footman could announce them. "There's trouble. The Brotherhood camp—something's brewing there."

"Men have been arriving for the last three days, Sire,"

Carlsohnn said. "Their numbers reach the thousands now. We believe..." Carlsohnn cast a cautious look at Sera.

Nicholas nodded curtly to her. " Kindly leave us," he said, without a hint of inflection in his voice.

Sera bent her head and walked to the door. He was beyond her for now, impervious to the truth of her argument. She could only pray that with time, he would choose to believe not what he had seen, but what his heart knew to be true. She was so afraid her prayers would not be answered.

That night, she crept up the secret stairway to Nicholas's chamber. He had not come to her, but she had no pride where he was concerned. His door was closed. She tried the handle, only to find it locked.

"Nicholas," she said softly and knew somehow, from the dead stillness in the air, that he wasn't there. "Nicholas," she whispered, while a numbing dread began to envelop her. "Don't do this to us."

Empty silence greeted her plea. Sera wrapped her arms around her stomach and curled over, bracing against the pain. Slowly, she sank to her knees and leaned her head against the door. After a long, long time, she rose and walked blindly down the stairway.

***

"I told you to remain at home, Andre. Damn it, man, who will lead the country should something happen to me?" Nicholas sat his mount, in a black mood from two sleepless nights—the first spent in his study with a bottle of brandy for company, the second on the road.

The army had marched for two days and crossed the border before Andre presented himself. In the gray hour before dawn, he now rode the forest path beside Nicholas with one of those maddeningly cheerful smiles just visible on his face. Nicholas knew just one perfect right to the jaw would erase that grin and leave Andre safely asleep in the forest until the battle was over. He wished he could use it.

"You were under orders, you idiot! You and Katherine were to remain at home. When the time came, you were to rule and keep her safe."

"I keep her safe by protecting you, old man. And lower your voice, Nikki. We're coming in on them soon."

Indeed, the first scouts slipped back like silent ghosts

in the chill December mist to report a few moments later. Carlsohnn, among them, wore a look of deep concern.

"From the number of campfires, it looks to be as many as eight thousand troops, twice our number."

Nicholas tapped his fingers against his saddle, his mind sorting out the information against what he knew of Galerien and the Brotherhood.

"It will be difficult to win against so many of them," said General Oblomov, who rode up beside them. The other generals clustered about Nicholas, all of them wearing expressions of doubt.

"We must," said Nicholas. "They're gathering in force to march on Laurentia. There's no other explanation for such numbers when their normal method of operation is infiltration in small, deadly gangs. If we refuse to engage, we'll face them and Galerien's forces together soon, and Laurentia will fall. We must move now, gentlemen, while the element of surprise is with us."

"In the darkness?" asked Andre.

"No," said Nicholas. "The darkness will confuse us as well as them. We'll follow the original plan. Gather above them to the east and wait until sunrise. The cavalry will charge the camp, followed closely by the infantry. Pray the sun blinds them. Once down, we fight like hell. If we succeed, we fan out in legions and surround their army."

General Oblomov nodded once, smartly. "It just might work, Nicholas Andreyevitch." The others, though still grave, nodded as well.

"Gentlemen. Kindly send the order along the ranks and move the men into position."

An hour later, Nicholas shut his spyglass and replaced it in his pocket. "I want you at the back, Andre," he murmured. "You must return alive to Montanyard. Marry Katherine and name your first son after me, eh?"

Andre's hand pressed his shoulder. "You will not die in this battle, Nikki. Do you understand me? You will not die."

Nicholas tried to smile, but the effort was too difficult. "I don't want to make an end of it, you dunce," he said. "I simply want to justify my taking up space on this earth. If I make it back, I'll go on to solve the next problem, and the next."

"Damnit, Nikki," Andre began as the first rays of the

sun struck the hills behind them.

"Save your breath, my friend. You'll need it."

***

"What is it, Grandfather?" Jacob Augustus entered Emmanuel Aestron's study and sat down across the table from the Mage.

Jacob peered into the scrying glass. Across the smooth surface, the sun rose above hilltops surrounded by forest. A band of horsemen gathered at the top. A tall, dark-haired rider who sat straight as a Hillman in his saddle raised his sword. It flashed in the sunlight and the band charged downward to a plain teeming with black-clad soldiers.

"Nicholas Rostov goes to battle," said Emmanuel. "Sera will never forgive us if we do not watch carefully."

***

Nicholas whipped his sword arm upward once more, meeting the jarring stroke of steel yet again. His horse had been shot out from under him eons ago. He had managed to jump free, only to come up against one of the black clad soldiers. A ball from a pistol to his right had downed the soldier and saved him. The sun, now past the zenith by a good, long time, revealed a field strewn with bodies, both in the blue and red of Laurentia and the black of the Brotherhood. Still the fighting went on, to the cries of the wounded and the metallic stench of blood. He pressed on, backing a man toward a steep drop in the land, somehow aware of where he stepped, when to turn, although conscious thought had disappeared hours ago.

He had lost sight of Andre when he lost his horse. He could only pray that his friend made it through this hell. The enemy sliced at him from the left. Nicholas parried, stepped aside to the right, and readied. The soldier, wild for the kill, lunged, and Nicholas speared him cleanly. The soldier fell, never knowing what had hit him.

He sensed a lull in the battle and stopped for an instant, breathing heavily and wiping the grimy sweat from his forehead with his sword arm. And heard, very distinctly, a deep, powerful voice shout inside his head.

"Rostov! Behind you!"

Nicholas whirled to find a tall, spectral man caped in black, whose sword rose to slice through his neck. He blinked and leaped aside in time to feel the cold steel cut through the flesh on his side. The wound was bad, but he still had strength to lift the sword and back away.

"Count Vladimir Laslow, at your service." The black-caped creature bowed, a mocking, graceful movement. "Why don't you give it up, Rostov?" The spectre's voice was cold as the gates of Hell. "You are dying, just as Catherine Elizabeth will die, just as your sister, your friend, and the rest of these men will die."

Laslow grinned, a tight, feral baring of teeth. "In a day, maybe two, I shall get the ruby from the witch's daughter. Oh, yes, we know she wears it now. As we speak, there are men inside Montanyard to bring her and the jewel to me. And with it, the Hills will belong to Galerien, and Laurentia will belong to us. Your time is up, Rostov."

The spectre came closer, sword glittering against the sun, eyes gleaming. "I didn't make it easy for the chit's mother, I can tell you. I enjoyed her screams. Do you believe I'll give your mistress an easy death, Rostov? Oh, yes, I can see I've got your full attention at last. I shall allow Galerien to watch while I cut her, bit by bit. I shall cut out her heart last of all, and give it to Galerien still beating. Won't that be a pretty sight?"

Nicholas spun away from the bright flash of the sword. His head felt light and dizzy. He blinked his eyes to clear them and swayed on his feet. He must have lost a lot of blood. He probably wouldn't survive much longer.

"That is what you must remember, Rostov, as you hurtle toward death. The picture of the witch's daughter butchered, her body desecrated. Our victory over the Devil and his whore."

Again, his body was jolted by a shock of electric recognition, as though a soul had just touched his own. "To the left," said a voice, deep and compelling, and Nicholas jumped. The spectre took a step, stumbled over a hidden root, and Nicholas lunged as Laslow tried to right himself. His sword slid deeply into flesh, between ribs, and struck the very heart of the beast.

"No," whispered the spectre. "I planned it all perfectly. I shall not die." Even as he spoke, the cruel light drained from his eyes, and the beast fell forward on the sword, his venom drained forever.

Nicholas swayed above the prone figure from Sera's deepest nightmares. He had done this much, anyway. "Thank you," he whispered to whatever saint or touch of magic had given him warning.

"Nikki!"

Nicholas blinked to clear his vision. Andre hurtled toward him with a division of soldiers at his back. Within seconds, they surrounded him in a protective phalanx, and two men half-carried, half-supported him off the field of battle.

Andre bent over him, his mouth a grim line in a face lined with soot and sweat.

"I need you to..." Nicholas could barely hear his own voice.

"What the hell do you want me to do, Nikki?" Andre leaned his ear close to Nicholas's mouth.

Nicholas grabbed his arm. "Go home," he told Andre. "Save Sera. You have to save her."

"All right, old fellow. Tell me how to do it."

Nicholas fought the rising darkness while he gave Andre the details of the plan that would destroy the one chance of happiness he was ever to have. At least, he thought, he got it all said.

"Good," he muttered. "Leave now. Not a mom'nt t' lose."

Darkness rolled in and took him under.

Fourteen

At the rap on the door of Nicholas's study, Andre stopped pacing and took his place behind the desk. It would be an understatement to say he was not at all happy to inform Sera of her fate, particularly after speaking to Katherine earlier that day. But there had been no time to argue with Nikki. The fierce intensity in his drawn face, as well as the gravity of his wound, compelled Andre. He had to do it, and do it right.

Andre took a deep breath. "Enter."

Sera preceded the footman, who quietly closed the door behind her. She crossed the room in quick steps. "How is he?" she asked him breathlessly. "Terrible rumors are flying through the palace this morning. I don't know what to believe. How badly is he wounded? You must take me with you, quickly, for he needs me."

Sera looked like hell, Andre thought. Her shadowed eyes were too big in a face gone pale and thin. The realization of just how much Nikki meant to her hit him hard, and he inwardly cursed fate and duty. But still, he forced his voice to come out in a clipped, impersonal tone.

"The wound is grave, but the doctor believes he has a good chance of pulling through, as long as he is not disturbed. The king expressly does not wish you with him, not now, and not in future." He unrolled a thick parchment and forced his hands not to tremble.

"In this year of our Lord 1812, His Majesty Nicholas Alexander Andreyivitch Rostov, tenth of that line by the Grace of God, Ruler of Laurentia, and of the counties of the eastern Arkadian range, hereby deems it fit and worthy to banish Lady Sera, of those mountains, from Lauentia now and forever."

Sera made a sound, a choked whisper, really. Her face, already pale, now looked as white as the parchment he had been reading. Andre rounded the desk in a hurry. He was afraid she'd faint and he wouldn't be there in time to catch her. But she waved him off and clutched at the high back of a wing chair. He watched her struggle for control and silently cursed.

"The king has ordered that soldiers take you to the mountains. He reminds you that this is what you wanted for a long time. He tells you to keep the ruby as a..." Damn Nikki, he thought, choking on the word. "douceur. You may give it to anyone you please."

She raised eyes that were tragic blue pools. "A douceur," she said in a voice devoid of all emotion.

"Yes, Sera. Do you understand what that means?"

Blindly, she stared past him. "It is money, or a valuable trinket, an Outlander gives to a woman when he rids himself of her."

Andre realized that she was in shock. "Come." He eased her into the chair and poured a glass of wine. "Here," he said. "Take deep breaths. It's not so bad, after all. You're going back to your homeland, Sera. You'll see all your friends, all your family. Think of it that way."

She pushed away the glass he offered. "He gave me a douceur to take the sting away, did he? As though I were just another discarded mistress." The last word came out in strangled sob. Sera pressed her fist to her mouth.

Andre stared at the floor. He couldn't stand watching her devastation.

"The king wishes you to leave immediately. Soldiers await you in the courtyard. They will see that you arrive home safely."

"Tell them there is no need," Sera said, and he heard the soft scrape of the chair as she rose.

Andre took a hasty step forward, in case she should falter and need assistance. But she drew herself up and raised her hand, palm out, to keep him back. Sera was a small woman, but somehow, at this moment, she looked tall and commanding. He saw strength radiating beneath fragility, holding her upright. Without thinking, Andre executed a deep bow—a minister's bow to his queen.

"Sera," he said holding out his hand to escort her from the room. He paused, not knowing what to say or do next.

She lowered her head and raised it again, a regal gesture, and looked him square in the eye. "I do not require your assistance, Count Lironsky." She swept from the room and down the corridor.

Andre waited alone in the study until he decided enough time had elapsed for Sera to gather her strength to face him again. He must arrange to pack her clothing. Nikki was very insistent that she dress warmly for the journey. He gazed out the high arched window into the park, sick at what Nikki had ordered him to do, and disgusted with himself for doing it.

A slender figure covered in a plain gray cloak ran from the palace to the stables. Within moments, she appeared again, upon Wind Rider. Sera lifted her head to look at the palace. From where he stood, Andre could see the glitter of tears on her cheeks. She raised the hood of her cloak, and horse and rider disappeared into thin air.

***

Nicholas groaned. Where was he? He could hear flames licking and crackling. Was he in Hell? He doubted it. The place was warm, but not burning. He made a vain attempt to keep himself from thinking of Sera, but his nightmares had been full of her. In scene after scene, he saw them coming for her, saw her dragged from the palace and tortured by Laslow's ghouls, and upon waking, the horrifying images still made his blood run cold. He turned his head and groaned.

He hurt, that was for sure. His head felt as though it had spent the last twelve hours inside an active cannon. His side throbbed, and it was difficult to breathe. Cautiously, he opened one eye and found himself on a cot in a crude hut. The crackling flames were, in reality, a warm fire in the stone fireplace at one end of the room.

A familiar face twinkled down at him—a blue-eyed with a broad smile.

"Baron Summers," he said. His voice cracked.

The doctor lifted his head and gave him warm beef broth to drink. "Hullo, dear boy. You've found me out."

"But how? And where...?"

"You are in a crofter's hut not far from the Laurentian border. And I've been a member of His Majesty's Forty-seventh for a few months. Got the urge to travel, see the world, do my bit for Laurentia, and all that. So here we are, together again, I'm afraid. Andre and Will Carlsohnn dragged you here after the battle, which, incidentally, you won. Any other questions?"

"How many of us survived?" Nicholas couldn't keep the fear out of his voice. He was too weary.

Andre's face came into focus above him. "Many," he said. "They had us fighting hand to hand, there were so many of them, but when you killed their leader, their discipline broke. It was easier after that."

"God, what a creature," said Nicholas. "I'll have nightmares for weeks about him."

"They thought he was invincible," said Andre.

"He very nearly was." His voice almost failed him, then. "Sera?" he asked, and it came out in a whisper.

Andre leaned over him. He looked haggard. Nicholas wondered how he had managed to ride to Laurentia and back in just two days. "She's all right, old fellow. Safe home by now, with that horse of hers. She had a gray cloak like that Hillman wore when he disappeared. I'll tell you more later."

The picture rose in his mind of Sera, small and sad in her ermine cloak, sitting in the straw-strewn stall and confiding to her horse in the Hill tongue. "No cloak," she had said, even though ermine and wool protected her from the cold night. Of course. The plain gray cloak that had never raised suspicion among Outlanders had enough power to hide both Sera and the horse from those who would harm her. He sighed, filled with relief even as his heart opened in a crack that could never be healed. She was safe.

"But there's more, Nikki, and it's an unsettling mystery," Andre said. "You remember the merchant who sold you the ruby. The municipal guard found his body. Whoever killed him made him suffer for a long time before he died. So they alerted the palace. Then, three nights ago, our guards captured four men attempting to breach the palace walls. All of them wore Brotherhood black."

"Damnation."

"One of them lived long enough to confess. The thief had given them the location of the entryway to Sera's Hills before they killed him. Laslow sent them in to capture Sera as well, and—this is odd—the ruby you bought from the merchant. It seems the ruby's some kind of key to Arkadia.

Nicholas nodded slowly. "Galerien wants to see Sera die. Painfully and slowly. He thinks she is still in Montanyard."

He shook his head, trying to keep the fragments of what he had just learned together. "Laslow said something, too, about the ruby. He said that with it, Galerien would conquer the Hills. She gave that Hillman the ruby, Andre, and I thought to myself, 'she doesn't care about what it means. She doesn't love me.' I thought she had thrown away my betrothal gift. I didn't understand."

Nicholas felt cold, and it had nothing to do with the wound or the temperature in the room. It had to do with despair. "But I think perhaps I just hurt her worse than I was hurt. Do you know, I never told her I loved her. How could I, when I couldn't afford to love anything but Laurentia? She told me, of course. She had the courage of a lioness when it came to loving me freely, without reciprocation."

He laughed, a sound bitter and thin to his own ears. "But I was always afraid she'd leave me. So I made her leave me before she could think of it, herself."

Nicholas stared into the fire, recognizing fully what he had lost.

Andre bit his lip. "I'm sorry, Nikki."

"I'm not. She's safe." Liar, he thought. "She's safe," he repeated, using the words like a mantra to soothe the harsh sting of loss.

"Laurentia's still in danger," he told Andre. "I want the men to return to Laurentia immediately, Baron Carlsohnn. Would you and young Oblomov ask the generals to gather here in, say, half an hour?"

"Sire," said Baron Summers. "Forgive me. You should not think about traveling for at least a few days. The wound is deep enough to be troublesome as it is. Kindly keep your men here, protecting you should your presence be discovered."

"I cannot leave Laurentia with only half the force necessary to guard the land against Galerien." Nicholas lifted his hand to his eyes and covered them. "Baron Summers, I am weary. This conversation is at an end."

Summers heaved a sigh. "Andre, try to talk some sense into him, will you? And convince him to take the laudanum."

"He's right, Nikki, and you know it." Through a foggy haze, Andre scowled down at him.

"Galerien will be desperate when he gets word of what we did to his terrorists. If you could have heard that commander—by all that's holy, I didn't know if he could be killed."

"Laslow. A fanatic, a madman."

"I noticed," said Nicholas with a wry twist to his mouth.

The generals filed in, grim-faced. Nicholas knew that, lying prone on his pallet after so much blood loss, he must look like a dying man. But he had no intention of giving Galerien that satisfaction.

He gave his orders in a voice he hoped sounded less hollow to them than it did to his own ears. "Count Lironsky will lead you home. Station men of the fifty-ninth along the border and take the rest to the passes at Selonia. We can hold Galerien there for quite a while. Put the citizen militia on alert. General Oblomov?"

The old general approached the pallet and knelt in a rather creaky fashion. "I am here, Sire."

"I may be weak, sir, but I am not blind," said Nicholas with a wry smile. He pulled at the ring on his finger, the blazing sapphire held in a golden eagle's talons. It held fast, and it took all his puny strength to draw it off. Never, since they had crowned him king, had it left his hand.

"Give this to my sister in front of all the ministers. Tell her to keep Laurentia safe in my stead. Tell her I shall return." Nicholas lay back on the pallet and shut his eyes. He had no energy left to fight the hot pain of his wound. "I'll take that laudanum now, Baron," he told the doctor as the generals left the room.

***

On the third day after the battle, Nicholas awoke feeling less as though an ox cart had rolled over him. The hut was quiet and warm. Carlsohnn and young Oblomov kept watch in the room. Oblomov had his knife out and whittled away at a small object. He turned it in his hand, inspecting closely, then used the knife again.

Nicholas heard low voices outside the door, and then it opened. Andre stood silhouetted against the light, his hair going in a thousand different directions, and the grin wide on his face.

"What the hell are you doing, Lironsky?"

Andre's grin grew even wider. "I'm the proverbial cat that came back. I sent the generals on to Montanyard and returned in record time. Rather impressive, eh?"

"You know damned well I wanted you in Montanyard with Katherine. Stop that infernal grinning and get out of here. Damnit, this is serious, Andre."

"I'm well aware of that, my friend. You, however, seem to be a bit muddled about your own safety. Do you remember our first days at Eton? How the bullies came at you, wanting to make the barbaric crown prince cower before English superiority? It might be illuminating to recall that you could not have beaten seven boys so soundly without me by your side."

Andre was no longer grinning. "I have always been there for you. It pleases me to think that may be part of why we have never lost. Galerien is looking for you. There's danger all around, Nikki. Do you expect me to turn tail and run, leaving you to get out by yourself?"

Nicholas shook his head. "I wanted one of us happy, Andre."

Andre shrugged a shoulder. "What chance of happiness could I have if I didn't bring you home safe? Do you think Katherine would ever speak to me again? Do you think I could live with myself? So tell me you're happy to see me and when the hell we can get out of here." The smile broke on his face like sunshine through a cloud.

"Now, I suspect," Baron Summers said sweeping into the hut. "If the king can ride, we must leave immediately. Galerien's soldiers are scouring the area."

"All right," said Andre. Lieutenants Carlshonn and Oblomov jumped to their feet. They were halfway out the door when Nicholas heard the sound of hoofbeats and the metallic ring of swords pulled out of scabbards.

Nicholas had made it up on one knee when the door of the hut was flung open and several figures appeared silhouetted against the bright light. Andre, Carlsohnn, and Oblomov went for their swords, but the fruity tones of the man in the middle stopped them short.

"My dear Nicholas Alexander Andreyevitch Rostov. I hold a very accurate pistol in my hands. Tell your men that if they do not lower their swords, you will be the first to die."

Nicholas's men slowly lowered their swords.

Anatole Galerien stepped into the hut, his weapon raised and aimed at Nicholas. "I am hurt that you have chosen to take shelter in this rude hut when you could have come to me. But I am not one to hold a grudge. I have a comfortable litter that will take you to my palace in Constanza, where you will recover in a peaceful chamber while you await my wedding to your sister. No, no, my dear brother-in-law to be. Do not jerk like that. You will open your wound if you are not careful, and I need you alive until the wedding, which will give me as much right to Laurentia as I need to accomplish my goal."

Galerien smiled coldly as his men tied Andre's hands. They did the same to Carlsohnn, the doctor, and Oblomov with efficient dispatch.

"My sister is no fool, Galerien," said Nicholas. A cold, relentless fury welled up in him. He would survive this, he vowed, and have Galerien's head for it.

"Oh, she will consent, believe me. When my messengers inform her that I have her brother in custody, and that her marriage to me will free him. Of course, I shall not reveal to her that you will have but one instant of freedom before I have you killed, along with your guards, here. Such details are not for the gentler sex, are they?

"And now, Nicholas, if you'll excuse me, I shall see that your traveling accommodations are made ready for you." Galerien swept out of the hut, leaving Nicholas to contemplate how he might get them all out of this.

***

Katherine sank slowly into her chair as she read aloud the message Galerien had sent her. The faces of the ministers in the council room turned grim and frightened.

"What do you suggest, gentlemen?" she asked, raising a pale face to them.

"We must keep Laurentia safe. That is the important thing. We have soldiers at the borders, at the mountain pass, and armed citizens through the countryside. Remain here, princess. Keep the throne safe. That's our advice."

Katherine felt the weight of the monarch's ring that hung from a heavy gold chain about her neck. She lifted it and stared down at it. The eagle was a fitting symbol of the house of Rostov, and not just for its power and courage. She thought of Prometheus and his sacrifice.

She didn't doubt Galerien's threat. She, too, was a Rostov. She raised her head and looked calmly at the men assembled. "I am, in my brother's absence, regent of Laurentia, and what I decide is law, is that not correct?"

The men gathered about the table assented.

"You will remain here, protecting our country against Galerien's invasion. For as soon as he has married me, he will come. I shall go to Constanza and wed this monster."

The ministers rose, shouting their denial. Katherine

quelled them with one fierce look and a raised hand. "If I do this thing, Nicholas will be alive until the ceremony is completed. Your king is clever and resourceful. As long as he lives, there's hope. I give him a week by consenting—time for him to come up with a plan. Do you understand, my lords? This is the only way to buy what we need. Time."

***

Nicholas paced the tower room, thinking hard. He had been prisoner here for almost a week. His wound was not completely healed, but he could hold a sword or a pistol, if only he could get hold of one. Andre leaned over the narrow sill, staring out, as he did each day. Nicholas glanced down and saw the bright banners hung from the palace's high walls to greet his sister who was arriving today for her wedding.

"We would need a flying machine to get out of here, Andre. Keep your mind on another way for us to get to the abbey. For that's the only hope we've got."

"I'm aware that escape is impossible, Nikki." Andre's eyes glittered like those of a man stretched too far. "How could she do this? To agree to this marriage. To put herself in danger. How the hell could she, knowing I love her?"

"She's giving us time. Remember, Andre. There hasn't been a fight we haven't won."

"If it hadn't been for Sera, we would have lost the one in Iman Hadar's palace."

Sera. He had thought of her so often, and each time he thanked God she was safely away from all this. "Damnit, Andre. Concentrate. You've got to give me a distraction. That's not too much to ask. Just one instant, and I'll get to the abbey and take down Galerien."

***

Sera knocked on the door to Emmanuel's study. "You sent for me, Grandfather?"

Emmanuel looked up from the scrying glass. Instantly, the glass fogged over. "Come in, my dear, and sit here beside me."

Sera closed the door behind her, laid her cloak across a bench, and took the seat her grandfather offered. Jacob paced the room, she noted, with a most peculiar look upon his face. He was flushed and frowning furiously. Normally cerebral and serene, Jacob looked very much the Outlander at the moment.

Jacob's restlessness grated on her today, perhaps because she was so weary.

"Jacob, why don't you take your bad mood elsewhere?" her grandfather said.

"Absolutely not. I have every right to be here. Sera is still unable to make reasonable decisions, and I should—"

"Oh, do cease storming about." Sera bent her head and tried to massage the throbbing out of her temples.

The last days at home had been difficult. Only the other night, Jacob pressed her to dine with him and his friend Lysander Antiocus, a man she'd always admired. He had made it clear that Lysander, with a little encouragement, would ask for her hand in marriage.

When the dinner party was over, Lysander had taken her aside. Smiling kindly, he said, "You need time to return to us, Seraphina. I shall not press you until you are ready."

From the time she'd reached the age of dedication, she'd known that Lysander was everything a man of Arkadia should be. He was brilliant, comely, and kind. His line and the Aestron line would breed beautiful children who would, perhaps, lead Arkadia into a golden age greater than the one Pericles knew.

Lysander would care for her. He would respect her. But he would never look at her as Nicholas did, with passionate intensity. He would never tease her, or move her to the heights and depths of every emotion within her.

Lysander was not Nicholas.

Fiercely, she reminded herself that Nicholas had broken her heart.

Her grandfather's serene regard somehow called her from her bitter musings. "I must ask you to look into the glass, Sera," he said in that gentle tone he'd been using with her since her return. "Tell me what you see."

"All right." The swirling fog dissipated slowly as a picture formed and sharpened, all its colors and movement hurting her eyes.

"It's Katherine and a host of the ministers. Katherine is dressed in white velvet. She and the courtiers are riding through a city. A very poor city. People in dull, patched clothing with pinched faces line the streets as they ride through. They don't cheer. They don't do more than stare.

What is this place, and what is happening here?" An icy chill of dread crept through her, and she trembled.

"Look again into the glass, Sera." Grandfather's face wore the look of the Mage. His voice was no longer gentle, but commanding.

The colors swirled, changed, resolved themselves into another scene, and this one took the breath from her body in a rush. She held to the sides of her chair so hard her fingers hurt. "It is Nicholas. He is locked in a small, gray room high above the city through which Katherine rides. Andre is with him." She put her hand to her heart. "Oh, Nicholas looks tired. See how pale he is? Thinner, too."

"They are in Constanza, a small city in Beaureve," said Grandfather. "Galerien holds them for ransom. The price he demands is Katherine's hand in marriage. They wed today. Of course, he plans to kill the king and his friend after the wedding. Then he'll claim both Beaureve and Laurentia."

Cold crept into Sera, settling deep in her blood. She couldn't move for a moment, she was so cold. Nicholas to die! And Katherine to wed that beast? "No, no. That must never happen!" Sera grasped her grandfather's hands. "There must be something you can do, Grandfather. You cannot let this happen!"

The Mage shook his head. "My duty is to Arkadia, Sera. I cannot help them."

Sera nodded slowly and straightened her back. Feeling returned to her body, and with it, the ability to breathe, to move, in spite of the terror. She felt that her life was a scrying glass, and she had finally allowed herself to look deep within it.

"Of course," she whispered. "This is not your responsibility. It is mine."

"By the gods, I knew you had lost all sense among the barbarians! Lysander, the best of all the men in the City, asks to address you, while that man treated you like a common doxy. And you decide to risk your life to save him and all those fops who laughed at you and called you whore. Where is your perspective? Where is your mind, sister?"

Sera stood slowly and squared her shoulders. She gave Jacob a brilliant smile. "I have been thinking long and hard about this. It struck me that even in Hadar's palace, when Nicholas thought I was a harlot, he treated me with respect. I don't believe he would have acted so discourteously unless he wanted to hurt me into leaving— perhaps for my own safety." She lowered her head and blinked to banish the sting from her eyes.

"Don't be a fool!" Jacob glared at her.

She opened her hand and held it out to him—a pleading gesture. "Don't you see? My whole life has led to this moment, this choice. The important thing is not what Nicholas feels for me, Jacob. I love him. I love Laurentia. I have no doubt that I could love my own people, those poor, hopeless men and women lining the road into Constanza.

Jacob made a sharp sound of frustration and wheeled away from her. She walked to him anyway and took his hands, willing him to understand.

"Do not fling yourself away from me because I am half Outlander. I finally realize it is not such a terrible thing to be. Jacob, remember everything we've learned. It screams out at us now.

"Evil threatens those I love, and I may be able to stop it with the truth. How shall I live afterwards if I do not try?" Sera reached up and tugged a lock of his hair in the old gesture she had used at parting since they were children.

With an angry sigh, he bent his head, and she kissed his cheek, hugging him fiercely. "Don't be too angry for too long, Jacob. I need to know you'll forgive me."

"I forgive you already," he said. "I shall come with you."

"No," said Sera. "You are the Mage to be. Your duties lie here."

"Sera," said Emmanuel as he rose to kiss her brow. "Remember, you may be half Outlander, but you are also half Arkadian, and an Aestron. The blood runs very true in our line."

"Thank you, Grandfather. It is a good thing to know when one goes to confront a monster in his lair." Sera picked up her cloak and left the room.

***

The door to the tower prison swung open, and Katherine burst into the room. Her gaze swept to Andre and Nicholas. "Oh, captain, I am so overcome with emotion," she said in a high, fluttery voice entirely unlike her own. "If I could have just a moment with my poor brother..." She smiled tremulously at the beefy guard, and he frowned but obligingly left the room, locking the door after himself.

"Quickly," whispered Katherine. She knelt on one knee on the flagstones, unbuckled a holster from about her calf, and whipped out two knives. Nicholas leaped from the bed and grabbed them.

Andre grabbed Katherine, pulled her to her feet and into his embrace. "You clever, wonderful girl. How did you get Galerien to let you in here?"

Katherine shrugged. "It was easy, actually. I simply played on my reputation. Who would fear a plain, awkward, frightened little rabbit like me? I also happen to be a little muddled in my thoughts, as you have doubtless told me during many a philosophical argument."

Andre laughed softly, and his lips covered hers in a long kiss. "Oh, my love, you are the wisest of us all. Now we have a chance."

"There are only three of them outside the room. My charming escort and the two guards who have brought you the slop they've been feeding you. Nikki, they told me you were still weak from your wound."

Nicholas felt a bit of modest pride, himself. "I suppose acting runs in the family. I, too, thought a complacent enemy better."

"Ah—the Rostov motto—take every possible advantage. But hurry, there isn't much time," said Katherine. "Galerien only promised me five minutes to assure myself that you were still alive.

"Galerien's soldiers are everywhere, Nikki, a veritable army of them. Galerien insisted I bring none of our own here. We are all alone with only one chance, and that a slim one. We must take Galerien out during the ceremony." She reached into her sleeve and another knife magically appeared.

"Oh, no, Katherine," said Nicholas. "I'll not allow my little sister to take part in any of this."

"Don't be ridiculous, Nikki," snapped a flaming Katherine he had never seen before. "I've been practicing all week." Her vengeful look wavered as some terrible thought struck her. Then she straightened her shoulders. "I assure you, my brother, if you do not reach Galerien, I shall."

Katherine cocked her head. Nicholas heard the guard's heavy tread outside the cell and returned to his bed. Katherine motioned to them both and called out to the guard in a timid, tear-choked voice. "I am ready to proceed to the abbey, sir. If you could but open the door for me, I believe I can manage the stairway."

The guard appeared at the door.

"Ah, me, I am so overset, my legs are trembling." Katherine sniffled into a lace handkerchief and looked up at the guard weakly. "If you would be so kind as to escort me, I shall try to walk by myself."

The guard kept his eyes on Andre, who stood by the window with his head in his hands. Nicholas lay in bed moaning and tossing. Satisfied that the one man who might give trouble was too overcome to do so, the guard gave Katherine his right arm and reached with his left to shut the door. Katherine tugged once sharply, and the man stumbled to his right, losing his hold on the latch. Nicholas lunged from the bed and covered the guard's mouth, holding him down with an elbow locked round his throat.

"Move, Katherine."

"But—"

The man flailed beneath him with all his might. "Katya. You're in bridal white, remember?"

"Oh." Katherine moved away, and Nicholas slit the guard's throat.

Katherine, stared, her face dead white. The man gurgled, and his limbs twitched wildly. Blood sprayed over the floor.

"Come on," whispered Nicholas, pushing Katherine toward the door. He peered through the crack to watch her performance. The two guards in the hallway barely had time to look up when an ashen-faced Katherine stumbled to the table, nearly collapsing.

"Oh, sirs, my brother—the kind guard who brought me here—please, in there!" The men leaped to their feet and ran into the tower room. Andre and Nicholas gave each a swift chop to the jugular. The guards dropped like stones. Grabbing their swords and the braided tunics off their backs, Nicholas and Andre quickly shrugged into those and the high beaver caps of the palace guard.

"Well," said Katherine as they locked the door and ran to her side, "I'm happy I didn't have to witness the rest of that." All three raced down the winding stone stairway. "So that's what you men do when you go to war," she muttered to Nicholas. "I should think you would have outlawed that particular international solution eons ago."

"When we're safe home, I'll abolish war in my next speech to parliament."

They had reached the ground floor. Here, soldiers milled about, watching out for any sign of trouble from the visiting Laurentians. Galerien paced the marble floor waiting for a sign of Katherine.

"Our soldiers are gathered at the border, Nikki," whispered Katherine. "That is the closest I could get them. I must go, now. Wish me luck." She squeezed his hand and threw her arms about Andre, holding him very hard. Then she was gone, walking toward Galerien in an awkward, hesitant manner, wringing her hands as she greeted him. Due to some trick of acoustics in the hall, Nicholas could hear every word clearly.

"M-m-my b-b-brother is v-v-very ill. Please, c-c-could you send the doctor to h-h-him after the c-c-ceremony?"

"Yes, yes, of course," said Galerien absently. "Now, hurry to the abbey, my dear. I shall see you in but a few minutes."

Katherine stumbled and sniffled her way out the door.

"Damned half-wit," muttered Galerien. "I'll get a couple of brats off her, and then she'll go the way of her brother."

***

It was dark and dim inside Constanza Abbey. Even the candles seemed to fight weakly to stay lit against the gloom. A fit cave for the beast, thought Sera. Hood raised, she walked down the long aisle, past disheartened nobility, clever ministers with their fox eyes and gold badges of office, and guards, in their blue and gold uniforms, everywhere. One of them, close to the far side of the aisle, stood with such straight grace that she took a second look. Nicholas! And beside him stood Andre, with his unruly gold locks hastily shoved beneath a beaver hat. They had managed to escape, after all, but they stood behind a large company of soldiers armed to the hilt. She turned her gaze to the altar, where two figures knelt like statues, and a third read from a book.

The man reading wore a tall hat and robes of crimson. His voice intoned a service over the bride and groom. As Sera drew closer, the words flowed to her through the incense clouded air. Something about marriage not being taken lightly. What irony, Sera thought.

The moment was coming, the one she had feared and run from all her life. How would the beast try to kill her? For indeed, he would try. Probably, he'd shout to the guards, who stood now to her left and right as she strode soundlessly up the aisle. Galerien was never one to do his own dirty deeds, although, as she recalled, he vastly appreciated seeing the results.

The soldiers would probably take her before she could raise the hood of her cloak and disappear. But perhaps her appearance could give Nicholas the time he needed to reach Galerien.

Sera had studied this ceremony at university, learning the reasons for the words intoned by the Outlander holy man. He came to the part of the ceremony she would take for her cue. She took a deep breath and slowly drew down the hood of her cloak.

"If anyone knows of any reason why this man and this woman should not be joined together in matrimony, speak now, or forever hold your peace."

"I know of several," she said in a clear, firm voice that echoed through the abbey and kept walking.

Nicholas's head jerked at the sound of that clarion call. A collective gasp went through the congregation as Sera walked like a queen down the long, white aisle, her cloak trailing gracefully from her shoulders. He heard the screech of metal on metal as soldiers drew their swords. A guard standing in front of him remembered his duty and drew a pistol. Nicholas's hand cracked against the back of the soldier's head. He grabbed the pistol from his slackened hand. Edging around the fallen guard, he slipped through the next rows of men in blue and gold uniforms who seemed riveted on what was taking place at the altar.

"Hold," said the archbishop in a commanding voice. "This is God's house."

The soldiers looked to Galerien, straining like hunting hounds before the cast. But the king had turned pale as a sheet. He stared at the woman walking toward him, and his mouth quivered. The men sheathed their swords.

"Who makes this objection?" demanded the archbishop.

"I, Catherine Elizabeth Seraphina Galerien, do make it." Sera's clear voice carried through the entire abbey. She turned to face those gathered, and at that moment, sunlight slashed through the clear, leaded window above her, lighting her features for those in the front of the abbey to see clearly. Men and women murmured to each other, and the whispers spread through the abbey from front to back.

"She is the image of her blessed mother," cried one woman.

"Aye," quaked an old man, "but with our beloved king's coloring. I remember exactly that golden hair and those deep blue eyes. It is our princess, returned to us."

Elderly ministers of Beaureve painfully went to their knees while the new ones installed by Galerien looked left and right uneasily.

Sera raised her right arm and pointed at Galerien. "This marriage cannot go forward because this man is a murderer and a traitor to Beaureve."

Galerien's face froze in a mask of malevolence and fear. "How does this imposter dare to interrupt my wedding? Guards!"

His army unsheathed swords again.

Nicholas pushed through the last row of guards separating him from the altar. His heart pounded against his chest. Sera was so small, so vulnerable standing alone in the vast, cold abbey.

She turned and slowly perused the abbey. Men gave cries of shock. Swords clanged dully upon stone as they dropped their weapons.

"Dear Heaven," said the archbishop, casting a fearful glance at Sera. He seemed to remember himself and his office, for he squared his shoulders and looked her straight in the eye. "Young woman, your charges are heavy, indeed. I must have proof that you are the princess Catherine Elizabeth before I listen to your accusations."

Sera climbed the stairway to the altar and held her hand out to the archbishop. In it was a man's ring, wrought in beaten gold, a crowned lion rearing.

"Dear Heaven," said the archbishop again. "The royal seal. We have been looking for this for seventeen years."

Sera turned to Galerien. "You never could find it, could you? My father gave this to me moments before you had him murdered. Mama hid me, for we heard the assassins killing the guards outside their door. The murderers broke the door down an instant later. She never had time to close the wardrobe door completely. I saw everything."

Nicholas was close enough to see Sera's face. Something painful and wrenching twisted in his heart as he watched her relive the worst night of her life.

"They were dressed in black," she said. "First they killed the king. He struggled, but they stabbed him again and again. My mother screamed, and they laughed as they plunged the knife into her heart."

There was absolute silence in the abbey. Sera's voice clearly cut through the silence, and she sounded as cold as the moon. "You came in shortly afterwards, didn't you, Uncle? 'Where is the seal?' you said. 'I need it.' And the tall man, the one who looks like Death said, 'Why must you have it when you have a whole country now?'"

A gasp of horror went through the crowd. "'And the girl,' you said. 'Why did you not kill her in her nursery? I told you, I wanted them all taken out in one blow.'"

Sera's voice gained strength. She pointed at Galerien. "You have murdered kings and innocents. You have plundered the riches of Beaureve. You have forced the people into a life of destitution. You are not fit to marry. You are not fit to rule this country."

Galerien's face mottled purple. Nicholas had seen that look before on a wild boar cornered by the hounds.

"Imposter!" he roared, charging Sera from his place. "Guards, take her!"

Sera squared her shoulders and faced the monster charging her. He would try to kill her, now, but Nicholas and Andre could escape with Katherine. A tall man stepped in front of her, his wide shoulders blocking her view.

"No, Galerien. Finally, it comes to just you and me, doesn't it?"

Sera's whole body went cold. "No, Nicholas," she cried. "You have been ill. He will not fight fairly. I can deal with him."

Nicholas pushed her aside, very gently. "This is my

battle," he said in a soft, chilling voice. She had never seen so much cold fury in one man's eyes before.

She wanted to stop him, to reason with him, but it came to her that Nicholas must do this for his own pride. Even more, he must do it for Beaureve, for who would rule her country after she left it if not Nicholas? And how would her people accept him as their king, if he did not save them now from Galerien? She only prayed he was well enough to win against the monster.

Galerien roared and unsheathed his sword.

Nicholas's face was calm and implacable as, blazing with rage, Galerien lunged. Nicholas parried easily. Sword rang upon sword as Galerien fought to push Nicholas back down the aisle of the cathedral. Nicholas stepped and turned without wasted motion. Sera thought he looked as graceful and as unconcerned as a dancer, but this dance was deadly. Galerien feinted, and his sword thrust down and sideways, but Nicholas had whirled out of the way.

He had that look of abstract concentration one saw on the faces of saints and warriors in Outlander paintings. Sera dared not speak to stop the killing for fear of breaking that concentration. He leaped aside again as Galerien's sword slashed downward. The deadly arc was a flash of jeweled color beneath the stained glass window. Sera shuddered, compelled to watch as every person in the prayer house watched, scarcely breathing.

They twirled and feinted, clashed against each other as swords met and held. And then Nicholas, almost insouciantly, gave a flick of his wrist, and Galerien's sword arced into the air. It sailed to the altar and embedded itself into the wood of the little cloth-covered table behind which the priest stood, transfixed. Nicholas smiled, a small, tight movement of the lips, and pressed his sword against Galerien's throat. Galerien backed. Nicholas followed. Galerien fell to his knees and fumbled in his sleeve. He surged up again, a knife in his hand.

But Nicholas gave a snarl of satisfaction. With a swift thrust of his leg, he kicked out and the knife went sailing. Galerien fell, tried to right himself, but the marble floor was slick. He struggled, back arched, while Nicholas held him there.

"Say your last prayers, Galerien. Not that they'll do you much good where you're going." Nicholas stood over his enemy. He was coiled to thrust.

"Stop." Sera's voice held his hand back from the final coup.

"What?" Nicholas tried to shake the battle rage from his brain. Sera stood beside him, staring down at the beast. Why did she ask—no, *command*—him to stop? How must she feel, looking into the eyes of the monster who had taken away everything she loved?

"Not death," she said. "Not in a prayer house. Not for this man."

"Sera, think. He took your loved ones from you. He hunted you and murdered your people. Think of Selonia, Sera, of Iman Hadar's palace." He could not believe she would hold true to her philosophy after all this.

She shook her head. "It is too easy a fate to let him die," she said. "Instead, he shall know, finally. He shall know just what he did." *Shall, not will.* She spoke in the language of the law, proclaiming herself judge and jury.

"Do you see them, Uncle? Your victims. My mother, my father, who did nothing to you but love you. Do you see their end, now?" She spoke very softly, and Galerien stiffened, moaning.

"Do you see the people of Selonia? The dead children, the old people who couldn't run fast enough from the black shadows that cut them down? Do you smell the blood?"

"No, no, please!" Galerien's neck was stretched like that of a man on the rack.

"Do you hear the infants wailing for mothers who lie dead on top of them, shielding their tiny bodies from the beasts you sent to wreak such terror?"

"God, no more! I see them. I see them! Take them away, please, please."

"I cannot, Uncle. You killed them, and now they'll haunt you for the rest of your life. You'll know your sins forever, and the sacred promise of each life you snuffed out."

Galerien rolled to his side and drew his legs up, curling his whole body together in agony. "I didn't know. I didn't realize." He began to sob, muttering and moaning to himself.

Nicholas looked at Sera and then at the figure cowering on the floor. Her beautiful face was stern. "Artemis," he whispered. "Goddess of the silver bow. You called the

Furies."

"I am no goddess," Sera said, still staring at Galerien as he writhed at her feet. "And I did not call them. They have been waiting for him, lo these many years."

And Nicholas knew that with all his modern understanding, his enlightened vision, he would never totally comprehend this woman whose magic could make a demon writhe in shame.

"Take him away," said Sera to the people kneeling before her. "House him comfortably. From now on, look upon him and recognize his suffering."

Sera looked at the men and women before her. She began to raise the hood of her cloak.

An old man richly dressed hobbled toward her as guards dragged Galerien out of the abbey. He dropped to one knee before her. "Princess, I am—"

Sera bent and helped the old man to his feet. "I recognize you, Baron Taurons. You used to let me play with your timepiece."

The old man's rheumy eyes grew bright. "Aye, that I did. Princess, your throne awaits you. Your people need you."

Sera looked at Katherine, at Andre who stood now beside Katherine. After a long moment, she finally raised her gaze to Nicholas's face, her expression inscrutable. She seemed to be waiting for something from him, perhaps an explanation, a justification. He was paralyzed by fear— that whatever he said wouldn't be enough. What could he tell her, this goddess from a golden world, that would keep her here, that would convince her he was compensation enough for what she'd lose?

Stay with me. Try to love me, in spite of my imperfections. If he were any other man, he could say, *I love you.* The muscles of his hand ached with the need to reach out and touch her, to tell her what was forbidden to him.

A movement from the corner of his eye made him turn. Another walked the cathedral aisle toward them, a giant of a man with golden hair, wearing a gray cloak.

Nicholas felt Sera's eyes still locked on his face. Why couldn't he say it? Why must he condemn himself to a life of hiding from what he felt? Everything in him fought to break free, to express in words what his heart had known, it seemed, forever. But her eyes fluttered shut and the radiance that seemed her very life seeped out of her face. Nicholas lunged forward an instant too late. The Hillman had already grabbed her. Sera slumped against his side, her face bleached of color. Even her hands hung lifeless from slack arms.

"Let me have her," Nicholas said—actually, begged— the man who had taken her away from him once. He raised his hand, half in supplication, half in preparation to take Sera in his arms. "I have to tell her. She has to know."

The Hillman's blue eyes bit into Nicholas with a chill that went bone deep. "This is what you have done to her, Outlander," said the Hillman. "The power she used to save you and these others has drained the life out of her until there is almost nothing left of her. Can *you* heal her?"

Nicholas dropped his hand and lowered his head. He had not a word to say in defense of himself. What had he done in his pride but harm the only thing that gave light and joy to his life? *My kind don't heal. We only wound*, he thought, *and call it duty.*

"She comes with me." The Hillman raised Sera's hood to her hair, and then raised his own. A faint breeze wafted past Nicholas's face. He shut his eyes, unwilling to face the empty space where she had been, but it didn't matter. He knew that she was gone. He knew because he felt the crack that rent his heart in two.

Fifteen

Andre hesitated outside the door to Nicholas's study. His friend had been busy all day with the problems of two countries, and if the last two weeks were any indication, he'd work on well into the night. Beaureve's ministers had asked him for help, at least until their princess returned to them. Poor fools, they really believed she would come back to them.

Nicholas seemed to know better. After the first week of difficult work in Constanza, Nicholas had appointed new officials, new justices, and new ministers to report back to him on a regular basis. He had been tireless in his efforts for Beaureve, attempting to exorcise his demons through intense work.

He had succeeded in giving Beaureve the beginning of a new age. People who had suffered under the iron rule of Galerien now hoped for better from Nicholas, and were content to wait for improvement, particularly now that there was food in the markets and only reasonable taxation to face.

But Nicholas, although physically recovered from his wound, carried scars that worried Andre. He never spoke of Sera, and he never laughed. He dined alone and ate little. The only sign of pleasure he had shown in the last week was his delight in Katherine's upcoming marriage to Andre. And even that was tinged with a hint of melancholy.

Andre bit his lip as he raised his hand to knock at the door. He must think of something that would smooth away the haunted circles from beneath Nicholas's eyes. A sound behind him, a brush of air quickly displaced, jarred him from his thoughts. He turned about and scowled fiercely. The man removing the hood of his gray cloak was the Arkadian scoundrel who had taken Sera from Nicholas.

"Does your king sit within his study?"

Andre bristled. The fellow had a hell of a nerve returning to the palace.

"Do you wish an interview? For what purpose? Will you tell him about your idyllic married life? Does it please you to rub his nose in it? Come," he said raising his fists. "I apprehend that you do not approve of weapons, at least those that only hurt the body. But perhaps I could interest you in a bout of fisticuffs."

The golden bastard gave him a mild look. "Count Lironsky, you do me and your king a disservice. I am unmarried at present, and intend to remain so for quite some time. I came only because I believe that Sera and Nicholas Rostov may have made a grave miscalculation—one in which I played a part. But I must see with my own eyes if he suffers in any way as greatly as she does from this separation. Knowing that, will you allow me to pass, or do you wish me gone?"

Andre blinked and lowered his fists. He could think of nothing to say or do other than step aside. The man gave him a curt nod. "My name is Jacob Augustus. If you would announce me to your king, I shall complete my task as quickly as possible."

***

Nicholas looked up from the book he had been trying to read for the past hour. "I am very busy, Andre," he said upon seeing his friend at the door. "Perhaps I'll see you tonight." He was growing more and more impatient with Andre's constant hovering.

Recently, Andre and Katherine had made it their sole responsibility to watch over him, interrupting the little time he had to himself to seek reassurance that he wasn't—what? Contemplating suicide?

All of their worry was utter nonsense, of course. A man didn't die for want of love. He simply no longer cared about living, which made sense when all about one was barren and gray as a landscape in Purgatory.

What he contemplated was worse. For months, he had ignored what was in his heart, telling himself he mustn't ever look at it closely, for fear it would weaken him. But living without Sera had shown him his own soul. Whether he admitted it to himself or not, he loved her, and he would love her forever. And out of fear, he had thrown it all away.

Too late, he'd discovered that strength came not from denying love, but from accepting it, and giving it back for every moment love was granted him. Oh, he would survive, and he would even be a good king. He was too duty bound not to. Survival without Sera, however, wasn't really living.

Nicholas stared blindly at the book, willing Andre to leave. In the silence, he could hear the sounds of an army unit drilling to music outside his window.

Andre didn't leave. He was too stubborn to get Nicholas's not very subtle message. He stood at the door looking... actually quite strange, and much too thoughtful, as though he had just been told that the moon really was made of green cheese, or that dragons did exist.

"A man wishes to see you, Nikki. His name is Jacob Augustus. I believe you'd better grant him an audience."

Nicholas sighed. The last thing he wanted to face was another courtier from Beaureve today. "My schedule is full. Perhaps you could see him in my stead."

Andre cleared his throat in a curious manner. "He needs to speak to you. It's rather urgent, Nikki."

Nicholas rubbed his eyes. "Very well. Send him in if you must."

Andre opened the door and spoke to this Jacob Augustus in a low voice. Nicholas rose and walked to the window, composing his expression. He heard the door shut and turned to speak to the man who waited before it.

Nicholas froze in place, his whole being caught in a flash of pain. He didn't know how long the two of them looked at each other, measuring, wondering. Finally, he felt he could control his voice enough to speak.

"Sera, she is well?" he asked, indicating a seat as he walked to his desk.

This Jacob Augustus shook his head and remained standing. "I do not believe so."

Nicholas felt all the blood drain from his heart and grabbed at the desk to remain upright. "She is not recovered?" he asked, remembering her deadly pallor in the abbey at Constanza.

The man nodded solemnly. "In a way of speaking. She is physically well, just as you are."

Just as he was, thought Nicholas. He was a mess. "But soon she will marry. And you will be good to her, I know." He looked down at his hands. "Else she would never agree to..." He couldn't go on.

"Marry me?" asked Jacob Augustus in an incredulous voice. "Nicholas Rostov, I am her brother, not her betrothed."

The sounds beyond the window dimmed in Nicholas's ears. "Her brother?" he repeated numbly.

"You have a sister, do you not?"

Nicholas slowly loosened his hold on the side of the desk. "Katherine. She is very dear to me."

"As Sera is to me. And that is why I am here. Sera told me quite recently that she was now certain you had no wish to see her again, that you would never change your mind. In the prayer house, she was too busy and too tense to see anything in your face but what she thought was a final rejection. And I—well, I admit it. I gave in to anger and judged you to be like all the rest of them, in spite of what I saw in your expression when she appeared and you fought to reach her. You looked like a man desperate to protect his woman.

"I acted wrongly," the Hillman continued, "and knew I must make restitution. So I made her listen to my observations. Although she is not at all convinced that I am correct concerning your—what do you Outlanders call them?—intentions toward Sera, I have come to place the choice once more before you."

Jacob Augustus reached into a pouch that hung by his side and placed something wrapped in velvet on the desk before Nicholas. He picked it up and unrolled the wrapping. The betrothal necklace he had given Sera the night of the ball lay in his hand. The ruby was gone. Instead, a great sapphire, as deep a blue as Sera's eyes, hung from the chain of diamonds and rubies.

Beside the necklace sat a man's large gold ring, fashioned by a master goldsmith. Nicholas's breath caught as he looked at the crowned lion, rearing. The royal seal of Beaureve lay before him.

"I must warn you. Sera knows nothing of my journey or its purpose. I also "borrowed" the ring without her knowledge. If you choose it, wear it, and return the necklace to her. That is the way of your betrothals, is it not?"

Nicholas felt the first stirring of hope deep in his chest. He touched the ring with one finger, feeling the warmth of the metal as a promise. Carefully, he slipped it on the third finger of his left hand. It was a perfect fit.

Jacob smiled and nodded as he picked up the necklace and stowed it back in his pouch. "I shall return this to my sister straightaway. Sera told me you can track a mouse through a forest. Is that true?"

Nicholas's lips quirked in a small grimace of irony.

"Your sister thinks more highly of my talents than she should, but yes, I'm a good hunter."

Jacob nodded and looked past Nicholas to the window, where the sun was breaking through the clouds. "It promises to be a fine, warm day," he said speculatively. "I believe I shall ride home without raising my hood." Without another word, he turned and walked out the door.

Nicholas stared at the betrothal ring on his finger. A slow grin spread across his face and through his whole body. He lifted his head as warmth and energy filled him, and he ran out the open door into the corridor.

"Which way did he go?" he shouted to Andre.

"To the left," said Andre, loping after him. "What's going on?"

Nicholas sprinted for the stairs. "You and Katherine are co-regents until I return."

"Good God, Nikki. Just like that?"

Nicholas yelled to a passing footman. "My horse and a pack of provisions. Immediately." He ran on, shouting orders, grabbing a warm cloak and gloves from a footman who raced to meet him as he made for the great stairway.

"Andre, you're slowing me down." Nicholas threw on the cloak as he took the stairs two at a time.

Andre grabbed his arm. "This is folly. You cannot go alone."

Nicholas easily broke his grip and turned to face his friend. "I'm following a dream, Andre, and it's getting a head start." He threw his arms around Andre and gave him a bear hug.

Andre grunted. And grinned. After all, what else was there to do?

The guard held Nicholas's horse for him. The bay pranced, as though he had caught his master's eagerness. "Farewell," called Nicholas. He felt giddy and light as air. As soon as he touched his legs to the horse's flanks, they sprang forward and cantered from the yard.

***

The snow whirled around Nicholas as he continued his ascent of the tallest mountain in the Arkadian range. He had been riding for three days and slowly climbing upward for two. Damned if Jacob Augustus wasn't a far better woodsman than his sister. Nicholas had to backtrack twice to find the man's trail. This cost him valuable time, but luckily, the snow hadn't begun until quite recently, when he hit the base of Mount Joy. He wondered at the irony of the name.

An hour ago, Nicholas had left the horse with a crofter who promised to take care of it. The peasant seemed to be the only man to live among these isolated, bare cliffs. Nicholas knew why. He was cold and wet clear through. His lungs began to burn with each breath, but he couldn't tell whether this was because of the double-damned pneumonia or the lack of oxygen as he climbed ever upward.

A storm had begun an hour before. Through the swirling snow, he could make out a horse and rider high above him. Amazing what those Hill horses could do, he thought with a twinge of envy. Hell, if he lived, which he bloody well planned to do, he wanted to ride one of those magical beasts. Provided Sera didn't throw him back out into the blizzard.

During the ascent, he felt curiously detached from his own body, his own mind. But as soon as he became aware of his laboring breath, all of his fears and doubts gained ascendancy. Jacob had said nothing reassuring about Sera's frame of mind. She was probably furious and hurt and far beyond his feeble attempts to convince her of his love. What trick could he use to move her when she had told him in every possible way that she loved him and he had never once said those words to her? Nicholas clung to the mountainside and heaved himself upward. Suddenly, it was abundantly clear that there was only one thing that mattered. It was in her hands to accept or reject him. It was in his to tell her what she meant to him.

Each breath seared his lungs. He stopped, giving himself a little time to rest. Sweat bathed his body and drained the heat from him. A deep, bone rattling cold sliced through his boots, his gloves, his wet cloak. Icy pain gripped his limbs. His energy seeped from his body with its heat, and his own moisture chilled him.

Cold shuddered through him. He pushed down the fear that surfaced with the cold—the panic that he would fail to reach Sera at all—and began to climb again. He'd make it, step by grueling step. He had to.

"In order to tell her," he whispered against the howling wind.

With grim determination, he bent against the storm. It screamed in his ears, howling a vengeful dissonance. He climbed on, stopping occasionally to look upward and gauge where Jacob Augustus was on the mountainside. One last time, he scanned the heights, his eyes narrowed against the wind and the snow. Jacob and his horse stood before a frozen waterfall. A flash of light and a fiery red burst from behind the fall pierced the gathering darkness, and Jacob...disappeared.

Nicholas marked the spot in his mind and trudged upward with renewed purpose, furious with his clumsy steps, his stumbles over rock on the narrow path. His boots slipped. Sleet stung his face with a thousand needles. And still he climbed.

The light began to fade completely as he hit the last hundred feet. Each breath he took felt like fire. His legs were numb, almost useless. He couldn't suck enough air into his lungs. He fell to his knees, and shook his head against the dizziness that threatened to engulf him. And he crawled toward the waterfall, measuring his progress in inches. Fending off the dark spots before his eyes, he gritted his teeth and struggled forward. With every foot he gained, he thought, *Behind that wall of frozen water, Sera is waiting.*

How long had he been climbing? he thought wearily. Forever? The waterfall stood before him, all its tumultuous power frozen in time and place. Slowly, painfully, he staggered to his feet, searching for the door behind the falls. He found only sheer, solid cliff wall.

Ah, God. His breath came out in a painful sob of frustration. Along with his muscle and sinew, his mind had turned to porridge in the last hours. How could Jacob Augustus have disappeared behind this wall of rock? He had seen it, the flash of fire, and the man no longer visible.

The flash of fire....

Nicholas carefully explored the rock with hands almost too frozen to feel. He forced his sleet-encrusted eyelids open and studied the pillars of rock to the left and the right of the falls. Think, he silently screamed at his sluggish brain. All right. Jacob Augustus still sat astride his horse when he disappeared. That meant the key to the door was high enough for a rider on a seventeen-hand mount to reach with ease.

Nicholas tore off his gloves and blew into his hands. As soon as his sense of touch began to return, he ran his bare hands up along an icy crevice in the pillars. He felt something solid, many faceted, on the right hand column, and it was warm to the touch. In the midst of this frozen world, it felt as warm as the ruby he had bought from the merchant, he thought muzzily.

And at his touch, the cliff wall split and slid open, as silently and cleanly as a pocket door in the palace. Through the swirling snow, he caught the rosy glow that emanated from the open cliffs. It bathed him in a warm radiance. He raised a foot and took a faltering step toward the light. It was suddenly very important that he walk upright through the gate.

Nicholas squinted against the light of the setting sun as he slowly walked into a large square. He tried to make out the dark silhouetted figures that stood waiting at the square's perimeter. Against the rose hues of sunset, one, a small, delicate shadow, stood frozen in place beside a larger shadow.

He thought he heard her say, "For the gods' sake, get him a cloak," but his storm-deafened ears couldn't make out the words clearly. He knew only that the voice was dear to him. On stumbling legs he made his way slowly toward her. He had to tell her.

A tall, upright figure stepped into his path, and Nicholas stopped as abruptly as a dog reaching the end of a strong leash. Try as he might, he could not break past the invisible boundary that hemmed him in. Nicholas half shut his eyes against the last rays of light and peered at the man who blocked his path by will alone. He could just make out blue eyes deep as an ocean in a face lined but powerful.

"What do you wish, Outlander?" asked the man who stood before him. Nicholas recognized his voice. He had heard it recently, on a battlefield in Beaureve.

Nicholas stood straighter and tried to swallow, but his throat burned like fire. He ran his tongue over his lips, but even his tongue was dry.

"I am Nicholas Andreyevitch Rostov," he said through a voice that cracked as his lungs strained for breath to speak. "I must speak to Catherine Elizabeth Seraphina Galerien."

"Say what you will to her in the presence of this company," said the older man.

A mass of shadows moved forward, surrounding Nicholas. He swayed, took a step forward, and hit the invisible wall hemming him in. He blinked and felt along the boundaries of his prison. His numb fingers traced out a flat, smooth surface, like crystal and steel welded together. Leaning his forehead hard against it, he fought the frustration and tried to think of a way out of the cage that trapped him, but his mind was as useless as his trembling legs. Voices came to him like the muffled sighs of the ocean through a conch shell. The amorphous figures murmured and slowly took shape before him.

Lights flickered on as torches flared. Nicholas could see buildings lining the square, the marble rosy in the light. Around him, men and women took their seats upon benches that led upward in a semi-circle. A fine irritation jittered along all his nerve endings. He felt as though he were a beast in a pit.

"Nicholas Rostov, you have formerly expressed a desire to wed Catherine Elizabeth Seraphina Galerien, of this country," a voice declared from midway up the rows of seats.

Desire, thought Nicholas, does not begin to cover it.

"If this is still your wish, by what right do you claim her?"

This answer, at least, came quickly to him. "I have no right."

Nicholas groaned, pressing against the invisible cage that held him. He couldn't coerce, or outmaneuver, or argue logically. But Sera was there, he had heard her, felt her presence. He had come to tell her—he had lived to tell her—and nobody was going to stop him now.

"I have no right to take you from the safety of this place," he said in a voice that tried for calm but shook with emotion. "All I have is my love for you. I love you, Sera."

The small shadow at the periphery struggled, whether to run to him or away, he couldn't tell. But the larger one touched her arm, and she quieted.

"Let her come to me," he called out to the dark shadows about him. "If just to say good-bye, let her come." But the invisible walls hemmed him in, as alone as he had ever been in the gray Outlander world beyond this light. He forced himself to go on, ignoring the listening ears, the strangers prodding him for all his secrets. It no longer mattered a damn who heard him, as long as she did.

"Sera!" His voice broke on a laugh that was half a groan. "I don't think you understand what it means to me that you see what I am, all of me and still you love me."

He cleared his throat. "You never let me off, did you? You never let me hide in logic or pretension, yet you believed in me when I doubted I would ever be good enough. Because of you, I changed into a man whom my people actually seem to look upon with fondness. Because of you, Katherine is no longer afraid of me—or anything else. Rather amazing, isn't it?"

He gave a low laugh that caught in his throat. "I have no right to you, Sera. Bloody shame, isn't it, because I love you with all my heart. I think I did from that moment in Hadar's palace, when you told me how you might have a terrible disease. Do you remember how you decided that if one was disgusting, two would certainly keep me away?"

Nicholas stared at his hands and muttered, "Now I've probably embarrassed you in front of your people and ruined my chances. But I came here so I could tell you. I shall love you until I die. That is all I have to say."

"Nicholas!" Her clear cry cut through the muffled air.

The barrier shattered into a thousand pieces. Nicholas turned blindly toward the sound of her voice. Sera burst down those endless stairs into the pit and flung herself against him. His arms whipped around her. She lifted her face. Her eyes were shadowed, and her face was thin. But she glowed.

Nicholas tried to grin. With the lump in his throat, it was too hard. He buried his face against her neck, breathing in the sweet scent of her body, fighting for control.

Sera tugged lightly at his hand. "Come away," she whispered, glancing about them, and he remembered himself, and where they were, and the scrutiny that she must feel from the inquisitors who stood witness. He followed her out of the square and on through a wide city street smelling of flowers and fresh, blessedly warm air, and he realized that Sera's elusive scent came from Arkadia, itself.

It was around them and part of her, and it was the earth that had nurtured her all her life. In the soft lamplight, the buildings rose about him in the classic Greek style, clean of line and perfectly harmonious. This was quite unlike any city he had ever seen, not even Montanyard. Sculptures stood everywhere, magnificent, finer than any he'd seen in Florence. The streets were broad, and the stone that made them perfectly cut. Somewhere singing in the back of his dizzy brain was the strangest feeling of ease exchanged for tension, as though he had finally, after years of exile, come home. The Temple Square was empty. The people must all still be gathered in the amphitheater beyond the mountain pass.

Nicholas pulled Sera behind the columns of a great marble building and wrapped his arms about her. She nestled against him, her own arms holding tight. This was what he craved, what he needed to live again. Bending his head, he covered her lips with his own, to take her joy and give it back again. He cupped her cheeks and planted kisses over her nose, her mouth, her eyelids. The words he'd kept boxed inside him flew from his lips. "I love you," he whispered. "I love you."

In the dim light, he fumbled for the necklace and clasped it around her throat.

"Blue and white," he murmured, tracing the oval of the brilliant sapphire, feeling the soft skin above her collar bone with the back of his hand. "The colors of Laurentia."

"Red and white," she said, drawing his hand to the rubies and diamonds of the chain. He could hear the smile in her voice. "The colors of Beaureve."

Laughing, he lifted her high and twirled her so many times, he lost count. "I love you," he said again, for all the times he had not said it. And then, because it was a serious decision she had, after all, made in the midst of high emotion, he asked, "Are you sure?"

The moon rose, silver and full, and he saw the radiance again on her face, and the teasing smile that he had seen before only rarely. It had the same effect it always did on him, turning him heated and eager in a flash.

"How many times must I agree to marry you, Nicholas Rostov? Indeed, I do not believe you have formally proposed even now."

He pulled her up against him, letting her feel his heat

and his need. "Once upon a time," he said between butterfly kisses to her cheeks, her chin, the soft, upward curve of her mouth, "a king got himself well and truly lost. And a beautiful princess took pity on him."

She threw her arms around his neck and kissed him back, ardent and joyful and sensual beyond his wildest dreams. "What happened then?" she whispered.

"She married him." He buried his face in her neck, breathing in her scent, which was the perfume of the flowers all about them. "And they lived happily ever after."

Epilogue

A week later, Sera watched the moon rise over Arkadia. The light shone into the room where she stood with Nicholas behind her, his arms wrapped about her waist. It was their wedding night, and there was nothing more she would have wished than this—to have him warm and strong at her back, sharing her world, whichever one it would be. Waiting to be wed would have seemed torment, for they were not permitted to be alone with each other for more than a few minutes at a time. But there were compensations for her body's hunger for him. This week she had seen Nicholas's face light at the sight of scientific discoveries at the academy, at the feel of a Hill horse beneath him, and at the sounds of intense, earnest debate among young men and women in the agora.

He had spent hours with her grandfather, discussing oligarchy and democracy, for Arkadia had been in transition from the former to the latter since the tenth century, when the eugenics program was discarded. Most of all, she treasured the look of relief and happiness on his face when he gazed through Grandfather's scrying glass and saw the French troops hurrying away from Laurentia's border, toward France.

Never, she thought with a blush and a shiver of anticipation, had he looked so young, so eager and relaxed, except after their bodies had met and merged in love.

This night, she had seen his even deeper joy at the sight of her, sitting suddenly shy in her crimson gown and veil when he came to "abduct" her from her home.

Her kinsmen and her friends had put up very little fight when Nicholas and Jacob Augustus appeared at Grandfather's. There had been much laughter and applause when he had swept her up in his arms and carried her from her childhood hearth while Jacob, as groomsman, ran ahead to bring the horses for the bride and groom to ride away.

Jacob had taken time to get to know Nicholas in the last week, as if to make up for the prejudice that had unwittingly caused her so much unhappiness. And in the end, he had confessed a genuine liking for the king, intensified by his study of Nicholas's genealogy. Hill blood ran in the Rostov line from Sophia, the daughter of a Russian prince and an Arkadian mother, who had met and fallen in love with Nicholas's grandfather. It was Queen Sophia's room that had the hidden staircase and the wondrous wallpaper that included a bird from the Hills.

This discovery explained many things to Jacob. He now knew why the king felt that little prickle at the back of his neck, why he could fend off recurring pneumonia with the force of his will alone, and why he was able to hear Emmanuel's warning on the battlefield in the Brotherhood camp. Jacob surmised that the Hill blood running in Nicholas's veins was what had toppled his sister into delirious love in the first place.

Sera could have told Jacob that Hill blood hadn't a thing to do with her love for Nicholas, but she wanted to encourage his new interest in the Outlander world. For if Jacob, the future Mage, became curious, others would follow, and the bridge between both worlds would strengthen.

"What are you thinking?" Nicholas wrapped her closer, his breath a warm, soft huff against her ear. She bent her head to one side, giving him access. A jolt of heat swept through her when she felt his soft kisses on the sensitive skin beneath her ear.

"Among other things, how delighted you were with the wedding present your groomsman gave you."

She could feel his lips curve against her skin. "The Hill cloak! Sera, did I ever tell you how much I wanted to travel? When I was a boy, all I could think about was what the Pyramids must look like, and the Great Wall of China, and the Taj Mahal. I never thought I'd be free enough to do such a thing. And now, we can go anywhere we want, and be back by suppertime."

How she loved his joy. Such a man as her husband would never grow old. "Do you remember Jacob's instructions?"

"I should hope so," Nicholas said with another huff of air, this time not so gentle. "They were certainly simple, although several months ago, I wouldn't have believed in such things as Hill cloaks and beautiful, magical, stubborn women."

She smiled at that last and turned to twine her arms about his neck. "Tell me how to use a Hill cloak," she said, rubbing her lips against the smooth skin just above his collarbone.

"Tomorrow," he murmured against her hair. "I can't think when you do that." His hand traveled up her side, cupping the fullness of her breast. She gasped as his palm grazed the nipple. Memory and privation sharpened her hunger, and she arched into his hand. But there was one last gift she wanted to give him before she surrendered to the need coursing through her body.

"Now," she whispered.

He sighed and drew her close. "Either I think very hard of the exact place where I want to be, or I hold your hand, and you'll guide me. Jacob also said that certain sensations would be... unsettling and that I should let you guide me the first time or two. But I know where I want to go."

"Where?"

"To bed. With you." Nicholas kissed her again, maddeningly exciting little teases along her throat and down, lower.

"There will be a bed, I promise."

The cloaks lay across the couch by the window. Sera carefully fastened one about Nicholas's shoulders. "Don't put the hood up until it's time," she said, with frightening visions of Nicholas lost on the wind.

"I have better things in mind for tonight than waiting for you to rescue me, Sera." His eyes danced with excitement as she fastened her own cloak. "Take me to a nice, big bed where we can make love all night."

"Hold on to me," she said, reaching out for his hand.

Nicholas lifted the hood over his head. The world disappeared in a whoosh and swirl of air. He held on tight to Sera's hand, sailing on the wind like a hawk high above the earth below them. The stars and the moon glowed, cold and remote above them. His nose was cold, but everything else was blessedly warm beneath the cloak's thin wool. What magic had they woven into the warp and woof of the fabric? His heart pounded, his eyes watered against the wind, and he brushed them with his free hand, to better see rivers below him like shining silver ribbons.

Excitement thrummed through him. This, then, to fly above the world at will, was the freedom he had always craved. He felt the earth beneath him coming up fast. For an instant, his insides lurched in sickening fear of a crash.

Wildly, he looked round him, but the place was a blur in the darkness.

Softly as a feather, they touched down into warmth and light. He blinked, disoriented. His feet felt boards beneath them, his hands the blaze of a fire. He drew down the hood of his cloak and looked about. His great, canopied bed with the crown at the top rose on the dais directly before him. Sera stood beside him, beautiful in the firelight as she unfastened her cloak and laid it carefully upon the chair in his room. For a moment, he didn't understand her, and thought this must be some joke she'd thought to play.

But she came to him with that radiance on her face and unfastened his cloak.

He caught her fingers in his hand. "Why? Why of all the places in the world, here, in my room?"

She raised his hands to her lips and very softly kissed them both. When she lifted her gaze to him, he saw that her eyes were that serene, deep blue of an ocean on a perfect summer morning, when the world is new again.

"I've brought us home, Nicholas," she said.

Home. It was such a simple word. And with it, she gave him everything—her allegiance, her happiness, her complete trust.

If he had learned one thing in the last months, it was to accept a gift of love without reservation. He scooped his wife up into his arms and carried her to his bed. She held on tight to the nape of his neck, warm and soft in his embrace. As he laid her down, she smiled up at him, a full, rich curving of her lips because he had understood her gift. Aye, he thought bending to her, a man who holds tight to the blessing in his arms may be flawed in a million ways, but he's no fool.

ABOUT THE AUTHOR

Mary Lennox grew up dreaming of places where magic and happy endings co-existed. She woke up long enough to leave graduate school, marry an irreverent lawyer and tour the world. Nothing could have prepared her for the medieval beauty of Europe's cathedrals, the grimness and glory of Russia, or the exotic mysteries of India. The only way to top that experience was to turn carpenter and build with her husband her perfect house on a tranquil horse farm in Appalachia, home-school her kids from grades K-12, and gallop her horses on the wooded trails.

Heart of Fire is Mary's second novel. Now back to dreaming full time, Mary spends her days creating worlds where magic and human endeavor vanquish evil and a happy ending is guaranteed.

Tired of mundane romance?

Dare to ImaJinn

Vampires, ghosts, shapeshifters,
sorcerers,
time-travelers, aliens,
and more.

Sometimes Scary. Always Sexy!

Find ImaJinn books online at
www.imajinnbooks.com

ImaJinn Books Catalog
Order Form

Please send me a free ImaJinn Books Catalog. My address is:

_____
Name

_____
Address

------------------   ------ ---

City   State   Zip

Mail this form to:

Catalog Offer
ImaJinn Books
PO Box 162
Hickory Corners MI 49060-0162